POST [illegible] ANGER

POSTCARDS FROM A STRANGER

Sally Stewart

PAN BOOKS

This edition published 1999 by Pan Books
an imprint of Macmillan Publishers Ltd
25 Eccleston Place, London SW1W 9NF
Basingstoke and Oxford
Associated companies throughout the world
www.macmillan.co.uk

This first world edition published in Great Britain 1999 by
SEVERN HOUSE PUBLISHERS LTD of
9-15 High Street, Sutton, Surrey SM1 1DF
This first world edition published in the U.S.A. 1999 by
SEVERN HOUSE PUBLISHERS INC of
595 Madison Avenue, New York, NY 10022.

British Library Cataloguing in Publication Data

Stewart, Sally
Postcards from a stranger
1. Love stories
1. Title
823.9'14 [F]

ISBN 0 330 39656 0

Typeset by Palimpsest Book Production Ltd
Polmont, Stirlingshire, Scotland.
Printed and bound in Great Britain by
Mackays of Chatham plc, Chatham, Kent.

One

She peered at herself in the mirror, hoping that something might have changed. Not so! Twenty-five she might be since midnight, but for Jane Kingsley, spinster of the parish of Little Fairford, everything else seemed just as usual – dark, fly-away hair, and straight black brows that refused to make the seductive curve she'd always yearned for; nose, contrariwise, tip-tilted when it ought to have been elegantly straight. Add in a stubborn chin, and nothing special in the way of mouths and the sum total was a face that made no claim to beauty. Uncle Edwin must have given up hope by now of any noticeable improvement in the small, lost creature he'd rescued fifteen years ago. She hadn't even grown a great deal since then and had remained somewhat thin, but at least she was no longer lost. Four years spent teaching in the village school had been an object lesson, exhausting but hilarious, in how to survive. Unlikely as it had once seemed, Jane reckoned that she was now definitely a survivor. A lot had been crammed into her first quarter of a century . . . more love and laughter, sadness and loss than some people experienced in a lifetime – but the rest of her days looked like being more ordinary. Other people might even consider them dull, but the poor things didn't know that village life and the village school rarely came within hailing distance of dullness.

She smiled as usual at the pictured faces of her parents hanging over the dressing-table, then went downstairs to get breakfast for her uncle and receive his birthday present. She knew already what it would be – one more perfect pearl to add to the fourteen she'd been given since coming to live with him at the age of ten. She'd have preferred something with colour in it – turquoise, jade or coral – but Uncle Edwin belonged in spirit to a past age, when pearls were what a lady wore in the way of daytime jewellery.

She put coffee and toast on the table precisely at eight o'clock and just as precisely he walked in, blinking in the bright sunshine that poured into the room. He sat down with a little sigh of relief, and she noticed sadly that the strong light made him look more gaunt than ever. There were times when she feared that he might not live long enough to see her necklace completed.

'Good morning, my dear . . . happy birthday.'

She took the little parcel he held out to her, grateful for the fact that they'd long ago agreed to give up pretending she didn't know what her birthday present would be.

'Number fifteen, Uncle . . . lovely,' she said, and was surprised to see him smile.

She opened the package and sat transfixed – not one pearl but a whole handful of them, beautifully matched and graded.

'I hope they'll make up the whole string now,' he explained gently. 'It occurred to me that the rate of progress needed to be speeded up a little.'

It was the closest he'd ever got to admitting that the heart attack that had cut short his university career had lessened more than that. She bit back an enquiry he wouldn't want and got up from the table instead to deposit a kiss on his thin white hair.

'Thank you, they're beautiful. I'll take them to the jeweller's this morning to be strung. Prepare yourself for the grand moment when I dazzle you by dressing up properly!'

He surprised her for the second time that morning. 'You're not obliged to wear them, my dear. They're meant to be an untaxable investment! Something you can always dispose of at a good price if you should ever be in need of ready cash.'

The kindness of it touched her to the point of tears, but he waved the subject aside. 'Judging by the pile of envelopes in front of you, every child in Little Fairford has remembered your birthday.'

'I can hear them all daring one another to send "Miss" a card!' First of all, though, she picked up an envelope with a French stamp on it. 'I think I recognise *Oncle* Marcel's spidery handwriting.'

Inside, with a rich man's usual thriftiness in small things, Marcel Colbert had enclosed another envelope addressed to her uncle.

'He has a suggestion to make,' Edwin Kingsley announced a minute or two later, looking at her over his half-moon spectacles. 'He wants his godson to spend three months here, learning Arabic and studying the Collection.'

'Here in this house, you mean, or here in England?'

Edwin consulted his letter again. 'Here with us . . . Marcel says quite specifically "*chez vous*". The godson is not French, by the way, but a French-Canadian called Jules Legrand. What do you feel about that?'

Jane didn't answer the question, being concerned with one of her own.

'Have you heard of Monsieur Legrand before? Did you even know that Oncle Marcel *had* a godson?'

'He's the son of someone Marcel met at the end of the war,

when Paris was liberated. I suspect that, having no child of his own, my old friend is grooming the young man to run the gallery for him eventually. Marcel has hopes of making a good scholar out of him.'

She couldn't help grinning at the comment, aware that if the French-Canadian had this merit her uncle would happily accept him. Even so, there was an anxiety to be registered. 'It's a lot to ask of you – a stranger here for three months, and teaching him into the bargain.'

A gleam of humour flitted across her uncle's thin face. 'Trust a Frenchman to be practical – Marcel wants me to pass on what I know before I pass on myself! I think we shall have to let the young man come.'

Jane nodded, still doubtful about the idea but taking comfort from the thought that no average young man would put up with even one month in the Kingsley household. Her uncle would see to it that any student of his learned what he was there to learn. By way of light relief, there would be health-giving walks along the river, and General Wolfe's battles refought over the backgammon board each evening. She gave Monsieur Legrand a week or two at most of this rather spartan régime. But clearing away the breakfast dishes, she realised that for once her birthday wasn't running true to form. Two surprises so far made her think superstitiously that there must be a third to come. There was, and it was even now standing on the doorstep.

The shock when she answered the ring at the door was heart-stopping. She hadn't seen the large man who stood there for more than six years. He looked older than she knew him to be, but she would always recognise him, however much time and experience had changed the youthful contours of his face. Her teenage years had been spent in hopeless hero-worship of him, and through every painful one of them she'd known that he saw her only as the lonely orphan who'd had to be inserted into Edwin Kingsley's bachelor existence.

'Remember me?' he enquired calmly now. 'Oliver Hatton, and not the ghost of times past, as you obviously seem to think.'

She made a tremendous effort, released her clutch on the door, and held out her hand. 'I'm taken aback,' she explained hoarsely. 'You're supposed to be in America. Why didn't Mary say you were about to honour us with a visit?'

'She didn't know. As far as my dear mama's concerned, her black sheep has sown his wild oats at last and come back to browse in the calm pastures of home.'

'Sheep graze,' she pointed out faintly, determined somehow to be true to her calling. 'Do I gather that a surfeit of wild oats isn't really what has brought you back to Little Fairford?'

'The real reason's not for public consumption. Father wrote to me a little while ago to say he'd been given an ultimatum by the doctor: a quieter life, or a shorter one. You know Richard almost as well as I do . . . he was so damned casual about it that I properly got the wind up. All in all, it seemed the moment to pack in my American adventure and come home.'

He looked from Jane's face to the posy of tightly massed jonquils clutched in his hand, and remembered why he'd been sent there.

'Special delivery – happy birthday from the Hattons!'

She stared at the exquisite handful of spring, then at the man who stood indolently propped against the door-post. He'd changed, but not in this deceptive habit he'd always had of ambling about the world as if he was on the verge of falling asleep. He must have succeeded in New York by misleading his competitors. It would have taken time to discover that toughness and self-controlled strength lay beneath lazy surface charm and affability. Jane dragged her eyes away from his face and considered the flowers instead.

'Richard's choicest blooms, I bet, and arranged by Mary's loving hands.'

'True, but who was it that crawled about the undergrowth, looking for them? I don't see why I shouldn't get some of the credit.'

He was solemn as a judge, and that was something else that hadn't changed. Oliver, when deadpan and serious, was always laughing inside.

'All that effort . . . it's quite worn you out, I expect. Will you come in and sit down before you tackle the walk home?'

Her face expressed nothing but gentle concern for an ageing visitor. He looked at her, thinking that of all the changes he'd noticed since coming back to England, the change in Jane Kingsley was the most astonishing of all. He'd left behind a gauche, dazzled adolescent who frequently embarrassed herself and him. There was nothing gauche about the young woman whose huge dark eyes now had the impertinence to laugh at him. Hero-worship seemed to have been been outgrown as well.

'A rest would be welcome,' he agreed with a wistful air that made her grin, 'but there's work to be done. I must soldier on unless I've managed to lose my shopping list already . . .' he broke off to rummage in the pockets of his jacket, '. . . no, here it is; a house seems to be the first item.'

'A house?' she enquired faintly.

'Somewhere to live,' he explained with gentle patience. 'I'm too old to fly back to the parental nest, wouldn't you say?'

'Much too old, and Mary would be worn out in no time,

putting up with you. Anyway, surely you want to carve out a niche for yourself in London?'

'There's a hopeful note on your voice, little one. You're supposed to welcome the returning prodigal with open arms, not push him out of the door again.' She left the suggestion alone, and he had to go on. 'You've also missed the point. I've come home to add another Hatton to the Hatton & Meredith partnership. I'll be living in the vicinity . . . Oxford, probably.'

She supposed it was something to be thankful for that he didn't propose to settle in the village, but Oxford was a bare eight miles away. Oliver's sleepy gaze registered the flicker of dismay in her eyes; this coolly grown-up Jane hadn't, at least, entirely lost the habit of giving her feelings away. But he looked away at his now empty hands, brow wrinkled in a frown. 'There was something else I was supposed to remember. I know! Mary wants you and Edwin to come to dinner this evening – combined celebration: your birthday and my homecoming. Are you free by any chance?'

'Provided an assignation over the backgammon board can be postponed until tomorrow, I believe we are,' she agreed sedately.

Oliver stared at her for a moment, then smiled. It was a smile he'd been careful never to offer an adolescent already far gone in love, and Jane was grateful for the fact. With that sort of encouragement at the time she might have disintegrated altogether. She could manage it very well now.

'It's unexpectedly nice to be home,' he said gently. 'See you, little one.'

She watched him amble down the path, thinking that her birthday's third surprise had rather outdone the other two; the temptation was strong to sit down and contemplate nothing except the extraordinary fact that Oliver was back among them, but she forced herself to go in search of her uncle instead, confident that she'd find him in the room that housed the Kingsley Collection.

Her great-grandfather, Edwin's grandfather, had sunk his wealth in acquiring the rare instruments that made up the Collection – astrolabes made in Muslim Spain, of brass so richly engraved and decorated that it gleamed like gold against hangings of blue velvet; armillary spheres whose intricately intertwining circles depicted all that medieval minds had been able to comprehend of the Universe; and treatises on astronomy and medicine penned in the exquisite, flowing lines of Arabic calligraphy.

Jane stood in the doorway, watching Edwin's absorbed face, and wishing yet again that she could feel some real interest in the Collection. The instruments were beautiful, and fascinating to historians like Uncle Edwin and Marcel Colbert, but for her they went too far back in time, and the civilisation that had created them was tainted by what had happened since. For Edwin the past still lived in these beautiful artefacts. For her the past was what she remembered of her laughing, loving parents, annihilated by a Middle Eastern bomb thrown in some futile fundamentalist vendetta. Ten years old at the time, Jane never saw either of them again. She'd never managed to look at the Collection since without seeing in her mind's eye a wreckage-strewn hillside outside Jerusalem.

'Are you trying to visualise all this with Jules Legrand's eyes?' she asked now.

'I suppose I'm hoping that a young man destined to go into a famous auction house won't just see the instruments with a price-tag on them.'

'*Oncle* Marcel doesn't, and it's his auction house,' she pointed out consolingly.

'I know, my dear. But he *is* a scholar, as well as a businessman.'

It explained the unlikely friendship between a retired and retiring don and a rich, urbane, pleasure-loving Frenchman. After her uncle's heart attack, it was Marcel Colbert who always did the travelling. He was a generous guest, arriving with out-of-season delicacies, expensive perfume for Jane, and books for Edwin that a retired scholar coveted but wouldn't dream of buying for himself. She doubted whether her uncle should have been asked to take on three months' intensive work, but there was no denying that the prospect of teaching someone again had brought a sparkle to his face.

'We're invited to dinner with the Hattons this evening – Oliver's home,' she explained briefly. 'Do you feel like going?'

'Of course. What a pleasure to have him back again!'

She was saved from answering by the *ping* of the telephone. Her uncle's side of the conversation, conducted in French, told her that he was speaking to his friend in Paris. The half she could hear seemed to suggest that their visitor was going to arrive a good deal sooner than she'd bargained for.

'That was Marcel, ringing from London,' said Edwin, putting down the telephone. 'He and his godson flew over unexpectedly to attend a sale at Sotheby's. I got the impression that the young man had come prepared to stay, in the hope that I would suggest it. When I did, Marcel jumped at the idea, so they'll both come down this afternoon, and he will go back alone tomorrow.'

Jane swallowed the comment that they were being hustled unfairly. It would only distress her uncle and waste time better spent on making up beds and restocking the larder.

'What about Mary's dinner party this evening?' she remembered suddenly. 'Do we not go, after all?'

'Oh . . . well, why not ring her, my dear? She and Richard know Marcel already. I dare say she won't mind an extra couple for dinner.'

'It's high-handed . . . I hope she says no!' Jane was stung to tartness on Mary's account even while she knew that half a dozen unexpected guests would be made welcome by Mrs Hatton and greeted with relief by her family, who would otherwise be eating for days afterwards the surplus food she always prepared.

The Owl House was ready for guests and so, just, was Jane by the time an elegant cream-coloured car slid to a halt outside the front door midway through the afternoon. It was perfectly timed and typical of Marcel Colbert's smooth ordering of his affairs. He roamed the world in search of exotic works of art for his Parisian galleries, but bore a charmed life as a traveller. She'd never known him beset by the trials that other people experienced. They could be airsick, strike-bound, or bereft of luggage, but never *Oncle* Marcel. He climbed out of the car now, a little ponderously because he was beginning to put on weight, and surged forward in a waft of *Givenchy pour l'Homme* to kiss her on both cheeks.

'*Ma chère, Jane . . . aujourd'hui plus belle que jamais,*' he pronounced gallantly.

She smiled and accepted the compliment calmly, aware that he would have felt obliged to offer it however she happened to be looking. She greeted him in the French they always spoke together, and waited for his companion to put in an appearance.

With a sense of timing obviously caught from travelling with his godfather, a stranger emerged from the driving seat of the car and sauntered deliberately towards them.

'Act one, scene one,' Jane said to herself. 'Enter Monsieur Jules Legrand.'

He bowed over her hand, then straightened up to make a thorough examination of a girl who was going to figure prominently in his comfort and entertainment for the next three months. A smile appeared, seeming to suggest that the prospect looked rather better that he'd had much hope of. The smile was also slightly rueful – apologetic, she thought, about the effect he couldn't help making on a sex-starved village maiden. Still, she acknowledged privately that, although not altogether young, he *was* a stunning vision of manhood . . . sun-bronzed skin acquired on some ski-slope or other, and the throw-away elegance that few Englishmen aspired to. If he looked a little too pleased with himself, she must put up with that. He was heaven-sent – just what she needed to convince a large, sleepy gentleman that it made no difference to her on which side of the Atlantic he now lived.

Beyond explaining the rambling layout of the Owl House to their new guest, and supplying Marcel with the China tea he always insisted was his real reason for visiting England, Jane left them alone with her uncle until it was time to shepherd them to the other end of the village for dinner. The Hattons' home had once been Little Fairford's vicarage and it was her favourite house among the architectural hotch-potch that made the village odd but beautiful. Two hundred years of weathering had mellowed its brick to a soft glowing red, and miraculously it had escaped the fell hand of the developer; the rooms and windows were as perfect as their Georgian builder had made them.

As they strolled towards the house she saw Marcel Colbert considering it with the approving eye of an expert. The inconveniently picturesque held no charms for him – elegance and proportional grace were what he asked for, in his surroundings as well as in the women he escorted. Aware of this, she'd done her best, knowing that her usual hasty preparations for a social occasion in the village wouldn't do. It had no connection whatsoever with Oliver Hatton; she was simply keeping England's flag aloft in front of two Parisian visitors! Her dress was far from new, but the yellow silk glowed against her dark eyes and hair, and perfectly matched a surprise birthday gift of antique topaz earrings brought her by *Oncle* Marcel. She thought with gratitude that they made her look unusually sophisticated.

'Tell me about our hosts,' he said as they walked slowly up the drive at a pace that suited Edwin Kingsley.

'You've met Richard and Mary Hatton here before, they're our dearest friends, and Richard's also my uncle's solicitor. It was he who found the Owl House for us when we needed to move out of Oxford. He's a fanatical gardener, while Mary collects every stray or damaged animal that crosses her path. There's an occasional clash of interest, but they're devoted to one another all the same.'

'They sound very English,' Marcel commented.

'The very *best* English,' she pointed out swiftly, hackles rising at the scent of condescension, 'they're staunch and kind.'

'Of course,' her companion agreed with haste, 'and their house is "very best English" too, by the way. I hate to admit it, but we never achieved this small-scale perfection in France. Cathedrals, grand palaces, yes . . . but not this lovely domestic architecture.'

Jane was mollified by the tribute, and uncomfortably aware

that she'd snapped at him when her edginess was not his fault; it simply had to do with the prospect of meeting Oliver again. But inside the house her confusion was unnoticed in the flurry of introductions, and she could even ignore Oliver's long, slow stare – brought on by the new earrings, she supposed, because he'd never bothered to stare at her before. Richard Hatton, as tall as his son but much less broad, gave her a shy birthday kiss, and Mary enveloped her in a hug that threatened to dislodge several of the floating scarves and shawls with which she always 'dressed' for dinner.

'Jane, dear, isn't it a gorgeous surprise to have Oliver home? I always prayed he'd get tired of New York; in fact I usually found myself praying for that when I was supposed to be concentrating on something else – like famine relief in India. But it doesn't seem as if God could have minded!'

Mary's conversation took a little getting used to and Jane stifled a grin at the startled expression on Jules Legrand's face; then she was startled in her turn by a strange girl coming slowly down the stairs towards the group still standing in the hall. There was nothing shy about the slow descent – this was a stage entrance by someone who knew the effect it would have.

'Another unexpected visitor,' Mary Hatton explained in a hurried murmur. 'Cousin of Richard's, several times removed. Estelle's an actress, sent here to recuperate after an illness, poor girl. Blessing in disguise, because she'll have no difficulty in keeping Oliver amused.'

Jane could believe it, judging by the way his eyes were on the girl coming towards them. Her own candle-glow of pleasure in her appearance flickered and went out in the face of this flaming competition. A mane of carefully disordered red hair framed enormous green eyes made up to look larger still, and a catsuit of some faintly irridescent material clung to her like a second skin; it added up to something more exotic than Little Fairford normally saw at close range.

'Should I have heard of Estelle Harding?' Jane whispered to Richard Hatton, while the newcomer was being introduced to Edwin and his French friends.

'Doubt it – she's budding rather than full-blown! Two walk-on parts in provincial rep so far. Still, we must say this for her – she walks down a staircase very beautifully!'

The smallest of grins touched his mouth for an instant, reminding Jane of Oliver, and she was suddenly resigned to her yellow silk again.

Back in the drawing-room after dinner, handing round Mary's coffee, she was surprised to receive an inviting smile from Estelle.

'Mary says you *live* here.' The actress voice held a note of wonder that made Jane grin.

'Quite a lot of people do – it's a large village, not the Sahara desert!'

'I know, but what can you find to do? There isn't even anything that could be called a shop apart from that gruesome little emporium known as the General Stores.'

'I keep house for my uncle, but my job is to help teach the next generation – all forty of them – in the village school.'

'My God,' Estelle murmured faintly. 'I thought an actor's lot was hard.'

She stared at Jane, looking for some visible mark of a fate that must certainly be worse than death, then smiled with the relief of finding the French-Canadian visitor at her elbow. At least he came from a world that she could understand. Jane was free to return to the coffee tray, but found Oliver there, waiting for her. It was an effort to pour coffee and cream unconcernedly, but pride insisted that she didn't allow her hand to tremble.

'You're looking very gorgeous, little one. I still haven't quite got used to the new Jane Kingsley.'

'*Oncle* Marcel's birthday earrings, I expect,' she explained solemnly. 'I dare say they'd beautify a hippopotamus.'

Her literal-minded friends would have felt obliged to point out that hippopotami hardly ever wore topaz earrings, but she knew she was safe with Oliver – a delight in the absurd was a pleasure they'd always shared, and it was one of the things for which she'd missed him most.

'Your own house guest is truly gorgeous,' she said wistfully. 'I doubt if it matters whether she can act or not.' Oliver's glance followed hers across the room to where Estelle was now getting into her stride with Jules.

'Your uncle's friend must be a relief to her,' he said with a reminiscent grin. 'Little Fairford's brand of entertainment so far has been unfamiliar, to say the least. Mama had her holding a blackbird this afternoon while she put a splint on its broken wing. This afternoon it was my father's turn to amuse, which he did with a detailed lecture on the propagation of camellias! What did *you* say, by the way, to take her aback just now?'

'Only explained that I manage to exist here quite happily. I think she found it hard to believe, but it was the village school-marm bit that really threw her!'

'*Is* it a happy existence, Jane?' The quiet question was asked without his normal undercurrent of amusement for once. 'I heard from Mama, of course, about Edwin's illness and the move from Oxford, but I don't remember you dreaming long ago of a life spent teaching in the village school.'

She was surprised into answering truthfully. 'The dream rather fell apart, I'm afraid, and I felt resentful to begin with, because the glorious visions disappeared too suddenly . . . three years of untrammelled bliss at Cambridge to be followed by the world-shaking novels I was going to write! Instead, there was the Owl House to be made habitable, and Uncle Edwin to nurse. But as soon as he was well enough I took a teaching diploma at the Oxford Poly. I was on the point of starting to look for a job when dear Miss Prentice retired, and Jim Watkins offered me the vacancy . . . pure luck!'

'Was it?' Oliver asked sceptically.

Jane nodded her head. 'Oh yes – I wouldn't change jobs now, even if I could. The children are willing to learn simply because they know I belong here, whereas they'd be thinking up all kinds of devilment for a stranger. In return, they're a continual education to me, and in the process we all seem to have a good time.'

He smiled but made no comment, still coming to terms with the fact that a silent, awkward waif should have blossomed while his back was turned into this new Jane Kingsley . . . a girl to be reckoned with, who came startlingly close to beauty when she smiled, and certainly didn't stand in need of help from expensive earrings. Jane was unaware of his silence, having her own thoughts to wrestle with. Among them was the question of whether or not she should touch on something personal with a man who'd never been one to invite comment on his private life. Mary had relieved her own distress by confiding in Jane about his short-lived marriage in America. Its ending had been particularly unpleasant, and a proud, reserved man had had to endure a very public legal battle to get free of a woman with a beautiful face and the morals of an alley cat. He hadn't lost the lazily relaxed air of someone who didn't take the world very seriously, but Jane wondered what it had cost him in self-control.

'I'm sorry about what happened in New York, Oliver . . . the divorce . . . and everything,' she muttered.

'Thank you. Kind of you not to think I got what I deserved.' His tone of voice rather than the actual words told her that it was to be the end of a subject which was not for chewing over endlessly by all the ladies in the village. He changed the subject instead by gesturing across the room to where Estelle still flirted happily with Jules.

'Our foreign Adonis is carrying all before him, I see; an irresistible mixture of transatlantic verve and French polish!'

'Don't worry,' she recommended sweetly. 'Estelle will remember solid English worth eventually and come back to you.'

If it had been meant to comfort, all she got in return was a quelling stare.

'You've become very pert while my back was turned, little one.'

'And you have become a trifle pompous, dear Oliver!'

His shaken expression made her relent to the extent of giving him a kindly smile, but she walked away to talk to Mary while she still had the upper hand. Her victories over him in the past had been few, and they had also been brief; she had no intention of staying to let him wrest this one out of her hand.

Two

The morning after Mary's dinner party, Jules drove his godfather back to London Airport, and work started in earnest with Edwin as soon as he returned. Jane wasn't one to give up her prejudices without a struggle; it took her several days to admit to herself that when Oliver wasn't in sight she could stomach their visitor at all, and several more to decide that he might actually be an asset to the household. But from the very first day it was clear that he wouldn't have to be dragooned into working. He spent each morning in his own room, studying the Arabic that inscribed so many of the early instruments, and only emerging when he needed his teacher's help. The afternoons were given over to studying the instruments themselves; the times and places in which they had been made, and the ways in which they had been used. Jane knew that intelligence alone would have endeared Jules to her uncle, but he was diligent and courteous as well, and the combination earned him the complete approval of an exacting man.

'Marcel's fortunate to have such a protégé,' Edwin said wistfully one morning. 'Jules will be more than capable of running the galleries when the time comes, and although he likes to consider himself a businessman, I think he may even have the makings of a genuine scholar as well.'

At the weekend it was decreed that there should be some relief from study, and Jules immediately invited them out to lunch. Edwin declined on the grounds that he was going to earth in his study with a book he longed to read, and Jane was equally reluctant to waste the first sunshine of the year shut up in some dim restaurant. Instead, she countered Jules' suggestion with one of her own.

'It's too lovely to be indoors; why don't we take a picnic on the river? We could go along the backwater. It will be sheltered there, almost warm, in fact.'

If he thought a river excursion in March sounded insane, he managed not to say so. He'd had time enough already to register the fact that Jane Kingsley was not quite like the girls he was used to; a speculative glance now and then he didn't mind, but derision in her eyes wouldn't do at all.

'The river sounds fine,' he managed to say cheerfully, and was rewarded with a friendlier smile than usual.

Warmly dressed as she recommended, he even found himself enjoying the absurd picnic. Winter hadn't yet given way to spring, but the quiet stretch of water *was* sheltered, and he was strangely aware of both peace and gratitude.

'I'm lucky to be here,' he announced abruptly. 'I haven't said that before, and should have done.'

'Perhaps you weren't sure,' Jane suggested with a small grin. 'Little Fairford must be about as far removed from Paris as anyone could get, in terms of exciting daily life, and apart from that Uncle Edwin is working you very hard.'

'I'm here to work hard – I owe it to Marcel Colbert, as well as to your uncle.'

His eyes were fixed on a water-vole, scurrying along the bank beside them, and it was safe to inspect the contradictions in his face – youthful, but not young; expressive, but only when he wanted it to be; often smiling, but not necessarily amused. Altogether, he was a puzzle that she was beginning to find interesting.

'I know you're Marcel Colbert's godson,' she said suddenly, 'but how did that come about?'

Jules abandoned his nature study to smile at her. 'More luck, in a way! My father was in Paris at the end of the war, doing liaison-work with the free French. He met Marcel, managed to save his life in fact, and afterwards they became friends. Then it was time to return to Canada, but they stayed in touch until my father died. I grew up in Quebec, but I knew all along where I wanted to be.'

'So you left home for Paris, and a godfather you'd never met? It was adventurous, I think.'

After a small pause he startled her with his answer. 'I *am* an adventurer, Jane, but not a stupidly rash one. I studied what I knew would be helpful to Marcel . . . am still studying, to make myself *more* helpful, and we understand each other very well.'

She nodded, vaguely troubled until he reached out to cover one of her hands with his own.

'We like each other, too, and that has become important to both of us.'

She smiled then, and said they'd been idle long enough; it was time to start moving again. He didn't revert to talking about himself, but she had the pleasant feeling when they went home that because he'd been honest with her their friendship had advanced a little, slowly but surely.

The following morning he announced that he would like to go with her to morning service in the village church.

'More education?' she enquired with a smile.

He looked put out for a moment, then had the grace to grin. 'You guess that I don't normally do such a thing. It's true, but I'm interested in Little Fairford.'

The Hatton pew looked unusually full, and Jane found herself smiling inwardly at the picture they made. Mary's happiness at having her son home again lit up the morning, and Oliver bowed gracefully to all the ladies who inspected him. Estelle wore an outfit that would have graced a London party, and Richard, by her side, pretended bravely that he didn't mind being stared at by the rest of the congregation.

Out in the churchyard after the service, Jane was trapped by the Vicar in a discussion about the forthcoming village fête. By the time she was free again Jules was in the middle of the Hatton party, obviously enjoying the sight of Estelle's black-veiled face. Over-dressed, Jane decided austerely, but her new friend didn't think so. She watched him for a moment, intrigued by this different view of him from the one they saw at the Owl House. Which was the real Jules Legrand – the eager student who hung on her uncle's lips, or this smoothly charming man who could so easily keep his end up with Estelle Harding? She hadn't made her mind up when Mary Hatton's voice distracted her.

'Jane, my love, you're looking delicious this morning . . . lucky girl to be able to wear that colour! Isn't she gorgeous, Oliver?'

Oliver took his time about answering. 'Like the best kind of lettuce, I'd say,' he agreed at last, 'all crisp and green.'

Jane supposed it was the best she could have hoped for, but Mary saw nothing to cavil at and smiled happily at her son. She'd made it plain years ago what she wanted most in life; if only he would marry Edwin's orphaned niece, they could all live happily ever after in Little Fairford. That loving blackmail had helped drive him away to practice law in New York instead of Oxford. Jane knew she hadn't been intended to overhear the terms in which he was finally driven to make the matter clear to Mary – Jane Kingsley was a harmless little thing, but he was *not* going to spend the rest of his life looking after a tongue-tied, sexless waif even to make his mother happy. She doubted whether either of them now remembered that cruelly dismissive sentence, but it was branded on her own memory so painfully that she was obsessed with the need to show him that she'd grown out of hero-worship, along with measles and spots.

'Come back to lunch with us, Jane,' Mary was suggesting hopefully. 'Bring Jules as well. He seems to be getting on very well with Estelle, and I'm afraid Richard finds her a bit overpowering.'

Jane smiled but shook her head. 'We left Uncle Edwin to his own devices all day yesterday, and there's no lunch prepared for him.' She sent a glance brim-full of mischief in Oliver's direction. 'I'm sure your son is more than a match for Estelle.'

Oliver heard and answered the note of challenge. 'She isn't all he's a match for, my dear Jane. You're living very dangerously.' His voice was an amiable drawl as usual, but a glint in the eyes holding her own suggested that they now met on equal terms. Little Jane was long since gone; if she wanted to cross swords with him she must be prepared to take the consequences.

It was something to think about, but meanwhile the matter of lunch still remained to be settled. She beckoned to Jules and he wandered over with Estelle.

'Mrs Hatton is asking us to lunch, Jules. I must go home, but there's no need for you to do so.'

He hesitated for a moment, smiled regretfully at Estelle, then bowed with charming grace in the direction of Mary Hatton.

'Another time, if you permit, Madame. Today I think I must conduct Jane safely back to the Owl House.'

Jane saw the danger in the nick of time. The grin on Oliver's mouth told her clearly that he was about to enjoy himself, enlarging on the variety of perils that might lie in wait if she attempted to cross the village green on her own. Before he could embark on them she leapt into the conversation.

'We'll be on our way, then,' she said hastily. '*Bon appetit*, everyone!'

She walked home hoping that it wouldn't be long before Oliver found himself a house away from Little Fairford. It was unsettling to have him around, and tiring to have to keep her defences constantly manned in case he should suddenly appear. There was no danger of falling in love with him again; that particular virus was like lightning, never striking in the same place twice. But he wasn't a man to be overlooked, even in a crowd. Established in a home of his own, he'd do no more than check up on his parents occasionally; better still, a home of his own would probably need a wife of his own as well. If he could summon up the energy to crook his little finger at them, there'd be no shortage of women falling over themselves to keep him amused, but Jane reckoned it was time he settled down and labelled himself a staid married man.

Jules returned to his Arabic mysteries after the weekend break and Jane was plunged into planning the second half of the school spring term. Fine weather always brought the risk of a rise in the truancy rate, and the only way to counter it would be to take the children on as many outdoor expeditions as possible. It was beyond the wit of any teacher to hold their attention for long once April sunshine flooded the classroom, and a cuckoo in the woods behind the church mocked the poor creatures who were cooped up indoors.

The longer evenings were also hard to resist. Jules got into the habit of sharing Jane's after-dinner stroll, or sometimes they would take the punt out on the river in the last of the day's light. They occasionally met Oliver, entertaining Estelle in the same way, but Jane didn't know whether to deduce from this that he was in no hurry to leave home or in no hurry to leave Estelle. Their separate excursions sometimes merged into one, though Jane avoided it as far as possible. It was obvious that the two men didn't like each other, and the more proprietorial Jules became, the more sardonic amusement she detected in Oliver. It wasn't anything he said, but she saw his raised eyebrow when Jules helped her over stiles or in and out of the punt with exaggerated care. She wasn't used to such treatment, having been raised in the knowledge that she must learn to fend for herself; still, it was pleasant to be squired, and know herself the envy of the rest of Little Fairford's female population.

Given the normal tempo of social life in the village, they might have seen little more of the Hatton household than church on Sundays, but with Oliver home again and a charming French-Canadian around as well, the local ladies were spurred to a frenzy of entertaining. Cocktail parties and dinners abounded, and at all of them Jane could see Oliver partnering Estelle with obvious enjoyment. She gave thanks for Jules, who stayed devotedly by her own side, and enabled her to smile at Oliver with a friendly indifference he found extremely irritating.

Edwin Kingsley took no part in the social activity, but kept his frail store of energy for teaching. He looked increasingly tired, but Jane knew how much he was enjoying himself and refused to nag him into resting. It was Jules who raised the subject of his health when they were out in the punt one evening. She had been silent, content to watch a family of young moorhens in the roots of a willow tree that sprawled into the river, but she looked up to find him staring at her.

'You look very solemn . . . something bothering you?' she asked gently.

'*You* bother me,' he said with sudden emphasis. 'I've never met anyone so alone in the world.'

'I've got Uncle Edwin,' she pointed out, not yet ready to share with him the fact that her parents remained vividly alive in her memory.

'Mr Kingsley is a sick man, Jane. In fact I keep wondering whether I should go on staying here. I know Marcel suggested three months, but I'm beginning to feel a burden.'

Jane shook her head. 'Please don't think of leaving. My uncle's perfectly capable of saying if he wants you to go. I know he looks fragile, but he's happier helping you than he's been for several years. He wouldn't thank you for trying to spare him exertion and prolonging his life; quality is much more important to him than quantity.'

A little silence fell between them until Jules asked another question.

'What will you do . . . eventually?'

'Stay here, I expect. I'm a creature of habit. The Collection is left in my uncle's will to one of the University museums in Oxford, of course, but I think he'd expect me to go on living at the Owl House.'

Jules hesitated for a moment. 'Don't you really mind about losing the Collection? It's an incredibly valuable possession just to give away.'

'Uncle Edwin knows that I wouldn't want to keep it, and

even if I did, it wouldn't make any difference. He'll do what he thinks is right, and he believes the Museum is the place for it.'

Jules put that subject aside and asked another question. 'I know we always see Oliver Hatton with Estelle, but I seem to sense a link between you. Does he have anything to do with your decision to stay here?'

She would have liked to say that it wasn't a question he had any right to ask, but he'd been kind enough to feel concerned about her and it was hard to snub him. Nor, in any case, was *anyone* to think she had an interest in Oliver Hatton.

'What you sense is the remains of childhood affection. Oliver was very kind to me when I first came to live with Uncle Edwin. Losing my parents shocked me into almost total silence for a long time, but he used to drag me around the countryside with him, explaining things, taking no notice when I said nothing in return. Of course, as an adolescent I fell in love with him, but it was a dose of hero-worship so violent that it couldn't possibly have survived, even if he hadn't gone off to America. Now that he's back I'm "young Jane" again, familiar and unnoticeable! He seems rather serious about Estelle, but even if he's not, there'll be plenty of other women ready to distract him from being the hardworking solicitor he's supposed to be.'

She was pleased with this airy summing-up, but glad when Jules decided to change the subject.

'Marcel told me something I find it hard to believe. Is it really true that the Collection is as unprotected as it appears to be?'

'Yes, it's true,' she confirmed unconcernedly. 'We couldn't afford even a fraction of the premium any insurance company would ask for, and my uncle wouldn't agree to have it locked away in bank vaults. He thinks the instruments are beautiful, of course, but their real value for him is what people like you can learn from them. He'd never allow them not to be available. Anyway, in a sense the Collection *is* protected: everyone knows where those instruments belong and no thief would get a reputable dealer to touch them.'

'I agree with you, but it leaves out of account a good many disreputable dealers.'

'It's a chance my uncle takes,' Jane said calmly.

'And you wonder why I worry about you!'

The intense remark made her smile at him. 'There's no need. Heaven has a special department looking after innocents like Uncle Edwin and me!'

When she got home from school next day Jules was out, and she remembered that he was due to spend the evening in Oxford with an acquaintance of Marcel's. Supper could be simple for once, and there would even be time to do some work in the garden before she need think of getting it. She was struggling in the middle of an overgrown flower-bed when someone spoke behind her. Oliver, sounding amused and half-asleep as usual.

'"A garden is a lovesome thing, God wot" . . . especially when it includes the view I now have of such a delectable small behind!'

Jane shot upright, cheeks flushed and temper not improved by the fact that he'd startled her into jabbing her toes with the fork.

'I don't know what brings you here, but it would be helpful if you didn't creep about like the villain in a Victorian melodrama.'

'I could go away and make a noisier entrance if you like.'

She brushed the suggestion aside but still frowned at him. 'What *are* you doing here, anyway?'

'Attending to your uncle's affairs. I've taken them over from my father.'

'Oh . . . he didn't say.' She sounded slightly aggrieved.

'He didn't know until this afternoon,' Oliver explained, trying not to smile. 'I offered him my services in future and he was kind enough to accept, so you'll be seeing a little more of me from now on.'

Recovered now, Jane managed to bow like a duchess. 'How very delightful.'

His mouth twitched, but there was a different subject on his mind. 'I thought Legrand was here to learn Arabic? He seems to work on the Collection too, I see. In fact he'd got one of the astrolabes in pieces when I arrived yesterday morning.'

'He's here to study the instruments as much as to learn Arabic; of course he has to handle them.'

Oliver gave all his attention to a camellia that was about to burst into flower. 'Does our friend know what is going to happen to the Collection?'

The question sounded casual but Jane knew him too well. She was suddenly angry for Jules, and enraged on her own account for the credulity she was being charged with.

'Why not say what you really mean, Oliver, instead of phrasing it so delicately? Does Jules know it's no good running after me because I'm not going to inherit the Collection?'

She'd forgotten how fast an indolent man could move when he wanted to. He closed the gap between them in one swift stride and took her shoulders in a grip that made her wince.

'God help you if you ever shout at me again, Jane Kingsley. My question wasn't intended to be offensive, as it happens. Given the value of the Collection, Legrand's obvious interest in it, and my professional connection with Edwin's affairs, I've a right to know the answer. So cool down and tell me – does he know or not?'

'Marcel knows, and so does Jules,' she conceded reluctantly.

'Excellent. So if he does propose to you, we shall know that his intentions are honourable!'

The blandness of it almost goaded her into shouting at him again, but discretion finally got the better of valour, helped by the fact that she'd thought of a reply that would surely irritate him.

'Such admirable concern for your clients' interests, Oliver . . . how fortunate we are to have you.'

He accepted the tribute with a smile that would have done credit to a crocodile. 'Don't be too sure, little one. I should, of course, advise Edwin not to let you marry Jules Legrand. You need someone *much* more capable of keeping you in order.'

A bow and he was gone, leaving her to wreak havoc among the weeds in the herbaceous border.

Three

The following Saturday was the day of the 'little' village fête, so-called to distinguish it from the Grand Fête that always rounded off the summer. Jane spent an entire evening trying to explain to Jules what would be expected of him, but it was hard to make him understand why people were prepared to work so hard for no personal reward.

They woke to the ominous patter of rain, but 'Curly' Clark, village odd-job man and infallible weather prophet consulted in the shop after breakfast, scratched his absolutely bald head and pronounced that the skies would clear by mid-morning. At ten the rain was still sluicing down, by eleven a slight rift in the clouds was visible, and at lunch-time Curly's reputation was safe. The Manor grounds – time-honoured setting for the fête – were steaming gently in the warm sunshine.

Jane's allotted task was the plant stall, for which she'd been potting up seedlings and cuttings all the week and wheedling contributions out of neighbours. She and Jules shared an early lunch with Edwin, then loaded up the car and set off for the Manor. Feverish activity finally won against the late start, and by the time General Harcourt led his 'celebrity' out to declare the fête open, the stalls were more or less ready for their first customers. The celebrity in question turned out to be Estelle Harding, easily making up in glamour anything she lacked in reputation. The village didn't particularly mind that it had never heard of her; all that mattered was that she exactly matched its communal idea of what an exotic actress should be.

Business at the plant stall was brisk but chaotic, owing to Jules' inability to tell one piece of merchandise from another. Still, on balance Jane reckoned he was more of a help than a hindrance, since the ladies of the village were charmed into buying whatever he offered them. By half-past three the stall was sold out and they were free to inspect other people's efforts. Oliver was still pinned to his hoop-la duties, drumming up clients with a line of patter so dreadful that his customers were too weak with laughter to get anywhere near the objects they aimed at.

He looked relieved to see Jane. 'Just the girl I was needing. Be a honey and ferry Gran Parsons home for me. I promised to take her as soon as she got weary, but I can't leave this damned stall. Alternatively you can stay and mind the shop while I do the ferrying.'

'I think I'd rather take Gran home,' Jane said frankly. She handed Jules over to Estelle, and by the time she got back the proceedings were almost over. The Vicar had made the speech of thanks he delivered every year, and the village was straggling contentedly home to high tea. Only the helpers were left, being fortified by the General's home-brewed beer before they put his garden to rights.

'I missed the egg-and-spoon race,' Jane said regretfully. 'An epic of its kind,' Oliver commented, overhearing her. 'Mrs Hughes-Watson was in the lead and running well, to the consternation of one and all. But just when it seemed all over, the foolish woman got over-excited and was firmly ruled by Curly to have fouled Mama! She was disqualified, and my dear mother ran on gamely to finish last, having lost her egg on the final lap and been sent back to the start again.'

Jane wiped the tears of laughter from her face, forgetting for a moment that she'd intended to be on her dignity with him. 'Poor Mary . . . though I suppose we really ought to say poor Mrs H-W. She'd work so hard for the village if only it would let her.'

'Frightful woman,' said the General frankly, then blushed under the Vicar's reproachful eye, '. . . means well, I dare say.'

A silence greeted this doubtful statement until Jane thought to ask what the afternoon's efforts had done to help swell the organ fund.

The Vicar cheered up immediately. 'Best yet, my dear – we took in three hundred and seventy-one pounds, not including five Irish pennies and a button which I fear could only have come from Curly's grandson.'

'You forgot to mention that a good time was had by all,' Oliver added with a smile. 'Estelle, especially, enjoyed it – her first starring role!' Then he put down his tankard and set about organising the work-force with ruthless efficiency. It wasn't until she'd been sweeping up rubbish for ten minutes that Jane realised he was no longer there at all. By the time he finally reappeared they were tiredly putting their tools together and the Manor gardens were neat again.

'What happened to you? I suppose you wore yourself out at the hoop-la stall and had to go and lie down somewhere?' she suggested coolly.

'Not at all, beloved. I thought the most useful thing I could do was to take the General off your hands. You know how the old boy gets in the way. We've been discussing a spot of blight in his orchid house.'

Jane stared at him with a fascinated eye. 'You felt able to advise?'

'No, but I listened very intelligently.'

She gave up the struggle and told Jules it was time they went home. His face wore such a deep frown as they walked back to the car that she felt obliged to apologise for taking him to the fête.

'I know it's a strange way to spend an afternoon, but I hoped you were enjoying it,' she said diffidently.

'Of course I enjoyed it . . . I wanted to help you. My difficulty is that I find myself hating Oliver Hatton more and more.'

For a moment or two she told herself that he was joking, but his set face denied the possibility. There was also her strong feeling that the dislike was mutual. An Englishman would shy away from using the word 'hate', but she thought Oliver's own antipathy was real, all the same. She tucked a hand in Jules', wanting him to look less unhappy.

'I don't think you've any right to hate Oliver,' she said gently, 'and certainly no reason.'

'You're wrong, *chérie*; my instinct tells me that I have both.' He didn't elaborate on it, and that in itself was worrying.

It was time to register the fact that she'd been too thoughtlessly grateful for his friendship. She could insist, of course, that he was wrong about Oliver, but it wouldn't help matters to explain why. The two of them were poles apart enough already without her suggesting that it amused an Englishman to provoke a foreigner he found uncongenial.

'Oliver refuses to take the world very seriously,' she tried to say instead. 'We're all specimens, observed under his microscope for the amusement we give him.'

'Perhaps, but he mustn't expect us to share his enjoyment.'

She agreed that the objection was reasonable, but gave a little inward sigh. Jules was often more French than Canadian, and it seemed useless to point out that she couldn't help seeing some virtue in Oliver's philosophy.

Worn out by the excitement of the fête, the village took life easy the following week. So peaceful was it – humdrum, even – that Jane convinced herself she'd been unnecessarily alarmed about her guest. It was ridiculous to feel a prickle of foreboding just because he expressed his feelings more intensely than she was used to. Even if it was true that two civilised men could grow to hate each other, it would scarcely matter if they did; Oliver would soon be safely out of the way in a house of his own, and Jules would return to France. Without them to unsettle everybody, herself included, life at Little Fairford would go back to being what it always was – happy, but uneventful.

But things were *not* ordinary one morning the following week. Edwin Kingsley didn't appear for breakfast as usual and when Jane knocked at his door she found him still in bed – something she had never known happen except in the days immediately following his heart attack.

'Nothing to fuss about,' his voice insisted, faint but definite, 'I've taken the pills.'

She knew better than to fret him with her own alarm. He needed time for the pills to take effect; all she could do for him was put more pillows behind his back so that he could sit upright without strain, and then sit holding his hand. Gradually she felt the rigidity of his body relax and knew that he no longer braced himself against another onslaught of pain.

'Shall I call Dr James now?' she asked at last.

'No point, we know what he'd say – rest more!' her uncle whispered.

'Jules keeps wondering whether he should go away and leave you in peace. Shall I ask him to?'

Edwin shook his head slightly. 'Like having him here. He's doing very well, but I haven't finished with him yet.'

Jane's opinion was that Dr James, if consulted, would certainly say that a visitor should be sent away, and she was debating whether to insist on it when her uncle spoke again in a stronger voice.

'Been thinking of your parents, my dear, remembering how complete they seemed together. A companion's a good thing. I like Jules very much, and my impression is that he likes you. I should be happy to think he was going to take care of you.'

It was, in all respects, an unusual speech for her uncle to have made. It had never crossed her mind that such a self-sufficient man might, after all, have regretted a bachelor life. Even more vividly than he did, she remembered her parents' happiness in being alive together; it had been enough to light up whatever dingy rented apartment they happened to be living in. Jane could recall an ever-present shortage of money, and a lack of what other people considered necessary comfort, but what remained most vividly in her memory were days coloured golden with love and laughter. William and Genevieve might have been complete together, but they'd also found ample room in their lives for a small daughter.

'I like Jules, too,' she said at last. 'But it's only elderly ladies who are supposed to matchmake, uncle mine. In any case, he may have some fond attachment in France, for all we know.'

'Hasn't . . . told me so,' Edwin whispered with a triumphant smile.

Jane judged that recovery had reached the stage where her

uncle could now drink some tea. She went away to fetch it, left him to drink it in peace, then went downstairs again to the dining-room. She opened the door on tension so strong in the air that it was almost visible. Jules sat over the remains of breakfast, looking flushed. Oliver was propped against the fireplace, hands in pockets as usual. Still worried about her uncle, Jane felt nothing but irritation with two men who seemed intent on adding an unnecessary complication to her life.

'Good morning, Oliver,' she said curtly. 'If you had an appointment with my uncle, he won't be keeping it. He had what Curly would call a "bit of a turn" this morning.'

She collapse into a chair, grateful for the coffee Jules poured for her. Then he perched himself on the arm of her chair, looking protective and proprietary. Oliver, she now noticed, seemed grim, not his normal imperturbable self at all.

'Doctor needed, Jane?' he enquired briefly.

'I don't think so. There's nothing Dr James could do, and we know already what he'd say – "Edwin, old friend, you must rest more."'

Oliver didn't comment, but his raised eyebrow sketched now a different question.

'Jules has been agitating to leave,' she said hurriedly. 'Uncle Edwin won't hear of it.'

'Monsieur Legrand is full of agitation, it seems,' Oliver commented blandly. 'He seems to think we leave you too much to cope with here. I've tried to explain that Edwin wouldn't thank you for trying to fuss over him, and that if you did need help, you've only to pick up the telephone and half the village would come running.'

'I'm concerned all the same,' Jules said in a voice tight with anger. 'I shall soon be returning to France, leaving Jane here alone with a very sick man.'

His hand clenched on the arm of her chair made her give it a grateful little pat.

'It's very kind of you to worry about me, but I keep telling you there's no need,' she insisted gently.

Oliver surveyed them both with a thoughtful air, then heaved himself upright. 'As the lady says, there's no need to worry yourself. There may not be much of her, but she's become really quite capable and she's surrounded by *old* friends.'

It was clear to Jane that his intention was to point out to an encroaching foreigner that he didn't understand the workings of English village life, but she doubted whether Jules understood that either.

'Is there any message for Uncle Edwin?' she asked pointedly, hoping that an uncomfortable meeting could be brought to an end.

'No. I'll come back for my chat with him another time. But if you'll walk as far as the car with me, I've got a pot of something or other for you from Richard.'

She smiled at Jules, then followed Oliver to the door.

'You don't seem in any hurry,' she pointed out as he ambled along the path with his usual air of having all the time in the world at his disposal. 'Haven't you any work to do?'

'Case piled upon case, like Ossa piled on Pelion . . . or was it the other way round? Right now, though, I'm resting my poor old eyes, looking at you!'

Oliver minded to be provocative was hard to deal with, and Jane opted for a frontal attack in the hope that it would disconcert him.

'You don't like Jules, do you?'

'No more than he likes me, let us say,' he agreed with lazy indifference.

She said nothing, but when he'd delved in the boot of the

car and fished out one of Richard's prize azaleas, potted up and ready for planting, his glance took in the air of strain about her.

'Don't worry, little one. It's just the age-old stupidity of a couple of males squaring up to each other over a female; you should enjoy the spectacle of us making fools of ourselves!'

'Yes, but you're needling Jules just for the fun of it. I wish you wouldn't, because he doesn't understand.'

She couldn't read the expression on his face, but the flower pot was put into her hands, leaving *her* powerless and Oliver free to force her face up towards him. His mouth was suddenly on her own in a kiss that had little to do with neighbourly affection or childhood friendship. It left her breathless, and suddenly sick with anger when he lifted his head and smiled at her.

'Just for fun,' he finally agreed.

He didn't wait for the reply she was incapable of giving, but got into his car and drove away. She looked at the pot still clutched miraculously in her trembling hands, not even seeing the beautiful plant Richard had sent her. During all the agonising years of adolescence she'd dreamed of being kissed by Oliver Hatton – woven round it the magical possibility that he would then stop seeing her as a boring responsibility, and a lovesick pain in the neck. Now that it had happened at last, she was only aware of the humiliation of her own surrender, and rage at what had prompted Oliver to kiss her at all – nothing but male assertiveness because he was piqued by her friendship with Jules Legrand. Damn, damn, damn Oliver Hatton!

Edwin had recovered sufficiently next day for the normal routine to be resumed, but even that slight attack had been enough to remind them that his hold on life was uncertain in the extreme. She thought it explained why he began to take for granted, in ways so subtle that she could scarcely pin them down, much less contradict them, the idea that Jules would figure permanently in her future. She hoped their guest was unaware of this subterranean pressure, but there was so little he failed to notice that she finally decided he was a willing pawn in her uncle's game of 'getting Jane looked after'. The idea was distasteful, however kind it was of both of them. Fifteen years of genuine gratitude to Edwin Kingsley had already been required of her. She couldn't spend the rest of her life feeling grateful to someone else because the burden had been handed on. She didn't need looking after – could go back to clambering over styles unaided if she had to.

Rage with Oliver got mixed up with a coolness towards Jules that he'd really done nothing to deserve. Irritation made her short with him, amd remorse then forced her to make amends. She suggested one Sunday that they should drive to Waddesdon Manor to inspect its treasures in case he should be feeling homesick for things French. They dawdled homewards after a pleasant afternoon, and stopped for supper along the way.

Jules suddenly flung an intense question at her in the French he preferred to use when they were alone together.

'Jane, how do I strike you – as someone completely sure of himself, confident, even a trifle arrogant?'

It was a difficult question to answer, sounding rather unkind if she said yes, even so, she had the impression that it was what he expected.

'Not arrogant,' she said after a moment, 'but you certainly give an impression of . . . of self-confidence.'

'An impression only?' he was quick to ask. 'You spot the poor vulnerable creature underneath?'

She hesitated, then decided to offer him the truth. 'I'm not sure I know what the real man is, but I can't help sensing in you some dissatisfaction with yourself. I don't why that should be – most men would envy you. Perhaps Canada has its own kind of frontier spirit, always driving people on!'

She'd spoken lightly, hoping to see him smile in return, but his face wore the intense expression she was coming to know.

'My mother was pure-French, from a stiff-necked Catholic family of minor aristocrats. They never forgave her for marrying to please herself, even cruelly pretended that they couldn't understand the sort of transatlantic French my father spoke. She did her best to settle down with him in Canada, but he couldn't make her happy however hard he tried.'

'What happened in the end?' Jane queried gently.

'She died before I was old enough to help, but I came to Europe determined to do more than escape the provincial life that satisfied my father. I'm going to become the sort of success that her family *can't* despise. I'll even buy up their tin-pot little château before I'm through.'

He stopped again, reading in her expression what she was careful not to say.

'You dislike that idea? Think it sounds un-English? I should wish my mother's hateful relatives health and happiness? I can't do it, Jane, not even to stand well with you. Don't compare me with a man like Oliver Hatton, born with the certainty of who he is, with no need to fight for *his* proper place in the world.'

She overlooked deliberately the reference to herself, and recollected instead the ribald tones in which Oliver was liable to refer to various blue-blooded relatives scattered around Oxfordshire. It was impossible to explain that such a man was totally unconcerned about what his 'proper' place might be; it would simply be wherever he happened to feel comfortable.

But that attitude, so far removed from Jules' own, only seemed to confirm what he'd just said; in his true world, Oliver hadn't had to fight, only when he'd stepped outside it to marry unwisely in New York.

'I was remembering my father,' she answered at last. 'He would have understood your point of view, because it seemed to me that he understood everything. But he'd have insisted that material success never mattered in the long run – he and Uncle Edwin were alike in that. The important thing for him, as an archaeologist, was to unravel the past; the important thing for *you*, he'd have said, was to love and understand what *you* are dealing with.'

Jules managed to smile, converting the bitter retort he might have offered her into something less hurtful. '*Chérie*, your father was a devoted scholar, no doubt, just like Uncle Edwin, but forgive me for thinking he should have considered *your* welfare a bit more – not left you alone and empty-handed to be rescued by his brother.'

'*Not* alone,' she said very firmly. I have some precious friends; and I wasn't left quite empty-handed, either. I'll show you when we get home.'

It put an end to a conversation that she realised had been important, substantially adding to what they knew about each other. Jules accepted her lead when she began to comment on what they'd seen at Waddesdon, and suspected that she would change her mind about what she'd promised to show him.

He didn't remind her of it when they arrived back at the Owl House, and was pleasantly surprised when she invited him to follow her upstairs to her bedroom. Saying nothing more, she led him to a glass-fronted cabinet and pointed at the tiny objects that lined its shelves.

'I call them Father's little dears,' she murmured. 'I expect you know what they really are.'

'Oh yes – I know,' he said rather breathlessly, 'Japanese netsukes, carved out of ivory; each one a little masterpiece not more than an inch square, each one more beautiful than the last. My dear girl, it's a priceless collection that ought to be locked up in a bank vault somewhere, like the instruments downstairs.'

She simply shook her head. 'Father didn't like lovely things locked up, and nor do I. Choose one to sit on your bedside-table. I give them all a turn!'

For a moment she couldn't read the expression on his face – doubt, dismay, regret even? Then he seemed to shake it away and smiled instead, with a kind of triumphant tenderness. 'You're mad . . . do you hear me, Jane? But I'm beginning to love you very much indeed.'

His lips touched her own, lightly and sweetly, before he walked out of the room.

She was left with a muddled mixture of things to think about – he'd gone without making the choice she'd offered him; his voice a moment ago had sounded unevenly sincere; and, by no means least of all, *his* kiss had certainly not made her angry. She would have given much to be able to convey that news to Oliver Hatton.

Four

It was Mary Hatton, encountered in the village one morning, who offered the news about Oliver's new house.

'He's just like his father – so casual that I know he's delighted,' she said sagely. 'It's a Queen Anne gem, according to the estate agent; not a bad bargain according to my son! Don't ever let your children become solicitors, Jane dear; it kills *all* romance in them.'

'I'll remember,' she promised, trying not to smile. 'Where is this gem of a bargain?'

'No distance – the other side of Sutton Courtenay. Not near enough for us to be always falling over each other, but close enough for me to dash over if the babies need minding.'

'What babies?' Jane asked, fascinated.

'My grandchildren, of course. What's the point of Oliver buying a house if he doesn't settle down and begat . . . beget should it be? . . . a family to put in it?'

There was an alternative – that he might want to live in the house alone, or if not solitarily, at least in extra-marital seclusion. But it wasn't a theory to lay before a lady who yearned to be a grandmother, and while Jane was still thinking of something else to say Mary was in full flight again. 'Estelle's having a lovely time, advising him how the house should be decorated and furnished. It's such a *blessing*, Jane! We've got her for the whole summer and I've been at my wits' end to keep her amused, but this answers the purpose beautifully.'

Jane hesitated, then decided to risk the comment that occupied her mind.

'It sounds as if Estelle's becoming a fixture in his life. Don't you think so?'

Mary's kind face looked distressed for a moment. 'We rather do,' she admitted sadly. 'Estelle's beautiful, of course, and kinder than you'd imagine by looking at her. But I can't say she's the wife we'd have chosen. Richard says he has the feeling he ought to break into applause whenever she appears – he swears she's waiting for it.'

'With her face, I think I'd be waiting for it too,' Jane confessed. 'Still, the staginess won't survive permanent life in the country. By the time she can tell a carnation from a camellia, Richard will be eating out of her hand.'

Mary smiled but her disorganised mind was following a train of thought of her own. 'We always hoped . . .' then she broke off, realising that the object of their hopes was the girl she was talking to. Her sentence was left hanging in mid-air, but fortunately the Vicar stopped in front of them to enquire after the health of a hedgehog he'd watched her rescue from certain death in the middle of the road the day before.

Jane walked home, still thinking about Oliver's new house. It explained why they'd seen so little of him recently. She'd imagined him toiling in Oxford, nose to grindstone, but it was much more likely that he'd been at Sutton Courtenay with Estelle, looking at house plans and interior decoration. She still remembered with painful vividness the despair of learning years ago that he was marrying in New York. Well, not a trace of suicidal sadness this time, she told herself approvingly – the business of growing up had been accomplished at last.

Self-examination wasn't to be pushed too far, but she could, at a pinch, be genuinely glad to be rid of a man who'd muddled up her emotional life for far too long. If he was to be happy again, married to Estelle, it was no more than he deserved; she would be glad about that as well. With gladness all round she need pay no heed to a small, shameful twinge of something that felt like regret – jealousy, even. Oliver would make sure that he didn't allow a second marriage to fail. This time his going from Little Fairford would be for good, and as the years passed Jane Kingsley would become simply a recollection of the past, not worth the trouble of remembering.

A week of blazingly hot weather arrived with the suddenness that happened nearly every May and, as with every other May heatwave, took them by surprise. Jane blamed it for the tiredness that made her crawl home after school one afternoon, thinking longingly of the summer holiday ahead. She found the Owl House empty and remembered that Jules had enticed her uncle into making a rare expedition away from home. Edwin had described to him an Aladdin's cave of a house called Snowshill Manor in Gloucestershire, filled with an assortment of treasures that attracted them both as a magnet attracts pins. For once she needn't plunge into preparing a meal more elaborate than the one she and her uncle would have eaten alone; for once she would simply not think about Jules at all. The thought brought such relief that she collapsed on a seat in the garden, for the pleasure of just being there alone, with the afternoon sun warm on her face, and a blackbird practising his song in the prunus tree beside the front door.

She was eventually woken by the sound of footsteps on the flag-stoned path, and a dreaming memory of someone's lips against her own.

'Wake up, little one . . . a sun-kissed skin is one thing, a peeling nose quite another.' The advice was delivered in Oliver's usual lazy drawl, ruling out the possibility that his had been the kiss she remembered.

'I never peel,' she said crossly, 'having as my only claim to beauty a complexion that turns a beautiful bronze.'

'You sound irritable, though, and look tired. Why is that, Jane? Are you more in need of help here than I told Jules Legrand you were?'

The sudden gentleness in his voice disturbed her almost to the point of tears – there was never anyone like this large, slow-talking man when he decided to be kind.

'It's been a busy term,' she said huskily. 'I shall be my sunny self again as soon as school breaks up for the summer holiday.'

'Or as soon as a demanding guest departs and leaves you alone.'

'Uncle Edwin will miss Jules – and so shall I,' she insisted, but Oliver looked unconvinced and she had to try again. 'He's become so much a part of the family that I can't imagine how we'll manage without him.' Now, probably, she'd protested too much, but before Oliver could point this out she cast around hurriedly for something else to talk about.

'Mary told me about the house. Are you pleased with it?'

'I rather believe I am,' he agreed. 'There's a lot to do to it because the previous owner was infirm, and neglected it for years, but it will give my wife something to occupy herself with while I'm sweating away in Oxford, earning our daily crust.'

'Your . . . your wife? Actual, or notional, as they say?'

'No contracts exchanged yet,' he said solemnly, 'but I hope it's only a matter of time.'

Jane concentrated on the blackbird's arpeggios, no longer

joyous-sounding but tinged with the sadness that seemed to be welling out of her own heart. Mary and Richard were clearly going to have to make the best of Estelle as a daughter-in-law. They would manage to love her in time, because Oliver had chosen her. Only Jane Kingsley might always continue to feel that she'd known better than he did himself what her friend needed for happiness. That was the trouble, of course. However hard she pretended to the contrary, Oliver could never be anything but her friend . . . the man who'd bothered to take a desperately unhappy child in tow and bring her back to sanity.

'Well, when the marrying time comes, don't sneak off to Oxford or London and do the deed when our backs are turned,' she told him severely. 'The entire village will expect to be invited, and you'll have to give us warning so that we can get the dust of ages blown off our wedding hats.'

Oliver unfolded himself slowly from the end of the bench and stood up to go. 'You'll get warning,' he promised gravely. 'Now, nice as it would be to idle away the rest of this lovely afternoon, I still have work to do. I've left some papers in the porch for Edwin – I'll call and collect them in a day or two.'

She watched his tall figure stroll away down the path, then after a moment or two got up herself. To think about him in his gem of a Queen Anne house with a green-eyed, flame-haired wife should have filled her with rejoicing; if she couldn't manage that her only alternative was not to think about him at all. She had her own pleasant life, and the gratifying suspicion that Jules hoped to be allowed to make it still pleasanter. The future was something she was very far from sure about, but the certainty was growing in her mind that whatever it turned out to be, the man Marcel Colbert had sent them would have to be included in it somewhere; they'd progressed, almost without being aware of it, beyond the point where anything else was possible.

The remainder of the summer term dragged on slowly, with the children restless in class, wanting to be fishing or swimming in the river instead. *They* needed to be assured each day that the weather wouldn't change the moment the holidays finally began, while she and Richard Hatton bemoaned to each other plants wilting in the record-breaking drought, and searched the brilliant skies for some wisp of vapour that might grow into a cloud capable of producing rain.

The days left before the the school holiday now roughly equalled the remainder of Jules' stay at the Owl House, and Jane blamed her tiredness for the fact that for once she couldn't make up her mind about wanting him to go or stay. For her uncle's sake it would be a relief when the visit ended. The stimulus of having an intelligent and interesting pupil to teach had now worn off, leaving him even frailer than before, but he was too courteous and too stubborn to let Jules know that his little hoard of strength was almost gone.

On her own account Jane knew that she would miss him very much. She felt as restless as the children in class, but freedom to spend the long summer days out of doors wouldn't be a sufficient cure for what ailed her. In moments of depression she remembered that she was on the way to becoming twenty-six, doomed to dwindle into another Miss Prentice, perhaps declining into lonely and virginal old age! She didn't feel as if she'd been born to end her days a spinster; her heart longed to give itself to someone. But it had been attached to the wrong man for so long that the poor yearning thing now didn't know in what direction it should go. She wasn't quite in love with Jules; she was fairly sure of that.

But he'd become more than just a friend she valued. There was pleasure in knowing that she was admired and wanted, and pride in the disciplined self-control that kept him hard at work during the gorgeous summer days. If occasionally his determination to succeed seemed to be obsessive, she reminded herself of the outline of his life that he'd given her; success wasn't an option for him, but a necessity. More puzzling were her glimpses of some kind of nervous tension in him that nothing in the placid life of Little Fairford seemed to account for. If he'd begun by seeing Oliver as a rival, he certainly didn't do so now when it was taken for granted in the village that Mr Hatton's future was mapped out with Estelle. She decided in the end that it was just the way Jules was – still haunted by the past, and feverishly intent on the future. It probably had nothing to do with her, and he might even go back to France without her having to decide what she really felt about him.

She was proved wrong on both counts soon enough. An old *Madame Albertine* rose that wanted to clamber all over the house had to be dealt with, and she perched herself on a ladder, the better to talk to it severely. The breeze dragged a long stem across her bare arm and she jerked away from the clutch of some particularly vicious thorns, forgetting the precariousness of her position. She lost her balance just as Jules appeared round the corner of the house and managed to break her fall as she keeled over. They landed in a heap on the ground, Jane laughing until she saw that his face had gone pale and anguished.

'Providential for me, but I think I may have winded you, poor Jules,' she gasped.

He didn't smile back and she realised that sudden fear had made him angry.

'You were mad, *chérie,* to climb up there and not ask me to do it for you. Am I not here to help?' he almost shouted at her. 'You might have damaged yourself badly.'

His strained expression prevented her from saying that she quite often needed to climb ladders and didn't usually make a habit of falling off them.

'I was doing very well,' she explained instead, 'until I got impaled on some wicked thorns. I will allow, though, that your arrival was very timely!'

It was also time, she thought, that they sorted themselves out and got up off the ground, but Jules had other ideas. His arms tightened instead of releasing her; he bent his head to kiss her scratched arm, and then found her mouth. When he finally let her go she knew that the episode with the ladder had shaken him out of his usual self-control. Even his black hair, normally smooth as a seal's head, was now ruffled and untidy.

'You've been so careful to ignore your uncle's delicate hints that I decided I should leave without saying anything of this, because it seemed as if *that* was what you wanted. But it's clear to me now that I *must* take care of you. Marry me, please, and come to live with me in France.'

His face was full of tenderness and entreaty. She was quite sure of not needing to be taken care of, but it was heart-warming to know that a charming man wanted to offer himself for the job. Even with this vulnerable and ardent Jules she wasn't in love, but what was that condition except a snare to the unwary? A marriage based on shared liking, tenderness and respect had more chance of growing into the partnership her parents had known than the brief *coup de foudre* of a passionate love affair. In any case, the society of Little Fairford didn't exactly overflow with young men queuing up to sweep her off her feet. Between old General Harcourt, widowed a year ago, and a bunch of teenage schoolboys, the only unmarried males were Jim Watkins – headmaster of the village school and a confirmed bachelor – and a newcomer of whom the village was frankly doubtful. What were they to make, they asked each other, of a man who didn't wear socks and spent his days designing silk cushions? In this discouraging review Jane was careful to leave out Oliver Hatton. He no longer lived in the village, and it wouldn't have made any difference if he did. She sensed in Jules Legrand not only physical need, but some deep-seated unhappiness that it would be an achievement to mend. The more she considered it, the more worthwhile and even desirable the prospect became.

'We need each other,' Jules said earnestly, so exactly echoing her own thoughts that she smiled more encouragingly than she'd meant to. 'I want you very badly, dear Jane, but I'm not thinking only of myself. I don't wish to . . . to denigrate Little Fairford, but it's slightly like being buried alive. In Paris we could have a lovely life together – I'd make a true Frenchwoman of you in no time!'

His arms tightened again and he set about confirming the surrender he thought he sensed in her. Jane was aware of passion rising in him and did her best, despite the lack of leaping excitement along her blood. It would come in time, she promised herself. Fifteen years of living under Uncle Edwin's loving but austere regime hadn't accustomed her to giving free rein to passion, that was all. She wondered whether it would make matters better or worse to explain this to Jules, but he'd found his own reason for her disappointing lack of response.

'*Ma pauvre*, you're still shaken . . . not in a state to be made love to at the moment. Don't be afraid that I won't make you happy, though . . . all your funny English inhibitions will melt away as soon as we're on our own.'

He was going much too fast, and this at least she must pull herself together enough to explain. 'Jules . . . dear Jules . . . you'll have to let me think about it. It will sound stupid, but I shan't know for certain until you're no longer here! Will you go back to France and let me make up my mind then? I *shall* know, when I'm without you again.'

Her eyes scanned his face, trying to read from his expression whether he was hurt or merely puzzled. Then he gave a little shrug, and made himself smile. 'You haven't said no, *mon amour*. It's not happiness, but it's something!'

She leaned forward to kiss his cheek, grateful for a patience she hadn't been sure of, and by way of apology for what she had to say next. 'You might decide that you can't wait for me anyway,' she confessed ruefully. 'I couldn't possible leave Uncle Edwin, Jules. For as long as he is alive, I must stay here.'

His answer came so slowly that she half-expected him to say his offer to make a Frenchwoman of her had been withdrawn, on the grounds that a Frenchwoman would never behave so unreasonably.

'I realise that he cannot be left alone,' he said at last. 'But I doubt if he would enjoy the idea that our happiness was being sacrificed. Money isn't a problem, you know. We could afford to have someone take care of him.'

'He could have found someone to take care of me,' Jane pointed out steadily, 'but instead of farming me out, he allowed a small child to turn his quiet bachelor life upside down. I couldn't possibly do less for him,' she insisted.

Jules didn't argue, nor make the other mistake of suggesting that she wouldn't have to stay for very long. 'I can't pretend that I'm patient by nature, *chérie*, but to have you in the end I *shall* be patient!'

She smiled at him – he was behaving so beautifully that she couldn't bring herself to mention again that she'd so far done nothing but promise to think about marrying him. Then she was lifted off the ground, and Jules shinned up the ladder to deal competently with *Madame Albertine.*

It was Uncle Edwin who suggested they must give a party to mark Jules' return to France. He didn't ask her outright whether she'd agreed to marry his old friend's godson, but there was an air of contentment about him, as if he felt confident that this was how matters would end. She had no way of knowing what he said to other people, but his attitude at the party coupled with Jules' strongly possessive air led several guests to congratulate her on a marriage that was obviously going to take place.

Jane was aware of being left severely alone by Oliver until the party was almost over. He'd been propped against a wall for most of the evening, happy to talk to anyone who put themselves to the trouble of walking over to him. She remembered of old that he didn't go in for the exhausing business of circulating at cocktail parties, and could even recall the exact words in which he'd explained it to her when she'd chided him for being indolent.

'You've got it wrong, little one. I stay in one place for everyone else's sake, not mine. The kindest thing I can do is take root somewhere; then anyone who wants to talk to me knows where to find me.'

'The fact that it leaves you comfortably lounging near the bar has nothing to do with it, I suppose.'

'Nothing at all,' he'd agreed virtuously.

Still, for once here he was, standing in front of her.

'Everyone keeps telling me I should be offering you congratulations,' he murmured vaguely, as if he could scarcely remember what the congratulations were for. Then his eyes suddenly found her own and she was disconcerted by the intentness in them. 'It rather takes me by surprise to be told that you're going to marry Jules Legrand.'

'I don't know that I am – yet,' she said a trifle sharply. '"Everyone" is taking too much for granted.'

'Including Legrand himself, in that case,' Oliver pointed out smoothly. 'I've never seen a man who looked more pleased with life.'

It was too true to be argued with; Jules was brimming over with gaiety and the indefinable confidence of someone for whom things were going extraordinarily well. Jane met Oliver's glance and impulsively plunged into something that had long needed saying between them.

'You ought to feel relieved – the ghost of young, hero-worshipping Jane Kingsley finally laid to rest! I must have been a great embarrassment to you for years.'

'Yes, you were,' Oliver agreed after a slight pause.

It was more brutal than she'd bargained for – and still hurt more than she would have believed possible. But she couldn't burst into tears at Jules' party and, with an enormous effort of will-power, she made herself smile brightly at her tormentor.

'What about your own plans . . . the house and the wife to go inside it?' she asked.

'Slight hitch,' he confessed coolly. 'Nothing to worry about long-term . . . I hope.'

She realised that she hadn't seen Estelle all evening, and said so.

'Dashed off to London unexpectedly,' Oliver explained. 'The miraculous happened, and her agent rang about some part she might have a hope of getting. Health and strength were magically restored, and we took her to Oxford this morning to catch the London train.'

It explained his cruelty of a moment ago, and Jane even managed to forgive him for it. One bitterly unhappy marriage was enough for any man. Oliver deserved better luck with the next one, and was due a woman who would learn to put his happiness before her own.

'I'm sorry,' Jane muttered. 'I can see she'd want to take a chance if it was offered, but I hope she isn't going to rush off too often – it would make for a rather unsettled domestic life, I'm afraid.'

'My dear girl, I doubt if she'll be given the chance,' he said with a frankness Jane hoped he didn't offer his beloved. 'She's beautiful, knows how to wear clothes, move gracefully and, at a pinch, make herself heard at the back of a theatre. There's a little more to being a successful actress than that.'

He was probably right, but he usually tempered the truth with a little more kindness all round than he seemed diposed to do this evening. Jane's large eyes fixed on his face spoke the thoughts she didn't put into words, and he suddenly smiled at her in rueful apology.

'Do I sound a little acid, Janey? Sorry . . . I must be getting past the age for enjoying for cocktail parties!' He looked across the room to where her uncle was sitting and changed the conversation abruptly. 'Edwin's tired; I should wind up this affair as soon as you can.'

He allowed himself to be pounced upon by Mrs Hughes-Watson, leaving Jane no time to point out that the guests were there at her uncle's invitation. It was typical of Oliver, she thought, to issue a lordly instruction and then walk away without explaining how it was to be carried out. Nor, she realised, had he bothered to congratulate her on the marriage he assumed, like everyone else, to be going to take place. She remembered him saying once that he would advise Edwin not to let her marry Jules. It had been said merely to provoke, of course, but she felt saddened to know that it no longer mattered to him *what* she did with the rest of her life. Janey Kingsley – he hadn't called her that for years – was now old enough now to paddle her own canoe. She put the painful thought aside, and didn't talk to him again for the rest of the evening, but she occasionally glimpsed the withdrawn expression on his face and found herself offering a little prayer that Estelle Harding would make him happy.

Five

Jules left for Paris two days later, refusing to let Jane go with him to Heathrow. She hadn't confessed to a subconscious dread of saying goodbye to people at airports that she'd never been able to grow out of, and she was all the more aware of the things he perceived without having to be told about them. If he'd wanted to reopen the subject of marriage before he left, it was another temptation he resisted, and he went away only reminding her that she was to miss him very much. Miss him she discovered she certainly did; the house without him now felt too quiet and empty and, dearly though she loved her uncle, he was becoming less and less of a companion. It was also clear that his strength was draining away, and that he felt not resentful but strangely content about it. Her future was taken care of, he believed, and he'd had the joy of completing a last piece of work to his satisfaction. The prospect of death didn't frighten him and Jane even suspected that he looked forward to finding out what would come after it. Discussions on the subject with the Vicar had been one of his intellectual pleasures in recent years, and it gave him a certain satisfaction to know that he was going to be the first to learn which of them was right.

Jane did her best to cosset him without his being aware of the fact, and went through the days holding her breath for fear of seeing his life blow out, like the last remaining candle on a child's birthday cake. He now spent more time than he liked to admit in just dozing, instead of reading the book that was always in his lap. This fact explained why a skilful burglar was able to come and go at the Owl House without his knowledge that rooms were being ransacked.

Jane got home late on the last day of term, and opened the front door on the heart-stopping knowledge that something was different about the house. She fled upstairs to her uncle's room, but he was sleeping peacefully in his armchair by the window – nothing wrong there. Downstairs again she could still smell that some alien body with no right to be there had been in the house. The Collection sprang next to mind, but when she went into the room nothing had been disturbed – no shattered display cases, no gaping holes. The burglar had had no interest in the fortune that gleamed and shone there. Things were different in the drawing-room: all the rugs were askew and she registered the first theft – a lovely, small Sisley watercolour that should have hung above the fireplace was missing. Silver was gone from the oak buffet in the dining-room, but raging despair only washed over her when she got to her own room. The cabinet that had held her father's tiny ivory figures was empty – not a single netsuke remained.

She forced herself out of the paralysis that had clamped itself round her legs and went downstairs to dial Richard Hatton's number.

'Richard . . . I don't know what to do . . . we've been burgled, but Uncle Edwin's asleep. If I wake him with that sort of news I'm terrified that he'll . . .' she stopped to swallow the tears clogging her throat, and heard him say,

'Hold tight, Jane love. I'll get hold of Oliver and we'll be over straightaway. Don't do anything – don't touch anything – until we get there.'

She was sitting in the kitchen, ashen-faced, when Richard and Mary walked in ten minutes later.

'The b-bastard's taken my little dears,' she told them hoarsely.

Richard disappeared in the direction of the dining-room and returned with a small glass of neat brandy.

'Drink that and don't argue,' he said, sounding so like his son that she hovered for a moment on the edge of helpless, hysterical laughter. 'I've rung the police,' Richard added, 'and Oliver's on his way. You two stay here while I take a look round.'

'The Hatton male in action,' Mary whispered respectfully in the silence that followed his departure, and it made Jane grin more normally to discover that even Mary, who idolised her husband, might also occasionally find something to smile at in him.

'You mustn't let Oliver get too bossy, though,' Mary added as an afterthought. 'It's bad for him.'

'Oliver's marrying Estelle,' Jane pointed out gently.

Mrs Hatton looked distressed for a moment. 'Yes, of course . . . silly of me.' The sight of the glass in Jane's hand made her sound suddenly decisive. 'That's not the right thing for shock at all; we'll make some tea.'

They were all in the kitchen drinking it when Oliver walked in, soon enough to have broken every speed limit between Oxford and Little Fairford. He threw a brief glance at Jane, then accepted the mug of tea she handed him.

'You're all right, I see. Father didn't stop to tell me over the telephone whether a thug had hit you over the head, or something.'

She was minded to say that he could have sounded less indifferent about it, but remembered that at least he'd come when they needed him.

'What shall I do about Uncle Edwin?' she asked instead. 'Wake him and try to explain why policemen are soon going to be tramping through the house?'

'Have you any idea what's gone, Jane?' Oliver asked.

'One painting, some silver, and the netsukes from my bedroom – for which I hope the thief rots in hell. The Collection is intact as far as I can see.'

'Well, let me go and break the news to Edwin; you stand by with a reviving cup of tea.'

When she went upstairs ten minutes later, leaving Richard to talk to the police sergeant who'd just arrived, it was obvious that Oliver had performed the miracle of telling her uncle without upsetting him unduly. He looked calm, but very apologetic.

'I'm so sorry, Jane dear . . . I've let you down, dozing here while a thief helped himself to your most precious possessions.'

'A thief would probably have hit you over the head,' she said with a loving smile. 'If I was made to choose, I think I'd rather have you still intact!'

His thin face flushed with pleasure, but he said nothing except that he would pretend not to notice if a policeman began to crawl about the landing outside his door. An hour later a methodical inspection had confirmed that the Collection hadn't been disturbed, and the sergeant was scratching his head.

'Don't understand it,' he confessed. 'A fortune here under his hand and he didn't bother with it.'

'It's perfectly understandable if he knew that the instruments are too well-known to be saleable,' Jane suggested.

'It's *still* odd,' Oliver insisted. 'A queer miscellany of things to have pinched, even for someone who wasn't just a casual cat-burglar. What did he really come for out of that mixture of things? Or was he simply trying to tell us that he *wasn't* interested in the Collection and took the other things to prove it?'

This argument caused the policeman to shake his head again and look relieved when no one else seemed to know the answer either. He and his colleague finished their painstaking search and finally went away. After failing to persuade Jane and Edwin to go home with them, the Hattons also departed, promising to telephone in the morning to see how they were. Jane forced herself to prepare the supper they had no appetite for, and then telephoned Jules. If Oliver hadn't seemed overly concerned, Jules more than made up for it by sounding heart-broken. It was too late to catch a plane that night, but he'd come by the very first flight in the morning. He was so distressed that she was taken by surprise – touched by his concern for her, and grateful to discover that he considered her problems to be his own.

'Jules, dear . . . it's wonderfully kind of you, but there's no need to come,' she insisted quickly. 'Richard's got it all in hand, and Mary's keeping an eye on us. Uncle Edwin is very calm, and there's really nothing to do except let the police ferret away as they do. You mustn't think of bothering to come racing over.'

'What exactly has been taken, *chérie*?'

Jane repeated the odd list again, and there was a little silence at the other end of the line.

'No instruments at all?'

'Not a single one. According to the police who've been

searching the house, it doesn't look as if the thief even bothered to go into that room.'

'*Pauvre petite* . . . I know what those little figures meant to you,' Jules said with quick sympathy. 'Don't despair of getting them back, my darling. I keep my ear on what's happening in the art underworld, and if they surface here I'm sure I shall hear about them. If I can get them back for you, perhaps they would make a wedding present you couldn't resist.'

He sounded wistful as well as tender, and suddenly it seemed stupid and unkind to keep him in suspense any longer. It was no way to treat a man who could feel entitled to an answer.

'You've gone very quiet, *chérie*,' he said after a pause. 'I think I *should* come over and take care of you.'

'No need, Jules,' she murmured, on the edge of tears. But I think I'd rather like you to take the job on in future!'

'Are you saying that you *will* marry me, Jane?' he asked slowly.

'Yes . . . yes, please.'

'Then, my dear one, I shall have to bless that thief to the end of my days.'

He made no attempt to persuade her to abandon Edwin, or to hurry over to France; he didn't even propose to come to Little Fairford himself until she suggested a suitable time. But she put the telephone down at last, feeling comforted by his love and understanding. Uncle Edwin had been right all along to edge her into Jules' arms, and the news she could now take upstairs would send the burglary clean out of her uncle's head.

Life at the Owl House returned to its normal holiday routine, no morning rush to get ready for school, no juggling act with lessons and meals to be prepared. The village was peaceful, too, with many of its regular inmates taking it in turns to go away to more exotic holiday spots. Jane didn't crave excitement abroad; there'd be time enough in the future to travel with Jules, and she wasn't even impatient to begin living in Paris. With the knowledge that her days in the village were numbered, each one suddenly became precious, something to be fixed in her memory against a time when she was no longer there to watch the slow unfolding of the year. It seemed unreal to think that, in some not very distant future, neither she nor Uncle Edwin would sit in the Kingsley pew in church, that Jim Watkins would be able to run the school without her, and even the dreaded Mrs Hughes-Watson would be encountered in the village shop for the last time. The knowledge induced in her a feeling that was uncomfortably close to panic, and it needed her regular telephone conversations with Jules to remind her that she was going away towards a happy future.

The excitement caused in the village by the news that the Owl House had been burgled gradually died down, and her pupils forgot to rush up to her in the High Street to ask if the thief was about to be hauled before the local Bench. The police sergeant had become a friend in the course of several visits, but she could see that he wasn't very hopeful about catching a burglar who behaved so irrationally.

Matters stood thus when Jane went up to her uncle's room one morning to take him a letter just arrived from France. The room was empty, and so was his adjoining bathroom. It was several weeks since he'd come downstairs for breakfast, and she ran down to the instrument room wondering what had roused him to make such an effort. He was there, as she'd felt sure he would be, sitting at his desk, an astrolabe in pieces and its separate gleaming plates spread out in front of him.

Even before she could say anything, or reach him, some quality of absolute stillness in the room denied the possibility that he was still alive. She fumbled deperately to find a pulse in the wrist that lay on the desk, failed to find it, and fled to the telephone. Dr James, mercifully caught before he left the village to attend morning surgery in the community hospital, arrived five minutes later, without even stopping for the jacket and tie he'd been about to put on. His nod confirmed was she was already certain of.

'An hour or so ago, my dear,' he said gently, 'nothing you or I or anyone could have done. Every time I saw my dear old friend I told him to avoid exertion. Did he make a habit of getting up so early?'

Jane shook her head. 'He hasn't been down to breakfast for weeks. This morning I thought perhaps he was feeling better . . .' her husky voice faltered and died, and she turned to stare out of the window, hardly aware of the doctor's hand resting on her shoulder for a moment.

'I'll be off, my dear. Tiresome formalities to put in hand, but there'll be people along to help you very soon.'

She nodded at him, not trusting her voice to function. The sound of the front door closing told her that he'd gone, but she stayed sitting where she was, conscious of nothing except the simple fact that she couldn't go away and leave her uncle alone.

The first friend to appear was Mary Hatton who, when Edwin Kingsley had left the Owl House for the last time, tried to persuade her to go back to the Vicarage.

'I think I'd rather stay here, Mary dear,' Jane said slowly. 'It's kind of you, but I shall be better doing things. I'm full of grief but not desperation, so there's no need to worry about me. Uncle Edwin was right to want to attach me to someone else. I'm so grateful to know that I've got Jules to anchor myself to.'

When Mary had gone she picked up the phone to call the Colbert galleries in Paris. It was a disappointment to be told that Jules wasn't there, but a moment later Marcel came on the line. He was hardly surprised to hear her news, but shocked all the same.

'My dear Jane, I'm so sorry. What can I do to help you?' he asked immediately.

'Only tell me where I can get hold of Jules. Everything is under control here, but I *would* like to speak to him, and I gather he's not in the Galleries.'

'I'm desolated to have to say it, my dear, but he left Paris this very morning, with a long journey in front of him, and a difficult negotiation at the end of it. It was left that he would contact me, but that may not be for several days until he has something to report.'

Jane was puzzled by the suddenness of it. 'He didn't mention having to go away when I spoke to him two evenings ago.'

'It blew up almost overnight,' Marcel explained apologetically. 'Jules was approached by a Spaniard with whom we've had some excellent but rather secretive dealings before. He's an odd, awkward customer, so it wasn't surprising when he insisted that Jules must meet him in Andorra. There are some priceless instruments on offer, it seems, and Jules wouldn't hear of jeopardising our chances of getting them by arguing with him.'

It sounded just like Jules, she thought; no effort would ever be too great to make sure of the will-o'-the-wisp success he craved. And a cloak-and-dagger rendezvous in Andorra would have appealed to him rather more than a decorous business deal in the Galleries in Paris. But she realised how badly she wanted the comfort of hearing him say that he'd take the next plane to England.

'Well, never mind; I must be patient, that's all,' she said at last. 'But I'm afraid it will grieve him if he has to miss Uncle Edwin's funeral. Will you just ask Jules to ring as soon as you do hear from him?'

'Of course, *ma chère* . . . and you must let *me* know, please, when I should come to . . . to pay my respects to my dear friend.'

She put the telephone down, wandered aimlessly out into the garden because nothing she could think of doing seemed relevant, and afterwards spent the rest of the day answering calls from people who wanted to be told what they could do to help her. Her last visitor of the interminable day was Oliver, who arrived just as she sat staring at an omelette she'd made and now knew she couldn't eat.

'Go and get your bonnet, or whatever else it is you need – we're going out,' he said briefly.

A small murmur that she'd rather stay where she was was borne away like a wisp of paper on the summer breeze. Oliver was in his *God-knows-best* mood, and it would be less tiring to do what he said than go on arguing with him. She got into his car five minutes later, folded her hands on her lap, and waited for the next commandment. Instead, as he got in beside her, he covered her hands with one of his own.

'Sorry I wasn't around this morning, Janey. I'd just left for London when Father tried to get hold of me.'

The gentleness in his deep voice threatened to pitch her into the tears she hadn't shed all day, and for fear of weeping she said nothing at all until Oliver stopped the car on the outskirts of the neighbouring village of Sutton Courtenay. Through a wrought-iron gate she could see a small, graceful Queen Anne house – he'd brought her, she realised, to his own home.

'It's lovely,' she commented quietly. 'Mary told me the

estate agent said it was a gem. He was quite right, for once.'

'Don't expect too much of the inside yet,' he warned her. 'I've only been able to get the outside attended to so far.'

He led her on a conducted tour, through the confusion of replacement timbers, wires, and pots of paint, as if it was a perfectly normal day, and this a perfectly normal visit. As he'd said, the inside was still chaotic, but it didn't need much imagination to appreciate the serene and lovely home that would eventually emerge. She didn't feel envious of Estelle Harding, only doubtful of the sanity of a woman who might choose the ephemeral excitement of the theatre to the life she could have here with Oliver. Aware that it was a long time since she'd spoken, she cast around for something safe to say.

'Mary said Estelle had been helping you. Part or no part, I don't think I could have torn myself away at this stage – I should have had to see what was going on.'

'She gave me a lot of advice, which I didn't always feel obliged to take!'

'I see,' Jane said uncertainly.

An odd little smile touched his mouth for a moment. 'I don't suppose you do. Never mind; we'll adjourn to the kitchen and find some food. I missed lunch altogether today, and you've definitely shrunk since I saw you last.'

Remembering how the day had begun, she realised she'd missed breakfast as well. She felt hollow but still disinclined to eat until Oliver began carving slices from a succulent-looking ham. He presided over the grill, which he insisted was his culinary forte, but allowed her to wander round his overgrown vegetable garden in search of what she might find. She came back with parsley and chives to chop into a mound of cold cooked potatoes she found in the refrigerator, put them on to fry gently, then sliced tomatoes, dusted them with sugar, salt and basil, and gave them to Oliver to join the ham under the grill. The aroma of hot appetising food suddenly made her feel ravenous, and the pair of them ate in concentrated silence until hunger was appeased and they were sipping coffee from large earthenware mugs.

'What happens now?' he asked out of a friendly silence. 'I take it you'll stay on at the Owl House?'

It was the moment her thoughts had been avoiding all day, the moment when she had to consider a future that had little to do with the familiar world of Little Fairford, and nothing at all to do with this unfamiliar house that she could so easily get to love, and this man sitting opposite her who'd been for so long at the heart of her life.

'What happens now,' she said with difficulty, 'is that I . . . I become a Frenchwoman.'

'So you *are* going to marry Legrand.' The expression on his face was unreadable, but she was suddenly breathing air so cold that it was a sharp pain in her lungs. A moment ago she'd been enveloped in warmth; now she knew what a cat felt like when it was put out of doors on a January night. Oliver, in some way she couldn't define, had simply abandoned her.

'There hasn't been a chance to make it common knowledge,' she explained stiffly. 'We settled it a few days ago over the telephone. I'm glad Uncle Edwin knew about it, though . . . it was what he wanted to happen.'

'So your fiancé will be coming over, of course?'

'As soon as he knows, but Marcel told me this morning that Jules has had to set out on a trip down to Andorra. He's out of touch for the moment, and we have to wait until he rings Paris.'

She said the words calmly, felt the sudden prickle of tears, and then was helpless to prevent them overflowing. Faster than she could blink them away, they poured silently down her cheeks and she was powerless to stop them. A moment later she was picked up in Oliver's arms and she turned her face into his shoulder in the blind certainty that comfort would be found there when she needed it so badly. Just for a minute or two the cat was in from the cold again.

She raised her head at last and smiled at him apologetically. 'Sorry about that . . . your jacket's soggy, I expect I am, too.'

'Yes, but sweet with it,' he told her gently. 'My dear mama would say that a good weep is probably what you've been needing all day. I'll begin sorting things out tomorrow, by the way. It won't take long, because your uncle left his affairs in apple-pie order.'

He drove her home soon afterwards and Jane found nothing to say until he pulled up at the gate of the Owl House.

'Thanks for putting me together again, Oliver. I shall be all right now . . . and Jules will come as soon as he can.'

He nodded but didn't say anything, and she cast around for something that would cover the fact that he still hadn't congratulated her on her engagement. 'I forgot to mention it, but your house is going to be utterly beautiful.'

'I hoped you would like it,' he agreed quietly. In the silence that followed she could hear the words dropping through space, down and down into the well of things that might have been, if all that had happened had happened differently.

'Good-night,' he added, and there was nothing for her to do except get out of the car and watch him drive away.

Six

She got up next morning determined to start grappling with her affairs. By the time she heard from Jules she must be organised, calm, and ready to start her new life with him in France. A first step was obviously to go and call on Jim Watkins. His little house lay not far away, but progress was slow because everyone she met wanted to say something kind, and something nice about her uncle. Even her pupils, not noted for thoughtful behaviour during the freedom of the holidays, indicated rather bashfully that they were sorry. Jim showed no surprise at seeing her when she finally got to his doorstep.

'Been expecting you,' he said briefly, showing her into the parlour of his cottage, which remained in a state of unnatural neatness because he used it so rarely. 'Sorry about your uncle, Jane. Quiet man, but the village will miss him, all the same.'

He put coffee in front of her, in no hurry to hear her confirm what he guessed she'd come to say. Jane was in no hurry, either, being concerned with realising how much she'd grown to like this small, unsentimental man who had watched over the well-being of the village school for nearly twenty years. The legend, carefully fostered but never put to the test as far as she knew, was that he was a karate expert. She'd occasionally suspected that he didn't know any more about karate than she did, but the legend, or something in his pale blue eyes, had

had a marvellously quelling effect on young village tearaways coming up against him for the first time.

'Jim, I've come to hand in my resignation,' she said slowly at last. 'I'm going to marry Jules Legrand. With Uncle Edwin still alive, nothing was going to happen immediately. Now, of course, there is no reason not to go to France as soon as I can.'

'S'pose not,' he agreed. 'We shall miss you, young Jane, and the children won't be best pleased, either, but what Little Fairford wants is neither here nor there.'

He'd have liked to say that he couldn't think why she wanted to live in a God-forsaken place like France when she could stay in the Thames Valley, but he wasn't a man much given to pressing his opinions on other people, and the strained face of the girl in front of him made him wish that he could give her a hug instead. He wasn't a demonstrative man either, and contented himself with picking her a handful of the most perfect roses he could find in his garden. Jane thanked him and walked home, feeling that her most decisive step had now been taken. With her job surrendered, her face was surely turned towards France.

At the end of the week her uncle was buried in the rook-haunted churchyard beside the river. The village was present almost to a man, and between them and the host of Edwin Kingsley's former colleagues at Oxford, the little church was packed to the doors. There were so many people to greet and thank for coming that Jane had no time to dwell on the fact that the only person missing was her fiancé. Marcel Colbert had come alone, deeply apologetic for the fact that he had still not been able to contact Jules. Jane thought it a strange and unsatisfactory state of affairs, but if he chose to run his galleries in this peculiar way it was hardly up to her to say so. It was also odd that Jules should have gone so completely out of touch when he'd known that her uncle's health was precarious. But she would have to learn to accept his absolute preoccupation with the job in hand. If he'd known about Edwin's death, he would have come at once, she felt sure; not knowing, he was clinging to his 'awkward' Spaniard until their deal was completed.

She struggled through the day of the funeral, dimly aware that Oliver Hatton was never far from her side, magically there whenever she needed him. When it was finally over and the very last visitor had gone, he astonished her with a fleeting kiss and a quiet, 'You did very well, little one.'

'With much help from the Hattons,' she commented after a moment's hesitation. 'I couldn't have coped without them.'

'Colbert told me that you still haven't heard from Jules. It seems odd, but obviously we don't understand how these high-powered dealers work.'

Jane managed a careless shrug. 'Marcel isn't worried, so I suppose I needn't be either. Poor Jules is in pursuit of a Spaniard in Andorra, who's known to be difficult but must be borne with because of the rare objects he has to sell.'

'That explains it, of course . . . there's no telling how long a Spaniard can drag out the business of haggling – very Moorish people, the Spaniards!'

This, uttered in tones of strong disapproval, made her smile, as he'd intended it should. She refused an offer of dinner on the grounds that she was too tired to do anything but take herself off to bed, but her real intention was to prove to herself that she could manage without his help. She was aware of having leaned heavily on him all day, and it was the sort of dependence that could easily become a habit. It was time to start managing on her own.

* * *

Among a heap of mail in her letter-box next morning was a postcard with a French stamp, postmarked Orléans. She pounced on it, saw Jules' name scrawled at the bottom, then went back to read a message that she found puzzling. He'd obviously stopped at Orléans on his way out of Paris, perhaps simply long enough to send a card that would explain his unexpected trip; but the message emphasised the excellence of a certain *Hôtel Richelieu*, pictured on the back, and recommended her to be sure to see it for herself. She decided that it was slightly odd, but more disappointing than odd, because it left her no wiser about where Jules was going next. She put the card aside to tackle the rest of the mail, and was only half-way through when Oliver knocked at the front door. He was dressed for a day at his office in Oxford, and a slightly brisker manner than usual seemed to stress that this was merely an official visit between executor and client.

'Probate's being hustled through, Jane. There's no reason why you shouldn't put the Owl House in the hands of an estate agent immediately. I assume that's what you have in mind – to sell it?'

'It's the only sensible thing to do. What's the good of a house in England when we shall be living in France? I've asked Jim Watkins to use the rest of the summer holiday to find a replacement teacher, so there's only the house to worry about.'

'And the Collection,' Oliver reminded her.

'Of course, but I don't think of that as being anything to do with me.'

He thought she sounded blithely unconcerned about the assortment of almost priceless objects under her roof, and his private anxiety on the subject made him speak more sharply than he meant to.

'It's to do with you to the extent that it's still here. It shouldn't be, and I'm bulldozing sleepy Authority into transferring it to the Museum straightaway.'

She remembered the burglar of a few weeks before, who certainly now knew what the Owl House contained, even if he hadn't wanted the Collection for himself. Oliver was right, as usual, and she had to tell him so with a reluctance that made him smile. His gaze lingered on her face for a moment. 'You've lost weight,' he remarked suddenly. 'If you get much smaller, you'll disappear altogether. Anything bothering you?'

Jane shook her head, thrown off balance as usual by that rare note of gentleness in his voice. 'I think I feel a bit limbo-ish at the moment . . . not really belonging here any more, but not yet settled in my new life.'

She thought Oliver hesitated about whether or not to enquire whether anything had been heard of Jules, and felt relieved to be able to say that a postcard had arrived.

'It doesn't help us to get in touch with him, because he was obviously just passing through, but at least he remembers that he's got a fiancée,' she said cheerfully. She did *not* propose to share with Oliver the fact that she looked strained because she was sleeping badly, and dreaded sleep in any case because of a recurrent nightmare in which she walked blindfolded along a tightrope stretched high above the ground. She hadn't fallen off yet, but the fear that she would do so in some culminating terror went with her to bed every night. Her disorientated life at the moment was the cause of it, she felt sure; if only Jules could subjugate his Spaniard and get back to Paris, all would be well.

By the time Oliver came again, to supervise the transfer of the Kingsley Collection to Oxford, she'd received a second postcard. This time the *Auberge Arc-en-Ciel* at Châteauroux was, apparently, another place she must on no account fail to visit. The message seemed as pointless as the previous one, except that Jane recalled with a feeling of disquiet the fact that Jules never did things that were pointless. Odd though it seemed, she began to feel that he actually *wanted* her to follow the route he'd taken himself, in imagination if not in fact.

She was so abstracted when Oliver next arrived that he misread the cause of her thoughtfulness. 'Sad to say goodbye to them after all, Jane?' he asked, as the last gleaming astrolabe was tenderly packed in layers of tissue paper and polystyrene for the brief journey to Oxford.

The shake of her head was very definite. 'Not sad – relieved. Jules couldn't quite believe that I don't regret losing such an inheritance, but it's true. I don't know enough to value the instruments for what they can explain about the past, as Uncle Edwin did. They're beautiful, but I don't even covet them for that; for me they represent a culture that has betrayed itself by bigotry and senseless violence.'

Oliver nodded, but knew that if the loss of the Collection wasn't worrying her, something else was. He wished very much that she would confide in him, but there was an air of reserve about her nowadays. The Jane Kingsley he'd known as well as he knew himself had gone now. He blamed Jules Legrand for that, whether it was fair to do so or not.

'What news from the Great Wen?' she asked cheerfully. 'Is Estelle about to leap to stardom?'

'I think not. To nobody's great surprise, the part finally went to a *soi-disant* "niece" of the impresario! Estelle is returning to the fold at the weekend to lick her wounds in rural solitude and once more consider Giving Up The Stage!'

'I'm very glad, Oliver,' Jane said earnestly. 'Not glad for

Estelle; I suppose she's disappointed. But I'm very glad for your sake.'

He couldn't help smiling at this comment, delivered in her sweet, husky voice; she totally misunderstood the nature of his interest in Estelle Harding, but that scarcely mattered now. She was generous, his little one, and damnably staunch. He didn't know the extent of her attachment to a man who had obstinately disappeared; but great or small, he knew she would keep the information to herself.

'Come and see Mary soon,' he suggested. 'She was bemoaning the fact that you've gone into purdah recently.'

'I've started packing up books and things – one of the more endless labours of Hercules – but I *will* go and visit her,' she promised.

She watched him walk down the path to his dark-green Rover parked at the gate, thinking that life was extraordinarily perverse. It had taken so many years to achieve this pleasant, grown-up friendship with Oliver, and now that she had, their paths were about to diverge for good and all.

The new-found friendship lasted two and a half days by her subsequent reckoning. She was in the middle of clearing out cupboards and bookshelves when peaceful co-existence with her lawyer exploded into more fragments than could ever be put together again. The floor of the study was littered with piles of books when he strode in. She was still puzzling, while she worked, over the messages on the postcards Jules had sent. The obvious step of ringing Marcel Colbert to ask his advice had just occurred to her when the sight of Oliver standing in the doorway made her heart give an unexpected lift. But happiness didn't survive a second glance at the expression on his face. She'd seen him irritable in the past, even angry when he thought she'd done something stupid; but she'd never encountered this grim-faced stranger who confronted her like an executioner.

'Getting ready to go, I see,' he remarked of the air somewhere above her head.

'Why sound surprised about it?' she asked reasonably. 'I can't sell a house stuffed with books and furniture.'

'And your instructions are, of course, to get over to Paris quickly.'

'I have no instructions,' she pointed out with some coldness, nettled by his tone. 'You look angry, Oliver – tell me what's wrong.'

'What's wrong is that I resent being had for a mug.'

The astonishing words dropped with icy emphasis into the silence in the room.

'I'm afraid I don't follow you . . . you'll have to explain.' It was an effort to speak calmly when her pounding heart was surely sending blood pumping round her body at twice its normal rate.

'I need someone else – Jules Legrand, perhaps – to do some explaining to *me*. I need to know how it comes about that ten of the instruments examined by experts at the Museum, that's to say all those supposedly originating in Muslim Spain, are judged to be fakes. *Fakes*, Jane.'

'Don't bellow at me,' she said sharply. 'Are you saying that Uncle Edwin – Edwin Kingsley of all people – didn't know the difference between a replica and the real thing?'

She saw Oliver answer with a shake of his head.

'So you're suggesting that he knowingly bequeathed the Museum a lot of rubbish?' Anger swelled inside her at the implications of what he'd said and made her shout the question at him.

'You didn't listen,' Oliver said, as sleet-cold as she was hot. 'There's no question of Edwin being involved. All those instruments were handled in the past by the very people who examined them today. They were accepted then as bona fide instruments, rare and irreplaceable.'

'What *are* you saying, in that case?' she enquired hoarsely.

'That they've recently been substituted for the clever beautiful fakes we packed up with such care the other day.'

Jane digested this calm, cold statement, trying to find some way of denying it and finding none. Then she remembered how the conversation had begun. 'You said you wanted . . . you wanted *Jules* to explain. If you think of suspecting him, the idea's almost too monstrous to put into words.'

Oliver could scarcely hear the horrified whisper, then he saw her face change. 'The *burglary* . . . that *was* just a blind. The instruments were changed then, only we were intended to think the thief had ignored the Collection . . . you said so yourself!'

Oliver's own sombre expression didn't change. 'Yes, that was when the substitution was made, but it was planned before then – had to be, so that the replacement instruments could be made. And it was planned by someone who knew precisely what was here.'

'Not by Jules,' she insisted steadily. 'Dozens of people over the years have come here to study them.'

'After which they were still here. I need to talk to Legrand, Jane.'

'Assuming that your theory is even worth arguing about, which I don't accept, how could the switch have been made without my uncle knowing? He was the one man who could have been sure to spot a fraud.'

The anguish in her face moved Oliver to sick despair. He

wanted more than anything in life to strangle Jules Legrand, but there seemed no doubt now that she truly loved a man who might turn out to be a criminal.

'I'm guessing, Jane,' he said more gently, 'I can't prove any of what I say at the moment. But I must tell you how it looks to an outsider. Edwin's strength was fading with every day that passed. How much did he handle the instruments himself, even towards the end of Legrand's visit? He died sooner than expected; the exchange might not have been discovered for months – was intended not to be discovered at all, of course.'

'Jules was in Paris – I spoke to him an hour after the police were here. Even without that I'd be certain he wasn't the thief. He loves me . . . loved my uncle.'

Then, suddenly, her expression changed, and Oliver knew the terrible truth that had occurred to her.

'The morning Uncle Edwin died he was looking at an astrolabe . . . it was in pieces in front of him . . . he must have known then about the substitution . . .' She couldn't go on and walked away to stare out of the window. After a moment or two she wheeled round again to face Oliver. 'I don't believe it,' she said proudly. 'Jules could never have done what you're suggesting.'

Oliver would have given all he possessed to believe that she was right. 'Well, it's vital that we talk to him,' he was forced to point out. 'For the moment I've persuaded the people at the Museum to do nothing, but I can't hold them off for long. Where can I get hold of Legrand?'

'I don't know.'

'Oh, come on, Jane, you're engaged to the man! You must have some idea.'

'I repeat that I do not know.' She was near breaking point,

her voice climbing to a shout again. 'Even Marcel doesn't know, he said the Spaniard insisted on secrecy. If it sounds absurd to you, I can't help it. Talk to Marcel if you don't believe me.'

'I most certainly will,' Oliver said grimly.

She ran to the desk and scribbled out a telephone number. 'Take it and go; I won't talk to you any longer.'

She flung the words at him, intending to run past him out of the room, but his hands caught her in a grip that held her trapped in front of him. Her friend had disappeared; in his place was an implacable stranger whose eyes glittered in a chalk-white face.

'I thought you'd be reasonable. I underrated your devotion – or Legrand's prowess as a lover. I suppose he's deliciously fierce and French, give or take a bit of Canadian blood!'

He regretted the jibe even as it was spoken, but Jane's hand flew up to avenge the insult. Before it could reach his face it was caught and imprisoned behind her back. They stood for a moment breast to breast, and then she was being kissed more thoroughly, ruthlessly, hurtfully than she'd known a woman could be kissed. But the final humiliation was the knowledge that the fire that hadn't leapt along her blood for Jules now leapt for Oliver. She was almost lost when he lifted his mouth from hers and pushed her away, in a contemptuous gesture that said his only intention had been to punish her.

'Hurrah for *English* prowess,' she whispered through sore lips, determined that she wouldn't leave him with victory.

A nerve jumped in his temple, warning her that she might have taunted him too far. A civilised, self-controlled man had been pushed so far off balance that anything could happen. But Oliver rubbed an unsteady hand across his eyes, changed his mind about something he almost started to say, and was gone from the room in three long strides. Jane heard the front door slam, and the sound of it echoed hollowly in her mind. Door after door seemed to be closing as far into the future as she could see.

Seven

The nightmare that night was much worse than usual. She was still inching her way along the tightrope, hands outstretched in a desperate attempt to keep her balance, but now hideously thorned stems caught at her, threatening to drag her off the narrow wire she crept along. She was no longer blindfolded, but dazzled instead by a a golden disc suspended in front of her like some monstrous sun. It wasn't the sun – the intricately worked filigree all over its face told her that she was staring at a giant astrolabe that grew and grew to mammoth size. She was blinded by its brightness and put her hands up to her eyes, forgetful that she must keep her balance on the tightrope. The sensation of plummeting down through space finally woke her, choking with terror.

The cold bath of perspiration in which she lay finally drove her out of bed to wrap herself in a cotton robe. It was still dark in the room, but a thin line of gold just above the horizon outside held out hope of dawn and daylight. She stood at the window dragging cold sweet air into her lungs until the thumping of her heart returned to something like normal. Mary Hatton's voice came back to her, insisting that tea was good for shock, and when she went downstairs she was calmed by the mere ritual of making it. Then she wandered out into the garden, hands cupped round the hot mug, grateful to discover that she wasn't alone in the world. A thrush was tuning up in the willow tree, and although he stopped singing immediately, he decided that she meant no harm and went on with his rehearsal.

Sitting in the dimness of the garden, Jane sipped her tea, telling herself that if she didn't allow her mind to panic like a terrified animal, she would be able to decide what it was she must do. After Oliver had walked out of the house the previous evening she'd spent hours trying to reach Marcel Colbert. There's been no reply from the Gallery number she'd given Oliver, none from Marcel's own apartment. Oliver would have achieved the same nil result, and she didn't doubt that he'd soon be on the doorstep again, trying to shake out of her knowledge she didn't have. The news he'd brought had bludgeoned her into stupidity; now, in the calmness and quietness of dawn the obvious solution occurred to her. The Spaniard had caused the instruments to be stolen, and they were precisely what Jules was doing his level best to get back. His postcards had been more than the result of a simple wish to keep in touch with her. They'd contained oblique messages she had been witless not to understand. With that certainty came the knowledge of what she must do, and the huge relief of standing on firm ground again.

She went indoors, showered and dressed, and sat at the kitchen table forcing down toast and coffee while she studied her uncle's large-scale map of France. The Dover-Calais crossing was by far the shortest, and once on French soil the drive to Paris looked straightforward – Abbeville, Amiens and Beauvais and she was practically there. With Heaven on her side to see that she didn't get obliterated by some vast camion the moment she set wheel outside the port, there was no reason why she shouldn't get herself to the Colbert Galleries successfully. Her passport was in order, and the car insured for foreign travel on the Continent.

Half an hour later, almost ready to leave, she walked along the lane to Jim Watkins' house. It was still only half-past seven, not an hour when she'd have felt it permissible to call on anyone else, but she knew Jim's habits. He was an early riser, and on a fine summer morning he was certain to be outside already, working in his garden. Apart from growing some of the loveliest flowers in the village, he produced enough vegetables to keep an old people's home just outside Oxford supplied the whole year round. He preferred his good to be done by stealth, and only Jane knew why he simply grinned when people teased him about the bushels of vegetables he got through.

'You're bright and early,' he said by way of greeting. 'Well, *early* anyway; now I come to think about it, you look a bit washed out, not bright at all.'

'Bad night,' she explained briefly. 'Jim, will you do me a great favour?'

'I expect so . . . what is it?'

'Keep an eye on the house for me while I make a quick trip to France? I'm not going for good yet, but there's something I have to do there immediately.' She hesitated, then told him the truth. 'There's been some trouble about Uncle Edwin's Collection – our burglar exchanged the instruments for fakes, although we didn't realise that at the time. If anyone comes asking for me, will you just say I've gone away for a few days – you don't know where? I expect it will look odd, but I can't help that.'

His eyes inspected her face while he made up his mind. 'I'll say whatever you like, and they'd better not tell *me* it sounds odd.'

Her strained expression relaxed briefly into a smile and, one foot in the car, she turned round again to plant a kiss on the rough cheek he hadn't got round to shaving – a liberty she wouldn't have dreamed of taking while she still worked for him. He looked taken aback but not displeased, and didn't immediately go back to watering his cabbages when she'd driven away. Something was very wrong with the little maid, but he'd known better than to ask her what it was. He thought she'd wanted him *not* to know, so that he wouldn't have to lie for her when someone started asking questions.

She got back to the Owl House to find a tall figure waiting in the porch. Her heart missed a beat for a moment, but it was Richard Hatton standing there, not his son. He was a conventional man, not given to making social calls before breakfast, and she knew at once that Oliver had been in touch with him.

'May I talk to you, Jane?' he asked quietly as she came up to him.

'If you're simply going to repeat what your son said last night, I think I'd rather you didn't.'

His arm round her shoulders urged her back to the wooden bench on the lawn, which at least meant that she didn't have to take him into the house where he'd have seen her suitcase standing in the hall. His eyes glanced at her, noting the pallor of her face and a cut lip that lipstick didn't quite conceal.

'Oliver's told me that he made a mess of things yesterday – not the sort of mistake my son likes to confess to. He's old enough to do his own apologising; I'm only here to see if I can help.'

'Did he have any luck in trying to get through to Marcel Colbert?' she asked.

'No . . . tried for hours, apparently, and he'll begin again this morning. Jules has to be found, my dear, if only to tell us when the genuine instruments were last there for certain.'

'*You* may put it like that, but Oliver doesn't. He's convinced Jules is the thief, and he's not very sure I didn't have something to do with it as well.'

Richard Hatton would have given years of his life to deny it, but the stark comment left him nothing to say. The look on Oliver's face the previous night was etched into his memory. His son had appeared very late, just as Richard wandered back indoors from a last moonlit stroll round the garden.

'Thought I'd see if you were still up,' Oliver had said briefly. 'Something to talk to you about if you're not too tired.'

'Of course not . . . like old times, a jaw and a glass of whisky. Let's go inside.'

He'd waited until his father was settled with a glass by his side.

'We're in deep trouble, I'm afraid. Some of the Kingsley instruments have been replaced by fakes. The only person who could have arranged the switch seems to be Legrand – either on his own account or possibly at the instigation of his boss. They aren't buying instruments from a mysterious Spaniard – my guess is that they're selling the the damned things.'

There was a long silence before Richard Hatton said anything at all. 'I think you'd better tell me the whole thing,' he suggested at last.

At the end of a bald recital of the facts Oliver's voice had suddenly cracked. 'I simply don't know what to think about Jane. I'd have sworn that she was truly shocked this afternoon, but God knows I've had proof enough that a woman can look one thing and be another. She's too intelligent not to see that Legrand must be questioned, but she won't even admit that she knows where he is . . . her own fiancé! Is it remotely credible?'

'It's possible that she's deliberately blinding herself to the truth,' Richard said quietly, 'but I refuse to believe she herself had anything to do with it.'

'I'd agree with you except that you're forgetting something: she's going to marry Legrand. Her loyalties are formidable, and we have to accept the fact that they now lie with him, not here.'

Richard stared at his son's drawn face; thinking that he'd now seen it at last without the mask of smiling detachment it normally presented to the world.

'Give it up for tonight – you look all in. I'll go and have a chat with Jane in the morning, while you keep trying Colbert. He must surface before long – he has a business to run.'

That had been the extent of their conversation but as a result of it, Richard Hatton couldn't perjure himself now by telling Jane that Oliver was convinced of her innocence.

'He's a lawyer, my dear, and the executor of your uncle's will,' he said instead. 'Don't blame him too much if he goes by the evidence, not the heart . . . he's obliged to, you see.'

'The heart has its reasons, too,' she quoted sadly. 'But Oliver's not prepared to trust them.'

'It's precisely *your* heart's reasons that bother him, my dear. He can't help remembering that you're about to marry Jules Legrand.'

'There is that,' she agreed, staring at him.

'I suppose I'd better go, Mary'll be wondering why I don't appear for breakfast. We'll see you soon, won't we?'

She nodded, unable to put the lie into words, but the sadness in her face went with him as he walked away. He told himself he'd go straight to Oxford and beat into his son, if necessary, the conviction that she *couldn't* have known about the fraud. Oliver probably half-knew it too, but his ex-wife had destroyed his confidence in women.

Jane watched Richard Hatton lope down the path, wondering when or even if she would see him again. It felt strange not to be open with a man who'd been almost as much of a surrogate father to her as Edwin had been, but she hadn't dared tell him she was going to France. What Richard knew, his son would know soon afterwards, and she had to be across the Channel before Oliver got wind of what she was up to.

She fetched her suitcase and coat from the hall, and collected from the doormat the mail delivered while she was visiting Jim. It was no surprise to see another postcard from France – postmarked Limoges this time – but for once the message was more explicit than the others had been. Jules needed to see her, but must rely on her to come to him because his movements were so uncertain. If she would only follow him down, he'd make sure of finding her somewhere along his route. She was thankful for the confirmation that she was doing the right thing, but the message suddenly prompted her to pick up the telephone and dial Jim Watkins' number.

'I've got another favour to ask, Jim. It sounds rather cloak and daggerish, I'm afraid, but Jules is travelling at the moment, and occasionally sends a rather important message on a postcard. If I leave the key under the tub by the kitchen door, will you look in occasionally and see if anything else has arrived? I'll ring you when I can.'

'Will do . . . take care of yourself, young Jane.'

When Oliver drove along the lane an hour later he was surprised to see Jim Watkins making a circuit of the Owl House.

'Morning, Jim – what brings you here?'

'Keeping an eye on things for Jane. You know what women are – usually remember to lock the doors, then go and leave a window open.'

'Kind of you. Do I take it that Jane has gone away?'

Jim wished someone would tell him what was going on. First Jane, now Oliver, both looking like the wrath of God.

'She called early this morning . . . wanted me to know the house would be empty for a few days.'

'Did she happen to mention where she was going?'

'France. Just a quick visit, she said; not going for good yet.'

'You do surprise me. Well, I'll be on my way. See you, Jim.'

Oliver put the car into gear and roared away at a speed quite different from his normal method of driving through the village. He'd been tempted to let Richard convince him that Jane was not involved in what was going on. The truth made him feel sick, but he had no doubt now what the truth was.

Jane drove her Metro onto the ferry at Dover obedient to the commands of a traffic-controller who wheeled and swooped over his customers with the autocratic precision of a ballet-master. She finally managed to place the car exactly where he insisted it must go, then climbed up on deck, grateful that the first hurdle was over. She'd banked on the fact that a mid-week, midday crossing might not be fully booked, but late-August was still high-season for holidaymakers and she might have been turned away. It would have been a real setback to have to kick her heels in Dover, and there was the fear lurking at the back of her mind that Oliver would suddenly appear and haul her back to Little Fairford. To make entirely sure, she hung over the rail, examining the long line of cars still being fed into the bowels of the ship. Behind them the juggernauts waited their turn, presumably patient in the knowledge that, last on, they would be the first off the other side. The stuffy saloon and restaurant didn't tempt her to go below, and she sat huddled in her coat on deck, feeling the coldness of apprehension rather than any chilliness in the late-summer air. There was nothing more to be done for the moment; it was time to think quietly instead.

She abandoned the tempting but unrealistic idea that a mistake might have been made; if the Museum experts said the Muslim instruments were fakes, that was undoubtedly what they were. Jules might not have been experienced enough to tell the difference, so there was no certainty about when the exchange had been made, but it seemed obvious that it had been at the time of the burglary. The other things had been taken to make them all believe that they were what the thief had come for. The Spaniard was the most likely person to be at the bottom of it . . . a fanatic devoting himself to the task of recovering the treasures he considered belonged to Spain, or simply wanting them for himself, to gloat over in secret. There *were* such people, and it was the thought of them that had made Jules behave so secretively – they were rich enough and ruthless enough to go to any lengths to get what they wanted.

It seemed reasonable to think that Jules was now on the track of such a madman, but if he hadn't taken Marcel Colbert into his confidence, could it possibly mean that he feared his godfather might be implicated? By going to Paris was she driving straight into a trap? Her stomach heaved, despite the calmness of the Channel. The world was going altogether mad when *she* could suspect Edwin Kingsley's oldest friend, and Oliver Hatton could suspect her or Jules. She swallowed the nausea in her throat, struggling for self-control. But the moment of panic had given her the answer to another of her questions: Jules had wanted her out of reach of people he wasn't sure they could trust; that was the reason for this strangely mapped-out journey. She must still start at the Colbert Galleries, but she must go to discover what she could, not to give anything away.

The ferry docked punctually at Calais but there was the usual endless wait before anything happened at all. Then at last the ship's bow-doors were opened up, and cars hurled themselves away like greyhounds suddenly released from their traps. She was rigid with nerves to begin with, hands clenched on the wheel. An impatient lorry-driver behind her hooted because she steered too gingerly away from the quayside, and then blasted her over to the right side of the road when she automatically sought safety on the left. A previous journey with her uncle prepared her for the alarming junction of roads, and finally she was safely out of the town, on the road running south.

By late afternoon the accumulated stresses of the day were beginning to tell. She was hungry, tired, and well aware that it would be madness to tackle the evening rush-hour in Paris when she was stupid with exhaustion. Beauvais offered a suitable staging-post, and when she stopped the car outside a pleasant-looking hotel called *La Résidence* her trembling arms and legs confirmed that she couldn't safely have gone further.

Food and a night's sleep did her good, and she set out at half-past eight the next morning feeling calm enough to regret not visiting the beautiful Cathedral of St Pierre. But there would be time for such things when the present nightmare was over and she and Jules could visit them together. Her route into the capital still lay more or less due south, through the *Porte de Clignancourt*. The *Sacré Coeur*, gleaming on its hilltop above Montmartre, appeared on her right, and the sight of it made her suddenly feel at home again, instead of a stranger in a hostile city. This had been a *quartier* she had stayed in more than once with Uncle Edwin.

About to cross the traffic roaring along the wide spaces of the *Boulevard Haussman*, confidence was rudely shattered by the sight in her driving mirror of a dark-green Rover nosing its way into the traffic behind her. Her hands went nerveless on the wheel and her foot instinctively hit the brake pedal, until an outraged roar on the horn of the car behind her jolted her on again, hands clammy with perspiration and a nerve jumping in her throat. Just for a moment she'd been reminded of Oliver's car, and it took a moment to convince herself that he couldn't possibly be there. She was at the *Rue Saint Denis* at last and, by the grace of God, could see an empty parking space almost outside the *Galéries*. With the car safely tucked alongside the meter, she could relax for a moment from the strain of the past twenty-four hours. The quiet country bustle of Little Fairford belonged to another world a lifetime away; but at least she and her car were here in one piece, and if Heaven continued kind, Marcel Colbert would be there to set her mind at rest from its worst anxiety.

She stepped inside elegant premises that indicated how greatly he had prospered. A tall, *soignée* girl stood up from the reception desk to look her over, and in that cool glance Jane read confirmation of a much smaller fear. Her face *was* flushed and shiny from the morning's drive, and her shirt and skirt were definitely travel-worn.

'Monsieur Colbert, if you please,' she said with as much self-possession as she could muster. 'My name is Kingsley.

I'm well-known to him in England, and it is important that I speak with him.'

Her French, at least, was crisp and flawless, and the mention of the name Kingsley warmed the atmosphere a little.

'I regret, Mademoiselle, Monsieur Colbert is not yet back from a trip to Brussels . . . I don't know exactly when he will return.'

Jane struggled with a strong inclination to burst into tears. It explained why she hadn't been able to get hold of him, but was no help at all in settling what she ought to do next.

'Is it likely to be today . . . tomorrow?' she asked.

A Gallic shrug perfectly honed to combine regret with the fact that a receptionist couldn't predict the vagaries of her employer left Jane no wiser than before. She was still debating what to do when the door opened and Marcel himself walked in, a valise in one hand, his briefcase in the other. His face, never revealing what was in his mind, expressed now only the surprise that was reasonable.

'Jane, *ma chère . . . je suis enchanté de te voir, mais quelle plaisir imprévu!*'

'I tried to telephone,' she spoke in English, hoping the receptionist wouldn't understand. 'I needed to talk to you rather badly about something that's happened.'

His eyes took in the signs of strain in her face and the way her hands gripped the bag she held. He barked a brief question at the receptionist, who shook her head, and then swept Jane into the seclusion of his own room.

'Sit down, Jane, and then I shall insist that you sip a glass of wine while you tell me what has brought you all the way to Paris.'

'In a way it's . . . it's worse than losing Uncle Edwin,' she said hoarsely. 'You know he willed the Collection to an Oxford

Museum. My uncle's executor, Oliver Hatton, arranged for the instruments to be transferred, and it was then discovered that the most priceless instruments – all the Moorish ones – are nothing but clever fakes. Oliver wants to talk to Jules, and he doesn't believe that I don't know where he is.'

It was her turn to examine Marcel's face; this time she could read only shock, cushioned by a slight disbelief.

'Are you sure you cannot be mistaken, my dear Jane . . . have the Museum officials not made some absurd mistake?'

'There's no misunderstanding, no mistake,' she said baldly. 'But the worst thing is that Oliver thinks Jules is responsible, that no one else could possibly have known how to instruct a burglar to substitute fakes for the genuine instruments.'

The dreadful words were out, and she waited to hear what Marcel would say.

'I simply cannot believe this. I confess that I've begun to feel anxieties of my own, because Jules left here with a very large sum of money – our Spanish contact, you see, had insisted on a cash-only transaction. But my fear has been for Jules himself, and it worries me now that he is so completely out of touch.'

Jane dropped her face in her hands, fighting the dizziness that swept over her. Life seemed to have become a continuing nightmare in which she stumbled blindly from one terror to another.

'You are faint, *ma pauvre*,' Marcel said gently. 'You need food to restore you. After that you will take heart, and we shall decide together what we must do.'

She glanced at her watch and saw that it was indeed the time in France for eating lunch. Since nothing short of an earthquake would prevent Marcel eating what he regarded as the most important meal of the day, she must eat too if she wanted to go on talking to him. She was offered the use of his black and gold bathroom in which to 'refresh' herself, and that was typical too. Even in a crisis Marcel Colbert was not a man to share a luncheon table with a woman whose appearance offended his eye. She could do nothing about her crumpled linen skirt, but felt undeniably better for a cool wash and the knowledge that lipstick and perfume were in place again.

They walked the few hundred yards to his usual restaurant, where Jane agreed to struggle with an omelette and salad while Marcel ordered with less ceremony than usual a minimal meal of *choucroute*, veal, salad, and Brie. When the waiter had disappeared, he took a sip of wine, and at last seemed prepared to revert to the subject that dominated her mind. She shifted her chair slightly, and saw the rest of the room suddenly tilt and fall away from her.

'Jane . . . what is it . . . you've gone so white,' he said hurriedly.

She ducked her head for a moment, saying nothing at all, then looked up to find Oliver Hatton now standing by their table, smiling and immovable.

Eight

'Good morning, Jane . . . Monsieur Colbert. We met once, if you remember, at my parents' home.'

Marcel bowed to the inevitable with a good grace.

'Of course, I remember. Join us, please, Monsieur Hatton, since I can guess why you are here.'

Oliver pulled out a chair and sat down, unmoved by the sight of Jane frowning at him across the table.

'Have you been following me all the way?' she asked abruptly.

'No, I've been virtually camped outside the Galleries; you must have stopped the night somewhere along the road.'

He looked from her stormy face to his host's unrevealing one. 'I need your help, Monsieur, in finding Jules Legrand, since Jane insists that she doesn't know where he is.'

Marcel's shrug was as expressive as the receptionist's had been, thought Jane, but it managed to say even less.

'May we come to that in a moment? First of all, the instruments. Is there the slightest doubt about the fact that a substitution has been made?'

'None at all,' Oliver replied politely. 'Nor, to be frank, is there the slightest doubt in my own mind that it was Jules Legrand who had the exchange made, either on his own account or at the instigation of someone else.'

Jane stared at him, aware that the man who'd seemed to amble about the world half-asleep had disappeared. This was an Oliver Hatton she hadn't seen before – coldly courteous, alert, and inexorable.

'Someone else,' Marcel repeated, 'myself, perhaps being an obvious candidate?'

Oliver borrowed the Frenchman's own shrug. 'I'm not in a position to suggest any such thing; my only concern at the moment is to find Jules Legrand.'

It was the moment when Jane knew for a certainty that her uncle's old friend was not involved in the fraud. He pushed aside his food, and fumbled for his wine-glass with a hand that trembled.

'I wish I *could* help you find Jules, if only to destroy this infamous suspicion. I know nothing about the fraud, and I am convinced that my godson doesn't either. He left Paris with a large sum of money in order to deal with a Spaniard who wished to sell us some rare instruments, and I have not heard from him since. Now, of course, I fear that Jules guessed where the instruments had come from. It was madness to try to deal with the situation on his own, but my godson is hot-headed as well as brave.'

Oliver stared at the Frenchman's grey face. 'But you can't help wondering how many other people would have been in a position to have put in hand replicas so perfect that only an expert could spot them. There was also the fact that the burglar who exchanged them must have been given precise information as to how to get at them.'

Marcel's face moved Jane to such pity that she deliberately moved into Oliver's line of fire.

'That's where I came in, of course,' she suggested coolly.

'Who better placed than me to ease a thief's path by unlocking and locking up display cases for him?'

'The thought does keep occurring,' Oliver agreed with a smoothness that merely accentuated the anger consuming him.

'Thrust and counter-thrust . . . it's meaningless,' Marcel said tiredly, 'except to confirm that we all seem to distrust each other. The truth is that, for the moment, Jules has disappeared. Our arrangement was that he would contact me. If there had been an accident, I should have heard. But I prefer an alternative possibility to yours, Monsieur Hatton. It is that Jules has discovered the whereabouts of the instruments and is doing his best to retrieve them.'

'Exactly,' Jane said swiftly. 'It's the obvious solution, so simple that the tortuous legal mind can't grapple with it.'

'I shall, of course, be the first to apologise if you are proved right,' Oliver agreed, so blandly that it would have given her relief to hit him. 'Meanwhile, what do you suggest we do next?'

Marcel rubbed a hand across his eyes. 'If Jules does not contact me, I must go in search of him, but that will take time. Unless you are able to stay indefinitely, I suggest you return to England. Rest assured that I shall contact you the moment I have news.'

Oliver's glance moved on to Jane. 'What about you, little one?' The use of the nickname was deliberate, and she hated him for using what had belonged to a time when they were friends. She felt no friendship now in this inimically hostile man.

'Marcel's right,' she mumbled, not looking at him. 'There's nothing for *us* to do here. We must just trust him . . . and wait.'

Oliver hesitated, then nodded his head. 'I can't afford to hang about, nor am I inclined to put much faith in trust, but I'll agree to leave things to Monsieur Colbert for the time being. If news isn't soon forthcoming the police must be called in, but I should like to avoid a public scandal if we can. So, for the moment we'll both go home.'

'You'll stay the night as my guest, Jane?' Marcel asked, smiling at her for the first time.

'Thank you, but I'd rather start back straight away. If I miss the last ferry of the day I'll stay the night in Calais. Is that your route as well?' she asked Oliver.

'No, I shall be making for Boulogne. See you back in Little Fairford, Jane.'

They left the restaurant together. The dark-green Rover that she *had* seen crossing the *Boulevard Haussman* was parked fifty yards along the road. Both men walked with her to her car and waited while she strapped herself in and said goodbye. By the time Oliver had parted from Marcel she was already pulling away, the route she must take clear in her mind – across the Seine, along the embankment past the *Jardin des Plantes*, and out of the city by the *Porte de Vitry*. Once there, the road to Orléans would lie in front of her: the route Jules had taken.

It was simple enough to follow: the N20 through Étampes brought her to the outskirts of Orléans by early evening. Jules' postcard of the *Richelieu* had clearly shown a riverside hotel, and she headed in the direction of the Loire. She found the hotel without any difficulty and liked its peaceful atmosphere and pleasant garden overlooking the river. A pile of postcards on the counter where she stood waiting to register were just like the one that Jules had sent, confirming at least that she'd come to the right place. She was about to launch into an explanation when the receptionist stared at the name on her passport and then delved in the cupboard behind her. The small package she handed Jane was addressed in Jules' handwriting.

'Monsieur Legrand explained that you might come,' she said with a smile. 'If not, I was to return it after a month to an address in England.'

Jane hoped afterwards that she'd thanked the girl adequately and confirmed that she'd be dining in the hotel. But she climbed up to the little attic room she'd been offered in a peculiar state of numbness. It should have been a relief to have confirmation that she'd done what Jules clearly wanted her to do by coming to Orléans, but she felt strangely reluctant to open his package all the same. For a moment she was almost suffocated by the feeling of being in a web of intrigue that was enclosing her more and more. Common sense insisted that she was simply suffering from a lack of air in the stuffy room, and she got up to wrestle with a dormer window that hadn't been opened for a long time.

With soft evening air flowing in, and the sound of doves murmuring to each other in the dovecot beneath her window, the moment of panic subsided and she picked up the parcel again. Inside the wrapping, a small cardboard box had been carefully lined with cottonwool. Within the box nestled something she recognised – an ivory figure no more than an inch high of a smiling man resting against a rock – her favourite among the collection of netsukes stolen from the Owl House. It was a joy to have it back, but also a puzzlement. The little figure's smile seemed mocking for once, underlining her sense of helplessness. If Jules had imagined that she would find her journey an intriguing adventure, she was going to disappoint him. She was floundering in a morass of doubt and steadily increasing fear . . . about his own safety, about the fate of the stolen instruments, and about what she was meant to gain from this wild goose chase across France. Engrossed in opening the box, she'd failed to notice a sheet of paper carefully folded to fit underneath it. It was a letter from Jules.

My dearest Jane,

I hope that you will read this in Orléans, not in England, because it means that you will have done what I so badly wanted you to do. I knew when I left England that I needed you, but these weeks without you have shown me that you are now my whole life. Together, there is nothing we can't do, my dearest, but first there is this task to be completed, and it's vital for our future. The netsuke will show you that I'm on the right track, I hope. I didn't dare explain things on my postcard, in case other people should read it as well; and there is no time to explain here. Please just trust me. Keep to my route, I beg of you, because in that way, I know where to find you, but no one else can reach you. Do I sound mad? Melodramatic? Bear with me, we shall soon be happy together. I'll *make* you happy, Jane, I swear it.

A bientôt,

Jules

Jane put the letter down, picked it up and read it again, then wandered over to the window. The evening sunlight lay over the garden and the broad silken ribbon of the river, but she was hardly aware of what she saw. In her mind's eye she was seeing Jules instead – a dashingly handsome, self-confident figure to the ladies of Little Fairford, to herself a man full of unexpected doubts and tenderness. Away from him, she'd begun to forget how intense he was. His letter didn't sound mad, but it had an excited note that brought him vividly to mind. She longed to see him, to say that she didn't expect him to recover her and the Museum's stolen property at the risk of his own safety. If he knew something about the missing instruments, the police could be given the information and the responsibility for hunting the thief from then on. What she and Jules needed was not this sort of derring-do, but the chance to plan a peaceful, happy life together. But until she could catch up with him there was nothing to do but follow the route he'd mapped out for her. She tucked letter and netsuke into her handbag and went downstairs to the dining room, aware that she'd eaten very little in the past two days. She was doggedly examining the menu in the hope that it contained something she felt like eating when a chair scraped on the flagged floor. Someone sat down opposite her and she felt slightly irritated by an unwanted companion when the room was half empty – he could surely sit somewhere else. But when she looked up she found herself staring at Oliver Hatton. Her face went so white that he half-rose, thinking that she was about to faint, but she was full of murderous rage, not faintness.

'You were supposed to be going to Boulogne,' she threw at him in a furious whisper.

'True . . . but only because *you* were advertised as heading for Calais. After five minutes it was perfectly obvious that you were going south.'

She was incapable of returning his bland smile, being concerned with an inclination to shout, beat her hands against his chest, or even run him through with the knife on the table in front of her. None of these things seemed possible in a French provincial hotel where the diners about them were getting down to the sacred business of selecting their evening meal. She took a steadying breath instead, reminding herself that her only hope lay in guile. It took a moment or two, but in the end she managed to smile at him.

'Poor Oliver, I can hear the creaking of the legal brain from here! "If I follow the silly creature long enough, she'll lead me to Jules Legrand." Well, I'm sorry to disappoint you, but the truth is that I don't know where Jules is, any more than you or Marcel Colbert do.' It *was*, essentially, the truth, and her husky, mocking voice was marvellously convincing.

'So you're just doing a little carefree sightseeing?'

'Taking an indirect route home, let us say,' Jane corrected him lightly. 'I suddenly couldn't bear to turn round and go straight back. We have to kill time until Marcel can contact Jules, or hears from him, and it seemed silly to rush back for the next ferry when I was feeling very tired, and have nothing particular to do at home. I'm sorry you're having a circular tour for nothing, but you've only yourself to blame.'

Being still busy with her menu, she didn't have to look at him, which Oliver knew she couldn't do *and* lie to him. Some women undoubtedly could, but not Jane Kingsley. But still there wasn't the slightest shadow of a doubt that she *was* lying.

'Had-for-a-mug Hatton,' he murmured thoughtfully at last. 'I can't say I'd normally choose to call at Orléans en route for Boulogne, it's a bit like going to Birmingham by way of Beachy Head! Still, on the credit side, there's this delightful dinner with you, little one. Let us eat, drink and be merry, for tomorrow we part!'

The effort on top of a long, exhausting day was almost

more than she could make, but she'd cast herself in the role of time-killing, careless traveller and she was stuck with it. The delicious chilled *Saumur* wine Oliver ordered for both of them helped matters. She drank two glasses quickly, relying on the wine to blunt anxiety and tiredness enough to convince him that she was anxious about Jules, but not at all concerned with the fate of a Collection that had very little to do with her. She ate enough of her melon and sole to escape comment, and followed Oliver's lead in talking about the wines and *châteaux* of the Loire Valley.

'I suppose you feel perfectly at home over here?' he enquired lazily when they were sipping the white dessert wine he'd also insisted on ordering. 'It's a country you know well, I remember. No problems about adjusting to the life of Madame Jules Legrand – assuming, of course, that all the other problems besetting us at the moment can be sorted out.'

'Jules and I have no problems,' she insisted steadily. '*You* have a problem, which I'm very much afraid he's trying to help you with; otherwise he'd be in Paris. I expect I shall miss Little Fairford for a while, but already I feel as if I belong here.' If it was another lie, one more scarcely seemed to matter, but she couldn't go on talking about her own future. It seemed safer to spear him with a question instead.

'I should have thought you were the one with problems of adjustment – Oxford, and village life after years in New York – isn't it going to seem unbearably slow and uneventful?'

'Village life uneventful? Come now, Jane – you must know better than that.'

Her eyebrow lifted in slight disbelief. 'The yearly round? Cricket matches and church feasts, garden fêtes and Guy Fawkes' Night?'

'Exactly! You can look as sceptical as you like, but after frenetic years in the Big Apple I find the ritual immensely reassuring and only ask of Heaven that it should never change. But it isn't the familiarity that makes it valuable.'

'I suppose you mean the people themselves do that . . . what Curly calls "yuman natchur"!'

He smiled at her over his glass, and she thought that just for a moment or two he'd forgotten they were enemies.

'It doesn't matter what you call it, but what makes village life irreplaceable is the fact that the whole gamut of experience is there, in manageable quantities.'

The wine's lift had come and gone too quickly, leaving her painfully homesick for the place he'd just conjured up. Had he done it deliberately? Very probably, in the hope that she'd be enticed into some reckless confession of Heaven knew what. She emptied her glass in a last desperate gulp and got up from the table.

'It's been a pleasant evening, Oliver, so I'm rather glad I led you astray. But a long day is now catching up with me. I'll say good-night and wish you a safe drive home tomorrow.'

On his feet too, he stood looking down at her, the glint in his eyes signifying something she was too tired to fathom.

'It's a beautiful night . . . I can't believe there wouldn't be a nightingale. Shall we stroll along the river and find out?'

'Thank you, but I shall stroll only as far as my virginal couch!'

'Chickening out, Miss Kingsley – afraid that the couch might seem lonely if we'd listened to the nightingales together?'

Acutely aware of him, she was aware too of one new improbability in this journey she was caught up in. Little, lost, sexless Jane seemed finally to be desired – though, of course, only briefly – by the man she'd once confused in her mind with God. Life was nothing if not perverse. She took a firm grip on the chair in front of her in case her body should weaken, and made herself smile at him.

'Time was when I might have agreed with you to forget Estelle. But I'm a big girl now, engaged to Jules Legrand, and you, if you remember, don't trust either of us. So I'll say good-night again.'

She made a creditable stab at walking firmly to the door, but out of his sight it was hard to force trembling legs to carry her up the stairs. The virginal couch looked very cold and lonely, and virtue, like patriotism, was not always enough! She needed Oliver Hatton to go away, and Jules to come very soon.

Oliver sat down again when she'd gone, with problems of his own. It was no time to discover that he'd wanted very much to walk with her by the river, listen to nightingales, and then take her to bed. Desire was even sharpened by the knowledge that she was doing her level best to make a fool of him. But this he could deal with; more disturbing was the knowledge that pure anxiety was growing inside him. During the long afternoon drive, when he'd been keeping a discreet distance behind her, it had borne in on him that he wasn't the only person taking an interest in Jane's route. He'd first noticed a nondescript black Renault on the outskirts of Paris only because three of its registration numbers happen to run in the same sequence as his own. From then on the car had stayed ahead of him, never quite losing contact with Jane's cream-coloured Metro, never overtaking it.

To begin with, he'd been grateful for a car that kept *him* hidden from view, but the sight of it this evening, neatly backed into the hotel car park, had rung a little warning bell in his mind. The alarm had been real enough to make him change his mind about letting Jane know he was there. He didn't trust her, he didn't like or trust Jules Legrand, and he wished to God that none of them was mixed up in whatever it was they *were* mixed up in; but he couldn't let anything happen to her. He would probably even forgive her if she'd only tell him the truth; but she was stubborn as well as stupidly loyal. It wasn't even any good trying to frighten her into being sensible; it would simply make her more cussed than ever. He could do nothing but wait and see what happened tomorrow. If the same procession took place, he'd know beyond any doubt that they had company; time enough then to decide what he was going to do about it.

Nine

Jane got up very early and spent half an hour poring over maps. Oliver had seemed to accept her story of a detour on the way back to Calais, but she couldn't count on the possibility that he wasn't becoming just as devious as she was herself. In case he was hanging about in the hotel, waiting to see which way she went, she must leave looking like the casual sightseer she pretended to be. The road for Blois and Tours would be the obvious one for a tourist to take. She must set off on that, and find some way or turn southward to get back onto the N20 for Châteauroux and Limoges.

There was no sign of Oliver in the dining-room when she went down at seven o'clock. Sloth had probably kept him in bed, and would do so for another hour. But a careful inspection of the car park as soon as she was ready to leave convinced her that she'd wronged him. There was no sign of his dark-green Rover – Oliver had washed his hands of her, and finally set off for Boulogne. It was tempting to go straight to Châteauroux after all, but a plan was a plan; she'd finish up a disorganised wreck if she kept changing her mind.

The road to Blois ran alongside the Loire. The morning and the world around her were so lovely that it seemed criminally wasteful not to be enjoying them. Her eyes were glued to her driving mirror in the expectation of seeing Oliver's car materialise behind her, but after half an hour there was still no sign of him. She could relax a little, and begin to look for a road that would take her west and south. What she was searching for came into view almost immediately – signposted Romorantin and Châteauroux – and she turned on to a long straight road so empty that she could put her foot hard down on the accelerator. Another car had turned off the Blois road behind her and at the speed she was travelling she was faintly surprised to see that it was catching up with her . . . not only catching up, but even intending to overtake. She edged over to the side of the road, anxious to make room for the car behind her but conscious of a deep drainage ditch bordering the edge of the road. He was directly behind her now, then running level and forcing her dangerously near the gulley. Her fist found the horn in a desperate reminder that he was guilty of a lunatic piece of driving, but he was deaf as well as mad. She tried to slow down to drop behind him, but he simply kept pace with her, and the truth hit her just as her near-side wheels left the tarmac and the car juddered in a desperate downward tilt. There was a moment of terror, then the relief of darkness as her head crashed against the side of the car.

She was roused by the sound of a voice muttering sadly, '*Mon Dieu, Mon Dieu . . .*', but, being tilted at a strange angle towards the sky, had no way of knowing who this regretful voice belonged to. She was incapable of moving, and there was nothing she need do to try to help; with perfect calm it occurred to her that the solution to all her troubles would be to stay for ever where she was, lying in a French ditch, looking at the clouds. It was almost an irritation when a sharp squeal of tyres announced that another car had stopped too abruptly on the road above her. Then a different voice repeated much what the Frenchman had said, only in English this time.

'Oh, my God . . . Jane!' It was Oliver, of course; why had she imagined even for a moment that he was nearly at Boulogne?

The Frenchman yelled for his colleague, working in a neighbouring field, and the three of them fought to manhandle the car into a slightly more level position. It enabled Oliver to reach the driver's door and wrench it open.

'Feel like getting out?' he asked in a conversational tone quite unlike the ravaged voice of a moment before.

'I can't move,' she pointed out crossly, wondering with the small segment of her brain that seemed to be functioning whether any of this was really happening at all.

He reached in, hesitated momentarily at the sight of something that had spilled out of her unzipped handbag on the seat beside her, then unfastened the seat belt that held her trapped. She was lifted out and put on the grass verge of the road. Her face was ashen-white except for a gash on her forehead and a broken weal on that side, from her hair-line to her chin, but otherwise he could see no sign of damage.

'I'm going to be sick,' she said suddenly, and promptly was, while he held her with a matter-of-factness that astonished her when she remembered it later. He wiped her face afterwards as if she was a child, and only the fact that his hand trembled slightly told her that he was less calm than he appeared to be.

'What happened, did you fall asleep for a moment?' he asked.

Jane shook her head, unable to explain what she had known in the moment before the car left the road . . . that she'd been shoved in the ditch deliberately. She shut her eyes, determined not to be sick again, and Oliver changed his mind about questioning her.

'We'll leave this helpful chap in charge while I run you to the nearest hospital,' he said instead.

'There's no need. I've got the makings of an almighty headache, otherwise I'm all right.'

She was picked up again and put in his car as if she'd said nothing at all, and Oliver went across to the farm workers, now marvelling to each other that anyone who'd been inside the Metro was still capable of being sick by the roadside. After a moment or two he got in beside her, but apart from a brief instruction to close her eyes and not talk, said nothing more until he handed her over to the casualty department of the hospital in Châteauroux. A check-up and an hour later, she was released with a supply of headache pills, a dressing on her temple, and a stern injunction to drive more carefully in future. Oliver was waiting for her, apparently asleep on one of the brutally hard chairs lined up outside the casualty department door. She couldn't help feeling thankful to see him: just for the moment she'd shot her bolt and needed someone to take her in charge. It should have been Jules, but Oliver would have to do.

Outside in the car again, he turned to look at her. 'You're a mess, little one, but I gather they said you could go?'

She nodded, undermined by the gentleness in his voice.

'Where do we go from here? I can't help feeling that you had some reason for coming to Châteauroux.'

'The Auberge, *Arc-en-Ciel,*' she said stiffly. It gave away more than she wished, but it was the next stage of her route and must be visited, and she was now without transport of her own.

'What will happen to the car?' she asked by way of changing the subject.

'I've reported it to the police. At some point your insurers will get a hefty bill from whatever garage they put on to salvaging it.'

She closed her eyes again, in the hope that Oliver would think that she felt too weak to be questioned. It was the truth, anyway. She was overwhelmed by the anxiety of wondering what she was going to do next. He asked for directions to the hotel from a passer-by, but left her in peace until they were outside the *Arc-en-Ciel*. Jane left him to park the car and retrieve the suitcase he'd thoughtfully collected from the battered Metro for her, and forced herself to almost run into the reception office . . . had they any message for Mademoiselle Kingsley? Indeed they had, in fact a package left for her by Monsieur Legrand. She thrust it into her big shoulder-bag just as Oliver walked into the hotel. If he'd seen her being handed something, he made no comment on the fact; simply gave the receptionist his charming smile and suggested they needed a room where his friend could rest after a slight accident. Nothing could be simpler, if the hotel had been packed to the roof, for Monsieur something would have been arranged, Jane felt sure. She was instructed to get into bed while Oliver stretched his long legs in a gentle stroll. After that, he would come and see her in her room. She wasn't tempted for a moment to think that his intention would be to enquire tenderly after her health. Oliver would want the answer to some questions.

When he'd walked away she first of all climbed groggily into the bath, convinced that she would feel better if she could physically wash away all trace of the horrendous morning. She brushed her teeth and the taste of sickness from her mouth, and got into bed, as instructed. It was heavenly to relax for a moment, but almost immediately she dragged herself upright again and pulled out of her bag the parcel that had been handed to her downstairs. It was no surprise to find another missing netsuke inside, but Jules' accompanying letter this time was even more tender, and more insistent about his need of her; a love-letter, in fact, such as she wouldn't dream of showing to Oliver.

A quarter of an hour later a knock sounded at the door; then he walked in, carrying lunch on a laden tray.

'I bet it's a good many years since you had a dorm feast,' he said, kicking the door shut behind him.

'I didn't have one at all – Edwin's finances didn't run to plush boarding schools.'

He delved in his pockets for the glasses he hadn't found room for on the tray. 'A sip or two of wine to calm your nerves before you eat.'

She watched him serve food onto a plate for her as calmly as if they were having a picnic at home. There was lot to be said for English phlegm after all. It was suddenly such a relief to have him there that she felt obliged to tell him so.

'I'm very glad you're here, Oliver.'

The simple confession sent a flicker across his face that came and went too quickly for her to identify, but after a moment's silence he spoke with a deliberate lightness that seemed to deny the sincerity of what she'd just said.

'All part of the incomparable Hatton service . . . at our clients' beck and call twenty-four hours a day, if need be. Well, not *all* our clients, perhaps. I can call to mind an elderly dowager or two in whose bedrooms I hope never to find myself!'

He saw a grin chase the look of strain from Jane's battered

face, and then left her to eat as well as she could with her bruised jaw. By the time he'd removed the empty tray and returned with coffee, he thought she was recovered enough to talk.

'Now tell me what really happened this morning.'

The quiet but insistent question made her close her eyes, seeing again imprinted on her memory the bonnet of a black car rocking along beside her, almost welded to the side of the Metro like a Siamese twin.

'I was pushed into that ditch,' she said bleakly.

'By a black Renault, by any chance?'

'Yes, although I can't imagine how you know. I doubt if the driver was hanging around afterwards to enquire about my health.'

'He followed you out of Paris yesterday afternoon, and I followed *him*. There was a chance, then, that it might have been accidental, but when you went past the turning where I was parked this morning and he followed twenty seconds later, I knew that the procession was deliberate. Ten kilometres outside Orléans a large lorry barged its way in front of me and I damned nearly lost you both. It wasn't until I came to a long straight stretch of road that I knew for certain that you'd turned off it. I wasted fifteen minutes coming back to find the road you'd taken.' He stopped talking, confronted by the vision in his mind of her car lying on its side in the ditch. When he spoke again his voice sounded brutally curt.

'Heaven seems to be on your side, even though I can't think why. The ditch was providentially damp and soft, and a very leafy hedge acted as a shock-absorber.'

'Otherwise I'd probably have been killed? I wish I knew why.'

She sounded astonishingly calm, but his gaze went from

the livid bruise on her face to the hands that trembled as she tried to pick up her coffee cup. If she'd only known it, English phlegm was wide of the mark – he was a seething mass of emotions inside. He wanted to shout that if she insisted on consorting with criminals she stood a very good chance of getting hurt; he wanted to kiss away the strain in her face, and most of all he longed to kill the man who'd hurt her.

'There are other things I want to know as well,' he said at last. 'First of all, let us abandon the fiction that you're doing a light-hearted bit of sightseeing. You left Paris with a definite purpose in mind. You've still got it in mind, and you're wondering how the hell to do it without a car. One other thing . . . I saw one of the stolen ivory minatures that had fallen out of your handbag this morning. It leads me to suppose that you know where the rest of the "stolen" things are. Was the burglary a complete farce?'

For brief moments she'd been tempted to think he was concerned about her – tiny shoots of tenderness had poked their heads through a thick blanket of mistrust. But the life of the poor little things had been pathetically short. There was no kindness for her in this cold, single-minded man, who would help *her* only because it might help him to recover the Kingsley instruments.

'You still think it's Jules, don't you? And you still think I'm involved in the fraud as well?' Hurt made her cool, but Oliver misread it for a taunt that set light to the rage that had been smouldering inside him for days.

'I'll tell you exactly what I think, little one, because I'm getting very tired of this maze of deceit. I think Legrand arrived at Little Fairford with an idea in his mind. It hardened into something inevitable when he saw how easy it was going to be to get the better of an invalid man, and a girl whose loyalty he could soon count on. You got drawn into it because you fell in love with him. It made it much easier to have you involved, but perhaps he's also infected by a mad sort of logic that says the instruments should rightly be yours and he's stolen them to share the proceeds with you.'

He saw her eyes dilate, and could almost have sworn that the theory he'd just aired had come as a shock to her. But after a moment or two she had herself in hand again.

'You're wildly, cruelly wrong about Jules,' she insisted steadily. 'I know instinctive dislikes are hard to overcome, but you're supposed to be trained to distinguish truth from falsehood with an impartial mind. I wasn't lying to you when I said I didn't know where he was. All I know is where he's been, on his way down to Andorra. He sent postcards mapping out a route that I finally realised I was meant to follow. He'd identified the thief because he's got the netsukes back – there was another one waiting for me here. His letters hint quite plainly that he knows where the instruments are. Presumably he's going to trap the Spaniard . . . buy the things back from him, then turn him over to the police. It seems extremely dangerous to me, but all the thanks he gets are your filthy suspicions.'

Intelligent as she was, she'd never accept that Legrand *had* to be the thief, he thought despairingly. To admit that would be to admit that she was in love with a man who'd been instrumental in killing her uncle.

'That driver this morning,' she said with an abrupt change of subject. 'Who could he have been? And will he be able to discover that . . . that I'm still alive and kicking?'

'I have no idea who he is,' Oliver said roughly. 'A nut, maybe, who can't see a GB plate on a car without wanting to smash it up. But all he has to do is call at the *gendarmerie* and make tender enquiries about his "friend", whose car he's just recognised wrecked in a ditch.'

The bruise stood out lividly against the chalk-whiteness of the rest of her face. He wanted more than he'd wanted anything in life to pick her up in his arms and say that he would let no more harm come to her. But she *had* to be involved with Legrand, and he must continue to distrust her.

'So what happens next?' she whispered.

'We go on with the tour, beloved. I assume that you have the next stopping-place already lined up?'

'The *Montrouge*, at Limoges.'

Oliver conveyed delight at the idea. 'I've always wanted to see Limoges . . . do they still make that hideously over-coloured porcelain, I wonder?' he asked chattily. Jane thought she wasn't obliged to answer, and when he spoke again after glancing at his watch, it was in a different tone of voice. 'You look wretched, little one. It's three o'clock now. Provided you feel up to it after a rest this afternoon I'd like to push on this evening. If our friend is still hanging around, I want to make things as difficult as possible for him by doing the next stage in the dark. If he came here, he'll know now which car he has to follow in future.'

It was said casually, but Jane was suddenly swept by a feeling of sheer disbelief that any of this nightmare could really be happening. What were either of them doing here? She ought to be in Little Fairford, discussing the new term with Jim Watkins and taking her turn with Mary Hatton, arranging the altar flowers in church. Mary! The thought of her made the nightmare ten times worse. She and Richard loved Oliver to the point of idolatry. Suppose *his* car was the next one to be wrecked?

'Oliver . . . if I promise on my honour to talk to Jules and find out what he knows about the instruments, will you go back to England and leave me to continue alone? I can hire a car here. Jules said he would find me somewhere along the way – but he may not do so if I'm not alone.'

'Kind thought, Janey, but we'll stay together, I think. I'll hand you over to Legrand in one piece and he can hand me back the Kingsley instruments. A fair exchange, wouldn't you say?'

Jane gave a little gesture of defeat that hurt him even while pride refused to allow him to take the words back. 'For God's sake go to sleep now,' he shouted at her suddenly. 'We'll start again at seven.'

Ten

When Oliver tapped at her door that evening Jane was ready to leave, and glad to go because sleep had been out of the question. If she closed her eyes, it was only to see a mental picture of a long straight road along which two cars careered, insanely yoked together. Eyes open or closed, her brain persisted in trying to make some sort of sense of what was happening. Had Jules simply wanted to be sure she would join him somewhere, there were less complicated ways of arranging it than this mad treasure-hunt across France. It was true that she now saw why he'd wanted her to stay hidden, but that part of the plan had seriously misfired. Who was the man in the black Renault? Had he, like Oliver, waited for her to show up at the Galleries in Paris, or had he been dogging her all the way from England? She longed to hear from Jules that *he* was somewhere in the vicinity, but agonised inwardly over the probability that he would run straight into Oliver. She didn't doubt that Oliver intended sticking to her like a burr to a sheepdog's coat, and however much she urged him to go home, the truth was that for the moment she was thankful to be going on in his company.

But going on where? The knowledge that her postcard trail would soon be exhausted made her pick up the telephone by her bed and call Little Fairford. She got Jim Watkins at the second attempt, and knew immediately by the sound of his voice that he had news for her.

'Glad you rang, Jane,' he said quickly. 'Two postcards at the Owl House. One from the *Auberge Chèvre d'Or* at Toulouse; the second from a place called Foix – the *Hôtel Audoye*. The message is pretty much the same on both, but the second one finishes up "Last port of call, my dear, so please come soon; there's so much to talk about. All my love, Jules." Does that help, Jane?'

'Thanks, Jim. It helps a great deal,' she said slowly. Something positive at last – the knowledge that Jules was bound to find her at Foix.

'Are you all right?' Jim Watkins wanted to know. He was too reticent a man to pry into anybody else's life, but something worrying was surely going on, and in his own way he loved Jane Kingsley.

'I'm fine,' she said, trying to sound bright and unconcerned. 'Tell you all about it one day, Jim, when I'm back in Little Fairford. Thanks for going to the house for me.' She hung up hurriedly, before tears could get the better of her. Her only reason for going back to the village would be to dispose of the Owl House, and the realisation threatened to submerge her in a drowning wave of homesickness. Aware of disloyalty to Jules, she acknowledged sadly to herself that she was going to remain much more English than French . . . her roots lay in a misty river valley, shaded by willow trees, among people who were *her* people. She'd tried to jeer at Oliver for being content with the humdrum village round, but that had been her own life too, predictable and precious.

She grimaced at her bruised face in the mirror and blamed her appearance and the hospital pills for her present state of misery; they'd helped a throbbing headache, but done nothing to raise her spirits. As the heroine of this sort of adventure, she was scoring rather poorly; tradition had it that she must remain beautiful and unbowed, no matter what happened. She could do nothing about the lack of beauty, but unbowed she *would* be if she died in the attempt.

She opened the door to Oliver's knock with a smile pinned to her face that he thought was the most heartbreaking thing he'd ever seen. He took the suitcase out of her hand, but instead of leading the way downstairs, stared at her for a moment, then bent and lightly kissed her mouth.

'What was that for?' she asked unsteadily, grateful for a voice that was always known to be husky.

'Comfort, I suppose. You looked as if you needed it.'

This gentle Oliver was what she needed least of all. It was downright cruel of him to be kind when her defences were so wobbly. She was about to insist, however unconvincingly, that she was enjoying the adventure when he spoke again in a deep, sad voice.

'Jane . . . I've been thinking while you've been asleep. One way and another I've been rather rough with you, I'm afraid. It's no good pretending that I don't think Legrand is involved in the fraud, or even that I'm still uncertain about *you*, but I keep forgetting the fact that you're in love with the man. For one girl you've had rather a lot to cope with recently.'

'Handsomely said, Mr Hatton.' She managed to grin at him and told herself that perhaps she was a heroine after all. His distrust felt like a knife-point draining away her heart's blood, but she must smile and look unconcerned.

'Handsome is as handsome does,' Oliver said quietly. 'I'm still intent on finding your fiancé, but I'd give a great deal for you to be honest with me before I wring the truth out of him.'

For all his care and kindness it came back to the same agonising impasse: he was determined to think ill of them.

'You of all people shouldn't need reminding of our judicial system,' she said stubbornly. 'Jules and I are innocent until you prove us guilty. We *are* innocent . . . there is no other truth that I can give you.'

Oliver's shuttered face told her only that she wasn't believed now any more than she had been at the Owl House. 'Then we must go on as we are – old friends who no longer trust each other. What a pity, Jane.'

It was heart-break, not a pity, and all she could do was nod in reply.

'On to our next port of call,' he said in a different tone of voice, 'the *Montrouge* at Limoges, if I remember rightly.'

They covered the one hundred and twenty-odd kilometres without stopping, and without seeing any sign that their shadow was still with them. Oliver drove through the twilit countryside with a speed and certainty that reminded Jane again of how incomplete her knowledge of him had been. She'd been intending to keep him at a distance, but a compliment insisted on being spoken, which he waved aside.

'My sense of direction's reasonably good, but I spent a large part of the afternoon studying the map!'

They got to Limoges just before nine o'clock, and by now it was apparent to Jane that her companion was entirely in charge of their progress. She was instructed to go into the hotel, explain that she was unable to stay, and see if any messages had been left for her. By the time she returned, clutching the usual small box, Oliver had the car turned, waiting to leave again. She would have preferred to leave her parcel unopened until she was by herself, but Oliver had decided not to spend the night at Limoges, and the package might include a message from Jules. It contained another missing netsuke and a charming love letter, obviously written in haste, but begging her to look forward as much as he did to their life together. Jane folded the single sheet and tucked it away in her bag without saying anything. Oliver glanced at her pale face, then concentrated on the road ahead of them.

They'd driven in silence for half an hour when he swung the car into a tree enshrouded lane and cut the engine. She turned to stare at him, and the dim glow of the dashboard lights showed him the tear-stains on her face.

'Supper time,' he said briefly, as if he hadn't noticed them. 'Don't know about you, but I'm ravenous.' He disappeared to rummage in the boot of the car and came back with a carton of food and a thermos.

'Obliging maid at the *Arc-en-Ciel,*' he explained in answer to Jane's enquiring look.

'Of course! The usual Hatton touch. No wonder you've been indulged from the cradle up. You've only got to smile at women and they crumple up immediately, I suppose.'

'Not always,' Oliver pointed out, handing her a chunk of bread stuffed with ham, lettuce and olives. 'I have my failures, unfortunately.'

The crusty loaf was difficult to eat with her stiff jaw, but she nibbled the filling, and hoped in vain that he wouldn't notice.

'Fool . . . I should have asked for junket.' His fingers stroked her sore cheek for a moment, gentle as a piece of thistledown, then he poured coffee and handed her the first mugful. Jane sipped it, thinking that she would remember this journey if she lived to be an old, old lady. Life would never again hold this mixture of anxiety and fear, hurting suspicion and occasional heart-easing tenderness. She would have liked to hate Oliver for distrusting her but she couldn't; and she must love Jules as his letters said he loved her, but even that was difficult while he subjected her to this uncertainty.

They'd been driving again for half an hour when she surfaced from her own thoughts sufficiently to notice that Oliver was often staring into the driving mirror.

'Something bothering you?' she asked at last, having observed this performance for another five minutes.

'The headlights of the car behind. I can't swear that it's the same car, but something has been keeping exactly that distance behind us ever since we left Limoges. When we stopped for supper it disappeared. Now it's behind us again – exactly the same station as before. We'd better prove it one way or the other – hold on, Jane.'

For the next fifteen minutes they alternately roared through the sleeping countryside or dawdled to the point of scarcely moving. Whatever they did, their phantom companion did as well.

'No doubt about it, little one. We've got company,' he commented grimly. 'I suppose the bastard has been keeping a discreet distance all the time, but now he's anxious not to lose us in the dark and he's had to creep closer.'

'So what now?'

'We drive like hell for Toulouse, though I doubt if we shall lose him.'

It was the last thing he said to her for the next four hours, while he drove with a silent concentration that would have defied conversation even if she'd felt talkative. Life had reduced itself to this strangely isolated little interval of time and motion . . . there might never have been a different existence not spent in this car with Oliver, saying nothing, but linked to him in a way that had no need of words of physical contact. If it was hard to remember anything before this extraordinary journey had begun, it was downright impossible to do what Jules' letters asked and think about a time when it would be over.

They began to cross a network of rivers – the Dordogne at Souillac, and the Lot at Cahors. With the third one, the River Tarn, came a stroke of unlooked-for good fortune. The warning light of an antiquated level-crossing began to glow in front of them. Instead of slowing down, Oliver rammed his foot hard down on the accelerator, and the Rover leapt forward like a thoroughbred horse resentful of an unnecessary spur. They bumped and rattled across the railway line just as the gate clanged shut behind them. Oliver looked in the mirror, saw the headlights of another car securely pinned behind the barrier, and turned to smile at Jane.

'God be praised! From what I remember of French railways at night, our friend will stew there for the best part of half an hour while a very delayed goods train arrives, and the driver consults his friends about the weather, the cost of living, and the state of the Government before he finally departs.'

They ran into Toulouse twenty minutes later, with the road behind them innocent of anything but the occasional large lorry already making a dawn move.

'Now we need one more stroke of luck,' he murmured, as Jane directed him thorough the outskirts of the city with the aid of a street plan in her Michelin guide. 'If Legrand chose an hotel that bolts its doors at night in case an invading army should camp outside, we shall have lost our advantage waiting for them to open up.'

'I think not . . . it's well-starred . . . the sort of place that's likely to have a night porter.'

She turned out to be right; the hotel's doors were already open.

'We need sleep, but not here,' Oliver said briefly. 'Go and see if anything's waiting for you . . . but make it quick.'

She came running out five minutes later, clutching a parcel that was noticeably larger than the others she'd collected. Oliver barely gave her time to get in with it before he was driving away again. Jane tore away the wrapping and sat staring at a boxful of little ivory figures – all that were still missing. She fingered them blindly, unable to see for the tears that filled her eyes.

'Jules said he'd . . . he'd get them all back for me,' she whispered. 'I'll never be able to thank him enough.'

For a moment she was unaware of the man beside her. Just as well, Oliver thought, because if she'd looked at him she'd have read his in face the certainty that her fiancé had been able to return the figures because he'd had them all along. Rage, hatred, love and longing consumed and confused a man who, even in the worst days of his divorce fight, had always been clear about what he was feeling.

'I'd be grateful if you'd drag your mind away from that damned box,' he said sharply. 'I can't drive and study the guide at the same time, and we need a quiet hotel on the southern side of the city.'

'All right – I'll do my best, but don't snap at me,' she flared, overwrought by tiredness and too much emotion.

'Dear Jane, for God's sake don't choose this moment to have an attack of the vapours,' he commanded roughly. 'We need a hotel and we need it now. I want to get this noticeably foreign car off the street before it's full daylight.'

She brushed away her tears and concentrated on the tiny symbols dancing on the page in front of her.

'The *Cheval Blanc*'s the best I can suggest,' she offered coldly. 'Turn right at the end of this street, and I can direct you from there.'

Ten minutes later they were at the door of a small ivy-covered hotel pleasantly concealed from the road. A row of plane trees shaded a courtyard that was set about with white garden chairs and tables, and a marmalade-coloured cat washed itself with slow deliberation in the warmth of the rising sun. There was nothing to be heard except a cockerel in full cry. Peace lay over the place like a benediction, and after the strain of the past day and night it was like stumbling by Heaven's grace into paradise. Oliver wound down the window beside him and sweet fresh air flowed in on them, bringing with it a mouth-watering smell of freshly-baked bread. Jane sat perfectly still, scarcely daring to breathe in case she broke the spell that held them. Then Oliver put out a hand, lifted hers to his mouth, and left a kiss in the palm of it.

'Sorry I snarled at you back there, little one. I had no right to – you're an excellent companion in a tight spot.'

She could find nothing to say at all, because for once there was no amused or mocking undertone to his voice. His expression, for some reason she couldn't understand, was only sad, as if he was saying goodbye to something that had been immensely important to him. Then he smiled at her. 'It's a shade early for breakfast, but I'm ravenous again. Let's hope the well-known Hatton charm works this time!'

She made no attempt to follow him inside. There would be no message here from Jules; there wasn't a thing she need do, but sit still and relax.

'Wake up, sleepy-head,' his voice said in her ear. 'Our friend inside has promised to provide breakfast in fifteen minutes. I agreed that we'd like it out here.'

Jane climbed stiffly out of the car and wandered into the hotel, looking for somewhere to wash. A small round woman who introduced herself as Madame Lamartine led her to a spotless bathroom, looked curiously at her damaged face, but said only that she was welcome to use the shower. Clean and refreshed again, she went outside to find Oliver talking to Madame Lamartine while the table was being laid for breakfast. The marmalade cat had now rearranged himself on Oliver's knees, and both of them looked very content with each other. Freshly baked croissants were brought out, so crisply delicious that it was sheer greed to heap butter and apricot conserve on them as well, a huge pot of coffee, and a bowl of early peaches. Jane finally withdrew from the contest, leaving Oliver at work on his third peach. Neither of them referred to what had brought them there, it was enough to share the sunlit morning at peace with each other for once, and feed the lordly marmalade cat with small pieces of buttered croissant.

At last Oliver could eat no more. He stretched out long legs, accepted a final cup of coffee that she poured for him, and steeled himself to wipe the serenity from her face by reminding her that they must soon go on with their journey.

'Dr Hatton recommends a little stroll round the garden, followed by four hours in bed,' he said gently. 'I've told Madame that we'll lunch here before we leave, and she's promised to exert herself on our behalf.'

'On *your* behalf, I suppose you mean,' Jane corrected him. 'Yet another slave willingly enrolling herself for duty!'

'Sickening, isn't it! Never mind; if it's any comfort to you, my one failure cancels out all the rest.' His face was suddenly sombre, and Jane called herself a fool for reminding him of his disastrous American marriage. He'd been looking remarkably content until then, but now the lovely spell was broken.

'Oliver, this man who's been following us . . . what do you suppose he's doing? Combing every hotel in Toulouse, looking for a dark-green Rover?'

'Could be, but it depends on who he's working for. If it turns out to be the mysterious Spaniard we kept hearing about, he almost certainly knows where Legrand is, or at least where we're heading for. From here, Foix is the obvious, probably the only sensible, jumping-off point for Andorra. I imagine that's where he'll make for, to start checking on the hotels.'

'We can't play hide-and-seek with him there,' Jane pointed out quietly. 'I must go to the *Hôtel Audoye*, or Jules won't know where to find me.'

'True . . . it's quite a little reunion we have to look forward to.'

They reached Foix towards the end of the afternoon, and she had almost convinced herself by then that she would find Jules waiting for her. It would mean that she'd led Oliver straight to him, but there'd been too many hours spent sitting in the car for her not to have done some thinking on her own account. A criminal fraud had been perpetrated, the discovery of which had certainly hastened her uncle's death. As Edwin's executor and lawyer, Oliver was bound to notify the police. For the sake of Edwin's reputation, he'd persuaded the Museum authorities to leave the matter in his hands, but it couldn't be for long, and she was unable pretend to herself any longer that it was unreasonable of him to want to see Jules. If the genuine instruments *had* been retrieved, she would have the pleasure of throwing Oliver's suspicions in his face; even if Jules only knew where the instruments were, it would be some repayment to Oliver for exertions that had gone a long way beyond a lawyer's normal devotion to the welfare of his clients. Her smile as they got out of the car suddenly reflected the gratitude she felt, and her forgiveness – late but whole-hearted – for the fact that he'd been obliged to distrust her. The smile was beautiful, transfiguring her tired face, but it confirmed to Oliver only what he'd been afraid of all along. She *was* in love with Jules Legrand, and simply happy at the prospect of seeing him again.

They walked into the hotel, and were right in thinking that someone was waiting for them . . . but it was the bulky figure of Marcel Colbert heaving itself out of a chair that now came towards them.

Eleven

For the first time in her knowledge of him, Marcel seemed ruffled and taken by surprise.

'Jane . . . and Monsieur Hatton! For two people supposed to be going back to England you've both chosen a remarkably indirect route.' He spoke with such unusual sharpness that Jane supposed him to be driven by the same anxieties and suspicions that they struggled with themselves.

Oliver seemed unperturbed as usual, and smiled affably. 'I don't recall that *you* advertised a visit to the Pyrenees, either.'

Jane looked from one to the other, aware of mutual distrust thick in the air. It was suddenly more than she could bear. She was sick of the whole stupid, dangerous charade, and even if they were prepared to shadow-box indefinitely, she was not.

'Could we please just trust each other?' she suggested quietly. 'I'm tired of deceit. The truth once and for all is that I didn't know about the fraud; I am just as certain that *you* didn't either,' she said to Marcel, 'and Oliver obviously wasn't involved. So could we please start from there?'

There was a moment's silence which Oliver finally broke. 'Out of the mouths of babes and sucklings . . . !' Shall we sit down and talk, Monsieur Colbert?'

'Yes,' Marcel agreed heavily after a moment, 'but not here. Come upstairs to my room.'

Jane turned to go with him and the light fell on the damaged side of her face, healing now, but the skin turning a yellowish-green as the bruise gradually faded. He opened his mouth to say something, thought better of it, and led the way to the lift. Installed in a bed-sitting-room that reminded her with a twinge of amusement of the comfort in which he always insisted on travelling, he first of all ordered tea to be sent to them. His questioning look in Jane's direction made her smile wholeheartedly for the first time.

'Thank you – how did you guess that my soul craved a cup of tea?'

'You look in need of something, *ma petite*. At the moment tea is all I can offer you.'

He smiled back, as if forgiving her for that moment of suspicion in the hall, but it was Oliver who took charge of the conversation.

'There's a lot to say, but may we know first of all, Monsieur Colbert, what brings you to Foix, and to this hotel?'

Marcel gave his usual little shrug. 'My purpose is the one I thought we agreed on in Paris – to find Jules, and the missing instruments. I came *here* because it is the obvious staging-post for Andorra, one we have always used in the past for rendezvous with Spanish clients who have a tiresome national addiction to conspiracies.'

Oliver accepted the explanation with a nod, then looked at Jane as if to say that the floor was now hers.

'I'll leave Oliver to tell you the story from the point at which we joined forces, but I must begin it,' she said in a voice made huskier that usual by strain. 'The day he came to tell me the fakes had been discovered we both tried to telephone you. Jules had left Paris by then, but I'd already received a postcard from him, sent from Orléans. It was oddly worded, and it wasn't until I got a second one, from Chateauroux, that I began to understand Jules' intention that I should follow his route. I didn't tell Oliver because I was angry with him for suspecting Jules, and I didn't mention it to either of you in Paris in case you tried to stop me. One of the missing netsukes from the Owl House was waiting for me at Orléans, another at Chateauroux, and each parcel enclosed a letter from Jules hinting that what he was supposed to be doing – buying instruments – wasn't what he was doing at all.' She finished the bald recital having apparently been making it to Marcel. It was Oliver she had really been talking to but his face was impassive still, and even now she couldn't tell whether or not he believed her.

After a moment his quiet voice took up the story, beginning with the black Renault that had followed Jane out of Paris. Marcel listened in silence, but his hands were clenched on the arms of his chair, and his normally florid face was colourless. A whispered '*mon Dieu*' gave away his feelings when Oliver calmly described finding her in the ditch; otherwise he said nothing at all until the tale was told.

'I don't recognise the Renault, but I've no doubt that Vicente Fernandez is behind it. I've known for years that he coveted Edwin's instruments, and he's rich and unscrupulous enough to do exactly as he likes.'

'So *he* could have arranged the burglary at the Owl House?' Jane suggested quickly.

Marcel looked at her with so much pity in his face that her own went white in the expectation of what he was about to say, but he began differently.

'Now it's my turn. When I left you in Paris I started my

own investigation at the obvious place – with the man who'd made the fraud possible by fabricating the fake instruments. I knew of only one with the necessary knowledge and skill. It took a little while to persuade him to confide in me, because he was alarmed to discover that I was not a party to the fraud. Jules, you see, had given him the impression that I was.'

Oliver glanced at Jane's face, and looked away again, unable to watch her trying to come to terms with what Colbert had just said.

'Jules . . . Jules brought the fake instruments with him to England?' she whispered.

Marcel shook his head. 'I think it was left to the burglar to make the exchange. Jules selected the instruments to be copied, drew the plan of where they were to go, and then waited for the originals to be brought back to Paris so that he could arrange a meeting with Fernandez.'

'It's clear so far,' Oliver said dispassionately, 'but what was the point of involving Jane in this mad journey?'

Marcel gave a little shrug. 'So that they could disappear together, I suppose, as soon as the sale had been completed. But my guess is that there was a hitch. Fernandez isn't the man to fall into a trap. He'll have had an informant in Oxford who has told him by now about Edwin's death and the discovery of the exchange. He wants the instruments, but not at the cost of having an incompetent fraud laid at his door.'

Jane stared at him with horror in her face. 'You sound calm about it. How *can* you be? Jules is your godson as well as your protégé.'

She saw Marcel's thickset shoulders lift in another resigned shrug. 'Will it achieve anything to shout . . . to rage to high Heaven that my friend's son has dragged me into this disgrace? I don't think so. Pierre Legrand saved my life a long time ago; when the chance came to help Jules I didn't hesitate. I also grew to like and value him for himself, but greed makes men blind to everything else, and I've been punished for forgetting that.'

She got up and walked over to the window, unable to bear the discussion any longer, and struggling with a strong desire to be sick. But amid all the emotions that assailed her it was strange to find hatred of Jules not included. Oliver and Marcel would probably find it impossible to understand the demon of ambition to succeed that drove him on, but what did either of them know of the insecurity that made a man desperate to prove himself? She couldn't condone what he'd done, but at least she understood why he'd done it. Wealth had seemed essential, not for its own sake, but to humble his mother's family and to avenge their contempt of his father.

She turned round to face the two men who stared at her across the room. 'What happens now?' she asked steadily.

'We wait for Jules to contact you,' Oliver answered before Marcel could reply. 'I doubt if we shall wait long, because he'll have been checking with the hotels along the way, and probably knows by now that you're here in Foix.'

'Then I'll leave you, if you don't mind,' Jane said abruptly. 'I feel tired and scruffy.' It was true enough, but her most desperate need was to get away by herself to think about the future.

Oliver got up to open the door for her, and it was impossible not to look at him as she walked out of the room. There was no triumph in his face for having been right all along, she could see nothing but a sympathy that tempted her to burst into tears. She forced herself to go downstairs and arrange to be given a room; took possession of it by hanging up clothes that had been jammed in a suitcase for days; and finally took advantage of the halt at Foix to wash hair that felt sticky after days of travel. She was towelling it dry when a knock sounded at the door. Surface calm splintered immediately into a network of anxieties, but Oliver's unmistakable drawl sounded on the other side of the door. She opened it to find him standing there, yet another tray in his hands and an unidentifiable bundle under one arm.

'Madame Lamartine of revered memory lunched us exceptionally well, but it seems a long time ago. You didn't seem disposed to come down, so I've brought up sandwiches and coffee for us both. Colbert missed lunch altogether, apparently, and is now restoring his strength in the dining-room.'

Her strained face broke into the semblance of a smile. 'I thought lunch and Marcel were inseparable! Thank you for the kind thought. I'm not hungry, but I should love some coffee.'

She poured it for them both, beyond care that her hair was a damp, tousled mess, and that she was scarcely dressed for receiving visitors. Only when she noticed Oliver's eyes on her bare, brown legs did it occur to her that her cotton robe was brief, and not as enveloping as it might have been.

'You look as if you'd come intending to stay,' she said lightly, pointing to the bundle on the floor beside him.

'I have,' he agreed.

She waited for her heart to recover from its panic-stricken stumble and start beating normally again. 'I wasn't aware of having issued any invitations,' she said hoarsely at the second attempt.

'No more you have, but I'm staying anyway, with only the most virtuous intentions, I may say, so there's no need to look outraged about it. If life weren't so fraught at the moment, there's no telling what my intentions might be, but I don't suppose you're feeling up to seduction, in any case.'

She thought she saw his real intention and managed to smile naturally at him. 'Dear Oliver, it's kind of you to think that my self-esteem might need a little bolstering, but I'm not available for seduction at any time; until I've talked to Jules I'm still engaged to him.'

'I keep forgetting,' he agreed affably.

She watched him prowl about the room, trying out the two hard upright chairs and putting them together to produce a makeshift bed. The situation was fast getting out of hand, but she took a deep breath and fought to stay calm.

'Oliver, I'm grateful for the coffee, and much else besides. I don't know how I'd have managed without you the last couple of days. But I'm tired, and I'd like to go to bed. Could we stop this silly game and say good-night?'

'It isn't a game, Jane, There's a black Renault sitting in the car park outside, and somewhere around, therefore, a man I have every reason to mistrust.'

'Why not say what you really mean?' she flung at him. 'You don't trust me either, and you imagine that I'm waiting for Jules so that we can slink out together during the night!'

'That isn't what I was going to say,' he pointed out mildly.

She didn't even hear him; tired, afraid, and overwrought, she wanted more than anything in life to hurl herself into his arms and weep away the misery that threatened to overwhelm her. Since that was out of the question, she shouted at him instead. 'I'm sick to death of the whole wicked business. I just want to be left alone – not spied on every minute of the day and night.'

She might not have spoken for all the difference it made.

He stretched himself out on his impromtu bed and gave her a seraphic smile.

'You'll get no sleep and you'll be as stiff as a board tomorrow,' she told him crossly.

'Right on both counts, I'd guess, but never let it be said that a Hatton put creature comfort before the call of duty.' Then he closed his eyes, putting an end to the conversation.

Jane resisted a strong inclination to tip the chairs from under him, and stalked to the bathroom instead. She returned five minutes later, and climbed into bed still wearing her robe, without saying another word. Eyes firmly closed, she nevertheless knew that he'd clambered off his perch and walked over to stand looking down at her.

'Bed-time story,' he said gently. Her eyes flew open and fastened themselves on his face. 'Listen carefully, Jane. There was once a stupid fool of a man who was almost destroyed by a dishonest cheat of a woman. He decided that rather than make the same mistake again he'd see to it that he never trusted a woman in future. It was a reasonable idea, but it led him to make a much more dreadful mistake, for which he now most humbly apologises.'

Her eyes were huge and questioning in the pallor of her face.

'Are you saying that you . . . you *don't* think I knew about the fraud?' she whispered.

Oliver nodded. 'Heart and head have been fighting it out for days, but the heart won, as I should have known it would. Someone else made the discovery long before I did . . .

"It is not wisdom to be only wise,
and on the inward vision close the eyes,
but it is wisdom to believe the heart".'

The words fell into a complete silence in the room, till Jane asked huskily, 'Who said that?'

'A man who *was* truly wise, a Spaniard called George Santayana. Forgive me for doubting you, little one.'

There didn't seem to be anything to say, and she only nodded and turned her head away so that he couldn't see her face. It took very little self-control to walk away from her; hadn't he been amply reminded that she still belonged to Jules Legrand? But when he returned from his own visit to the bathroom his chair-bed had been dismantled. A long French-bolster had been placed with mathematical precision down the middle of the bed, and Jane was apparently fast asleep on one side of it.

Oliver surveyed the new arrangement with a rueful grin. She meant to be kind, and couldn't know how hard she made things for him. He switched off the light and stretched his long body on the half of the bed allotted to him. It was a relief to be spared a night's torture on the chairs, but sleep was still far away.

Against all expectations, Jane *did* fall asleep, without bothering to work out that it was because she had only to stretch out her hand to touch Oliver. Men in black cars, Spaniards with evil intent, in fact all the forces of darkness put together could do their worst; it didn't seem to matter while Mary Hatton's large son lay stretched out beside her.

She woke while the room was still dark, but a paler rectangle at the window hinted that dawn was near. The bolster had disappeared, and she was lying enfolded by Oliver's arm. It was the only night of her life that she would ever spend with him – a night too ridiculously pure for either Estelle or Jules to believe in if they ever needed to know about it. She turned her head away from the sudden bitterness of the thought, and at the same moment felt his arm gently withdraw itself from under her shoulders. Five minutes later he padded quietly out of the room and closed the door – guard duty over now that the night was nearly done. Tears forced themselves between her shut eyelids, ran down her face, and soaked her hard French pillow. She wept herself into a brief doze and woke again to find stronger light seeping into the room. Her heart began to hammer because someone was sitting in the chair by the window, watching her, but it wasn't Oliver come back to resume his watch. The man who now sat looking at her was Jules Legrand.

Twelve

Melodrama and French farce were becoming inextricably mixed. She wondered after a stunned moment whether Marcel would be the next one to appear, probably looking like Noel Coward in an expensive silk dressing-gown. Too much emotion and too much strain produced a choke of near-hysterical laughter. She stifled it almost at once but it told Jules that she was awake. He sprang out of the chair and threw himself down beside her.

'Jane! Jane . . . I thought you'd never come!' His grip on her hands conveyed the feverish tension that consumed him, and she couldn't be sure whether he was about to laugh himself or burst into uncontrollable tears. 'I nearly bumped into Marcel last night. Dearest, I didn't mean you to bring him as well – he's the last man I want to see.'

She stared at Jules in the slowly strengthening light, seeing a different man from the one she remembered. He looked ravaged by lack of sleep, more fine-drawn than before, and even shockingly unkempt, as if some inner demoralisation had set in that was destroying him.

'I didn't bring Marcel,' she answered. 'I went to see him in Paris because I was getting desperate to find you, but he seemed to know less than I did, because by then at least I'd received two of your postcards. He's here to find you on his own account.' She hesitated a moment and then went on. 'Oliver Hatton is here, too.'

'*Hatton*? In God's name, Jane, why did you tell *him*?'

'He told *me* that the Moorish instruments in the Collection had been taken and replaced by fakes.' She held up her hand as Jules started to speak. 'Just listen, please. It will save time, and we've got a great deal to sort out. When my uncle died, Oliver had the Collection moved to Oxford, as an Executor was bound to do. The exchange was discovered immediately, and he felt certain that you must be involved. I preferred to believe from your postcards that you knew who the thief was and were doing your best to find him.'

Jules' ashen lips framed a question. 'You don't believe that now?'

'I can't. Marcel Colbert tracked down the man who made the replicas for you.'

His hands fastened on hers in a grip that made her wince. 'Jane, believe me now, please. I never thought your uncle would die so soon, and Bonnard in Paris *promised* me the copies looked so flawless that no lazy museum official would bother to inspect them twice. I never meant to harm you or Edwin Kingsley – if it seems like a crime now because it's all gone wrong, I did it for *us*.'

'Not for us,' she said slowly. 'Wasn't it all planned even before you came to England? Don't lie, please – we have to face the truth now.'

She doubted whether he was capable of that much effort, but after a moment's struggle he seemed to regain enough control of himself to release her. He gripped both hands together instead, like a child about to recite a difficult lesson.

'It began as a joke, Jane. Marcel and I used to laugh about the game it would be to fool Fernandez – the worst kind of fanatical, greedy collector – with fakes he couldn't spot. Then, at Little Fairford, I saw how easy it would be to change the game a little. Fernandez was right, after all, that the Moorish instruments belonged in Spain; I would sell him the real ones, and let the copies gather dust in some unvisited Oxford museum. The Collection *should* have been your inheritance – I always felt that; but this way we could share the proceeds together and make ourselves a lovely life. It seemed the perfect scheme.'

'But something went wrong with it here, as well as in Oxford,' she pointed out.

'Fernandez had an agent check there. I expected he would, and wasn't worried. But the Moorish astrolabes weren't on display and the man was refused when he asked to see them; the fakes had been removed. Fernandez cried off, of course, waiting for the fuss to die down. He still wants the instruments, but eventually he'll expect to get them for a much lower price. It's all a mess now, Jane, and I thought I was being so clever for us both.'

She wondered fleetingly how he would have arranged matters with his conscience if she hadn't agreed to marry him. Perhaps he didn't know himself whether he'd have gone on with his less than perfect scheme. But it scarcely mattered now. She *was* involved in it, however involuntarily. She'd accepted his offer to take care of her, had even been grateful for it, and she couldn't disbelieve him now when he said he'd been thinking of her as well as himself. She could walk away from him, but feel despicable for the rest of her life. Left alone, he would disintegrate, and she would be no better than the Pharisee in Christ's parable who'd crossed over to the other side, so as to be out of the way of trouble.

'The price you can get is immaterial,' she said at last.

'Oliver Hatton is here to take the instruments back to Oxford. I didn't bring *him*, either,' she added, watching the flush of anger in Jules' face. 'He followed me to Paris, and then down here. As a matter of fact I was rather glad that he did. Another car deliberately pushed me into a ditch, at which point I needed a friend badly.' She turned her face towards the light so that he could see its still discoloured bruises. 'Perhaps your Spanish friend was responsible?'

'I should like to kill whoever it was,' Jules said fiercely. 'But it can't have been Fernandez, my dear – he knows nothing about you.'

It left a small mystery unsolved, but there was a more urgent question to ask. 'Where are the astrolabes now?'

'In Andorra, in a safe-deposit box in your name at the Hotel *Galicia*. I had to be sure no one else could get at them, and I couldn't bring them back here myself. The Customs inspect French-registered cars very closely coming back across the frontier.' He spoke calmly now, pushed far beyond the point where self-deception or any other lies were possible.

'Then Oliver and I must go and collect them. He'll want to take them straight back from there.'

She expected another outburst but Jules merely nodded his head, almost as if there would be merely relief now in getting rid of what had brought him to ruin. Her own most recognisable emotion, to her own surprise, was the pity she couldn't help feeling for his abject condition.

'Marcel insisted that you were driven simply by greed,' she said quietly. 'I think it was more than that – you were trying to get even with life for past unhappiness.'

'That was how it began, but after I got to Little Fairford I truly wanted to impress *you* . . . wanted to heap treasures in your lap, look after you and make you happy. All I've done instead is to ruin everything.'

He spoke so simply and so sadly that she stretched out a hand to cover his own cold ones. 'What will you do?'

'I don't know – try to start again somewhere, I suppose; not in Paris; Marcel will make sure of that. I don't mind much about not working for him, though I'm sorry to have let him down as well; I never really enjoyed those old instruments.'

'What *do* you enjoy?'

She saw a glimpse of the old Jules in the flash of enthusiasm that lit his eyes for a moment. 'Paintings, Jane – they're what I know something about already, and I'd work and work at learning more. But I shall have to take whatever job I can get, and bury the dream I had of starting up a small gallery somewhere. The wages of sin aren't roasting in hell – they're simply knowing that you've brought disaster on yourself, and hurt the one person you wanted to hurt least of all.'

She believed him to be sincere, and it made what she said next sound right and inevitable. 'I've got the Owl House and its contents to sell. How much would it cost to get a small gallery started?'

His face went so white that she thought he was about to faint, but at a second attempt he managed to articulate words she could barely make out.

'You . . . you aren't serious, Jane . . . you *can't* be . . . not after what I've done.'

She produced a smile that might convince him. The road she was determined to follow was of her own choosing; it must be travelled, her father would have said, with generosity and cheerfulness, not by placing Jules under an intolerable sense of obligation.

'The Hattons won't let you do it,' he said hoarsely, 'and they'd be right.'

'My friends can't stop me, but we shall have to prove together that they *aren't* right.'

'We will, Jane, my dearest, we *will*, I promise you.' He leaned forward to kiss her bruised cheek very gently, and then began to smile himself. 'I've had one stroke of good luck here. It didn't seem to matter when I thought I'd lost *you*, but everything looks different now. I won't tell you about it now – I might be wrong, and I want to make sure first.'

She didn't press him – it wasn't time to think about the future yet. 'I must go with Oliver to Andorra, but I'll be back this evening,' she said instead. 'You look desperately in need of sleep, but you'll rest more easily if you don't go on trying to avoid your godfather. Talk to him as soon as he gets downstairs. Then, presumably, he'll go back to Paris.'

The prospect wasn't enticing, and she half-expected Jules to refuse. But after a moment he nodded his head. 'You're right, Jane, I'll do it as soon as I've cleaned myself up. Take care of yourself today, my dearest – I'll be waiting for you to get back.'

He smiled bravely at her, got to his feet, and let himself out of the unlocked door, just as he must have come in. She waited a few moments and then asked on her room telephone to be connected with Oliver.

'I've seen Jules,' she said baldly, as soon as she heard his voice. '*He* can't retrieve the instruments very easily from a hotel in Andorra, but we can – they're in a safe-deposit in my name.'

A small silence was all the response she got. Then finally Oliver spoke again. 'Order breakfast in your room, Jane, and then meet me in the lobby in an hour's time.'

The slam of the telephone sounded as terse as Oliver had been; he was not, she thought, in a mood to have his instructions argued with. On time to the minute, she went downstairs, relieved to see no sign of Jules or Marcel. She could only take one step at a time now, and the first ordeal in front of her must be to endure this final excursion with Oliver. In silence she was led outside to the travel-stained Rover, and in silence they threaded their way through a town that was still scarcely awake.

She concentrated on the map, directing him to the *Aix-les-Thermes* road that would lead them to the frontier post at the *Pas de la Case* and the route over the mountains.

'I hope your elegant car has a good pair of lungs,' she said to break the silence. 'It's going to have to climb to nearly 8,000 feet.' Then her voice suddenly changed. 'Oh, dear God, we're *still* being followed. I'm sure I glimpsed that horrible black car again.' She thought of the road ahead of them, full of serpentine loops and twists, and began to feel rather sick. Oliver, to her utter astonishment, merely looked in the driving-mirror and smiled for the first time that morning.

'Nothing to worry about. He knows we're merely taking him to his leader! I caught him unawares this morning and he has things to think about.'

What things? she wondered, but decided not to ask. Oliver was right, though . . . it was soon clear that their follower had no intention of doing anything but just keeping them in view. She realised something else – that Oliver was enjoying himself, even to the extent of giving an ironic toot of greeting on the horn whenever the two cars passed on parallel loops of the road. The end was in sight, of course; he could soon go home with his mission safely accomplished. She thought of Jules, crushed by defeat, and knew again how impossible it would have been to disown him.

She was quiet for the rest of the journey, and hoped Oliver would put it down to enjoyment of the dramatic scenery they were climbing through. But a sudden transition from bare, empty mountain ranges to a tree-lined valley and the crowded strip of town that lay at the bottom of it surprised her into speech again.

'It's like a Wild West frontier town gone wrong,' she commented. 'It ought to be full of saloons, and shops selling guns and rolls of gingham, instead of cameras and high-fi equipment. What an extraordinary place!'

But Oliver was concentrating on steering the car through the crowded street. Directed by an operatic-looking policeman to stop, he turned to grin at her. 'Thank God we didn't come on a Saturday . . . it's bad enough now.'

'What happens on Saturdays?'

'It seems to be day the Andorreans choose to get married. The traffic grinds to a halt while merry wedding parties chase one another up and down this street with every horn and klaxon blaring!'

'There you are, you see,' Jane pointed out. 'With guns instead of horns, it would be *just* like the Wild West.' She sounded rather regretful, then gave a little cry as she stared out of the window again. 'There it is – the Hotel *Galicia*.'

Oliver offered the policeman a sweet smile in return for the instructions being screamed at him, ignored the oncoming traffic and steered towards a little cul-de-sac at the end of which an opulent-looking hotel was jammed against the hillside.

Inside, sumptuously modern armchairs, marble floors, and a jungle of potted plants suggested that business was booming in Andorra. Oliver was in charge again, explaining to the young man behind the reception counter why they were there. He spoke quietly, but she was sure that the mention of her name hadn't gone unnoticed by a man who sat in one of the comfortable chairs, newspapers scattered around him, and a tray of coffee on the table by his side. She was aware of being stared at in a way that she didn't like. A pair of dark eyes considered her legs, but that, she felt, was purely a reflex action, this was a man who considered a woman's legs automatically. His interest in her was something other than amatory. She caught the gleam of gold on hands and wrist, and the unmistakable aroma of wealth that surrounded him like perfume in the air.

'We're here on business,' Oliver's voice murmured reprovingly in her ear. 'Stop ogling the residents and fish out your passport for me.'

'One of the residents is interested in us,' she whispered, digging in her enormous bag.

'In you, I expect, you know what Spaniards are!'

'Yes, but because I'm *me*, not because I wear a skirt. Do you suppose he could be Fernandez?'

Oliver's lazy glance lingered for a moment on the man who was now openly staring at them. 'Lombard Street to a china orange that he *is*, I'd say.'

'Well, how are we going to—' her agonised whisper was cut short by a hotel minion now beckoning them into the Manager's sanctum. Their credentials were examined, and then an aluminium case was handed over to them. Oliver asked for it to be opened, so that he could check the contents with his list of missing instruments. He pronounced himself satisfied, the Manager looked happy to be relieved of a responsibility he hadn't cared for, and then they were escorted back to the lobby again. Before they could walk out of the door, a voice spoke behind them.

'Will you join me in some coffee, Señorita, Señor?'

'Señor Fernandez, I presume?' The little smile on Oliver's mouth told Jane how much he enjoyed saying the classic line. 'No coffee, thanks, but I'm glad of this chance to talk to you. We're getting rather tired of being chaperoned by your watchdog outside. Call him off, please, and chastise him for severely exceeding his instructions to the extent of hurting Miss Kingsley and wrecking her car. She's entitled to institute criminal proceedings against you.'

'The fool told me – his orders were to delay her on the road; no more than that. My man in England had warned me that the Señorita had set out for France, and it seemed essential to keep her in view. I am deeply apologetic for the mishap, and want, of course, to make whatever amends I can. In my own defence I will only say that I thought I was involved in a legitimate purchase of objects that were neither faked nor stolen.'

A small silence followed this statement – masterly, Oliver admitted to himself, in what it left unstressed.

'No amends required, thanks,' he said finally, 'except to get Miss Kingsley's car repaired and sent back to England. But I'm afraid you must give up hope of getting the instruments – they're going back to Oxford where they belong.'

'Some people, myself included, would argue that they belong in Spain – they're part of our national heritage. Are you sure we can't come to . . . to some *arrangement*?' A delicate hint flowered in Fernandez's smile.

'I'm quite sure,' Oliver said bluntly.

The Spaniard's shrug expressed regret and resignation. 'One can do nothing, I'm afraid, when stubbornness goes hand in hand with high principles! Tell the Museum in Oxford, please, that if it ever wants to dispose of its assets, it should get in touch with me.'

He bowed, turned on his heel and walked away, and Jane let out the breath she discovered she'd been holding. 'As simple as that?'

Oliver smiled at her. 'What did you expect – pistols for two, coffee for one?'

Back in the car, they threaded their way out of the town again with Jane turning round every so often to make sure that there was no black Renault in sight. Convinced at last, she gave a huge sigh of relief and settled down in her seat.

'Pity we have to go back to Foix,' Oliver said after a while. 'I don't know about you, little one, but I've had my fill of driving around *la belle France*. What would you say to going up through Spain? We could put the car on the ferry at Santander and enjoy a little sea voyage home.'

Jane had known that breaking her news would be difficult; now that the moment had come it seemed almost impossible and she had to make two attempts to find her voice.

'I'm not going to England straightaway . . . I must go back to Paris with Jules.'

She felt the car falter, then swerve sharply as Oliver swung it into the next lay-by. When he'd cut the engine he turned to face her.

'Now say that again.'

'You heard me the first time.'

'I heard, but didn't believe. You can't be serious, Jane.'

The contemptuous note in his voice stiffened her into anger. 'I'm engaged to Jules . . . remember?'

Propelled by emotions that took no account of tact or

caution, Oliver went on to ensure disaster. 'Your engagement was never anything but a mistake, now it's madness.'

'That's not for you to say,' she insisted steadily. 'Jules knows that what he planned was all wrong and he regrets it deeply, but he wouldn't have gone on with it if he hadn't wanted to gain wealth that he could lavish on me.'

'My dear Jane, you don't . . . *can't* believe such rubbish!'

'I do believe it,' she shouted at him. 'Jules was right – he said you'd try to talk me out of marrying him.'

'He didn't need a crystal ball to figure that out! Of course I'd try to stop you ruining your life.'

She stared out of the window, mentally beseeching Heaven to prevent her from bursting into tears. After a moment or two she spoke again, calmly, and with a note of finality in her voice that Oliver recognised. Just so had young Jane delivered herself through all the years he'd known her of small decisions that, once taken, were unalterable. Having chosen self-destruction now, she would embrace it with all the fervour of an Early Christian going towards martyrdom.

'Try to understand, Oliver,' she said quietly. 'Apart from the failure of your marriage, your life has been a smooth, happy progression . . . loving parents, comfortable home, security, an enormous circle of friends, and a highly successful career. Jules has grown up knowing that he must make his own place in the world, determined to achieve success that other people *can't* despise. For the moment it's all been spoiled, but I want to help him put his life together again. We shall make each other happy.'

Oliver wondered why her decision should have come as such an agonising surprise; he'd known for long enough that she was in love with Legrand; he might have guessed that she wouldn't change . . . 'love is not love which alters when it alteration finds' . . . Shakespeare's words, but Jane's sentiments exactly. She risked a glance at his face and thought it might have been graven out of stone.

'Well, there doesn't seem anything left to say,' he remarked at last in a passable imitation of his usual drawl. 'We'll get the rest of this interminable journey over as fast as possible.' He steered the car back on the road again and drove from then on with a concentrated haste that stayed only just on the hither side of recklessness. Neither of them spoke at all until the Rover was braked outside the door of the hotel again.

'You'll be glad to reach home,' she said quietly. 'Estelle will be getting anxious – not to say lonely.'

He offered her a steely smile. 'You mustn't trouble yourself about us. Estelle's a broad-minded girl, not one to get upset about trifles.'

The whole heart-wrenching journey they'd taken together had been that, apparently – to her something she might have to remember for the rest of her life; to him merely a trifle.

'Give my love to Mary and Richard, please,' she said between stiff lips. 'I'll say goodbye now, Oliver, and thank you for all you've done.'

A moment later she was out of the car, and walking away from him for the last time.

Thirteen

Inside the hotel, she went up to her own room, and stayed there for a while staring into space; thinking of nothing at all because for the moment there seemed nothing worth thinking about. At last, when she felt sure that Oliver and Marcel would have gone, she roused herself to go downstairs, but the first person she saw was the Parisian, obviously waiting for her to reappear.

'I met Oliver Hatton, in fact waved him on his way to Boulogne at last!' Marcel said, with an attempt at lightness. 'Jules tells me that you're going back to Paris with him.'

'Yes, although we haven't had time to make any plans yet, of course.'

He didn't know whether to decorate her for gallantry, or implore her not to be fool. In the end he did neither; just tugged at his lower lip in a fit of indecision that was quite foreign to him.

'Jules doesn't expect you to . . . to overlook what he did,' Jane said in order to help him, 'and Bonnard knows that you weren't involved in the fraud; so the *Galéries Colbert's* reputation needn't suffer in any way.'

Marcel was in doubt no longer about what he must say.

'You don't have to worry about me, *ma petite*. It's *you*

who bother me. Are you sure you're doing the right thing?' His pudgy hands gripped hers and found them ice-cold.

She nodded, touched by a concern she'd scarcely expected.

Marcel hesitated a moment, then decided to be honest with her. 'I shan't, of course, take any action against Jules, but, my dear, I can't have him back at the Galleries. How will you manage?'

'Sell the Owl House, start something of our own, we're thinking,' she said firmly. 'Not in Paris, though; we need a fresh beginning.' She thought he tried hard not to look relieved.

'Well . . . you know where I am. You must come to me if you need help at any time; remember, please, that your uncle was my friend.'

She smiled her thanks, was kissed on both cheeks, and waited long enough this time to wave *him* on his way. When his car had disappeared onto the road she felt so lonely that it would have been a comfort to see the familiar black Renault waiting outside, but the car park was empty now and she went back to wait for Jules. Another long journey ahead of them – she would think of *that*, not of Oliver and a dusty green Rover, roaring up the motorway to Bordeaux.

When she saw Jules again he looked rested, and restored to something resembling the debonair appearance she remembered. The news that Oliver and Marcel had both left the hotel reassured him still further, and he suggested almost cheerfully that they should spend one more night at Foix before starting out themselves. Jane explained briefly that the instruments had been collected safely and that Fernandez, encountered in the Hotel *Galicia*, had been instructed to forget about a purchase he was never going to make. Jules shrugged aside the report as if the Kingsley instruments no longer concerned him, and she was warned not to ask a question that still bothered her; life would be unbearable for him if she kept harking back to the past. Then, with one of the sudden changes of mood that she was to become familiar with, Jules reverted to the very thing she'd promised herself she wouldn't mention.

'I'm sorry about your ivory figures, Jane.'

'You had them all the time?'

He nodded. 'I had to make it obvious that things *had* been taken from the Owl House, so that if the exchange *was* ever discovered, it would look as if it had been done at the time of the burglary. I described to my . . . my friend . . . a few things that he could find easily and recognise. But it was a brilliant idea, wasn't it, to return the things to you one by one? You were bound to go on to the next place once you'd started!'

The recollection of how neat the idea had been cheered him up again and she chose not to say that it had been cruel to steal, even temporarily, the only things she'd valued because they'd been her father's. Instead, she put her hand over his, as it crumbled bread on the table.

'If we've tidied up all the loose ends now, let's not talk about them ever again. We must look forward, Jules, not back.'

'You're right, as always.' He lifted his glass and smiled at her. 'To the future, my sweet!'

They made an early start the following morning, kept to the motorways, and after one night on the road, got to Paris late the next afternoon. While Jules threaded through the rush-hour traffic, Jane calculated in her head how many days it was since she'd driven away from Oliver and Marcel outside the restaurant. She didn't believe the answer, but got the same result each time she counted it up on her fingers . . . five nights ago, and it felt like five years.

Jules looked disappointed when she asked to be taken to a cheap hotel in the vicinity of his Left Bank apartment, but she was grateful that he accepted the request without argument. For a reason she recognised as illogical but important, she was determined that they should now do things, as she put it to herself, properly. For her that excluded living with Jules until they were married. She knew that he didn't understand, because he smiled tenderly and said 'Poor little one, you're worn out, and no wonder,' but at least he realised that their chequered relationship had lost ground that needed recovering.

His flat, which she visited next morning, was unexpectedly charming, the top floor of an old house in a tree-lined street tucked away between the *Boulevard St Germain* and the Luxembourg Gardens. It was the *quartier* of the Sorbonne, magnet for the student population of the city. For the moment it was peaceful, sunk in the quietness of the last of the summer vacation, but Jules admitted that he preferred it in term-time, pulsating with life and colour. He took her up to his own part of the house, and led her through the rooms he'd furnished with elegance and the occasional flash of flamboyance that she now knew was typical of him.

'What's the verdict, *mon coeur*?' he asked anxiously.

'It's charming. I'm rather sorry that we're not going to stay here. Are you sure we can't?'

'I think not, but I know where we should go instead – the city that's become the centre of Europe, Brussels! I've been urging Marcel for months to open a gallery there, but now I'm thankful that he didn't feel adventurous enough.'

'How shall we manage?' Jane asked hesitantly. 'You have

this apartment to sell, I have the Owl House, but Brussels won't be any less expensive than Paris.'

She saw him smile and knew that his recovery from the demoralised man she'd found at Foix was almost complete. Failure had been put aside and he was becoming confident again.

'Listen, sweetheart. Do you remember the stroke of luck I wasn't ready to talk about? Well, this is what it was. I hated hanging about for several days at the *Audoye*, with nothing to do but stare at the walls, but that was how I came to spot it – a dreadful painting that had belonged to the *patronne's* father. There was something odd about it, but when she told me its story I thought I could guess what it was. Her father had been given it at the end of the Spanish Civil War, when thousands of Republican refugees streamed across the Pyrenees, escaping from Franco's army. The painting was worthless, and she was delighted to get rid of it for the one hundred francs I offered her.'

Jane stared at him in bewilderment. 'You bought a bad painting very cheaply – was *that* your stroke of luck?'

He didn't answer immediately, but went to the suitcase he'd brought in from the car. Then he handed her several sheets of paper carefully interleaved with tissue.

'*These* are what I bought. They were hidden behind the painting – I found them when I dismantled the frame the day you went to Andorra.'

Jane looked from the sketches in her hand to Jules' excited face. 'Don't bank on them being genuine: Picasso's signature seems to have been found on so many things.'

'I know, I *know*; but they look *right*, Jane – they've got the energy and brilliant craftsmanship that only he had. He'd gone to live in Paris by the time the war started, but he went back to Spain to help the Republican cause. My dear, of course, they'll have to be authenticated but I think our fresh start might well be here, staring us in the face!'

Her face looked troubled now, not bewildered. 'If that is so, shouldn't you tell the *patronne* at the hotel? Otherwise we shall seem to be cheating her.'

Jules gave a little sigh, but clung to patience and a reasoned reply. 'Sweetheart, I bought something she didn't want, *still* didn't want even when I showed an interest in it. I took a gamble and risked my precious one hundred francs. There might have been nothing of value there – after all, the woman had had years in which to find out.' He tried to smile at her, but gave her a little shake. 'Don't look so anxious. Fate is smiling on us at last, giving us the kick-start we need!'

She nodded finally, accepting what he said and praying that she was right to do so.

They went out to shop for food in the neighbourhood, brought it home to cook, and in the process Jules recovered all his old gaiety. He was the tender, amusing companion she'd known at the Owl House, and watching him concentrate on the serious business of making their after-lunch coffee, she felt certainty return to her heart. Oliver had been wrong, she and Jules *could* make a life for each other. The thought of Oliver's name was enough to conjure him up in her mind's eye – fair hair usually untidy, grey eyes amused, and long body propped against some convenient resting-place – but she banished the picture from her mind. He would be home again by now, putting the finishing touches to the house he was going to share with Estelle. The name of Kingsley would soon mean nothing more than that of any other troublesome client whose affairs had been attended to . . . a bundle of documents tied with red tape, labelled 'file and forget'.

Jane wrenched her mind back to the present, to thank Jules for the coffee he put in front of her.

'Now, my love, it's the immediate future we have to talk about.'

'I know . . . I'll soon be running out of money, for one thing,' she confessed. 'But in any case I *must* go back to England and get things sorted out there.'

'That's what I want to talk about.' Jules played with her fingers, intertwining them with his own; then his grip suddenly tightened. The gaiety that had made their lunch enjoyable had disappeared, and he was suddenly tense again, white-faced and pleading.

'Marry me before you go, please, Jane. I daren't waste time and money in going with you, but if you leave without me I'm terrified that you won't come back.'

'My dear, I have to go *quickly*,' she reminded him. 'If I promise to come back, won't that do?'

'They'll find some way of stopping you . . . talk you out of it,' he said bitterly. His eyes devoured her face, looking for some proof that she couldn't deny what he'd just said. 'Perhaps that's what you intend anyway, not to come back? That's why you've refused to sleep with me here.'

'I've refused simply because I *am* going to marry you,' she insisted steadily. 'If it means so much to you, though, we'll do the deed before I go . . . Jules, you idiot, put me down . . . you'll damage yourself!' He took no notice; she was scooped up in his arms and waltzed round the room, and his face was transfigured with relief and happiness. When he finally restored her to the sofa again, he still didn't let go of her. 'I adore you, my dear one. I can't expect you to feel the same about me, but if I work and work for you will you *try* to love me, too?

Perhaps you do already, just a little, if you're prepared to marry me!'

She nodded, and was grateful that he seemed satisfied. It would have been hard to explain why she *was* marrying him – perhaps only out of a stubborn conviction that it was the right thing to do. But, with patience and effort of her own, love would come; it had to.

They were married four days later in a civil ceremony at which Marcel Colbert was one of the witnesses. She'd gone back to the Galleries on her own, to invite him to the wedding, and after the briefest moment of hesitation he'd accepted. Grown generous after the ceremony, he insisted that they must lunch with him, and if his manner towards Jules was still cool, she hoped that formality might eventually warm into forgiveness and friendship again.

When Marcel left them to return to the Galleries after lunch Jules smiled at the sight of Jane thankfully removing the white straw boater that had adorned her dark hair.

'Why take it off, *chérie* . . . it's charming.'

'It weighs me down!'

The solemn explanation made him grin, but he sobered again almost immediately. 'The hat, or the burden of being *Madame* Jules Legrand?'

'I'm not quite used to either,' she said honestly. 'Give me a little time.'

'It's exactly what I was going to offer you! The rest of the day is going to be a holiday. What would you like to do?'

She thought for a moment and then confessed to a yearning to go to Versailles, which she hadn't yet seen.

'Tourist stuff! But never mind. Versailles it shall be.'

Even if he disapproved of her choice, he was an excellent

guide – knowledgeable, and unable to resist enjoying the role of instructor. It was a light-hearted afternoon, and they loitered on the way back to dine, Jane remembering just in time that it wasn't the night to remind him that they could be eating more cheaply at home. She drank more wine than usual to keep him company and was glad of the fact afterwards, although Jules looked pleased when she confessed to being a virgin.

'It's archaic, I suppose,' she said ruefully, wishing she didn't feel so unprepared for the idea of a man having the right to walk into her bedroom. 'I'm about as up to the minute as high-button boots!'

'You're adorable, *ma cherie*, and I don't begin to deserve you. You're beautiful, Jane . . . how I do adore you . . .'

He was a tender lover – experienced too, she thought thankfully, because his skill helped to disguise her own lack of it. She did her best to respond, but doubted whether he considered their wedding night a success. Passion flowering between them wasn't something that could be had at once – that, too, would have to come with time and practice. She lay awake after Jules had finally fallen asleep, aware only of a terrible longing to weep. Too many unshed tears now seemed to weigh her down like that ridiculous white hat, but if once she started to weep, she might never be able to stop. Somewhere on the margin of her mind lay a memory of a different night spent, though not spent, with Oliver. She would never think of it again, she promised herself.

Jules seemed more cheerful next morning than she expected, and agreed at once when she suggested rather hesitantly that she ought to fly back to England as soon as possible.

'Of course, even though it's not the way we should be spending our honeymoon! But I shall be busy while you're gone. With this apartment on the market, I can make a quick trip to Brussels. I know exactly what we need – something we can turn into a small, exclusive gallery.'

'Exclusive?' she asked doubtfully.

'Of course, it's the first rule in this business – always look expensive and *never* be modest! We shall have to rent to begin with, but only until we get established.'

She was too glad to see him alive and interested again to mind a self-confidence that bordered on the dangerous. His self-esteem had been lacerated by the instrument fiasco, and they could scarcely begin a new venture by steeling themselves for it to fail. Rule two, presumably, was 'always be optimistic'.

She flew to Heathrow the following day, caught a bus to Oxford, and another from there to Little Fairford. It was late afternoon at the beginning of October when she walked up the lane to the Owl House, a day of golden, tranquil beauty. Someone – dear Jim Wilkins perhaps – had taken the trouble to keep the lawn mown, and the borders were ablaze with dahlias, chrysanthemums, and Michaelmas daisies. She'd forgotten already how beautiful it was, how quiet and peaceful.

Her bedroom was untidy, a reminder of the frantic sense of urgency that had driven her that morning when she set out to catch the ferry, but it was her own. She kicked off her shoes and collapsed on the bed – *her* bed, which she didn't have to share with anyone. The relief was so overwhelming that her body felt light enough to float up into the air; just for a little while she could be Jane Kingsley again, with the freedom to say and do what she pleased.

But it was Madame Legrand who set out next morning to keep an appointment in Oxford. She wanted to get the interview with Oliver over and done with before her return to the Owl House was known all round the village. The bus was almost empty, and hidden behind a pair of very large dark glasses she went unrecognised.

Oliver was warned, of course, by the name she'd given his secretary, but nevertheless this new version of someone he'd never been able to think of as anyone but little Jane made him stare at her in a silence she had just as much difficulty in breaking. She was thin, now, to the point of gauntness, the bone structure of her face more noticeable and more beautiful than before. Her unmanageable dark hair had been tamed and trimmed into something that resembled the fronded petals of a chrysanthemum flower, and the coral-coloured scarf tucked into the open collar of her pale-green shirt suggested a studied elegance that she hadn't bothered about before. Oliver noted the changes, aware that they were surface ones. Underlying them was some experience that had taken her across the frontier into womanhood, and he would have sworn that the journey had *not* been altogether joyous. Her face was reticent now, concealing what she felt. He felt such hatred of Jules Legrand rise in his throat that it was a moment or two before he could swallow it and get up to offer her a chair.

'The bush telegraph is not what it was,' he said unevenly. 'I hadn't heard that you were back.'

'Only last night,' Jane muttered, having difficulties of her own in talking normally. 'I hid behind my chic French sunglasses this morning . . . I wanted to see you first of all.'

'The total effect is *very* chic.'

'But very superficial, I'm afraid!' She grinned suddenly and he recognised Jane Kingsley again.

'What can I do for you, little one?' The epithet threatened her, but she managed to look steadily at him.

'I've come back to dispose of the Owl House and most of

its contents. Could you find someone to handle all that for me, please, Oliver? There is a lot to do in Paris, so I can't stay here for long. I'd be so grateful to be able to put it in hand and then leave.'

Oliver nodded by way of answer, then asked a question of his own. '*What* is there to do in Paris?'

'Arrange a move to Brussels, first of all. Jules . . . we, that is . . . are planning to open a small gallery there – modern paintings mostly, about which he's very knowledgeable. The money from selling his apartment and the Owl House will get us started.'

'A clean sweep here, Jane . . . no ties left in England?'

'It can't be done any other way,' she explained hoarsely. 'I'll store Uncle Edwin's books for the time being, and one or two items of furniture I don't want to part with. Otherwise, yes . . . a clean sweep.'

'Marcel parted company with . . . with your husband, I take it?' He forced himself to say the word out loud, in the hope that it might make the situation seem less unreal.

She nodded. 'But he was kind enough to come to our wedding, and I hope that he and Jules might eventually become friends again.'

'I'll arrange the sale, of course, and transfer the proceeds, but let me advise you, please, to keep a little of the money in England. It might be useful to hang on to a bank account here.'

He thought she was about to refuse, but suddenly she smiled at him. 'Stupid not to take the advice of one's solicitor . . . all right, leave a little of the money here, then.'

'You'll go and see Mary and Richard before you disappear again?'

'Yes, of course. How are they?'

'Much the same . . . no, not quite. Richard's looking rather frail, and my mama agonises about it in silence.'

'I'll go and see them,' Jane said again. Then she stood up. 'I'm taking up too much of your time. See you before I go, Oliver, and thank you again for more kindness than I can repay.'

Her smile hurt him, breaching the wall round the things he hadn't meant to say. 'Are you all right, little one?'

'I'm . . . I'm fine. I'll send my new address to Miss . . . Miss Farson, was it? . . . outside.'

'Miss ffarquharson – two f's and no capitals,' Oliver explained gravely. The deadpan solemnity of it transported her back in time more surely than anything else could have done, to days when she and he had always seen the same things as funny. Odd that it should transfix her now with pain when nothing else had. Then he took a step towards her and she almost ran to the door. Miss ffarquharson took in his usual cup of black coffee half an hour later, surprised to find him staring out of the window. It wasn't like him at all; despite an indolent air, he usually seemed to fill every unforgiving minute of the day.

Jane called in at the Hattons' house on her way home. Banished from the office for a week's rest by his son, Richard was pottering in the garden, and his wife was hovering nearby, trying not to look as if she was keeping an eye on him. They couldn't really have aged in the space of a few weeks, but Jane saw them with fresh eyes, aware that weakness was gaining on Richard, and anxiety about him on Mary. She gave them an expurgated account of what had happened to her since leaving the Owl House, apologised for concealing from Richard what she'd intended to do, and dwelt at length on the adventure in front of her and Jules. She didn't dwell on her marriage, because instinct told her that they weren't happy about it, but it reminded her of something she hadn't brought herself to ask Oliver.

'I saw my excellent solicitor this morning. There was so much business to talk about that I forgot to ask about his own affairs,' she said brightly. 'Have he and Estelle fixed a date for their wedding?'

Mary shook her head. 'You'll hardly believe it, but she finally got offered a part in a new play. Oliver says she hasn't got to do anything but wear some glamorous clothes very nicely, so there's no reason why she and the play shouldn't run for years.'

Jane now understood why Mary looked so discouraged. Estelle as Oliver's wife was much better than no wife at all – without whom there could be no grandchildren. But it was hard to think the prospect imminent, with Oliver living at Sutton Courtenay and his fiancée tied to a theatre in London. Poor Oliver, too. It explained why he'd looked so tired and stern this morning. Even the most patient of men would have found the situation frustrating, and though Oliver Hatton was a great many other things, he was probably the *least* patient of men.

She said goodbye to Mary and Richard at last, and remembered one more visit that had to be made before she went home.

Jim Watkins was in his garden as usual, throwing down handfuls of bulbs and planting them where they lay.

'It's . . . no . . . yes, it *is*, young Jane! I like the new hair-cut . . . very *Parisienne!* Time for a cuppa?'

'I'd love one, Jim.' She followed him into his spotless kitchen, aware that though she wanted no one else to know what had happened, Jim had a right to be told, and that it would be as safe with him as with a priest in the confessional. She told it almost all, and even found herself relieved to have shared it with someone not directly involved. Being Jim, he saw no reason to burden her with his opinion. All he said was, 'No wonder you look different . . . quite a voyage!'

'"*Heureux qui, comme Ulysse, a fait un beau voyage* . . . !"' she quoted, smiling at him. 'The voyage is only just beginning, too. Jules and I have to get our gallery started.'

She was brave and gallant, and Jim told himself he was an old fool to imagine that her friends should have found some way of preventing what had happened. He did his best not to make his next question sound disapproving.

'You're selling the Owl House, I suppose?' Her nod made him go straight on. 'Got a buyer for you, in that case. He's been trying to get into this village for years, so he won't haggle about the price. In fact, he's loaded with wealth, so give me a stiff figure to quote and I'll tell him he's getting a bargain.'

She saw him grin, but dimly, because her eyes had misted with tears.

'I owe you so much kindness already, but thanks, Jim. Will you ask him to contact Oliver Hatton? I've got a lot of clearing out to do, and most of my uncle's books will have to be stored for the time being. But will you come and browse through them first for anything that appeals to you? I should like to think of you enjoying Uncle Edwin's treasures. There's another thing as well. My Metro will be turning up soon, suitably repaired. I hope you'll keep it and use it yourself.'

Without meaning to, she'd managed to disconcert Jim for the first time. 'Kind of you, Janey,' he muttered. 'Just one or two volumes as mementoes . . . yes, I should like to pick just one or two. As for the car, well, my old banger's on its last legs, as you surely know.' He buried his nose in a mug of tea, then spoke more briskly again. 'You're off again soon, I take it.'

'Yes, as soon as I can. There's a lot to do, and I can't leave it all to Jules.'

'Hope he realises he's got himself a treasure.' It was the nearest Jim had ever got to saying what he felt about her, and she knew she'd been paid a rare compliment. But when she turned to tell him so, he was staring rigidly out of the window and she thought he would prefer his pretty speech to go uncommented upon.

'New teacher fixed up?' she asked instead, changing the subject.

'Yup . . . started at the beginning of term. S'ppose she'll do.'

He walked with her along the lane, as if in no hurry to part with her. 'I know you're all fixed up in Paris,' he said finally, 'but let me know if you need help any time.'

She thanked him as she had once before by kissing his cheek. He stared at her for a moment, then trudged home again.

For the rest of the week she selected what she wanted to keep, spring-cleaned the cottage, and spoke to the storers Oliver had put her in touch with. Then, at last, she made a round of farewells in the village. It was hard to say goodbye to the Hattons, but she was spared the ordeal of parting finally from Oliver. A family crisis had taken him unexpectedly to Scotland, and all she had to do was leave a farewell message with Mary. Curly Carter, in his role of local taxi-man, drove her to Heathrow, and that was another, minor blessing. Curly was capable of carrying on a conversation with no help at all from his passenger, and she needed only to drag herself out of her thoughts to say 'yes' occasionally.

Fourteen

Jules was waiting at the airport in Paris. He seemed delighted to see her back and settled her in the car with his usual care. The subject of the Owl House must have been heavy on his mind, but he was so careful not to bombard her with questions about it that she gave him the news the moment he could take his attention off the traffic.

'No problem about disposing of the cottage . . . dear Jim Watkins already had a client lined up!'

'A rich one, I hope, my love!'

'Jim says so, and Oliver has agreed to handle the sale for us, so we can be sure it will be done properly with the minimum fuss and bother.'

'Of course, with our paragon of a lawyer in charge.'

She bit her lip, reminding herself that he associated Oliver with the fiasco over the instruments. It was too much to expect that he would ever like him now, when he never had to begin with. Jules glanced at his silent passenger, and put out his hand in a little gesture of apology. 'Sorry – I've missed you, but that's no excuse. I've got some good news, too. The apartment's sold, and I think I've found just what we're looking for in Brussels. It's dilapidated at the moment, so the price is reasonable, but the neighbourhood is perfect: the *Rue au Beurre*, a stone's throw from the *Grand*

Place – home ground for the rich and fashionable clients we need!'

He insisted on cooking their supper, saying that she looked tired, and talked for the rest of the evening about the plans he'd made while she'd been away. She listened, looked interested, and struggled not to yawn. She felt deathly tired, and tried not to remember with yearning her unshared bed at the Owl House. Later, in a bed that wasn't unshared, she promised herself that Jules shouldn't know the effort she had to make to respond to him, but she was left more tired than ever, and unsatisfied in the deepest need of all, to give herself joyfully in shared delight.

She slept badly, finally overslept, and got up hurriedly to find him ready to leave. He looked keyed-up, but she had learned already not to prise things out of him; he would tell her when he was ready.

Her reward was to see him at the door, three hours later, his arms full of flowers for her and his face alight with happiness.

'Darling Jane . . . admit to me at once that you've got the cleverest husband in all the world, even if he doesn't deserve you!'

'They *are* Picassos,' she suddenly shouted. 'Jules – you've heard about the sketches!'

'Absolutely beyond doubt, my blessed. They're the real and genuine thing – drawings of the friends he spent his time with when he went back to Spain.'

'So where will you sell them – Paris, London, New York?'

He shook his head, smiling brilliantly at her. 'Where else but in Brussels, as the sensation of our opening exhibition? Can you be ready to catch the evening train, sweetheart?

I've seen some premises there but I want you to agree that they'll do.'

They dined late in Brussels, spent the night at a modest hotel that she teased him about – "never be modest"! – and set out the following morning to inspect the property he'd earmarked. Cheerfulness deserted her at the sight of its dirt and dilapidation, but he brushed the disappointment aside.

The ground floor had formerly been converted into a boutique selling women's clothes. The venture had closed down months before, leaving behind the debris and forlorn smell of failure, but Jules wasn't cast down; someone else's failure needn't bother them, and the asking rental was lower than it would otherwise have been.

'Look at this big room, Jane, *just* what we need, and the windows are interesting. There's a cubby-hole at the back that will make an office, a cloakroom off it, and best of all, a courtyard at the back – ideal for giving little receptions in the summer. The accommodation upstairs will put you off at the moment, but there's nothing there that a coat or two of paint won't cure.'

It needed the eye of faith to see any of it as ideal or even remotely promising, but she tried to match his enthusiasm and kept her doubts to herself.

They shipped the contents of Jules' apartment to Brussels, but moved temporarily into furnished rooms there. Their life was uncomfortable and, to eke out dwindling capital, they must do as much of the work on their new premises as possible themselves.

Slowly, as the weeks passed, Jane admitted that Jules had been right; the whole depressing place was being transformed. Instead of dirt and debris, there were now walls painted a pale silver-grey. The floor was carpeted in a slightly deeper shade of grey, and all the woodwork was sparkling white. Jules intended very little colour to detract from the canvases he would hang on the walls . . . an occasional low modern chair upholstered in dark-green velvet, and glass lamps in the shape of exquisite green water-lilies that he'd found damaged and filthy in a junk shop and spent hours cleaning and restoring. Jane laboured over the rooms upstairs, and, as a relief from painting walls and scrubbing floors, turned her energies on the pleasant green arbour of his imagining in the courtyard outside.

At last he was ready to scour the artists' colony for work he considered worthy to hang beside the sketches that would provide the climax of the gallery's launch. Jane addressed elegant invitation cards to the people he reckoned worthy to attend the opening of the *Galérie Legrand*, and added her private prayers that at least a few buyers would attend. Jules' remaining capital was almost gone, and they would soon be living on borrowed money. Even so, he insisted that they must serve good champagne at the reception, and it provoked their first sharp disagreement.

'It's madness – we can't afford it,' Jane said bluntly, forgetting in her anxiety that open opposition made him stubborn.

'We can't afford *not* to. Give me credit, my dear girl, for knowing this world better than you do.'

'I'll give you all the credit you deserve. The gallery's stunning, and you've done wonders with it. But we shall soon be heavily in debt, without spending a fortune on champagne.'

Jules' shrug told her that he was irritated by her persistence, and, as always, irritation produced a jibe at Oliver. 'Your paragon of a lawyer seems to be taking his time, after all. The simple business of selling a house seems too complicated for him.'

She refused to be drawn into another argument, but almost as if her need had been signalled to him, Oliver's awaited letter arrived the next morning. It announced briefly the completion of the sale, and the transfer of a large sum of money to their bank in Brussels. When she told him the amount, Jules looked disappointed . . . perhaps simply to underline his need to pretend that someone, anyone, else, would have done better for them. She didn't say that not quite all the money had been transferred – she felt ashamed of not telling him but it would have provoked an outburst that she felt too tired to endure.

Oliver's letter had to be replied to, but she wrote briefly, filling it with a glowing account of the gallery's launching party. It *had* been successful; even without the lure of the Picasso sketches the beautiful new room would have been crowded with just the sort of clientele, dealers and art critics that he'd insisted must be attracted to the *Galérie Legrand* if it was to succeed. Novelty was important in the hot-house atmosphere of a small capital where people got tired of seeing the same faces. They were intrigued by a charming new entrepreneur who combined Canadian zest with the polish he'd learned from Marcel Colbert in Paris.

The fine Indian summer dwindled into autumn, and as the city's tourists departed the winter social scene got into full swing. Jane learned to adapt herself to a round of parties and theatre visits, in which life became a blur of carefully graded hospitality through which she moved like an elegantly-dressed automaton – mere cocktails for acquaintances, little dinners for so-called friends or likely buyers. She struggled to redeem the sterility of it all by trying to take a genuine interest in the people she met, but more often than not she was defeated by the discovery that the rich and beautiful were like Tennyson's Maud: if not icily regular, certainly 'splendidly null'. She disliked the sophisticated idlers dabbling with Art, who might or might not become clients of the gallery, and feared the influential fellow-dealers who could become enemies or unreliable friends, depending on how the whim took them.

Jules, by contrast, moved through the shifting currents of the fashionable art world with the swift and darting precision of a goldfish in his true element. He knew by instinct when to flatter, when to disagree, even when, very charmingly, to bully a wavering client into making up his or her mind. Jane went less often now to the gallery, where he seemed to have no need of her, and occupied herself instead with the artists themselves. *They* provided the justification for the mad social merry-go-round on which she now lived, because association with a successful gallery saved several of them from starving.

The ordered chaos of their studios, and the smell of paint and turpentine always hanging in the air, seemed real when much of her own surroundings were not. The artists themselves, struggling to put their own private visions on paper or canvas, were usually odd but always interesting. She enjoyed enticing them to the apartment above the ground floor and feeding them the huge meals they always seemed in need of. For them she felt she had some use; in the gallery she seemed to have become superfluous.

The rarity of her visits explained why Oliver Hatton walked into the beautiful grey and green room one morning and found only Jules there, and the elegant receptionist who sat behind an antique desk.

'Good morning, my name's Hatton – we met at Little Fairford,' he said briefly.

Armoured with new-found confidence and success, Jules chose to forget that they had nearly met at Foix as well. He smiled and agreed that he remembered Monsieur Hatton. The man had become unbearably French for someone who was half-Canadian, Oliver decided, but if appearances were anything to go by, he had also become prosperous. The smell of success, indefinable but distinct, was in the air and in his smile. Thank God for that, at least; it removed one of Oliver's anxieties.

'What brings you to Brussels?' Jules asked with a show of interest.

'The troubled affairs of a client, but since I was here I thought I'd call. Is Jane around?'

Jules gave a little shrug. 'I rather doubt it, her social round is very hectic while I labour in the vineyard! How long are you here?

'Only for today, I'm afraid.'

'Let me ring through upstairs.' Jules gestured to the paintings on display that were there to be enjoyed, and disappeared into his small office at the back of the room. He returned almost at once – looking faintly apologetic.

'I'm afraid it's just as I feared – Jane is sad to miss you, but there isn't a free moment all day. Another time you must be sure to let us know you're coming.'

The smile that accompanied this little speech wasn't intended to conceal Jules' pleasure at being able to deliver it. Oliver resisted the temptation to hit the handsome face in front of him, and bowed ironically in return.

'My compliments, then, to Madame Legrand!' He started to amble towards the door but turned back to find Jules still watching him. 'A Lucien Freud, I see,' he said, pointing to a painting in the place of honour on the wall, 'fake or genuine?'

The affable question dropped into a silence heavy with mutual hostility and distrust. Jules' face went white at the thrust and try as he would he couldn't quite out-stare the cool, grey glance that said he'd been weighed in the balance and found lamentably wanting. He hated Oliver Hatton; always had, always would now.

'The painting is genuine,' he replied at last. 'The price will be fairly astronomical if you're thinking of bidding.'

'Quite above my touch, I'm sure. *Au revoir, Monsieur.*' Oliver sauntered out of the gallery, watched with so much interest by the receptionist that Jules bit her head off and she sulked for the rest of the morning.

The painting was, in fact, to be auctioned at an important forthcoming sale, but Jules had put it on display as a talking point at his Christmas exhibition. Jane's presence was required as hostess at the opening reception, and she circulated among the guests, slender and elegant in a sheath of holly-green velvet. She smiled often, and gave no sign of the searing row that had erupted with Jules that morning. It had arisen because of a six-line note from Oliver, informing her that all the details of her uncle's estate had finally been settled. Only the handwritten postscript was slightly less impersonal. He regretted that she'd been too busy to see an old friend when he'd called at the gallery.

'What does he mean?' she asked Jules. 'I'm not aware of his coming here . . . are you?'

Her husband gave a careless little shrug. 'I scarcely remember – perhaps Joséphine did mention that an Englishman had called one day when you weren't here. I can't see that it matters very much.'

'It matters a great deal,' she answered steadily, knowing that she would irritate him. 'Oliver is an old friend, and he's been wonderfully helpful to both of us. Please ask Joséphine to try to remember if someone asks for me in future.'

'Especially if Oliver Hatton shows up again?'

'Yes,' she agreed, stung into being honest with him, and saw Jules' face darken with rage.

'You need no reminders of Oliver Hatton,' he suddenly shouted at her. 'The man is never out of your mind. Do you think I don't know why you go rigid whenever I come near you? It's him you want to touch you.'

'You're mad . . . unfair,' Jane said hoarsely.

'I don't think so. But *you're* an alluring cheat. Every man who meets you probably dreams of taking you to bed. I could tell him not to bother. You promise a great deal and deliver nothing.'

She watched him stalk out of the room, but sat frozen herself until she heard the slam of the front door. Oliver's note was still gripped in her hand – such a poor little letter to have unleashed so dreadful a storm, but at least she now knew the reason for its curtness. She sat on in the quiet room, aware that it was the moment to face up to brutal truths she had been avoiding for months. The most important of them was the fact that her marriage was a failure. Instead of growing closer, she and Jules now shared nothing that seemed important. With the gallery firmly established, his only need of her was to run his home efficiently, to act the part of his elegant wife to the world at large, and occasionally to share his bed. This last point brought her to the most painful truth of all. She *was* the cheat he'd rightly called her. In her heart of hearts she was relieved that the child Jules insisted he wanted refused to be conceived; the blame was hers, he'd said more than once, and she was unable not to agree with him.

She got through that evening's reception as it seemed she might have to get through the rest of her life – smiling, pretending, locking away despair. No one had forced her to be where she was – she'd come willingly, and made promises that she must somehow keep.

The following day they left the city to spend Christmas with one of Jules' most faithful clients – Jeannine de Courville. She was wealthy, widowed, and the owner of a beautiful country house outside the town of Namur, in the valley of the River Meuse. She was also a woman Jane instictively disliked, and her house-party would consist of other people exactly like herself. Jules smoothly overrode a suggestion that, instead of going there, they might spend a quiet Christmas at home, and Jane's reward for not arguing about it was the discovery that *Madame* de Courville's idea of being the perfect hostess included giving her married guests separate rooms. It was such a relief to be left alone that she didn't even mind whether Jules stayed in the one allotted to him, or shared it with his attentive hostess. Her own relationship with him had crossed some invisible watershed and, for all her brave intentions, she could only follow the route he now marked out for them.

The pattern set by a distasteful Christmas remained when they returned to the *Rue au Beurre*. Jules now seemed too busy to remember that he had a wife; success was the chimera he pursued with wholehearted devotion, and it required him to be seen in the right places among the right people. Even Jane thought he deserved it when he was appointed in the new year a consultant to one of the great auction rooms. He had found his *métier*, he was an acknowledged expert, a man whose opinion the art world listened to.

She performed whatever part in the ritual he allotted her, and was saved from going mad with boredom and loneliness by her artist friends. One of them, a bearded, bear-like man called Georges Pothier, demanded to paint her portrait. She refused the request to begin with but Jules insisted, rather to her surprise, that she should change her mind.

'He doesn't do nearly enough work; for God's sake don't put him off if he wants to paint,' had been her husband's reaction.

Her first visit to Pothier's studio was an ordeal, because he examined her so intently, but she grew to trust him, and found herself grateful for his rough kindness.

'Why don't you do more work?' she asked one day. 'Jules says he could sell what you produce three times over.'

'I work to please myself,' Pothier replied indifferently. 'Damn you, Jane, sit still; you're fidgeting.' He glared at the canvas in front of him, then at her again. 'Beautiful mouth . . . but sad. I wonder why? A lost lover in England, maybe?'

'Wrong,' she insisted firmly, at the risk of being shouted at again. 'I'm a trifle under-occupied, if you want to know. Jules no longer needs my help in the gallery, and I suppose I'm conditioned to feeling useful. I miss my old job.'

'Which was?'

'Teaching in the village school! I don't mind if you think it sounds the sort of thing a sophisticated woman shouldn't admit to. I enjoyed it very much. Now, apart from keeping house, I lack something to do.'

'You lack a husband who appreciates you – would a lover do instead?' He saw the surprise and doubt in her face, and went on to make the offer plain. 'I'm volunteering myself, naturally! It would be a great pleasure, my dear Jane.'

'I don't think so,' she muttered after a moment or two, '. . . I'm afraid I really don't think so, but it was a . . . a very kind offer, Georges.'

She made it sound, he thought, as if she was refusing an offer to go out to tea, but her eyes were full of pain. He accepted defeat gracefully and put forward instead a suggestion that she might feel able to accept.

'I could find you a job, unpaid, I'm afraid, but interesting.'

'What is it?'

His bearded mouth smiled at her. 'You'd call it a reform school in England! I teach the delinquents to paint, but giving them English lessons might be more useful.'

'I'll think about it,' she commented slowly. 'Tell me where to write.'

He thought she'd put the idea aside, and told her so when she eventually reported that her services had been offered and accepted.

'*Mes compliments, Madame!* I doubted that you'd do it . . . I should have known better.' He stared at her. 'Are you nervous?'

'Yes, very.'

'No need to be; you'll have them eating out of your beautiful hands in no time.'

She wouldn't have put it quite like that, but her class of noisy teenagers did gradually progress from hostility to indifference and even in the end to a reluctant wish to learn.

Jules shrugged aside her attempts to interest him in what she was doing, preferring his own charitable efforts to be well-publicized and performed at a safe distance from the recipients. The children were tiring to teach, and it only needed one of them, hell-bent on self-assertion, to wreck the concentration of an entire class. But even the bad days were at least real, and the good ones sent her back to the goldfish bowl of her life with Jules feeling that she was achieving something. She still made desperate efforts to close the gap that opened steadily between herself and her husband, but they were becoming strangers courteously sharing the same roof, and she was aware of a terrible sense of isolation.

The letter from Oliver that had sparked off her row with Jules had finally been answered in such coldly formal terms that she knew he would now accept what had been made clear to him on his visit to the gallery – an old friendship was finally dead; Little Fairford had been written out of her life. Apart from her morning visits to the reform school and whatever social engagements Jules required her for in the evenings, her time was spent mostly alone, wandering about the city. She grew familiar with its museums and churches, and kept in touch with England only by reading day-old copies of *The Times* and *Telegraph* over coffee in the capital's cheap cafés. She had what most women wanted, she told herself – a comfortable, secure life, a position in society, and still some stubborn conviction that, if she abandoned him, Jules might go to pieces again. There was nothing she could safely change.

Then one morning in late Spring, as she glanced down the personal columns of the newspaper, the name of Hatton leapt out at her. Richard, beloved husband of Mary and father of Oliver, had died the previous Friday. Pain, not numbing as people always claimed, had the effect of wrenching her out of the peaceful detachment she had learned to float in, and it was like feeling a frost-bitten limb coming to agonising life again. Her mind fastened only on the futile regret that Richard would never see his garden in summer bloom again; she didn't dare to contemplate Mary's sadness, or the knowledge that the Hattons had accepted her separation from them so completely that they hadn't even let her know.

She walked slowly home, with a decision she wasn't even aware of making crystallising in her mind. The undertakers in Oxford answered her telephone call and gave her the information she asked for, and when Jules came in that evening her arrangements were already made.

'I'm sorry,' he said when she told him about Richard. 'You'll want to send flowers, of course?'

'I want to do more than that. I must go myself, Jules.'

'When *must* you go?'

'On Thursday afternoon. I'll stay the night somewhere in Oxford, Richard's funeral is on Friday morning, in the village.'

'You've forgotten that we're engaged on Thursday evening.'

She had indeed forgotten; remembering would have made no difference, but it *would* have warned her how seriously Jules would be displeased. He'd worked hard to win them an invitation to one of the most glittering receptions of the season. The square of thick white pasteboard engraved in gold that decorated the mantelpiece was the proof he craved that the Legrands were where they rightfully belonged.

'You must cancel your flight, if you've been rash enough to book it without consulting me. I'm sorry about Hatton, of course, but your appearance at his funeral is scarcely here or there. Your appearance here on Thursday, on the other hand, is a duty you owe me. I don't ask for very many.'

She stared at his pale, beautifully-featured face, wondering whether the man she'd imagined him to be had ever existed at all. It was an important point to decide at some quiet moment when she had time to think about it, because she needed to be fair; and it would be anything but fair to blame him for not being the man she'd created for herself out of loneliness and need and pity.

'I'm sorry to let you down, I know the Thursday thing means a lot to you,' she said at last. 'I'm sure you needn't go alone, though – Jeannine de Courville, to name but one, would be happy to partner you.'

He stared at her, aware as always of the confusing mixture of emotions she aroused in him. She looked, with her spare grace, just as he wanted his wife to look, more so than any other woman he knew; she made the impression on other people that Madame Jules Legrand *should* make; but it enraged him beyond bearing that beneath that surface allure she remained stubbornly the girl he'd met at Little Fairford, clinging to codes and convictions that were entirely her own. The long festering desire to change her in some fundamental way had never materialised, and frustration now goaded him into in an ultimatum he hadn't known was in his mind.

'You're using this funeral as an excuse – anything will do as long as you can see Oliver Hatton again. Well, let me make the position clear, Jane. If you insist on going on Thursday, I should prefer you not to bother to come back.'

'I *must* insist on going,' she said steadily. 'The Hattons were my salvation throughout childhood and when Uncle Edwin died; Richard was a dear friend. Those seem to be "excuses" enough, and I'm not going for the sake of seeing Oliver.'

'I don't believe you,' Jules shouted. 'Think about it, and then change your mind.'

He flung out of the room, and had already left the apartment next morning by the time she got up. She wandered about the rooms that had been her home for the past nine months. There was nothing in them that seemed to be hers, apart from the little ivory figures that still spoke of her father, and the pearl necklace that Edwin Kingsley had given her. Only the little courtyard garden had bloomed because it was she who'd tended it with love and care; now it would probably die of neglect again.

Nothing else could be thought about for the moment, except a fact that might dazzle her if she stared at it too closely – like trying to peer at the sun. She'd been trapped in inertia and resignation for so long that she could scarcely believe the cage door was open. All she had to do was walk through it to freedom, and it was Jules himself who'd offered her the gift of release.

The chiming of the carriage-clock in the hall reminded her that time was passing. She gave a long, shuddering sigh and then walked back into her bedroom. She must pack clothes, find a taxi, and get herself to the airport. After she'd said a final goodbye to Richard Hatton *then* there would be time to stop and consider how to fill the rest of a life that might look terrifyingly empty.

Fifteen

Mary Hatton walked home from her weekly visit to the churchyard one June afternoon, happy to find Oliver lounging on the wooden bench outside the kitchen door. She came quietly across the lawn and caught him unawares, but the expression on his face made her wish that she hadn't. She knew he preferred his feelings not to be examined by the rest of the world. Then he realised that she was there, and his sombre face lightened into the smile he offered no one else.

'I was passing; just thought I'd call to say hello,' he explained casually.

'I'll put the kettle on . . . I expect you've eaten nothing all day as usual.'

'Not quite true – a glass of very dry sherry and two fingers of anchovy toast with old Mrs Trumpington. "Come to lunch, dear boy," she said!'

'Who's she leaving her wealth to this time . . . the Friends of Richard the Third?'

'You're at least two wills out of date, but naturally my lips are sealed!'

Mary smiled, and abandoned the subject of Mrs Trumpington for one that concerned her much more.

'Oliver, there was another posy left on Richard's grave this afternoon.'

'Odd . . . or is it? The village, in fact the entire district, must be full of people who remember him with affection.'

His mother stared at him, wondering whether she was justified in giving him her next piece of news. On the whole, she thought she was.

'I happened to walk back the other way, and went past Edwin's grave . . . there was a posy there too, identical to the one left for Richard.'

Oliver's face registered nothing at all, but there was a moment's silence before he said anything. 'And what do you deduce from that, my dear Mrs Sherlock Holmes?'

'That it was Jane who put them there,' she said steadily.

'Wishful thinking, Mama, any one of a dozen friends could have felt moved to single out those two graves and put flowers on them.'

'That's true, but I have a feeling all the same.'

Oliver grinned at her. 'Not your prophetic Highland grandmother again!'

His mother smiled too at the old family joke, but refused to be teased out of the conviction that had now taken root in her mind.

'You ought to hope that you *are* imagining things,' he suggested, suddenly serious again. 'I don't believe it for a moment, but if Jane were back in England in any permanent way it would mean that something had gone very wrong with her life.'

'That had occurred to me,' Mary said quietly. Her eyes met his own, asking questions he couldn't answer.

'Let's have that cup of tea you were talking about,' he said abruptly. The subject of Jane was over, apparently; but it was Oliver who returned to it as he was on the point of leaving.

'I can think of only one other person our wanderer might have applied to . . . Jim Watkins. There are things to talk about with him anyway; I'll give him a look-in on my way home.'

Mary kissed her son goodbye, comforted by the knowledge that if the possibility of Jane's being in England were now implanted in his mind, he would find her, however long it took.

Oliver called on Jim, and spent the first half-hour talking about a scheme dear to both their hearts. The older children in the school were being encouraged to help take care of the fabric of the village. There was a lot to commend it – busy children having less time to look for ways of raising hell than bored ones; and what they were responsible for taking care of they didn't, in Oliver's experience, want to vandalise. It was only when he'd emptied the tankard of beer Jim had put in front of him and stood up to go that he lobbed an unexpected question.

'Heard anything of Jane lately?'

Mr Watkins' pale-blue gaze fastened on the glass in his hand. 'Supposed to be in Belgium, isn't she?'

'Supposed to be,' Oliver agreed levelly. 'But if you've got different news of her I wish you'd share it with me, Jim.'

'Can't . . . promised not to say where she was.'

'But she *is* back in England?'

Jim nodded reluctantly. 'She telephoned, soon after your father's funeral, asked if I'd keep my ears open for any school jobs that might be going.'

'Were you able to help?'

'Yes, as a matter of fact. She's fixed up now, and getting run in during this back half of the summer term.'

'Did she say what had gone wrong in Brussels?'

'No, and I didn't ask. Not my business. If she wants to tell, she will. As long as she's all right, that's all that matters.'

'If I thought there was the slightest chance that you'd break a promise I'd go on badgering you, but I know when I'm wasting my time. Promise *me* something, though? If you hear from her again, will you ask her to get in touch with Mary? My mama's convinced she's over here, and worried that she might be in some kind of need. It's also hurtful that she ignores old friends.'

Jim agreed to deliver the message, but in the end it wasn't needed. With a cunning that would have astonished her son, Mary judged her own visits to the churchyard to coincide with the time when fresh flowers were being left on Edwin Kingsley's grave. She came to the conclusion that it was early on Saturday mornings, and made her own visit at eight o'clock the following Saturday. All she got for her pains was a glimpse of a bicycle being wheeled out of the far end of Vicarage Lane. She went at seven o'clock the next Saturday and was waiting when the cyclist arrived. Neither of them found anything to say for a moment, and Jane went very white. Her face had changed, leaving lovely bones more visible and her dark eyes shadowed. The short-cropped hair was growing now, not altogether tidily. She looked rather tired, and extremely thin.

'Jane, dear . . . I *knew* it was you,' Mary said simply. She held out her hands, but instead of taking them Jane suddenly enfolded Mary in her arms. Then they stared at each other, both blinking away tears.

'I'm so *sorry* about Richard . . . I saw it in *The Times*,' Jane said huskily.

'We were afraid to let you know, in case you felt you ought to come rushing over.'

'I *did* come, but the girl I spoke to from Brussels gave me the wrong time. I got here to find the funeral over, and the churchyard deserted. In a way I wasn't sorry, except that I'd wanted very much to see *you*. Are you managing all right?'

Mary smiled at the anxious question. 'I manage quite well, because I talk to Richard as if he were still here. Strangers probably think I'm mad, but the people in the village expect me to be dotty, so it doesn't matter. Oliver says I work too hard in the garden, and wants me to leave the old Vicarage, but I don't think I can; Richard's closest to me there.'

'Of course. Where else would his spirit be but in that garden?' Jane hesitated over her next question. 'Oliver called in at the gallery one day, but unfortunately I . . . I missed him. Is *he* all right?'

'He grieves for Richard quietly, and rather rattles around in that large house of his. But of course I do the same thing here.'

'Give him time, Mary dear! Instant grandchildren aren't quite possible, even in these high-tech days!'

Mrs Hatton gave a despairing snort. 'Grandchildren! What hope have I got? Oliver's becoming a confirmed batchelor.'

'You mean he . . . he *didn't* marry Estelle?'

'I don't know whether he ever really wanted to, but in any case she married someone else in the end – a man rich enough to buy her a theatre all to herself to prance around in. I sometimes wish Oliver would sell his house and move back here, but I don't suggest it because he'd feel obliged to agree. I expect he prefers a home of his own, and you can imagine the loving interest the village would take in his affairs.'

Jane gave the sudden grin that made her familiar again. 'Curly would advise him on the running of his love-life, and Gran Parsons would inspect any girl he invited home and pronounce her not nearly good enough!'

Mary seized the opening she'd been looking for. 'Speaking of other people's affairs, what about yours, Jane love? We can't help being interested, and I'm tired of being tactful – but it's not just idle curiosity.'

'My affairs are . . . are fluid at the moment,' Jane brought out after some thought. As an understatement it bordered on the sublime, but she could see that Mary considered it inadequate. 'I've started teaching again, thanks to Jim, who told me about a vacancy that had cropped up unexpectedly. I'm staying near the school with a nice widow lady, but I'll find something more permanent eventually.'

She saw the expression on Mary's face, and it brought back her own smile. 'I can't bear the effort you're making not to ask questions! Well, my continental adventure didn't work out. Jules is established now and doesn't need my help any longer, so I decided to come back here. That's all . . . no great tragedy!'

No great tragedy, but Mary thought her eyes looked haunted. She longed to ask a dozen other questions, but she was a woman who let herself be guided by instinct, even though Oliver did tease her about her Highland grandmother. Instinct told her not to persist. Too much pressure now and Jane would hide herself away completely somewhere where they might never find her.

'Come back and see the garden, it's looking beautiful,' Mary suggested instead.

Jane hesitated, anxious not to hurt her by refusing, but still more anxious not to run the risk of bumping into Oliver. She glanced at her watch and saw that it was still not eight o'clock. He'd have had to change his habits completely to be paying social calls for at least another couple of hours. 'Just a quick glance,' she agreed finally, 'then I must be on my way.'

She changed the flowers on her uncle's grave, while Mary attended to Richard's, then they walked back to the Vicarage together. The garden *was* beautiful: the groupings of colour were sometimes delicate, sometimes dramatic, but Richard Hatton's sure instinct had never failed. Jane stared at a clump of crimson peonies glowing beneath the blue blossom of a ceanothus tree and imagined she could hear Richard murmuring beside her, 'Lovely, isn't it, my dear, did you ever see anything so perfectly lovely?'

She was firm about refusing Mary's offer of coffee, and hoisted herself on her ancient bicycle instead. A pleading face was turned towards her. 'Jane, I've been very good about not plaguing you with questions, but won't you let us know where you are? We can't lose touch again, and there's something a bit uncertain about chance meetings in the churchyard at the crack of dawn.'

Jane frowned at her handle-bars, hating to hurt Mary but desperately determined to cling to being independent and anonymous. 'I'd tell you willingly, but you couldn't bear to have a secret from Oliver. If I'd seen you all at Richard's funeral I was going to pretend that I was just in England on a visit. I'd much rather that was still what he thought. He told me I was mad to marry Jules. I don't mind him being proved right, but I will *not* have him thinking he must start feeling responsible for me again. I'll lick a few wounds in private and learn to hoe my own furrow; after that I expect I'll start feeling sociable.'

She spoke so cheerfully that Mary was almost convinced there was no need to worry; but doubt came surging back the moment Jane had pedalled away. Instinct, which *she* knew was to be trusted even if her son did not, insisted that some hurt had been suffered which might never be recovered from. She dithered over what to say to Oliver, even whether to say anything at all; but when he strolled in the following morning, announcing that he'd come to give her lawns their Sunday trim, the words she'd told herself she wouldn't say blurted themselves out immediately.

'I saw Jane yesterday, in the churchyard.'

'And I suppose you smiled at each other and walked on?'

'Not quite, but she's not feeling very sociable at the moment . . . a bit on the defensive, trying to work out her salvation without well-intentioned lectures or help from anyone else.'

'If that's aimed at me, I certainly *should* lecture her,' Oliver commented grimly. 'By the sound of it, Legrand has collared everything she possessed – all the money from the sale of the Owl House, and most of its contents as well. My impression there was that the gallery is very much a going concern, thanks to Jane's inheritance; now the damned man should share the profits with her.'

'We don't know that he doesn't.'

'No, but even *you* sound doubtful. For any particular reason?'

'Only that she spoke of renting a room in a house near the school where she works . . . and she was riding the wreck of a bicycle.'

Oliver bit off a word his mother wasn't meant to hear. 'Do

I take it that you're in on the secret, but I'm still to be excluded from knowing where she is?'

'I'm excluded too,' Mary said gently. 'She knew I wouldn't be able to conceal anything from you.'

'God in Heaven!' he exploded. 'It's beyond all reason – insane! I'll camp in the churchyard until she turns up.'

'You're shouting, but please don't apologise; just listen to what I say, instead. Jane *is* irrational at the moment, but she must be allowed to come to terms with whatever happened in Brussels in her own way. If you try to strong-arm her, she'll disappear for good . . . I'm certain of that, Oliver.'

It was rarely that Mary Hatton spoke with such quiet authority; when she did he knew that it was time to listen. His ravaged face confirmed something she'd known all along, but he finally dropped an apologetic kiss on her cheek and went out to vent the frustration that consumed him on the lawns.

Mary made no effort to coincide with Jane again in the churchyard, clinging to the belief that they would hear from her when she was ready to emerge from hiding. But the school term ended, August came in, wet and unusually miserable, and she still made no attempt to pick up the threads of her old life. Mary began to doubt that she ever would. Oliver's temper got alarmingly short, and being with him was like living on the edge of a not-quite-sleeping volcano. Then one gloomy Saturday afternoon he had to stop the car at the traffic-lights in the centre of Abingdon, and glanced out of the window to keep an eye on a cyclist who'd ridden up to stop beside him. It looked . . . dear God, not only looked . . . it *was* Jane.

She paid no heed to the large cream station-wagon alongside her, being deeply concerned with the thought that a bicycle was an undesirable form of transport on a wet, windy day.

She wasn't even aware that the driver had quitted the car until a remembered voice spoke in her ear.

'Get off, Jane – I'll give you a lift.'

Had her heart stopped beating for good? She thought it seemed so. 'Oliver! No . . . No need, thanks . . . I haven't far to go.'

'For God's sake don't argue, just get in the car.'

The lights showed amber, then green, but she could do nothing about riding away because he now stood in front of her, gripping the handle-bars.

'We're blocking the traffic,' she said desperately. 'I'll give you a ring, Oliver.'

'You'll come with me now; otherwise we both stay here.'

The line of cars behind his own began to get restive; a van-driver who managed to squeeze past called out something they fortunately couldn't hear for the chorus of horns now giving voice. She glanced at Oliver's implacable face and admitted defeat, knowing he was capable of doing exactly what he'd said. She dismounted and walked round the car, while he lifted her bicycle and stowed it in the back. Then he kissed his hands to the waiting traffic-jam behind them, like an opera singer acknowledging rapturous applause, and got in beside her.

Sixteen

'My place or yours?' The deadpan enquiry told her that his sense of humour, never far from the surface, was beginning to get the upper hand again.

It was going to be hard to remain on her high horse, safely offended and unapproachable, but she did her best. 'It will have to be yours,' she answered finally. 'My landlady doesn't encourage gentlemen visitors.'

'Quite right, too.'

The virtuous agreement made her struggle with herself, but her only defence against him lay in staying remote, even if she couldn't manage actual hostility any longer. Oliver glanced at the face turned away from him to stare out of the window, and remembered too late what Mary had said about the uselessness of strong-arm tactics.

'Wet for the time of the year,' he suggested conversationally.

She bit her lip, still managing not to enter into the spirit of the thing, and enquired gruffly instead, 'What happened to the Rover? I'd have known it was you if I'd seen that.'

'Exactly! I was tempted to go about in heavy disguise, but then I realised the change of car would be enough to fox you. I assume you know what happened to your Metro.'

'Jim Watkins told me – an elderly lady finally wrote it off for him, believing that she was entitled to drive fast in the middle of the road.' It exhausted the subject of cars and she had to find something else to talk about.

'How's Mary?'

'Bearing up . . . waiting patiently to hear from you.'

This brought her to a halt again and she went back to considering the passing scene with passionate concentration.

Oliver glanced again at her still-averted face and decided that his only hope was to drive to Sutton Courtenay as fast as possible.

When they turned in at the gate the name of the house worked into wrought-iron caught her eye. 'Why Winterbrook?' she couldn't help asking.

'Because a brook does materialise in winter. When the river's high, a little stream finds it way through the orchard at the back.'

Inside the house the peace and comfort of his home enfolded her, making it impossible to go on feeling belligerent. It looked just as she'd imagined almost a year ago that it would – serenely beautiful and comfortable. How could a sane woman, offered this and its owner besides, have turned it down for anything else in God's creation?

'It's lovely, Oliver,' she said impulsively. 'I always knew it would be.' She hesitated over whether or not to refer to Estelle; it might seem unkind not to say she was sorry about his bitter disappointment, but her own sore need at the moment was to keep the conversation strictly impersonal.

'You look half-starved,' he stated bluntly, taking a dive himself into the personal. 'I missed lunch, and you seem to have given up eating altogether. We'll have a nice fattening high-tea in the kitchen.'

'I can't stay,' Jane said desperately. 'Maybe just a cup of tea . . .'

'Boiled eggs, toast and honey, and the indigestible fruit cake my secretary insists on unloading on me. She feels a fatal longing to play the mother, God help me!'

'Not still Miss . . . Miss ffarquharson, with two small effs?' Jane brought out the recollection with a sudden grin.

'The very same.'

It was reassuring that the conversation should have got itself onto such a pleasantly ordinary level. The idea of boiled eggs suddenly seemed enticing, too, reducing the occasion to a tea-party so harmless that the lengths she'd gone to to avoid him seemed suddenly ridiculous. The reunion continued harmlessly until he pushed aside his plate, announcing that he could eat no more. Then, arms folded on the table in front of him, he fixed her with a grey stare. 'I've fed you up, you realise, for the serious business ahead.'

She saw the thin ice she'd been resting on crack all round her, but she managed to answer calmly. 'Sorry, but I don't want to talk about serious things. The tea was lovely, and I've enjoyed seeing you again, but now I'm going to climb on my bicycle and go home.'

'You no longer have a home,' he pointed out gently. 'I'm your solicitor, remember? The chap you're supposed to confide in freely. If I have to drag it out of you bit by bloody bit I will, but I'd much rather you just started talking. You might begin by explaining why you were too busy to see an old friend when he called on you in Brussels. That rankled, Janey.'

Her eyes met his for a moment, then looked away again. 'I didn't know . . . not until I got your letter,' she mumbled. The realisation was dawning on her that it would be a blessed relief to talk. There was nothing but stupid injured pride to prevent her crawling out of her dark little tunnel of isolation into the daylight of recovered friendship. All she had to do was sound brisk and unsorry for herself. As long as Oliver wasn't obliged to feel that he must look after her again, no harm would be done.

'You saw the gallery,' she began slowly, 'so you know how beautiful it is. You can't imagine what it looked like when Jules took the place over, but after a huge amount of hard work the opening exhibition was very successful – fortunately, because we were heavily in debt by then. The money from the sale of the Owl House eventually paid off the bank loan, and slowly but surely the paintings began to sell very well. Jules has slaved to make it a success, and there's no doubt that it is. He works all the time, and pays attention to even the smallest detail, but there's more to a successful gallery that that: running it *is* his proper *métier* – something he's brilliant at.' She stopped, aware that the easy part had been said.

'It all sounds hunky-dory so far,' Oliver prompted her. 'What went wrong?'

'I suppose Jules and I did,' she admitted painfully. 'But it was my fault, because what he found so enjoyable, I disliked more and more. I grew to hate the ceaseless round of entertaining, and I couldn't pretend to enjoy the fashionable rich people I was meant to make friends with. I was bored and rather lonely until an artist friend put me on to some work that I could do, teaching English at a reform school! It was hair-raising to begin with, but although I came to value it in the end, I knew it was only a stop-gap. Sooner or later I had to decide – whether I could bear to stay, or bear to admit that my marriage had become a failure.'

Oliver filled the next little silence. 'So you finally decided to go – walked out one day, just like that?'

'Not quite – I saw the notice about Richard in *The Times*. When I told Jules I wanted to attend the funeral he reminded me that we were committed to a reception he'd set his heart on. I dare say it sounds trivial to you, but you can't understand without knowing his past history. Jules needed a lot of convincing that he'd achieved his rightful place in the world. The proof was there at last, and I proposed to absent myself on one of the few occasions when he still had a use for me.' She glanced at Oliver's face, and forestalled what he might have said. 'The mistakes *were* mine all along. I can see that quite clearly now.'

'Go on,' he insisted harshly. 'Convince me that you deserve the treatment you've received.'

She chose instead to return to her story. 'We had an argument, of course, and Jules issued an ultimatum: stay, or don't come back. Well, I couldn't *not* say goodbye to Richard, and it seemed the moment to admit that I was trying to share my life with someone who would never think the things important that I did.' She smiled ruefully across the table. 'Even then, my grand gesture of independence misfired, because I was given the wrong time for the funeral and arrived when it was over. But it meant at least that you didn't know I was here, and so I decided to remain invisible.'

'Yes, and we take it amiss, I must say. It isn't the way to treat old friends.'

'I did contact one old friend – Jim Watkins. He helped me find a job at a school in Abingdon. I wasn't sure how Jules would feel about a divorce, so I didn't rush into asking for one. But he wants it himself now . . . at least, an annulment, on the grounds that our marriage wasn't properly consummated. Another of my failures!'

She even managed to smile as she said it, determined that

the solicitor she was supposed to confide in should know the extent of her inadequacy as a wife. But he seemed for once bereft of words, and she went on talking herself. 'I think the next Madame Legrand is probably lined up – a widowed lady with wealth of her own and all the right connections. I hope they'll be happy together.'

'I have a different wish myself,' Oliver said grimly, 'but leaving that aside for the moment, it's all wrong that things should remain as they are. Legrand gets everything, Jane, including what was your inheritance; you no longer even have a home.'

She shook her head in a gesture he recognised – Jane Kingsley with her mind made up.

'I won't have a squalid fight about money. Helping Jules to make a success of things is the only justification I have left for what is otherwise an awful mess. I can't regret it, or start haggling now over who owns what.'

The careful guard that Oliver had been keeping on self-control abruptly deserted him. 'Damn it, Jane, the man's not worth it,' he shouted. 'The truth is that you don't want him harassed because you're still infatuated with him.'

Her own schooled face broke into a look of such wincing pain that his anger died. 'I was never infatuated with him – *that*'s why I don't want him harassed. Jules called me a cheat, and he was right. Instead of marrying him, I should just have helped him get the gallery started. He wanted a child, but I seemed incapable of giving him one. In moments of real despair I used to remember Miss Prentice and come to the conclusion that I was just like her after all – born to be a spinster!'

'My dear girl, you're talking balderdash! You're no more like Miss Prentice than I'm like the man in the moon, and why be so bloody humble suddenly? Why shouldn't the failure to produce a child have been Legrand's, not yours?'

'I don't think so,' she said quietly. 'I was given to understand that it was my . . . my performance that was inadequate; other women hadn't found it hard to be responsive.'

Oliver understood at last the fullness of the damage that had been done to her. It would have given him infinite pleasure to batter Jules Legrand into the dust, but all he could do was set about rebuilding the inner confidence in herself that had been so completely destroyed.

'Listen, Jane, from the moment I came back to England last year you were determined to show me that the past was over and done with, but you might remember that once or twice I did get near enough to touch you. I promise you that I was *not* touching a woman incapable of passion, and I'll be happy to prove it to you now if you'll let me.'

He was watching her as she thought a stoat must stare at a rabbit it wanted to mesmerise. A small wrong move on her part now would pitchfork them into disaster. She forced her mouth to smile, and spoke with unbearable brightness. 'Dear Oliver, you're a lawyer beyond price, but there's a limit to the services you're supposed to supply. I think I *won't* take you up on your kind offer.'

She thought she sounded so repellently cheap that it was no surprise to have him abandon the subject at once. 'What about the annulment . . . shall I start that moving?'

'I want it over and done with as soon as possible, but please don't be offended if I give Jules the name of another solicitor.'

'Because you still don't trust me?'

'You know it's not that. But he will be more difficult if you are involved. He never forgave you over the instruments, and for no reason at all he was always jealous of you.'

'For once you're being less than fair. There *was* a reason, and he knew perfectly well what it was.'

'You mean he thought I hadn't outgrown my childish crush on you?' she enquired hoarsely.

'Much worse than that from his point of view – any man worth his salt can cope with childish crushes. What unsettled him was the knowledge that there was nothing childish about my crush on you!'

There was complete silence in the room for a moment or two; then came a reaction he certainly didn't expect. Jane was catapulted out of composure into shouting at him.

'Stop it, Oliver. I won't have you going to these ridiculous lengths to patch me up again. Next you'll pretend you want to marry me, because it's a way of offering me the home you think I no longer have.' She was trembling uncontrollably now, all the misery and loneliness of the past months flooding like a tidal wave over the careful little defences she'd built up against them. Then rage spent itself as suddenly as it had come, and tears trickled down her face instead, clogging her throat. 'You're kindness itself, but I won't have it . . .'

'As usual, you've got it all wrong, my darling.' His very quietness made her listen to him. 'Whatever I offer you is for my own sake, not yours. You *would* persist in the barmy notion that I was longing to marry Estelle. She knew perfectly well what the truth was, but she was kind enough to aid and abet the impression that we were having a desperate affair . . . quite her best performance so far, I'd say! You were so determined to throw Legrand in my face all the time that I had to try to persuade you not to bother. The truth is that I've loved you, almost without knowing it, since you were a lost and lonely child, but I think I fell in love with you on your twenty-fifth birthday. I offered you Richard's jonquils then, and if I'd had the slightest grain of sense I'd have offered you myself as well – much time wasted, and more misery than I can bear to think about.'

He so nearly made it sound the truth, she thought sadly. In a way it *was* true, but it wasn't the whole truth. She'd married Jules because she felt in some way responsible, and linked to him by the thread of events that couldn't be cancelled. That was exactly how Oliver thought about her, and she knew now that it wasn't a sufficient reason for marriage. She rubbed the back of her hand across her face, wiping away the trace of tears.

'You look about ten years old, doing that!' He smiled at her, remembering the lonely child who'd tagged uncomplainingly at his heels, refusing to ask him to go more slowly or walk less far. 'The trouble is, you're not ten years old . . . I can't browbeat you any longer, and you look alarmingly indifferent to a man who's just offered you his all.'

It cost him a great deal to sound light enough for her to be able to smile at him. But the shadow in her eyes warned him that he must be very careful. Her pride was great and it was the last thing she had left now.

'I'm not indifferent, I'm very grateful, and so should you be that I'm not taking up such a quixotic offer.'

Oliver hesitated a bare ten seconds too long, then it was too late. She'd opened the kitchen door and let herself out into the garden. He followed her, went to the car, and told her briefly not to argue about the fact that he was going to drive her home. There was nothing to do but direct him to a house on the outskirts of Abingdon. She scrambled out before he could come round to help her.

'Don't wait, I can see Mrs Cantripp at the window.'

'Damn Mrs Cantripp,' Oliver said savagely, and drove away.

Seventeen

Her bicycle was outside the house next morning, neatly lodged against the railing. In her hurry to escape the previous day she'd forgotten it in the back of the car, and suspected that Oliver hadn't remembered it either. She mentally thanked him for returning it, but regretted that he now knew where she lived. It probably no longer mattered; she'd refused the offer he'd felt obliged to make – now he could ignore her with a clear conscience in future. Mrs Cantripp, though rather too curious, was better than the devil landlady she didn't know, and in any case she couldn't keep on moving.

It was, at least, a comfort to be able to give up avoiding Mary Hatton. They'd been friends for too long for that not to hurt, and both of them were lonely. Her visits to the Vicarage were resumed, but it wasn't lost on Mary that they always occurred when Oliver was certain to be penned inside his office in Oxford. With a self-control that she was privately very proud of, she didn't ask why some other solicitor was dealing with the unravelling of the Legrand marriage; in fact, for all the mention she made of Oliver it would have been difficult to guess that she had a son at all.

One morning, though, over coffee in the garden, she approached the subject obliquely.

'Jim says the new school term starts next week – I suppose

that means I shall only see you at weekends in future. Sunday is the day Oliver tears himself away from Winterbrook to visit me.'

'I'll remember that,' Jane said with a faint smile. 'Guests are better as single spies, not as battalions!'

Fobbed off neatly, Mary made a more direct attack. 'Jane, dear, I'm sure the school in Abingdon is very nice, but are you going to be content with it forever, and rooms in someone else's house? Why not come and share the Vicarage with me – wouldn't I do as well as Mrs Cantripp?'

'Better by far,' she was assured unsteadily, 'but, dear Mary, I *have* to paddle my own canoe, not be rescued again by the Hatton family! I enjoy my job, but it may not be what I always do. I've resurrected an old ambition to write – I've made a start, in fact, and I'm even rather pleased with it, so perhaps I'll be a successful author one day after all.'

The subject of the future was allowed to drop, and in the flurry of getting ready for the new term it was a couple of weeks before Jane pedalled over to Little Fairford again, deliberately on a Saturday. She found Mary in Richard's conservatory as usual, among the flowering plants he'd loved, but for once she wasn't talking to them. Her face was wet with tears which she tried to blink away as her visitor appeared.

'What's wrong – tell me, please,' Jane said immediately.

Mary shook her head. 'Nothing's really wrong . . . I'm just being a stupid old woman.' She brushed a hand over her eyes and tried to smile. 'Take no notice . . . I'm being ridiculous.'

'We'll agree that you're a ridiculous, stupid, old woman; *now* tell me what's upsetting you.'

'Oliver's going away again,' Mary confessed, suddenly caving in. 'He's put Winterbrook up for sale.'

'I can't believe it!' Jane managed to mutter. 'How can he *think* of leaving you here alone . . . where is he going?'

'Back to America. He . . . when I asked him why . . . he said there was no future for him here, so he might as well try again over there.' She wiped her eyes again and looked ruefully at Jane. 'Mother hen with one chick syndrome! I *know* he has to live his own life . . . I just wish he wasn't going to the place that turned out so badly for him before.'

Jane spent the rest of the afternoon with Mary, turning over in her mind again the idea that had been mooted before. But before she offered to move into the Vicarage as a permanent lodger she needed to tell Oliver Hatton precisely what she thought of him. It had to be done immediately, before rage cooled, and she intended doing it on the way home. She pedalled herself into a state of flushed and breathless indignation, which was ignited into flames by the sight of the 'For Sale' board standing on the grass verge outside his house. She sailed up the drive, rehearsing in her mind what she'd come to say, and stopped abruptly as Oliver stepped out of the car parked in front of her.

'Jane – what an unexpected pleasure.' His manner was genial, but he took account of the fact that there was no answering smile, and that he was being regarded as she might have stared at a particularly poisonous reptile.

'It's not a social call,' she said stiffly. 'I've come to bawl you out, Oliver.'

'Then I think I'd rather you did it indoors. Inside, if you please.'

She obeyed the crisp instruction automatically, and then wished she hadn't; it would have been much easier to say what she'd come to say and leave again, while still clinging firmly to her bicycle.

He led the way into the drawing-room, and she had to follow him or shout at him from the front door.

'A glass of sherry, even though it isn't a social call?' he suggested courteously.

'No thanks, I'm not staying. I just want to tell you that I think you're . . . you're *rotten*, Oliver Hatton!' So much for all the telling phrases she'd rehearsed on the way there. The sheer, bathetic childishness of 'rotten'!

'Why? Because I'm about to sell a house that's much too big for me?'

'Because you're proposing to go dancing off to America again. Mary tries so hard to pretend that she can manage without Richard, but it's cruel of you to make her manage without you as well. I wouldn't have believed you could be so selfish and hurtful.'

'You find other things easier to believe – like the fact that I don't mean it when I say I love you, because you're too afraid to let me prove it to you.' He spoke calmly but his eyes were on her face, aware of the tremor of a different emotion she was now struggling with.

'You're changing the subject – stick to the point,' she said doggedly.

'It *is* the point. Let me convince you, and I'll abandon the idea of going to America. How's that for a bargain?'

'It's not a bargain, it's blackmail!'

Oliver appeared to consider the point. 'Technically, I think, it would be classified as coercion. We might as well get the legal niceties correct.'

She eyed him uncertainly, aware that the interview had somehow got out of hand. 'Whatever it is, you're joking, of course, but the joke's gone far enough.'

'Wrong again, my darling. It's no joke; just a simple

proposition: we go to bed together and prove whether you're a second Miss Prentice or whether I can rejoice my mama's heart by staying here after all . . . with you.'

She bit her lip, trying to find some way out of the terrible pit she'd dug for herself. Long knowledge of the man watching her so carefully told her that she would not be let off the hook; since childhood he'd taken care of her up to a point; after that she'd been allowed to reap whatever stubbornness or stupidity deserved. But he'd never been cruel, and she didn't suppose now that he had any idea of the mortal terror that consumed her. It would have been no hardship to give her life to make him happy, but to have him get up from her bed frustrated, disgusted, or simply bored would be a mortification she would never recover from. She couldn't say so; instead, she must take a deep breath and stare at him – he told her afterwards, like Marie Antoinette going to the guillotine – with the bedrock courage that is rooted in despair.

'Very well . . . let's get it over with.'

She saw his mouth twitch, break into a grin, and a moment later give a shout of laughter. 'I'm s-sorry, my dear one, but there must be more enthusiastic ways of accepting such an invitation!'

The outraged expression on her face made matters worse, but she couldn't continue to glare at him; she'd never in her life been able to resist sharing a joke with Oliver. A smile crept into her eyes, grew on her mouth, and a moment later she was in the same helpless condition as he was himself. For the first time in months and years she felt sadness and anxiety slip from her shoulders . . . she was young again, just happy to be laughing with him. Even when he walked over to her, with amusement still dying out of his grey eyes, panic didn't reassert itself. His hands held her shoulders lightly, making no demands.

'Forgive me, Jane. I couldn't hold you to such an infamous bargain. Why should it prove anything when I've already had one failure of my own?'

She didn't believe it, and the volte-face was worse than anything that had gone before; Marie Antoinette reprieved at the last minute when she'd screwed up courage to the point of accepting an heroic end.

'I insist on the bargain,' she said furiously. 'I'm going to be made love to *now*!'

A smile touched his mouth for a moment, and was banished with all the self-control he possessed. 'Then so you shall,' he agreed with the utmost gravity, scooping her up in his arms, and carrying her upstairs.

An hour later he raised himself on one elbow to look down at her.

'Ghost of Miss Prentice satisfactorily laid would you say, my love?'

'Poor Miss Prentice.' A world of pity was in her voice. 'Poor every woman who isn't me!'

'Content to *that* extent?' he asked, smiling at her. 'You look beautiful, and quite astonishingly happy . . . I pray I can always keep you so.'

'It won't be very difficult – just as long as you'll try to love me forever, and let me love you.'

'No effort involved, it comes as naturally as breathing. In fact the only fly in the ointment of utter bliss is the knowledge that I've soon got to admit to my dear mother that she was right all along. She would insist that all I had to do for perfect happiness was wait until you'd grown big enough to be marry-able.'

'I despaired of ever being big enough,' Jane confessed. 'I wasn't meant to overhear it, but I was the "sexless waif" you couldn't be expected to take care of for the rest of our natural lives! That's why I managed to convince myself when you came back from New York that I could love Jules – I had to look as if I'd finally outgrown *you*. But he knew all along that the wrong man was touching me, so you see I did *him* some damage, too.'

'And I was an intolerably arrogant young man to have said such a thing. I'm sorry you heard it, dear heart, but it was simply born of irritation – nowhere near the truth, as we've just proved so satisfactorily! Between us, we've taken some terrible risks with happiness . . . we shall have to do better in future.'

Far below, the faint ping of the doorbell made Oliver glance at his watch and give an agonised groan. 'Oh God, I forgot – someone was coming to be shown over the house.'

'At this hour of the night?' Jane asked indignantly. Then her face changed as a dreadful thought occurred to her. 'What on earth am I going to do about my landlady? Mrs Cantripp is so terribly particular. Would it be worse to turn up now, or not go home at all?'

'It's only eight o'clock, my love,' Oliver said, grinning at her. 'It may seem as if we've been here for hours, but I have every intention of staying a bit longer. I'll restore you to Mrs Cantripp at a still respectable hour, I promise.'

Another more insistent ring at the doorbell floated upstairs. 'Shouldn't you do something about whoever's there?' she asked. 'If you appear swathed in a dressing-gown, coughing heartily, they'll think you've got the 'flu and rush away.'

'They'll go away in any case in a moment or two. I normally refuse to let anybody come, but my daily thought she was being helpful this morning and told them to call.'

Still wrestling with the problem presented by Mrs Cantripp, Jane was slow in registering what he'd just said.

'Refuse to let people come? How did you expect to sell the house if you didn't show it to anyone?'

'I had no intention of selling the house, I like it,' Oliver explained. 'I hope you like it too, but if not, my love, we'll look—'

She reached out to put a hand over his mouth. 'You have a 'For Sale' board outside . . . I saw it.'

'Of course. My dear mother is almost as bad an actress as Estelle; I couldn't rely on *her* to convince you that I was leaving.'

She stared up at him, torn between the need to seem scandalised and a strong desire to give in to the laughter welling up inside her. 'Let me get this straight: you let Mary think you were going to America when you hadn't the slightest intention of doing so?'

'That is essentially correct,' he admitted, pushed into a corner.

'You're outrageous . . . totally unprincipled . . . and a *lawyer*, too! Mary was heartbroken when I saw her this afternoon.'

'I'm sorry about that,' Oliver mumbled, 'but I had to do something to flush you out of cover. She'll forgive me when she hears that we've agreed to toe her line at last.' He grew serious again, considering the future. 'I'm sure Mrs Cantripp is an estimable lady, but I'm not going to leave you with her while we wait for your divorce to come through. We've wasted too many years already, and my mama is fast losing hope of the grandchildren who were to brighten her old age.'

Jane's face clouded with the instant fear that Mary might still be disappointed, but Oliver kissed her mouth gently, knowing what was in her mind.

'How about Richard William for our first-born? After that *you* can choose.'

His grey eyes smiled at her, telling her that there was nothing to fear, and now she could be certain of it herself.

'It sounds very odd, suggesting that we should get up at eight o'clock in the evening! But let's go over to Little Fairford and tell Mary,' she suggested.

'Let's not, but I agree that we should telephone later on.' He climbed out of bed all the same, and swathed himself in a dressing-gown. 'Don't go away, my heart . . . I'll be right back.'

'What did you do?' she asked, when he returned again. 'Sneeze over the callers?'

'No, they'd given up and gone away, but I had the presence of mind to scrawl "SOLD" across the board. Now, *pace* Mrs Cantripp, the rest of the evening is ours.'

CURLEW ISLAND

CURLEW ISLAND

Sally Stewart

PAN BOOKS

This edition published 1999 by Pan Books
an imprint of Macmillan Publishers Ltd
25 Eccleston Place, London SW1W 9NF
Basingstoke and Oxford
Associated companies throughout the world
www.macmillan.co.uk

This first world edition published in Great Britain 1997 by
SEVERN HOUSE PUBLISHERS LTD of
9-15 High Street, Sutton, Surrey SM1 1DF
First published in the USA 1997 by
SEVERN HOUSE PUBLISHERS INC of
595 Madison Avenue, New York, NY 10022.

British Library Cataloguing in Publication Data
Stewart, Sally
Curlew Island
I. Cullin Island (Imaginary place) – Fiction 2. Love stories
I. Title
823.9'14 [F]

ISBN 0 330 39656 0

Typeset by Hewer Text Composition Services, Edinburgh
Printed and bound in Great Britain by
Mackays of Chatham plc, Chatham, Kent

The island of Cullin will not be found
on any Hebridean map . . . you must go there
by candlelight, and back again.

Chapter One

Fran usually enjoyed the walk from her tiny flat in Pimlico to Aunt Ernestine's mews house just off Berkeley Square. The waves of irritable commuters flowing out of Victoria always made her feel grateful to be living in the heart of the city. She refused to join in the fashionable game of lamenting London's decline; to her it was still whatever one's mood required – impressively grand, or intimately charming in its less-visited corners. If time allowed during her morning journey, she dawdled through St James's Park for a chat with the pelicans and ducks; if not, it was the quick route through Green Park and a suicidal dash across the traffic streaming along Piccadilly.

But today wasn't a day for walking. A cool, rainy summer was merging unnoticed into autumn, and she was getting tired of days of splashed tights, wet shoes and rain-soaked hair. Come to think of it, she was getting tired altogether. Aunt Ernestine's agency was becoming almost too successful, and visitors searching for help of one kind or another had streamed into the mews all summer, in varying states of need, bewilderment, or outright panic. Whatever they might have been expecting from an agency that called itself 'Campbell's Comfort', Fran suspected that it wasn't what confronted them in Ernestine Campbell. Six feet tall and very thin, with a decidedly Roman nose and an

Edwardian fringe of improbably bright red hair, she'd even overawed her niece to begin with. That was three years ago. Now they were friends as well as relatives and business associates. A helpful receptionist sifted the customers; two young Campbell cousins dealt with the common demands – met nervous grandmothers off trains, delivered boisterous children to airports, and acted as butler and waitress to crisis-ridden hostesses. Aunt Ernestine interviewed more interesting clients and handed their problems to Fran to deal with. She was, she said, too old for legwork herself.

Fran let herself into the house wondering what the day's harvest of oddities would be – nothing, she hoped, like yesterday's rainy research into half a dozen London houses known to have been lived in by Victorian poets. Ernestine was grinning when she went into the office – always a warning sign.

"Morning, Fran. You're looking bedraggled again." She patted her fringe, secure in the knowledge that every bright red hair was in place after the only journey required of her – a morning stroll downstairs from her living quarters on the top floor.

"I'm still drying out from yesterday. Could we add the cost of a ruined pair of shoes to the bill?"

"Why not?" Ernestine brushed the shoes aside. "Got something really nice for you next – a little trip to Scotland."

"You mean someone wants a tartan matched at the Scotch House?"

"Fran dear – Scotland, I said. Call yourself a Campbell and you've never been north of Manchester. Business ought to slacken off a bit now, so I've agreed to spare you. In any case, it will be a little holiday for you."

The smug expression on her aunt's face was irritating.

"I had nothing to do with being given the name of Campbell," Fran pointed out, "and if I'm allowed a holiday I'm going somewhere where it doesn't rain . . . ergo, anywhere but Scotland."

Ernestine gave her toothy, crocodile grin and spoke of something else, but two days later Fran found herself leaving London with a hired car and an American called Tod Harriman – destination Scotland! She might have preferred to be going almost anywhere else, but at least she'd liked the look of Mr Harriman. He was small and round, and clean as a new pin; everything about him, white hair, pink skin, and shirt with neatly buttoned-down collar, spoke of frequent laundering. But she suspected there was more to Mr Harriman than that. His eyes were bright and observant; nobody's fool was her American charge. He'd treated Aunt Ernestine like a duchess; in fact, misled by her manner and the Roman nose, perhaps thought she was one. Fran he treated like a princess. He settled himself beside her in the car, wondering what he'd done to deserve such a companion. Long, corn-coloured hair lay in a plait over one shoulder, and he found himself waiting for the smile that started in dark blue eyes long before it reached her beautiful mouth. Tod's luck they'd have called it, back in Nebraska.

Fran was wrong about the rain. From the moment they stepped off the overnight motor rail at Edinburgh the sun shone, and continued to shine for the two weeks they spent looking at the city. It was scarcely the holiday her aunt had promised, though. Apart from acting as chauffeuse, her job was to make notes of the information Tod was hellbent on collecting, and he went about it with the excited tenacity of a terrier hunting down rabbit holes. Out of all their work would come, she now knew, another of the guides that had made him a household name in America. 'Touring with Tod' had become the inseparable travelling companion of countless Americans setting out for the dangerous delights of the Old World. With Tod's chatty volumes to tell them what to see, what not to eat, and how to cope with the natives, it seemed that they felt both knowledgeable and safe.

Fran began the adventure by not taking it very seriously, but within two days she'd come to the conclusion that her funny little client was certainly not a joke; at the end of two weeks they were firm friends, and she was valuing properly the mixture of gentle courtesy, fun, and shrewdness that made up Tod Harriman.

They eventually headed north-west, skirted Loch Linnhe, and arrived one evening at Fort William after a long day's drive. It had been a perfect journey, Scotland at its rarely visible best – heather-covered moorland glowing amethyst in the October sunshine, sapphire-coloured lochs lying quietly in the folds of hills that were beginning to burn with the colours of autumn. Rather to her surprise, Tod failed to enthuse about it over dinner.

"You're quiet," she smiled at him. "Have you seen it all before in other places – grander perhaps . . . more beautiful?"

Tod shook his head. "Nothing better than today – ever. But from now on the trip isn't just another job, Fran – it's a pilgrimage. You've probably been wondering why I set my heart on going to an island most people have never heard of when we had places like Skye, or Mull, or Iona to choose from. Well, Cullin's a lifelong ambition for me . . . the crock of gold at the end of the rainbow."

"Why . . . family beginnings?" she queried gently. "Harriman doesn't strike me as a Scottish name."

"It isn't, but my granny was a McDougall. The Clearances were long over, of course, but poverty wasn't. She went out to America as a young girl to find work; married there, stayed for the rest of her life, and never went back to Cullin. She was a proud, reserved woman, taciturn you might say. But when a small boy cajoled her into talking about her childhood the result was poetry. I knew that I should have to go and see it for myself one day, but I've been saving it all these years."

Fran could only send up an urgent little prayer that he wouldn't be disappointed; an old lady's reminiscences were one thing, but fifty years later reality might be a cruel let-down.

The next morning they went on north and west to Mallaig and the steamer that would carry them up the Sound of Sleat towards Cullin. When they reached the port and garaged the car, Fran was entranced by the bustle of it, the smell of salt air, tar and fish, and the endless cries of the seagulls lining every roof. The morning was still sunny, but different from the golden days of the past fortnight. She thought the sea looked wonderfully inviting, then noticed that instead of his normal eagerness for their next adventure, Tod was showing an unusual reluctance to embark. While they threaded the channel between the mainland and Skye, he managed to stay fairly jaunty. A brief call at Portree was welcome, but with Raasay and Rona left behind the boat dipped into open water and a steadily freshening wind.

"Dammit, you're enjoying this," he said accusingly after a sharper lunge than usual made him anchor himself to the rail. "You keep insisting you're a city girl but you look as if you'd been born and bred to this kind of malarkey."

She couldn't help smiling at him. "I *am* a dyed-in-the-wool Londoner . . . natural habitat Bond Street!"

"Well, at that, Bond Street's a good deal nearer the ocean than Norfolk, Nebraska. Perhaps that accounts for it."

"Won't be long, Tod. Another quarter of an hour and we should be coming into Kirktown harbour. We could probably see it by now if the water weren't quite so choppy."

Tod closed his eyes and swallowed hard, determined somehow not to disgrace himself in front of an island race.

"Cullin Castle sounds pretty grand," she commented cheerfully, anxious to take his mind off the next ten minutes. "Just the sort of place you'd expect to see Lucia di Lammermoor haunting the battlements, wringing her hands."

Tod could spare no thought for poor, mad Lucia. "I don't care *what* it's like, honey, so long as it doesn't move up and down."

At last a sudden quietness in the wind encouraged him to open his eyes; they were chugging through smooth water along an estuary that ran into the heart of a little grey town. It huddled on level ground between the sea and the hills that provided its grand backdrop. They were coloured green, then grey-brown, and finally purple where the afternoon sun glowed on bare rock. Fran liked the look of Kirktown. There was nothing self-consciously picturesque about it; visitors could admire it or not, as they felt inclined. Kirktown had more important things to think about – like a living to be wrested from the hills and the surrounding sea.

Tod's face changed the moment he stepped onto

dry land, but it wasn't just because it stayed firm beneath his feet, and Fran was touched into sharing his wonder. It had taken a small boy a long time, but he was on Granny McDougall's home ground at last. She pointed in the direction of an antiquated minibus with the words 'Cullin Castle' painted on it, and they clambered apologetically on board over the legs, fishing rods, and golf bags of passengers who were already installed. The bus wheezed and wound its way up a road that snaked around the hillside. On one side the land dropped in rocky terraces towards the sea along the southern coast of the island. On the other, more hills rose above them, climbing inland to a great basalt crag shouldering its way into the sky.

"Beinn Mhor," Fran said knowledgeably, consulting her map.

They turned the south-western corner of the island and the landscape suddenly changed. Glens still vividly green after the summer nestled between gentle hills clothed in birch and rowan trees; higher up, as the slopes grew steeper, the dark green of pines took over. At last a grand gateway signalled the entrance to what must be the Castle; at least it had once been grand, but the stone pillars topped by supercilious-looking unicorns were pitted by the salt air, and the handsome gates that should have hung there were missing. A swathe of neatly mown grass bordered the drive, but it was the Castle's only concession to neatness; for the rest, the grounds were a jungle of wild rhododendrons, azaleas, and old roses that climbed rampant and unpruned over anything that could be climbed upon. The Castle itself appeared unexpectedly, hidden until the last moment by a twist in the drive. It was a hybrid sort of place – part tall and starkly beautiful Scottish keep, part miniature French chateau with pepper-pot turrets and curlicues rioting with the same abandon as the roses in the garden.

Busy looking round, Fran and Tod straggled through the door long after the other guests had disappeared. A vast, stone-flagged hall was redeemed from bleakness by a log fire burning in a cavernous fireplace, but nothing could redeem the bleakness of the rest of their welcome.

A tall man dressed in sweater and shabby kilt stood behind the reception desk, watching them cross the hall. Dark, unfriendly eyes inspected Fran's hyacinth-coloured slacks and suede jacket, switched to Tod and stared at his undeniably vibrant check coat. She found it hard to believe . . . they were paying customers, guests deserving courtesy, but she was aware that they were being weighed and found wanting. She waited for the man to speak, suddenly sure of what he'd say – there was no booking for them. Well, Londoner she might be, but the blood of a long line of fighting Campbells was beginning to rise – he would find himself confronting an enemy.

"Good afternoon . . . you have rooms reserved for us, I believe – Mr Harriman and Miss Campbell." The deliberate Kensington drawl sounded much more confident than she felt, and it was no surprise to see him shake his head.

"I'm afraid there is some mistake – nothing is available *here* . . . I am sorry." The apology was perfunctory enough to have been missed altogether, and she was maddened by the implication that the empty landscape between the Castle and Kirktown was littered with alternative places for wanderers to try.

"An agency in London made the booking. In fact it was my aunt, Miss Campbell, who telephoned."

"Then your aunt is the lady who rang off before

Jaime could explain the situation," he pointed out coldly. "What he would have said given the time is – yes, we have rooms; no, we cannot accept guests, being very short of staff."

Fran put aside the memory of Aunt Ernestine in fully cry. She could indeed be brusque to the point of rudeness on the telephone, and she never believed in wasting words in long-distance conversations. But the sight of Tod's despairing face said that something must be done. He couldn't be put off Cullin now by a scandalously unfriendly hotel-keeper; nor could he face that heaving stretch of water again between them and the mainland, at least for a little while.

"If rooms are free, please let us take them," she said as pleasantly as possible. "We'll make allowances for staff problems, as presumably the other people who've just arrived will have to do."

Dark eyes met and clashed with blue. "They are all old friends . . . accustomed to our ways."

Fran bit back the acid comment that friends were the last thing she'd have expected the Castle occupant to be rich in. Sauciness might get them rejected altogether; she wouldn't even put it past this surly Gael to dump them bodily outside the door.

"We'll be forbearance itself," she promised sweetly.

"For one night?"

"For one week." Once again their glance met and locked in battle; then, much to her surprise, he gave a little shrug and wrote something in the register in front of him.

"You'll be needing a ghillie, Mr Harriman," he suggested, casting an eye over the expensive luggage strewn all round them.

"Nope," said Tod, entering the conversation for the first time. "I'm not a fisherman."

"You play golf, then. The course is small – only nine holes – but you'll find it quite testing."

There was no hint of a golf bag either, and the Highlander's desire to needle was obvious, but Tod had a weapon of his own – he simply refused to be provoked.

"I haven't come to play golf either. But you don't have to worry about us. Fran and me'll have a lovely time."

"I don't think we're being worried about, exactly," she was forced to point out. The message she was receiving was indeed quite different. Tod wasn't the sort of guest likely to become an old friend, and she was even worse – not only a Campbell, which was probably a crime in itself in these parts, but an expensive-looking Sassenach who'd desert her elderly American if younger pickings offered themselves. She was enraged by the unfairness of it, and on tenterhooks in case Tod's introduction to his precious crock of gold should be completely ruined. It *would* have to be on Cullin itself that things began to go so badly wrong.

"We've done a lot of travelling," she said quietly at last. "Perhaps we could be shown our rooms?"

The man behind the desk bowed slightly and spoke through the open door to someone in the room behind him.

"Jaime will show you the way and see to your luggage."

Tod was decanted on the first floor, Fran taken through a rabbit warren of corridors on the second. This message was clear too: there was to be no nocturnal visiting. Humour was restored by the reflection that it would have taken Ariadne's thread to lead her to Tod's room through the maze of Cullin Castle, but her smile won no response from Jaime. He was polite but untalkative, and had the dark, closed face of the man downstairs. The island seemed to breed its menfolk dour when not downright hostile.

"What time is dinner?" Fran asked. "I forgot to ask."

"Himself said not before eight o'clock," the lad confessed reluctantly.

It seemed a long time to wait, with her appetite sharpened by a sketchy lunch and the sea crossing, but she took her mind off a complaining stomach with the chores of unpacking, and washing her long hair. Then she sat at the open window to let it dry, and found her irritation with Cullin dying in the sheer beauty of the landscape in front of her. The sea was not in view, but a flagged terrace led to parkland that ran down to a tiny, perfect loch. Beyond it the glen climbed up between the shoulders of adjacent hills until, towering over successive waves of green, she could see the great, shaggy head of Beinn Mhor, violet-coloured in the sunset light. Cullin might not be very friendly, but of its beauty there could be no question.

Chapter Two

She was downstairs on the stroke of eight, hair plaited and coiled into a shining knob, eyes made up dramatically, her dress the shimmering colours of the loch outside. Her determination was simple: at the risk of greatly puzzling Tod, she would flirt as blatantly as possible with her travelling companion, for the benefit of a pompous prig of a Highlander who had already drawn his own uncharitable conclusions about them. Tod ambled out of the bar as soon as she appeared, but their promptness did them no good. Dinner was late in coming, with long gaps between courses; worse still, the helpings might just have satisfied the appetite of inmates of a nursing home for the elderly and infirm. Their host, unfortunately, was invisible – she would have liked to point out that he was not only inefficient, but mean. She did what everyone else was doing and helped herself to a huge chunk of cheese, wondering by what miracle the guests continued to return if the catering was always as inadequate as this. Hunger more or less appeased, she said goodnight to Tod, declining to return to the bar to drink malt whisky with him. Days of driving over mountain roads had been tiring and she was content to go to bed early with a book for company.

Her bedroom was in the old tower part of the Castle, and it felt over-large and shadowy with night falling. She stood at the window watching the wind scouring the hillside, and shivered as the first fusillade of rain burst against the window pane. Her vast room needed to be fire-lit, and preferably shared with a companion; lacking either fire or tender Highland lover, a book was an absolute necessity, but search for it as she might the small handgrip in which her books and Tod's notes were stored was nowhere in sight. She buttoned herself resentfully into her robe and fumbled her way along the dimly-lit corridors. Guests not already in bed were obviously hidden away, watching television or playing billiards. There was no one else about, and the hall was in darkness except for the dying glow of the embers on the hearth. Only in the room behind the reception desk could she see a light, because the door leading to it was half open. She was stopped from knocking by the sound of a man's voice talking on the telephone. It was a voice she recognised even though its present warmth and gentleness hadn't so far been directed at her.

"Well, thank God Maggie and the bairn are well, Hamish. Don't let her know about the chaos here – we'll muddle through somehow. Goodnight, laddie."

Backing cautiously into the dimness behind her, Fran hadn't got very far when the door swung fully open. Himself stood there, startled by the unexpected vision in front of him . . . a golden-haired water nymph, perhaps, materialised by magic from the depths of the loch outside. He stared in silence for so long that she became aware of their isolation in the dark, deserted hall. She thought, too, of the possibility that the hostile man in front of her would have something else to disapprove of – a guest inclined to nocturnal wandering in a rather flimsy robe. But the light behind him showed her what she'd missed before. He looked mortally tired, and too strained by something beyond mere physical exhaustion to even notice what she wore.

"I came to find a missing piece of luggage," she explained as calmly as she could. "It's a small, zipped holdall with my books in it."

Neil McAlister rubbed a hand over his eyes. A Celtic imagination had played tricks with him. His water nymph was merely the troublesome English girl he'd crossed swords with that afternoon. He pounced on the handgrip, half pushed under the counter of the reception desk, still shaken by his own strange sense of loss.

"I'm sorry Jaime missed it," he said stiffly. "May I carry it up for you now?"

Fran hesitated on the brink of saying that he looked more in need of carrying himself. But the stern face in front of her refused sympathy, and she simply held out her hand for the bag.

"I can manage, but thank you, Mr . . ."

"McAlister," he said as she hesitated. "Neil Alexander Keith McAlister. Not Mr, though – just McAlister is sufficient."

"In other words, Himself, I suppose?"

"Yes." His worst enemy couldn't have accused him of using two words if one would do. Fran thought she was about to wish him goodnight and leave, but instead she heard herself say something entirely different. "I couldn't help overhearing the tail end of your conversation just now. I gather you're in some difficulty. I'd be glad to help if you'd let me."

His weary figure stiffened. "Kind of you to offer, and even more kind not to point out that dinner this evening was not only late but inedible. You're a guest here, however. We shall manage, Miss Campbell."

The dismissal was final, and if Highland pride allowed him to accept any help at all, it certainly wouldn't be from her. Should she mention that by breakfast time his half-fed customers were likely to be ravenous? His reticent, tired face prevented even that.

"Well, goodnight then . . . McAlister."

"Goodnight to yourself, Miss Campbell," he answered gravely, unable to say that gravity was tried by a sudden desire to smile at the mixture of grandness and doubt with which she'd struggled to bring out his name. But she groped her way back upstairs with the strange feeling that something had amused him, even despite the problems he seemed to be facing.

She climbed into bed with a book, climbed out again after a moment's thought, and set her little travelling alarm clock for half-past six. No conscious decision had been taken . . . instinct alone was operating, and Fran always believed in giving instinct its head.

On the way downstairs next morning she pushed a note under Tod's door to say that she would see him after breakfast. Jaime, vigorously polishing the hall floor, looked astonished when she asked him the way to the kitchen, but he led her to a room the size of her entire flat in London. A small, grey-haired woman was stirring porridge in a huge copper pan on the stove. McAlister sat at the table, deep in calculations that had to do with slices of toast per guest, divided into slices of bread per loaf. He looked up from his labours to frown at her as usual.

"Breakfast is not quite ready, Miss Campbell."

"I realise that." She took no further notice of him and went to stand beside the little lady stirring porridge. "Good morning, I'm Fran Campbell. I gather you're short-handed . . . can I help?"

After a measuring glance Elspeth McDougall scarcely hesitated. "If you mean it, lassie, there's the bacon and eggs to see to. Himself frizzled them yesterday while I was making the toast and coffee."

With a straight face Fran unhooked a large apron hanging on the kitchen door. She thought it prudent not to look at McAlister, and concentrated instead on laying out rashers of bacon for the thirty guests she'd counted the evening before.

"Do you always get your own way, Miss Campbell?" a cold voice enquired in her ear.

"Probably less often than you get yours," she answered, derinding bacon for all she was worth. She risked a smile that might turn away wrath, but his expression remained as unforgiving as before. He was stubborn to the point of stupidity, surely, but she was aware of being in the company of a man who wasn't in the habit of making life easy for himself. She could see that, unlike her friends in London, the hard way would be chosen by this stiff-necked Highlander; perhaps it was what existence on a storm-battered, sea-girt island had conditioned him to. She waited for him to seize the scissors from her hand and order her out of the kitchen, but after a glance at Elspeth's tired face he walked out himself, leaving the two women to exchange a little smile.

Two hectic hours later she scooped the last egg out of the pan, crisply frilled at the edges and succulently runny inside, added it to the remaining slices of grilled bacon, and put the plate in front of McAlister, now back at the kitchen table wrestling with more sums.

"This is *your* breakfast, I think," he said quickly.

"I'm surfeited with the sight of bacon and eggs! I might toss you for the last of the coffee, though."

He pushed the pot towards her, and then attacked the food in front of him with a relish that gave him away – it seemed that Himself had gone hungry to bed like the rest of them. She let him eat in peace, then risked the question that had been burning a hole in her curiosity.

"You don't seem to enjoy being a hotelier. In that case why do it?"

"I don't, normally. My job is to run the estate from Cullin House on the other side of the island. My sister Maggie looks after things here, but she's on the mainland at the moment, at the end of a difficult pregnancy."

"Can she possibly run it without help, apart from Elspeth, Jaime and the waitresses?"

"She *had* help – of a kind," McAlister said grimly, "a manageress who just happened to be cohabiting with the chef. The pair of them were swindling her right and left. As soon as I began to investigate what was going on the pair of them walked out. It was a pity – I should have liked the pleasure of firing them."

"Did Maggie not realise what was happening?"

"Probably not." He pushed away his coffee cup and looked up to see Fran's friendly but curious eye upon him. "Her husband was killed in a climbing accident six months ago. She hasn't been quite herself since then."

It was exactly the restrained phrase that he would use, Fran realised; tragedy had to be endured, and if it had to be described, only the fewest possible words were bearable.

"Poor Maggie," Fran murmured, aware that even the offer of that much sympathy would probably be rejected. She put aside the thought of a heartbroken woman left alone to bring her baby into a harsh world, and concentrated on what *could* be safely touched on.

"Can you replace the people who left?"

"Not now . . . it's almost the end of the season; but most of the guests will go soon – except for one or two people like old Colonel Forrester who make their home here. Maggie normally takes care of *them* herself . . . enjoys their company during our long winters." McAlister stared out of the window before fixing dark eyes on Fran again. "You've probably been too busy to notice, but there's another problem at the moment. Even if we *could* find anyone to come this late in the season, a full gale is blowing up outside – we shan't get anyone over from the mainland until the wind drops."

"And meanwhile there are thirty people to be looked after."

"Yes, but not by you," he said with a return to his stiffest manner. "I'm grateful for this morning's help, but Mr Harriman will be expecting your company."

"Mr Harriman, like the rest of your guests, will be expecting to be fed."

"Elspeth and I will manage. Leave us to our problems, Miss Campbell."

"Leave you to your stupid pride, you mean," she flashed, suddenly enraged by an obstinacy that seemed to border on the insane. "Elspeth is your housekeeper, she tells me, not a professional cook. Have you looked at her recently? She's *tired*, McAlister."

Too taken aback to answer with the same heat, he was still trying to find something to say when the door opened and Elspeth herself walked into the room. She gave them a cheerful smile, but the truth of what Fran had said was obvious. He knew her well enough to understand that she was not only tired but still harrowed by the memory of the previous night's fiasco.

"Come and sit down, Elspeth, and drink some

coffee," he insisted gently. "Otherwise Miss Campbell will take the cleaver to me. She thinks you need more help than either Jaime or I can provide, but you'll agree with me – it isn't seemly for a guest to be working in the kitchen."

"Campbell or no, if she offers I'm thinking we should be properly grateful and let her work," said Elspeth, making no bones about it.

He saw the smile that Fran offered her and accepted defeat. "Very well then . . . just while the storm lasts. After that I'll *drag* someone over from the mainland if I have to." An inspection of Fran's face showed no trace of triumph and he went on more easily. "Lunch would normally be sandwiches and a flask of coffee to take out, but I've warned everyone not to stray far from the Castle in present conditions. Allie and Morag can cope with serving soup and bread and cheese in the bar. It's dinner that will be the problem. I take it you're not a professional cook either?"

"No, but I shall just pretend that I'm at home, giving half a dozen dinner parties rolled into one," she told him calmly. "I don't see why it shouldn't work."

She was very conscious of his intent stare, but a carefully schooled face gave away nothing of the conflicting welter of emotions raging inside him. He was only certain of one thing – a mercenary and probably immoral Sassenach had no right to sound so kind or to smile so beautifully. She came from a different world from his own; familiar with the islanders, whose children he'd grown up with, he was anything but familiar with women like Fran Campbell. There was nowhere else in the world that he wanted to live, but he'd already had to learn a painful lesson: the seclusion of Cullin – the very thing he prized – was a drawback when it came to dealing with the sophisticated inhabitants of a wider world.

Remembering at last that it was his turn to say something, he thanked Fran with awe-inspiring formality, announced that he would go to Kirktown to replenish stores and look in on his own neglected house, and then stalked out of the room. Fran smiled at Elspeth behind his departing back and saw the housekeeper's solemn face relax into a sudden, unexpected grin.

"Himself isn't just used to accepting help, lassie . . . it's more often giving it that he is."

Fran was tempted to point out that what he wasn't used to was not getting his own way, but she abandoned the words before they were spoken; convincing Elspeth McDougall that there was any fault in McAlister would be like trying to make the earth turn on its axis the wrong way.

"Show me where the stores are kept," she suggested instead, "then we'll decide what to cook this evening."

Half an hour later, carbonnade of beef and apple pie having been decided upon, Fran went in search of her neglected employer. Tod was in the hall, talking to Colonel Forrester and a giant of a man he introduced as Dougal, piper and much else besides to McAlister. When they were by themselves again she apologised for leaving him to his own devices. "There's a crisis below stairs," she explained simply. "Would you like to lend a hand?"

Tod's enthusiasm was tempered with caution. "Anything you like, honey, just so long as I can do it on dry land."

She took him along to the kitchen to meet Elspeth, who was alarmingly polite to begin with . . . as McAlister had said, it wasn't seemly for a foreign gentleman to be asked to peel potatoes and apples. Tod's friendliness was hard to resist, but she was far from won over until a chance reference to Granny McDougall made her lay down the knife in her hand.

"Never tell me *you*'re a McDougall."

"On my momma's side," Tod explained proudly. "My maternal grandmother was Jeannie McDougall."

Elspeth did some lightning calculations. "Then you'll be second cousin to McAlister's piper, Dougal, and third cousin once removed to me."

Tod advanced on her with a wondrous smile and engulfed her in a hug from which she emerged flustered but not displeased.

"Land sakes," Tod breathed, "I *knew* Cullin was going to be something special – it had to be. But I didn't come thinking I'd find family here. I guess you could say I'm gobsmacked, Elspeth, and *then* some!"

She missed the full flavour of this tribute, but she was certainly aware of the joy that lit Tod's face. From then on he and his new-found cousin talked non-stop while they peeled and sliced. Fran prepared the carbonnade, and made pastry for the pies, happily aware that only brute force would now have wrested her employer from the warm, friendly kitchen.

Lunchtime came and went, and the only thing to disturb their peace was Allie's news that everyone had appeared for lunch in the bar except two young American women who were the only other newcomers among the Castle's guests. A day on the hills would normally be nothing to worry about, but after some fitful gleams of sunshine the rain was now slashing down again, and a wind beginning to work itself up to gale force was roaring in from the Atlantic. Allie looked concerned that two of the hotel flock were unaccounted for, and Fran began to wish that Himself would walk through the door so that they could unload the problem on *him*. By mid-afternoon there was still no sign of the Americans, and Colonel Forrester, now aware of their absence, appeared in the kitchen with even more worrying news.

"I came hoping to find McAlister," he said frowning. "He asked everyone not to go far today, but when those two young women were talking at breakfast I caught snatches of their conversation. Provided the steamer can reach Cullin tomorrow this is their last day on the island, and they were very set on climbing Beinn Mhor. I tried to explain how foolish such a thing would be in poor conditions. They listened very politely, but I could see what they were thinking – I was a decrepit old buffer who'd lost the relish he once had for walking the hills. They, on the other hand, were young, and experienced climbers as well. I can't swear that they were going to make for the Beinn, but it's my strong feeling that they might now be in difficulties up there."

Fran thought of the two girls she'd glimpsed setting out from the Castle that morning – confident, laughing, and all too probably determined to do the very thing that a member of the opposite sex, much inclined to the issuing of orders, had told them not to do. She found herself now praying for McAlister to come back. City life hadn't prepared her for this kind of situation. Maggie, almost certainly, would have known what must be done, but all Fran could think of was to ring Cullin House and implore its owner to come and take charge. There was no answer to her ring, and another hour limped agonisingly by before the door to the back courtyard burst open and he was almost blown into the kitchen on a great wet gust of wind. His hair was black with rain, and his tanned face shone wetly in the light of the room.

"Sorry to have deserted you for so long, but there was some trouble at one of the crofts." He looked from Fran's white face to Elspeth's worried one. "If there is also trouble here perhaps someone would like to tell me what it is?"

Fran answered him. "The two American girls went out at ten this morning – with the intention, Colonel Forrester believes, of climbing Beinn Mhor. They haven't returned, I'm afraid . . . we've been trying to reach you."

McAlister rubbed a hand over his wet face. "God in Heaven . . . climbing on a day like this. Why won't women *ever* do as they're told? Elspeth, find Dougal for me, please. He's unpacking stores in the cellars. Tell him we must be ready to leave in ten minutes."

"Can *I* do anything?" Fran asked quietly.

He hesitated a moment, then pointed to a list pinned up on the wall. "Those are emergency numbers. Try as many of them as you can. Anyone who's available must meet me at the bottom of the drive."

"The girls are probably sheltering somewhere," she insisted desperately, almost unnerved by the gravity of his face.

"Perhaps, if they've any sense left at all; but they should have been back at least two hours ago. *We* must start searching at once. There will soon be no light left in these conditions."

He disappeared into the hall to round up the more able-bodied of the male guests in the hotel, and Fran stationed herself at the telephone. Ten minutes later she'd contacted half a dozen men who promised to recruit what others they could. McAlister came back from heaving ropes and lanterns into the back of his Land Rover, and shrugged himself into his wet plaid again. The sight of Fran's pies lined up on the table waiting to be cooked halted him on his way to the door.

"Oh my God . . . dinner! I'd forgotten that."

"You can go on forgetting it," she said briefly. "We'll manage here."

He stared at her for a moment, not seeing her troubling beauty now, only the whiteness of her face and the fear that she strove to keep hidden.

"I'd leave you Dougal . . . but I shall need him on the hill."

Fran's mouth trembled into a faint smile. "He wouldn't stay . . . not when there's work to be done with Himself. Elspeth and I *will* manage." Still he hesitated for a second or two longer, and her next words were spoken involuntarily. "I trust you'll be careful, McAlister?"

The primness of it unlocked in him some hidden seam of amusement that she'd have sworn didn't exist in his stern, God-fearing mentality. It even produced a smile as unexpected and heart-warming as the gleam of sunlight that sometimes slanted through the island's usual coverlet of cloud.

"I'm always careful," he said solemnly. "I leave the heroics to Dougal."

He stretched out a hand – almost, she thought, as if to touch the shining plait that lay across her shoulder. But she must have mistaken the gesture, of course. He offered her a little bow instead, and a moment later he was gone, out into the racket of the approaching, stormy night.

Almost without conscious thought, she set aside food that would be needed later when the search party returned – hungry, but successful, she prayed silently.

Then she went on with the task that she'd undertaken to do. She couldn't help on the hill – that needed strength and expertise and local knowledge – but she *could* see McAlister's remaining guests fed and cared for, and it was a task she was suddenly content to be carrying out for him. Her mind travelled with a handful of tired men combing a windswept mountainside in the pouring rain, but her hands were busy. She even managed to smile at Elspeth when the housekeeper returned to announce with only the slightest tremor in her voice that Allie and Morag, being good lassies, had got everyone quietly assembled in the bar, with a splendid log fire burning to keep their spirits high.

Chapter Three

The carbonnade was a triumph, but unease lay nevertheless like a mist over the warm, comfortable room. The curtains were left undrawn, and first one guest and then another would get up to peer out, even though there was nothing to be seen except wind-tossed darkness and rain driving against the window panes. It wasn't until nearly ten o'clock that Tod, now permanently stationed in the hall, let out a shout and then rushed into the kitchen.

"Lights in the drive, Fran."

The courtyard outside was suddenly illuminated and full of the new and welcome noise of car engines; the next moment the kitchen seemed full of wet, hungry men. Elspeth settled them round the table and she and Allie served the huge helpings of beef stew that Fran dished out. The rescue party looked exhausted but content; even so she let the housekeeper ask the question burning on her lips.

"Don't just sit there grinning, Dougal McDougall. What happened, and where's Himself?"

"Still at the surgery in Kirktown, I'm thinking. We finally found the lassies in a corrie three-quarters of the way up the Beinn – one of them with a broken ankle, forbye. They are both now with the doctor, and McAlister will be getting Sandy to bring him home, but we were instructed not to wait."

Tod rushed off to the lounge with the news that everyone was safely off the mountain, and then went to help Jaime behind the bar. After hours of shared anxiety, gaiety was rising like a balloon; everyone suddenly wanted to talk and drink, and no one wanted to go to bed. Finally convinced that McAlister was unscathed, Elspeth allowed herself to be talked into going to her room. Allie helped stack the dishwashers, then departed herself, but Fran lingered in the kitchen. She was tired, too, but aware that sleep would be an impossibility. The lassitude that comes with relief from strain weighed down her body, but her mind had never felt more painfully awake. Cullin was teaching her things about herself that needed more careful consideration than she was capable of giving them at the moment, but sooner or later they would have to be faced and dealt with. Her life in London, so satisfactory and enjoyable until now, was beginning to seem not only too distant to be remembered, but thoroughly lacking in the demands and rewards that this small island was prepared to offer. Somehow, though, she must keep a hold on common sense . . . she was here with Tod to accomplish the service he was paying for; not to involve heart and mind with the problems of an overbearing, narrow-minded Highlander wedded to his inhospitable and storm-battered inheritance. She would forget both easily enough as soon as she was back in her natural habitat again; *that* was the certainty she must cling to.

She was needlessly wiping an already clean stove when the door opened and he walked in, bringing with him the clean, sweet smell of rain and an air of serenity she hadn't noticed in him before. The challenge of the last few hours, met and overcome, had released the tension she'd been aware of in him from the moment that she'd walked into the Castle.

"You're back then," she said unnecessarily, "and the girls are safe."

"Yes – they were lucky this time. Perhaps it's taught them a lesson they'll remember."

The tension no longer troubling him was now in herself. She felt absurdly nervous in the quiet room, because he stood watching her intently . . . noting, she felt sure, the signs of toil and strain left by the past few hours. She found it hard not to shout that the Americans had only been lucky because men like him and Dougal had willingly risked their own lives; but she could guess what he would say – they'd done no more than they always must. Stupid human beings, vulnerable animals in distress . . . all must be rescued when the need arose.

"The other men have been fed," she said hurriedly instead. "What about you? There's some stew left."

"Why not end the day as it began, with bacon and eggs?" he suggested with a faint smile. "That's what I should really like if I'm to be given a choice."

She rushed for the frying-pan, feeling slightly more in control of the situation with something so mundane in her hand.

"You're dripping rain onto Elspeth's floor," she pointed out in a voice she strove to make cool. "Would it not be sensible to get into some dry clothes while I do the cooking?"

She risked a glance at him when he solemnly agreed, but he walked out of the kitchen afterwards and she was left alone to recover from what she told herself was a perfectly natural reaction to the ordeal of a long and harrowing day. When he reappeared ten minutes later, hair brushed but still damply curling, she fancied she was able to put food in front of him with the calm briskness of a woman who'd been reared from the cradle up to cope with island emergencies.

McAlister applied himself to his plate, only stopping long enough to offer her a smile that threatened to destroy composure all over again. There was no fear of his making a habit of it, of course, but she reckoned that it was just as well. While he ate she drank coffee she didn't want because it seemed unkind to leave him there alone, even though it was probably what he would have preferred. Her conviction was strong that McAlister was accustomed to a solitary life . . . he neither needed nor wanted companionship; he was a thrawn, self-sufficient man only enduring the social demands of being an hotelier out of loyalty to his sister. About to ask for news of Maggie, Fran heard *him* break the silence in the room instead.

"I haven't thanked you yet for helping us today. How do you come to be so competent? Do you make a habit of pulling other people's chestnuts out of the fire?"

"In a way, I suppose. I help my Aunt Ernestine to run an agency in London. People with problems come to us and we do our best for them. The agency's called 'Campbell's Comfort'."

"Purely philanthropic?"

"No . . . we both have a living to earn. It started when her sister – my mother, that's to say – remarried an American and went to live in New York. She told so many people over there that Ernestine would help them if they got into difficulties that Aunt made a business of it in self-defence. It's a great success now." Fran hesitated a moment, and then went on. "It explains how I come to be travelling with Tod, by the way. He's one of our clients, employing me to organise his travels around Scotland and take notes for him. I think you might have got the wrong impression when we arrived."

The afterthought was gently said, but it made the colour rise under his tanned skin.

"I'm sorry . . . did I make it so obvious?" he asked after a moment.

"You stood behind your desk, glowering like the ghost of John Knox himself, and despising the pair of us. Tod may not have looked much like the guests you're accustomed to, but you could have given him the benefit of a little doubt. His granny came from Cullin, and it's been his lifelong ambition to stay here."

After another silence McAlister found something else to say. "I apologise to you both. It had been a bad day, but that is no excuse." He frowned at the empty plate in front of him before he spoke again. "Does it satisfy you . . . indulging the whims of rich travellers who ought to be able to take care of themselves?"

Fran examined the question, hearing in it a lingering echo of the disdain that had met them when they first arrived. "People don't need to be rich to come to Campbell's," she said sharply. "We don't charge the earth, or inspect their bank account before we help them. Nor do we send them away if they happen to look well-heeled . . . the rich occasionally have problems too."

"I'm sure they do, but they also have no lack of volunteers only too willing to run to their aid."

Suddenly angry as well as hurt, Fran stared at him with a flash in her blue eyes. "I wasn't proposing to send in a bill for helping today, if that's what is worrying you, nor for tackling thirty kippers for tomorrow's breakfast. I'll bid you goodnight, McAlister . . . it's been rather a long day."

She was on her feet and nearly at the door before

he caught up with her. His hands clamped to her shoulder made it impossible to pull herself free and she was obliged to look at him. The dark face too near her own was reticent no longer, but filled with strange, sad remorse instead. She could make no guess as to what he might do or say next, but the chance to find out was lost; she was immediately released as the door just behind her opened again and Dougal loped in to report that all was neat again outside. The castle could settle down for what remained of the night. She left the room unchallenged this time, but slightly regretful.

Next morning when she went downstairs only Elspeth was in the kitchen, already at work.

"Good day to you, lassie. Himself is away with Dougal, clearing a tree that's come down across the road. But the wind is slackening, he says."

"Does that mean that the boat will manage to get here?"

"I have my doubts about that," Elspeth said judiciously. "There will be a big sea running, you ken, between us and the mainland for a day or two yet."

Fran stared abstractedly at a pile of kippers without seeing them. "Have you heard how Maggie is . . . or when she'll be coming back?"

"All I know is she'll be here as soon as she can, poor wee girl. She hates to be away from Cullin. More's the pity Alan Harding didn't feel the same, but he would never refuse an expedition, and the higher and farther away the mountain the happier he was to climb it. His brother Hamish was hurt as well in the same accident; he's been here since, mending himself and helping Maggie."

"What do you suppose will happen, Elspeth?

McAlister has the estate to run. Will she be able to manage on her own here, with a tiny baby to look after?"

"I don't know, lassie." Elspeth's normally calm face was furrowed with an anxiety that it was suddenly a relief to reveal, even though she was aware of surprise at herself . . . confiding in an elegant young woman from London was very strange; but much that had happened recently was outside the quiet pattern of their days, and Fran Campbell seemed to be the least difficult of young women to confide in.

"The hotel closes at the end of October," Elspeth went on slowly, "but one or two people – Colonel Forrester and old Miss Milward – live at the Castle all the time now. My home is at Cullin House, but I dare say Himself will have to leave me here, as well as Jaime."

The calm acceptance in her voice made Fran look at her curiously. "Wouldn't you mind? It seems a bit . . . well, lordly – just to put you wherever he feels inclined."

"I doubt I should ever mind anything McAlister does," his handmaiden said simply. "It's always for the best, you ken . . . not for his own sake."

Fran went back to her kippers, aware that there was a lot to think about, and not least the kind of devotion that Neil McAlister had managed to inspire in his islanders.

As the morning wore on the weather steadily improved, although it grew colder as the wind shifted. With the sun shining again, the colours of the landscape outside looked freshly enamelled, tempting Fran to abandon her self-imposed duties for the first walk she'd been able to take with Tod since they arrived on the island. It wasn't, in fact, a very arduous walk because he insisted on stopping every few minutes to photograph a waterfall or a kestrel hanging in a sky washed clear of clouds. They munched sandwiches, sheltered from the wind by an outcrop of rock; then, out of the blue, Tod launched his bombshell.

"Fran, I've been thinking. Now that I've found Cullin I can't rush away from it again. You won't believe me if I say that I seem to feel I belong here; I don't quite believe it myself. But I *do* know that this is where I want to stay and get my book on Scotland written."

She stared at his round, pink face, familiar to her now after the weeks they'd spent together. He was still the kind, charming companion she'd got to know, always courteous, always interested, and always ready for the next bend in the road and the next adventure. But now something seemed to have changed; for the first time in her knowledge of him he *wasn't* ready to move on. Cullin wasn't to be let go of so easily.

Uncertain how to reply, she voiced the most obvious objection she could think of. "The hotel closes at the end of October, even if McAlister's sister comes back with her new baby. Where will you stay?"

"Why not where Colonel Forrester stays? He doesn't leave when the Castle closes – he told me so."

Fran swallowed the remainder of her sandwich with difficulty, reluctant to quench the enthusiasm in her friend's face. "Tod dear, the Colonel is an old friend of the family . . . it's different for him. What's more, he's familiar with a winter spent here – knows about the days when you can't set foot out of doors and it scarcely even seems to get light. It's a far cry from Nebraska, farther still from your life in New York."

For once she was aware of having disappointed Tod Harriman "I *know* that, honey. But I've got work to do

– a book to write; and I'm more and more sure that this is where I want to write it." He looked away from her, afraid to see rejection in her face when he put his next proposition into words.

"It's a lot to ask of a girl who has her own exciting life five hundred miles away . . . but would *you* stay as well, Fran? Three months' hard work together and we could get the book roughed out. But there's no disgrace in refusing . . . you've already given me more help and pleasure than I had any right to expect; and I know you can't feel about Cullin the same way as I do. All the same it would make things just about perfect if you *could* put London on hold for the next three months or so."

She thought she knew what a rabbit felt like when it bounded into a trap – free as air one moment, hopelessly caught the next. Tod's offer *could* be refused; he'd be disappointed but not harsh or bitter about it. He might even decide to stay on his own. But he wouldn't get the book written without help, and the sort of help he needed was unlikely to be found on Cullin. He hadn't, out of a sense of fairness, stressed what else she knew was true – that writing his Scottish book on Granny McDougall's home ground was what appealed to him above all. He'd probably convinced himself by now that it had been 'meant' all along – the perfect fulfilment of all his years of wandering.

Almost without knowing what she intended to say, she heard herself answer him. "There's nothing that I specially need go back for. I'd have to check with Aunt Ernestine, of course, but it's getting towards the end of the tourist season, and I doubt if she'd insist on my returning to London. *That*'s the easy part, Tod! The rest of it might be much more difficult. McAlister's sister, who normally runs the hotel, has recently lost her husband and just borne a child after a difficult pregnancy. More people here than usual to look after would probably be the last thing on earth she wants this winter."

"Maybe we could help, Fran. Have you thought of that?"

His cherubic face was now filled with the desire to help a woman he hadn't even met; it suddenly seemed the most important reason of all for staying on Cullin. Fran hesitated too long about pointing out that *their* help would, in all probability, not be acceptable. McAlister had brought himself to apologise for his lack of welcome, but with an effort that had been visible. He would be glad to see the back of a loudly-dressed American who didn't belong on Cullin, and even more relieved to see the last of Fran Campbell, who belonged no more than Tod did. She achieved a faint smile, but shook her head.

"I'm not thinking beyond the few days that we still have here. For as long as Elspeth needs help in the kitchen McAlister is obliged to put up with me. But don't let enthusiasm run away with you, Tod. Himself is more than capable of telling us very politely to leave his precious island. We seem to represent the sort of people he doesn't like."

Unable to believe that this could really be the case, Tod did a little Highland dance in the heather, already convinced that he was going to be there to see winter arrive on Cullin. Fran spread the last of the sandwiches on a convenient rock where the curlews could help themselves, and they took to the path again; but she shivered as they faced into the wind, gripped by sudden apprehension. Apart from the brief storm, October had been glorious, but almost overnight winter could set in. She knew a sudden longing to be back in a world she was familiar with, instead of on this beautiful but demanding island. She even found herself praying that McAlister would say they couldn't stay.

They trudged back to the Castle, tired by a walk that had taken them rather further than they'd intended. Tod made no bones about retiring for a snooze and a bath before dinner, but Fran changed out of her walking gear of sweater and trousers, and went down to the kitchen to start preparing cutlets and vegetables for the Lancashire hotpot she'd agreed on with Elspeth.

Neil McAlister was in the hall talking to a woman Fran hadn't seen before. She had a quick impression of a mane of red hair, and hazel eyes, large and baleful as a cat's, studying her as she walked by.

"Miss Campbell . . ." McAlister's voice halted her suddenly. "May I introduce you to an old friend, Fiona Mackintosh. You'd never think it to see her toiling in the kitchen, Fiona, but Miss Campbell is actually a guest. I'm not quite sure how we should have managed without her."

At close range Fiona Mackintosh was not as young as the flowing mane of hair suggested; she was probably much the same age as the man beside her – in her mid-thirties Fran decided. A brilliant smile didn't reach her eyes, nor did she intend to hold out a friendly hand.

"Having to be beholden to a Campbell, Neil!" she said rallyingly. "It serves you right; you should have let me know you were in such difficulties."

"McAlister doesn't have to worry about it too much," Fran pointed out, adopting her cool Kensington voice again. "My name may be one you don't like up here, but I'm scarcely a Campbell worth the hating. This is my first visit to Scotland, and I expect it will be my last."

She gave them a slight nod, and walked away confident that she'd been offhand to the point of rudeness. The memory of her last encounter with McAlister was sharp in her mind. She wasn't about to make friends with him, and if the woman with him resented anyone who looked like absorbing any of his attention, she might as well know that she could cross Fran Campbell off the list straightaway. A pox on them all, she told herself irritably. The sooner she could get away from Cullin the happier she would be. Then she remembered that if Tod got his way she wouldn't be leaving Cullin. It wouldn't be difficult to get Aunt Ernestine to insist on a return to London . . . at least, not unless she got into one of the perverse moods in which she galloped in the one direction she was required not to take. But Fran thought she owed it to Tod not to put any unfair rub in his way.

The stormy expression on her face as she walked into the kitchen made Elspeth look at her twice. She smiled at the housekeeper, but set to work in silence for once.

"Is anything wrong, lassie?" Elspeth enquired presently. "Ye seem a wee bit put out."

"Sorry, Elspeth. Was I looking grumpy? Mr Harriman and I walked too far this morning, I expect. McAlister is back, I see. I met him in the hall just now with someone called Fiona Mackintosh."

"Aye . . . Fiona's back too. She's been away to the mainland, and then staying in the north of Cullin, collecting and distributing work."

"What sort of work?"

"Knitting done by the crofters' wives. They make sweaters and hats and gloves and suchlike. Fiona works very hard. Himself thinks he must be grateful to her for running it for him."

It was hard to know what Elspeth thought, because her voice was completely colourless, but Fran wrestled with herself not to ask the housekeeper's real opinion of Fiona Mackintosh. She probably wouldn't have given it, in any case; the islanders wouldn't criticise one of their own to an outsider.

"Is Miss Mackintosh some sort of relative?" she asked instead.

"Maggie's cousin by marriage, but likely to become a good deal closer than that."

"You mean she's going to marry McAlister?"

"It looks that way, lassie." There was a note of finality in Elspeth's voice which said she wasn't going to be drawn further. But she looked as depressed as Fran suddenly felt. It was nothing to do with her whether he married Fiona or anyone else, she told herself. Her only reason for regretting his choice was the lack of kindness she'd sensed in a woman whose fiery colouring suggested that she ought to brim with warmth. A cold and calculating wife would bring out the very worst side of McAlister's character, instead of softening it, and he'd end up even more objectionable than he was now. Unaccountably, a tear slid down her cheek and she blinked to stop another one falling.

"Onions," she explained hurriedly to Elspeth, who was staring at her again.

The serving of dinner that evening went smoothly, without the undercurrent of anxiety of the night before. Allie reported that Himself was in the dining room with Fiona, but by concentrating fiercely on whipping cream to decorate bowls of lemon mousse, Fran managed to look serene and unconcerned. There was no sign of him in the kitchen when dinner was over, and she assumed that he'd probably left the Castle to take his lady-friend back to Kirktown.

She was sitting at the kitchen table, working out a menu for the next day, when he walked in and closed the door behind him.

"You look tired," he said abruptly. "I know you don't wish to be paid for helping us, but how else are we ever to say thank you?"

She wished he wouldn't stand there staring down at her; weariness, and she knew not what besides, was threatening her with tears again. The unaccustomed feeling of weakness made her feel irritable with herself, and with him.

"I've helped because I wanted to . . . forget it, please. Have you had any news from your sister?"

"Yes . . . the weather and the sea are settling down again, and Maggie can be discharged from hospital any time; so there's every chance that she'll be able to get across tomorrow."

"What happens after that? Will she be able to manage?"

"Not entirely on her own. I could always leave Elspeth with her for a while, but in any case Miss Mackintosh has also volunteered to lend a hand. She insists on relieving you tomorrow. I am more grateful to you than I can say, but happy that you can now return to being a guest."

For a man who wasn't accustomed to accepting favours, he managed to sound decently grateful, but Fran was left, nevertheless, with a feeling of having been pushed aside. Perhaps Miss Mackintosh had made it clear that she didn't want anyone else around with a claim on his gratitude.

"I didn't think my career as a hotel cook was going to end quite so suddenly," she managed to say lightly. "I was planning to go out in a blaze of glory – crêpes suzettes suitably flaming!"

He made no reply to the small joke and she looked up, surprised by his silence. When he did finally speak, it was to change the subject abruptly.

"What does Fran stand for – Frances?"

"Francesca. I rather like it in full, but my friends seem to think it's too much of a mouthful to use."

"It suggests to me a dark Spanish beauty," he said unexpectedly, "the stately kind; not a girl with hair the colour of ripe corn and eyes like gentians."

Far from feeling stately, she was conscious that her heart was trying to jump into her throat, and that the space between them was suddenly alive with electricity. Damn him for putting her off balance; she didn't normally have any difficulty in coping with the opposite sex, but with McAlister she could never seem to be at ease. The casual reply she'd have offered anyone else still hadn't been found when he abruptly spoke again.

"Mr Harriman buttonholed me after dinner. He wanted to know if you could both stay on after the hotel closes. I was in something of a hurry, with only time to say that I should have to consult my sister. Does Cullin please *you* so much that you don't want to return to London?"

Her heart was under control again and it was time to make things clear. "Cullin is beautiful, but it's Tod who wants to stay, not me. I'm anxious to get home, but he's got the idea that he wants to get his book written here, and he can't do it without secretarial help."

"He had no chance to mention a book. What does he write – detective stories, science fiction?"

"Nothing like that. He produces immensely successful travel guides – 'Touring with Tod', they're called. No American would dream of setting out without them."

From being highly-charged, the atmosphere in the kitchen was suddenly freezing her to death. McAlister's dark face was rigid with disapproval, and any thought of eyes like gentians had certainly disappeared from his mind.

"Do I understand that he is proposing to write about Cullin?"

"About Scotland generally. I have no idea whether he means to mention Cullin – but I should think he would when he finds it so beautiful."

"He won't if I have anything to do with it. If I could, I'd stop him writing the wretched book altogether, but he certainly won't write it here."

"Why not, for heaven's sake?" she demanded furiously. "Tod's less likely than anyone you can think of to subvert or pervert or whatever else it is that you're afraid of. Making judgements about people without any real knowledge seems to be your stock-in-trade. Why don't you *look* at one of his books before you pronounce on them like God Almighty?"

They were back in their usual position, glaring at one another across the kitchen table. At the back of McAlister's mind was the knowledge that he admired the way she leapt to the defence of her American friend; just so would he like a woman to defend him, if necessary. There was also the fact that, with flushed cheeks and eyes sparkling with rage, she was very beautiful . . . unfairly so. It made him more severe than ever.

"My 'judgement' has nothing to do with the quality of Mr Harriman's books, only their subject matter. The Highlands are already swarming with American and other visitors. To have more of them persuaded to come here is the last thing we need."

"That's your opinion, and it's an extraordinary one

coming from someone who owns a hotel. What do you call the people here if the aren't visitors?" she shouted.

"They're old friends who come every year, and love Cullin precisely for what it is: a place with its identity and its peace intact. The people Mr Harriman's book will bring are casual tourists 'doing' the Highlands. They choke the roads with their cars and coaches, and scatter money too freely. The result is that more and more people here forsake their natural way of life for an easier option, and the land slides slowly into ruin."

In other circumstances it was an argument Fran would have found it hard to disagree with, but she couldn't dismount from her high horse now.

"You're trying to swim against the tide," she said instead. "Who's going to work from dawn to dusk on a small patch of stony hillside when they can earn a better living elsewhere?"

"Enough people who share my belief, I hope."

"But on Cullin they're not going to be given any choice, I take it?"

"Not while I'm here," he agreed.

He was about as yielding as Beinn Mhor; collide with either and you meet sheer rock. Fran withdrew from an argument she was never going to win, but hoped she might at least have the last word.

"Tod came here for a brief holiday. If we promise not to spread discontent among the islanders, I take it we can stay for the week we came for? After that we'll find somewhere else for him to write his book, and I'll be as thankful to go as you will be to get rid of us."

"I doubt that. Beholden though I am to you, Francesca Campbell, I wish greatly that you had never come to Cullin."

She stared at him, unwilling to believe that she'd heard aright or that he could be so deliberately hurtful. But his face, like his voice, was sombre. She couldn't doubt that he meant what he'd just said. She looked down at the sheet of paper on which she'd written tomorrow's menu – chicken marengo and crêpes suzettes – crumpled it between trembling fingers, and walked past him out of the room.

Chapter Four

She got up early as usual the next morning, doubting that Fiona Mackintosh would be so anxious to help that she'd come rushing up from Kirktown in time to cook breakfast for the Castle guests. It was a temptation to let Himself stew in his own lordly juice, but that would have meant leaving Elspeth in the lurch as well. The housekeeper was already at work but looking, Fran thought, not quite her normal brisk self. When she picked up the salt jar, then hesitated, unable to remember whether or not she'd salted the porridge, it was obvious that her mind wasn't wholly on the job in hand.

"Are you thinking that you'll have Maggie and the bairn home today?" Fran asked, smiling at herself for the easy way the Scottish word now tripped off her tongue.

"Aye – it's happy we are about *that.*" A slight stress on the last word seemed to suggest that there was something Elspeth was *not* happy about, but whatever it was she proposed to keep to herself.

"You're getting a new assistant today, I understand . . . Miss Mackintosh."

"Aye," Elspeth said again. "But I've been the assistant, lassie, and you've been the chef. I hope the next one's as good and kind."

It was a long speech for Elspeth, and fulsome enough

by her sparing standards to take Fran by surprise. Not sure how to answer, she dropped a kiss on the housekeeper's cheek in passing, and then went on with spreading out sausages on the grill pan.

After breakfast she went in search of Tod, thinking that it was time she broke the news to him that they weren't going to be allowed to stay on Cullin. He was still in the dining room, chatting to Colonel Forrester, with whom he'd struck up an unlikely friendship. His face split into its wide grin at the sight of her.

"G'mornin', Fran . . . do you need me for something?"

"I was about to ask you the same question! I'm no longer needed in the kitchen and can now go back to the job I'm supposed to be doing."

"We're not working yet . . . this is holiday, and it's high time you had one. Is there anything special you'd like to do today?"

He asked the question with his usual courtesy, but something told her that he was hoping she'd say no.

"I thought of cadging a lift from Allie when she goes down to Kirktown. It would be nice to poke around the harbour there unless the idea doesn't appeal to you."

Tod's little shake of the head confirmed that it didn't fill him with joy. "To be truthful, honey, I'd rather put off facing that ocean again until I have to, but if you want to look at it, you go right ahead."

"What about you?"

"Dougal's promised to give me a lesson in playing the pipes . . . halfway up the glen, he suggests, so that only the birds need listen to the noise I make!"

Tod's delight in his newly-discovered family, in Cullin itself, and all things Scottish, made Fran wince inwardly. Now was *not* the time to say that he must make the most of what was left of his holiday; on the other hand, it was certainly high time that she tried to talk to Aunt Ernestine.

She shut herself into the little cubicle underneath the stairs and asked for a reverse-charge call to London. That in itself would probably be enough to put her aunt into an uncooperative frame of mind.

"Is that you, Fran? There was no need to ring – I got your card."

"Don't dare hang up on me," Fran said hurriedly, "I need to talk to you. Tod Harriman's fallen in love with the land of his grandmother and wants to get his book written up here. He wants me to stay and help him – three months' work, he reckons. I said I'd have to ask you."

There was a little pause at the other end. "You'd better tell me whether you want to stay or not," Ernestine Campbell suggested finally. "Now that the summer's over we can probably manage down here, but if you can't stand the idea, say so, and I'll hold him to the terms of the original contract."

Fran wished with all her heart that for once her relative had been less considerate. It would have been a relief not to have to make up her own mind.

"If you're sure you don't need me, I think I'll stay," she decided slowly. "He's a nice man . . . I'd like to help him."

"Stay where . . . on Cullin?"

"Anywhere but here. This island's owned by a stiff-necked autocrat who loathes the tourist industry and thinks that anyone connected with it is in league with the Devil. We shall be evicted before we start work, but if Tod wants to write the book in Scotland, that's what I'll help him do, if only to irritate Neil McAlister."

"Interesting," Aunt Ernestine observed after a moment's thought.

"What is?"

You normally like every man you meet and then promptly forget about them. At least this one seems to have made a more lasting impression. At the moment I'm not sure I don't agree with him about tourists, but that's only because it's the tail end of a busy season. We can't prolong this conversation, Fran – it's ruining me. Let me know where you're going to be."

There was a little click, then silence; Miss Campbell had hung up with her usual abruptness. Fran walked upstairs, turning over in her mind the places she could suggest to Tod as an alternative to Cullin; none of them would have the same appeal for him or lessen his feeling that he was being sent away from where he rightly belonged. Damn McAlister! She refused to remember now a moment when he'd returned from his mountain rescue briefly apparelled in the glowing garments of a hero. He was nothing of the sort – merely a stubborn, bigoted, but otherwise ordinary man. The conclusion did nothing to solve Tod's problem, but for the moment she must put it aside because Allie would be waiting for her.

They drove down the winding road to Kirktown in a series of blind, cheerful dashes that made Fran close her eyes, but somehow they arrived in one piece and arranged to meet for the return journey in three hours' time. It was a relief to be on her own, free to do just as she felt inclined . . . walk at her own speed, which wasn't Tod's, stand and stare, and even do some quiet thinking. There was necessary shopping required as well, but afterwards she wandered about the little town until the ocean that her friend so mistrusted drew her down to the quay, to watch the fishing boats unloading. The men's only notice of a girl standing alone nearby was to offer her a courteous good day. That in itself made Cullin a place to value, and uncomfortably reinforced what McAlister had said; the islanders *did* still live in their inherited way. It was a good way, and she wasn't so blind as to refuse to see why he didn't want it spoiled.

She was still there, watching the seagulls haggling over the rubbish and rejected fish spilled along the quay when the hoot of a ship's siren made her look round. The ferry from the mainland was swinging round to moor along the quay. The inevitable group of people attracted by its arrival had already foregathered . . . drawn to watch no matter how many times they'd watched the scene before. Her eye wandered over them, then stopped at a kilted figure half a head taller than the rest – Neil McAlister, dark hair blowing in the wind, and listening with grave attention to a diatribe from the ancient mariner beside him. Fran watched the two of them, wishing that she had a camera to capture the old man's eloquence and Himself's patient courtesy. He might have heard it a dozen times before, be longing to escape and look for his sister among the passengers waiting to disembark, but an elder had to be listened to. It shed an unexpected light on a man she liked to imagine riding roughshod over everyone on Cullin.

He detached himself at last and walked towards a tall, dark girl coming down the gangway, but at that point Fran turned away, anxious not to be seen watching them. She'd got no further than the little square leading away from the harbour when an estate car drew up beside her.

"A lift needed, Miss Campbell?" McAlister called, opening the door.

"No thanks – Allie's picking me up."

"Then tell her to keep her eyes on the road, and both hands on the wheel for a change."

Fran gave an airy wave and walked on, leaving him nothing to do but close the door and drive away, but she passed on his instructions when they were in the battered Mini again.

"Himself's inclined to be critical of my driving," Allie admitted with a cheerful crashing of gears. "In fact, he's been known to refuse to drive down the hill in front of me!"

The climb up was only one degree less nerve-racking than the journey down, and Fran climbed out in the Castle courtyard convinced that some heavenly agency must have Allie in its care. Inside the hall, intending to go straight to her room, she found herself facing McAlister again and a girl who could only be his sister. The same brown skin and bony features were unmistakable, but what in a man added up to spare good looks didn't work so successfully for Maggie Harding. She was thin to the point of gauntness; eyes, mouth, and nose all seemed too large for the face that contained them.

"You're Francesca Campbell, I think," Maggie said at once, holding out her hand. "Neil's just told me what's been going on here. I don't know what he was thinking of to embroil you in our troubles, but it's been wonderfully kind of you to help."

"My dear Maggie, please believe that I made every effort to stop Miss Campbell embroiling herself," McAlister pointed out before Fran could answer. "She's not the most biddable woman of my acquaintance."

Fran ignored the comment and smiled at Mrs Harding. "It's true," she confirmed cheerfully. "Apart from wanting to lend Elspeth a hand it was a new experience that I enjoyed very much. So now let's agree that the thank yous have been said, and get down to the more important matter of admiring your bairn."

The transforming McAlister smile lit Maggie's thin face. "I suppose I shouldn't say it but he's beautiful. Elspeth's keeping an eye on him in the kitchen, if you'd like to come and see."

The two of them walked out of the hall together, leaving Himself standing there, watching them go. The tiny scrap in the carry-cot was duly admired, then they sat down at the kitchen table to share the coffee Elspeth had made. Fran made cheerful conversation but she was inwardly shocked by Maggie Harding's frailness; still worse was an air of desolation not quite hidden by surface self-control. She needed more than a helpless child and a couple of elderly hotel guests for company during a long, northern winter. Then Fran remembered that someone else had been mentioned by Elspeth.

"Has your brother-in-law come back with you?"

"Yes, but only for the moment. He must go back to his school in Inverness as soon as he's properly fit . . . perhaps you know that he was hurt in the accident that killed my husband. His post is being kept for him, but they can't wait indefinitely."

"Elspeth did tell me what happened . . . I'm so sorry, Maggie," Fran said gently.

She saw the other woman's face suddenly crumple and, without conscious thought, got up and walked round the table holding out her arms. Elspeth quietly left the room, and found Dougal in the hall, talking to McAlister.

"Is the bairn here, then?" he asked eagerly. "I must go and pay my respects to Mistress Harding."

"Not just now, Dougal," she said with a quick shake of the head. "Leave it a wee while, I should."

He nodded and went away, leaving McAlister staring at her.

"Why not now, Elspeth? Is something amiss?"

"The bairn's fine, but Maggie's finally doing what she should have done months ago – weeping for her lost man. It's all right," she added as he moved towards the kitchen door, "she's not alone."

"You mean she's broken down in front of a stranger . . . Francesca Campbell?"

"Aye – she had the sense to choose a woman with a loving heart to help her," said Elspeth straitly.

He accepted this in silence, then changed the subject after a moment. "Will you remind Maggie that Fiona is coming up this afternoon to help with dinner? After that we must decide what's best to be done."

Elspeth's face looked anxious as she watched him walk away. Himself had sounded more confident than he felt, she suspected, and one way and another he had a lot that needed thinking about.

In the kitchen Fran waited for Maggie's sudden storm of weeping to pass, aware that in some mysterious and wordless way, they'd travelled in the last few minutes from being strangers to becoming friends. When Maggie had got to the point of being able to produce a watery smile the worst of the storm was over, and Fran judged it was time to remind her that a small son was awake and beginning to demand attention.

"What are you going to call him?" she asked, putting the baby into Maggie's arms.

"Keith Alan Alexander . . . we seem to like a lot of names up here! My wee lad is hungry. I'll take him upstairs and feed him." She looked at Fran over the thatch of dark hair on the baby's head. "Thank you for helping me just now. I hope you haven't to rush away from Cullin."

It seemed impossible to mention that departure wasn't a matter of choice. "We're here for a few days yet," she agreed instead.

Maggie smiled, and walked out of the kitchen with Keith Alan Alexander. Fran cleared the table of coffee cups, then absentmindedly started to wash them, her thoughts still on a woman who seemed badly in need of help. She was still there when the door from the courtyard passage opened and a stranger walked in. He was a slightly built young man, with the pale freckled skin that goes with auburn hair. A noticeable limp as he came into the room gave Fran a clue to his identity, but Hamish Harding stared in astonishment at the sight of Elspeth having metamorphosed into the dazzling creature who was now holding out her hand.

"Are you Maggie's brother-in-law, by any chance? I'm Fran Campbell, staying here for a day or two and making free of the kitchen, as you can see!"

"How do you d . . . do," he stammered. "Yes, I'm Hamish. Is Maggie around?"

"Upstairs . . . it's Keith's dinner time."

"Is she all right?" he asked anxiously. "I had the feeling that bringing the bairn home, with Alan not here to be with them, would be a terrible ordeal for her."

"I think it probably was," she agreed, liking him for his sensitivity. "She has to learn to accept that the poor wee boy will never know his father; I'm glad she has you here still to help her."

Hamish continued to stare at her. He hadn't the slightest idea what this girl was doing in Maggie's kitchen, but she had a smile you could bask in, feel warmed and comforted by. When the door from the hall passageway suddenly opened, he was smiling himself, and bemusedly looking at Fran. McAlister glanced from one to the other of them, with the shuttered expression on his face that she now knew meant she'd earned his disapproval yet again.

"I was just going . . . and hardly interfering at all, you'll be glad to know," she said cheerfully, as the only alternative to being intimidated by him. "Maggie's feeding her son, if you're looking for *her*." She walked past him to the door, unaware that Hamish's eyes followed her and that McAlister was sharply alive to the fact.

After a sandwich lunch with Tod in the bar, she spent the afternoon with him and Colonel Forrester, exploring the northern end of the island. The Colonel seemed relieved when she offered to drive his stately old car, and settled himself down happily to the task of answering the hundred and one questions Tod fired at him about Cullin.

The gales of the past few days had almost blown themselves out, but enormous seas were still hurling themselves against the line of cave-ridden cliffs that barricaded the north of the island from the Atlantic. It was a wild and marvellous sight in the afternoon sunlight, and even Tod's relentless demand for information died in the face of it.

When they got back it seemed strange to take her place at a table in the dining room again. Allie gave her a friendly wink and ten minutes later, when they were still waiting for food to arrive, a despairing shrug. It eventually did, but it came haphazardly, and reminded Fran of their first evening at the Castle. Morag looked tearful as the meal dragged on, and even the normally cheerful Allie began to look cross and flustered. Obviously there were still problems in the kitchen, and Fran felt sorry for Maggie and Fiona trying to cope with them. When dinner finally came to an end with an ambitious cheese soufflé that hadn't quite come off, she suggested to Tod that it was time to take their coffee into the library and talk about the future.

They settled themselves, waited hopefully, and were eventually served by Hamish Harding. He put the tray down in front of Fran and then lingered so noticeably that she couldn't ignore the fact that he was still there.

"Tod, this is Mrs Harding's brother-in-law, Hamish . . . Mr Harriman, Hamish, from Nebraska, USA."

"Join us, Mr Harding," Tod said inevitably, "unless you're having to act waiter this evening."

"I have been, but I'm free now."

Tod bustled away to the bar to beg another cup from Jaime and to order the beautiful malt whisky which he'd now learned to sip each evening after dinner as if it was some nectar provided by the gods.

"Was dinner very awful?" Hamish asked as soon as Tod had disappeared. "By the time I was dismissed Maggie was white with despair, Fiona scarlet with fury, and the waitresses on the point of walking out. It's another ten days before the hotel closes . . . Neil will have to do something."

Fran felt a reluctant twinge of sympathy for a man who was probably expected to 'do something' about whatever crisis arose. No wonder he often looked short-tempered and always tired.

"What about you?" she asked Hamish. "How much longer can you stay and keep Maggie company?"

"I've another month's sick leave; after that, if my leg continues to mend, it's back to Inverness, teaching physics and maths. I can't say I want to go very much . . . I wasn't born to be a dominie, I'm afraid, and children are quick to sense that. It's also true that Cullin now seems more and more desirable!" His eyes held hers, making sure that she hadn't missed the meaning of that last confession.

Fran wasn't unfamiliar with intense young men who flung themselves violently into love with her, and she recognised without the slightest difficulty the symptoms that seemed to be developing in Hamish. It would, she felt sure, be something else for McAlister to disapprove of, but she was also aware that Hamish Harding was still recovering from a tragic and frightening experience; he needed tranquillity and peace, not a fresh emotional strain.

"Tod and I won't be here much longer," she said as casually as she could manage.

"You mean you're . . . travelling together?" His face revealed what he thought about it, and again she registered a warning that he was tempted to take a brief acquaintance much too seriously.

"He's a client of my aunt's agency in London. I'm employed to help him write a book, but for the moment we're having a little holiday on Cullin."

Looking slightly happier, Hamish heaved himself to his feet to relieve Tod of the tray he was carrying carefully across the room.

"Here's to the Castle's son and heir," said Tod, remaining on his feet to give the ritual its proper solemnity.

Hamish responded politely by proposing a toast to America, and then they both decided to drink to the health of the Queen. By this time the glasses needed replenishing, and everyone else in the room was beginning to catch the spirit of the thing. They were all in the middle of a fervent toast to Robbie Burns when McAlister crossed the open doorway, en route to the front door with a stormy-looking Fiona. He managed to spare a glance for the revelry going on, and a dark look told Fran that he not only knew who the ringleader was, but blamed her as well for so blatantly encouraging Hamish to forget sorrow and rejoice instead.

Chapter Five

The evening was the happiest they'd spent at the Castle, but Fran went to bed aware that Hamish and the impromptu party had prevented her from talking to Tod. The longer she put it off, the worse his disappointment would be. Every day she could see him digging himself a little more firmly into life on Cullin, and every day she resented McAlister a little more for wanting to deprive him of it. She went down to breakfast next morning surprised not to find Tod already in the dining room. Allie was on duty, looking calmer than the evening before, but still less cheerful than usual.

"Chaos last night, Fran," she muttered, banging down a bowl of porridge, "and I'm warning you right now that tonight will be no better. The wrong kind of help's worse than no help at all."

Definitely all was not well 'below stairs'; but an extra cook spoiling the broth was the last thing they needed, even if she could have managed the miracle of working in the same kitchen as Fiona Mackintosh. She felt ashamed of herself for disliking on almost no evidence at all a woman who worked hard to keep a local industry going; Fiona was just the sort of driving force that a small, isolated community couldn't do without. That was all that mattered, *not* the indisputable fact that Francesca

Campbell found her more than she could cheerfully bear.

After breakfast she went upstairs and tapped at Tod's door. When he called out she went in to find him still not up.

"Hangover, Tod?" she asked with a smile.

"Certainly not, honey, but don't come any nearer . . . I guess I'm loaded with germs right now. I thought something was brewing yesterday, and this morning my temperature's up two whole degrees."

She looked suitably grave and asked what she could do for him.

"Nothing, Fran – I've got everything I need. I'll just stay here quietly and dose myself."

A battery of vitamin pills and bottles lined up on his bedside table confirmed that he believed in following the advice he gave his readers; he was equipped to cure himself of everything except dengue fever and housemaid's knee.

"Well, what about some tea to help the pills go down?" she suggested.

Tod emerged from a vast sneeze and agreed that hot tea would probably be beneficial. "Don't let Mrs Harding come to enquire, though, Fran . . . it wouldn't do for her to catch my germs and pass them on to the baby."

She went down to the kitchen, delivered Tod's message in the course of a friendly chat with Maggie, and collected a tray of tea and toast for the invalid. When she got back upstairs his room reeked of some powerful disinfectant spray, and Tod himself was sitting up in bed considering his medicaments like a general planning his next stage of assault upon the enemy. She grinned at him, thinking again how likeable he was, and then agreed to follow his instructions to take herself out into the health-preserving fresh air.

She'd been walking for an hour or so with the intention of finding her way to the shore north and west of the Castle when she studied her map for the tenth time and decided that she'd gone wrong somewhere. The landscape on this side of the island was wildly beautiful but apparently inhabited only by sheep, who rambled as unconcernedly as mountain goats up whatever hill happened to confront them. She retraced her steps to a track she felt reasonably sure of identifying on the map, and was staring at this yet again when a large spot of rain landed on the paper. Within five minutes the spot had become a shower, then a deluge. She'd just resigned herself to a very wet trudge back to the Castle when the welcome sound of car wheels spurting up stones on the track behind her offered rescue. She turned round as the vehicle slowed to a sudden halt.

"This time I think you *do* need a lift," McAlister's voice said calmly.

It was annoying to have to admit that he was right, but Fran wasn't one to cut off quite the whole of her nose to spite her face. He pushed a black labrador off the front seat and she climbed in, wet but dignified, beside him. She said nothing at all until he turned the Land Rover in what she thought was quite the wrong direction.

"Surely the Castle is behind us? If not, no wonder I missed my way."

"It is," he agreed, "but I happen to be going to Cullin House . . . and so, therefore, are you."

There was no question, apparently, of asking whether she felt inclined to go or not. Himself had spoken and the matter wasn't in doubt.

"It sounds extremely compromising," she said primly

after a moment's thought, in the hope of irritating him. He ignored the provocation and concentrated on threading a way through sheep who seemed to prefer the middle of the road to the hillside; at last he flung an unexpected question at her.

"How old are you, Miss Campbell?"

"Twenty-four . . . and a bit," she admitted, surprised into answering honestly.

"Astonishing!"

"What is?"

"The fact that someone hasn't strangled you before now."

It was said so grimly that she was more seriously taken aback. She knew she'd managed to seem troublesome from the moment they arrived, but *this* amount of dislike seemed out of all proportion to anything she was conscious of having fairly deserved. He hadn't until then struck her as a man who would be unjust – tyrannical and rigid, certainly, but surely fair. She was more curious than hurt but, unware of that, he suddenly offered an even more unexpected apology.

"I'm sorry . . . I shouldn't have said that to someone who has gone out of her way to help us. Elspeth would properly flay me for it, and so would Maggie."

The mention of his sister gave Fran an opening to mention something that had begun to trouble her. "Maggie seems far from strong yet, which is understandable; but I can't help feeling that she's soon going to be desperately lonely besides."

McAlister didn't answer while he steered them into a gravelled drive and stopped a moment or two later in front of a long, low house solidly built of grey stone. It was too plain to be picturesque, but it possessed the rightness of something that was perfectly suited to its surroundings. Storms wouldn't dismay it any more than they disturbed its owner; in fact nothing that came naturally to Cullin would be too much for either of them, it seemed to say.

With the engine and windscreen wipers suddenly still, McAlister made no move to open the door. They were isolated from the rest of the rain-shrouded world, and for an unnerving moment Fran was sharply conscious of his nearness. But when he broke the silence between them she understood that there was no need to feel apprehensive; his thoughts were elsewhere – not on her at all.

Maggie worries *me*," she heard him confessing slowly. "She married later than usual – perhaps when she'd expected not to find a husband. Now, with Alan dead, I fear that there will only be her child to concentrate on, much too passionately. She's a Highlander, you understand . . . we're not people to do things by halves."

Fran could believe it, but he spoke so sadly that she wasn't tempted to indulge in the rare pleasure of agreeing with him. Instead, she frowned over what he'd said, thinking only of Maggie. "She needs to be with lively, normal people. Colonel Forrester is very sweet, and so is Miss Milward, but I doubt if anyone could call them stimulating company." She was also inclined to doubt whether Cullin, despite its beauty, could ever provide a young, sad widow with the comfort she so desperately needed, but the man beside her would reject that as the opinion of a social butterfly, dependent on the pleasures she was used to.

"The Colonel and Miss Milward are Maggie's good friends," he said sternly. "You are also forgetting Fiona, who will not spare herself to keep my sister company."

With that he leaned across Fran to open the door of the Land Rover, but not before he'd registered the expression on her face. "You'd better run for it," he suggested coldly. "The rain isn't going to let up for the next hour or two."

Aware of having incurred his displeasure again, she leapt out and ran as instructed into a square hall, parquet-floored and shabbily welcoming. Bess, the labrador, told to stay on the doormat, settled down looking resigned but reproachful. Then McAlister led the way to a large, pleasant kitchen at the back of the house. Like the one at the Castle, it was obviously the heart of the home he normally shared with Elspeth . . . the place where neighbours dropped in, swopped news, and tasted whatever happened to be cooking. Pleasant as the room itself looked, it was the view from the window that took Fran's breath away. Cullin House was tucked into the lee of the hillside; at the back the ground fell away sharply and steps led down to a walled garden. Lower still lay a small, perfect cove – an arc of pure white sand lapped by a rain-flecked sea.

McAlister came to stand behind her as she stood staring out, too entranced even to speak. "On a fine day we can just see the Outer Hebrides – Lewis is more or less straight ahead," he explained.

Fran turned to smile at him. "On a fine day you must think you'd strayed into paradise," she said slowly.

He stared at her, as if to make sure that she meant what she'd just said. "Do you wonder that I don't want it spoiled?" he asked after a little pause.

"No . . . but there's the little matter of sharing what is so beautiful. Do you feel entitled to keep all this to yourself?"

"I don't – I share it freely with the people of Cullin and any others who I know will take due care of it. All

I insist on preventing is the sort of wholesale invasion that books like Mr Harriman's give rise to."

If Fran had had the slightest hope that he might change his mind about Tod, she now knew better. Himself wasn't given to changing his mind about anything, but about *this* he would be as intractable as granite.

"You look cold and damp," he said suddenly. "You could make some coffee while I hunt out the papers I came for."

He walked out of the room, leaving her to potter about in search of what she needed. Everything spoke of the loving care with which Elspeth normally looked after his house, and the larder could have withstood a siege. It conjured up a picture of life lived in a way that a flat-dweller in London could scarcely imagine . . . of weeks on end when the elements roared outside while its self-sufficient inmates were safely, happily isolated from the rest of the world. It wasn't for her, of course; Fran told herself that such an existence would be intolerable to anyone not born and bred to it from the cradle up. All the same, she had a sudden vivid image in her mind of Cullin House in times of winter storm . . . secure and inviolate and even extraordinarily tranquil despite the tempest outside.

She was still thinking about it when McAlister reappeared, shrugging off the waterproof he hadn't bothered to remove before.

"You have to spend a lot of time away from here at the moment," she said, pouring coffee for him. "Who looks after things?"

"I have a factor – farm manager, perhaps you'd call him. The livestock are mainly his responsibility, but I like to look after certain things myself; the breeding of Highland cattle, for example. We've perfected a strain here which is beginning to be exported all over the world."

She sipped her coffee, annoyed with herself to find that she was beginning to feel nervous again. His eyes were on her hair, in its usual thick daytime plait . . . a rope of bright gold against the dark blue of her sweater.

"You look much too exotic for Elspeth's kitchen," he suddenly observed. "I suppose you can't wait to get back to the fleshpots of London."

"It's where I feel at home," she agreed, wondering for how much longer that would seem true if she didn't soon leave this hauntingly beautiful island. "Cullin's lovely, but I'm used to shops and theatres, and a pavement view of great occasions."

His dark face looked unimpressed. "Our excitements are different, but they're real all the same," he pointed out. "You won't see a glen carpeted with primroses in London; eagles don't float there against a silver sky, or seals play like puppies in a bay outside your windows."

"I'm a Londoner," she insisted desperately, "and I'll be glad to get Tod off an island that feels as if it might be blown clean out into the Atlantic whenever the wind takes it into its head to do so."

"Miss Campbell nervous? Now that *does* surprise me. My impression was that nothing could faze her at all!"

He spoke with his usual gravity, but she had the uncomfortable feeling that he'd not only registered her present lamentable lack of unfazeability but was also amused by it.

"Right now Miss Campbell thinks it's time she got back to the Castle," she said as firmly as she could manage. "I left Tod nursing a bad cold, and Hamish promised to explain the finer points of curling to me this afternoon."

"So I'm required to deliver you back to an assignation with an impressionable man who's even more easily tipped off balance than usual at the moment. I think I'd rather leave you here where you can do less harm."

There was no glimmer of amusement in his face now; hard though she found it to believe, he meant what he'd just said.

"I don't think I'm in the habit of harming people," she pointed out more mildly than she felt.

His eyes beneath dark, frowning brows surveyed her without pleasure. "I'm thinking you're being less than truthful, Miss Campbell . . . you must be well accustomed to bowling young men over like ninepins."

Angry now, as well as hurt, Fran tried not to shout at him. "You make me sound like Mata Hari and Helen of Troy rolled into one! You're much too ready to stick labels on people, and I don't much care for being labelled a heartless adventuress." She was tempted to remind him that he'd been obliged to apologise once before for misconstruing her relationship with Tod Harriman, but it seemed more effective to suggest that his judgements were warped by the limited experience available on a small, isolated island like Cullin.

"Hamish doesn't spend *his* entire life here, McAlister. Inverness might not be quite a swinging metropolis, but it must have taught him not to go to pieces at the sight of a personable female!"

She knew as she spoke the words that they sounded unpleasantly cheap. Himself would doubtless think so as well, and he'd be confirmed in his all too obvious opinion that the sooner she and Tod left Cullin the better. She waited for him to say so, but after a moment or two he made the reason for his disapproval gravely clear.

"My only concern is not to see Hamish hurt. Helping me to look after Maggie has healed him to a certain extent; but he's far from recovered yet. What he least needs now is to get emotionally involved with someone as sophisticated as yourself. I don't say that you mean to be unkind or thoughtless; even the reverse perhaps. But in a week or two you'll go on your way and never spare another thought for Hamish Harding. That may not be how he can deal with you."

It might be true, but even if it wasn't she could see no hope of making the self-opinionated man in front of her understand that she might do Hamish more good than harm. Tragedy and grief still hemmed in his sister-in-law, and probably darkened his own private thoughts as well; to fancy himself a little in love with a passing visitor might at least remind him of the possibility of laughter and joy outside the small confines of the island.

"I doubt if we shall agree about Hamish," she said finally. "But since he's an experienced, adult man why not let him lead his own life? You may own Cullin, but you're not required to play God here to all its inhabitants."

It was a still worse error this time – she could see the flash of anger in his eyes, and registered belatedly the fact that self-control might sometimes slip even in this disciplined and undemonstrative man. For the space of an erratic heartbeat or two she almost expected to be grabbed and shaken into agreeing that he was entitled to play whatever role he chose; but at last he managed to master rage and pick up the jacket she'd thrown down.

"Don't let us keep Hamish waiting," he said between clenched teeth. "Or perhaps you must first minister to Mr Harriman. *He* is paying for your services, is he not?"

Afraid to trust herself to reply, Fran headed in the direction of the door, impelled only by the need to escape and trudge if necessary through whatever downpour still fell outside. But McAlister reached the door before her and held it open. She walked past him, blindly patted the labrador still waiting patiently in the hall, and stepped out into a rain-lashed world that seemed suddenly preferable to the unshakeable security of Cullin House.

Tod was still in his room when she got back to the hotel, but he insisted that he'd been most tenderly looked after. Jaime had been sent up with mid-morning coffee, and Tod was now looking forward to the light luncheon recommended by Mistress Harding.

"Everyone's so kind, Fran," he said contentedly. "It's almost a pleasure to be unwell here. I really feel as if I belong on Cullin."

It wasn't the moment she would have chosen to break her news to him, but it could be avoided no longer. "Tod dear, I've been wanting to talk to you, but there never seems to have been the right opportunity. The truth is that we've got to find somewhere else to write the book."

His fever-flushed face almost paled. "No, you're wrong, Fran – nowhere else could be as good as here. Don't you *like* Cullin?"

She bit back an acid comment on the island and its owner and tried to sound calmly reasonable. "Whether or not I like it scarcely matters. The fact is that Maggie

Harding is still far from strong, with a small child to look after. Extra guests won't be wanted once the hotel closes."

"But we wouldn't be any trouble, Fran. I was even looking forward to helping the poor lady." His face puckered like a baby's, with a mixture of disappointment and concern. "Perhaps I should talk to Mrs Harding . . . explain that we *want* to – what's the expression? – muck in!"

Fran shook her head, finally driven to the point where she must be entirely honest with him. "It's not just Maggie, Tod. McAlister doesn't wish for the book to be written here, and what Himself wishes, goes. He thinks tourists are a blight; the Highlands are better off without them, and Cullin above all must remain uncontaminated!"

There was silence for a while; then, much to her surprise, Tod nodded his head. "It's kind of feudal, I guess, but loving Cullin as I do, I can scarcely blame the guy who wants to keep it that way. I shall have this visit to remember . . . that will have to do."

Torn between regret for his disappointment and pride in his sheer niceness, Fran realised that she should have expected him to behave in this adult, philosophical way; there was nothing of the spoilt child about Tod Harriman, for all that he sometimes seemed like a white-haired schoolboy. He could even teach Neil McAlister a lesson or two in grace and sensitivity.

She smiled at him with more than usual warmth. "Dear Tod, the good news is that Aunt Ernestine says I can stay and work for you. We'll comb the mainland for some small pleasant place that you'll enjoy," she promised earnestly.

His own smile was like a good deed in a naughty world. "Honey, the worst setback of all would have been not being able to keep *you*."

She left him to enjoy the lunch Jaime brought up, and went downstairs wondering whether Hamish would have been warned off having anything to do with her by now. There was, she suspected, nothing in the way of high-handed interference that McAlister was incapable of when his Calvinistic blood was roused. But Hamish was waiting for her, intent on sharing lunch as well as the rest of the afternoon. She thought he stared at her curiously as they settled themselves in a window seat in the bar, but it took him a little while to risk a personal comment.

"Is anything wrong, Fran? . . . you don't seem quite your usual blessedly cheerful self."

She was tempted to say that cheerfulness wasn't what the survivor of his sister-in-law's tragedy was expected to relish. But it would mean relating her conversation with McAlister, and however repellent she found his attitude, she couldn't bring herself to complain of it to Hamish.

"I've just been breaking the news to Tod that we can't stay here. Can *you* suggest somewhere on the mainland where we can be comfortable for the winter while he writes his book?"

"Of course . . . Inverness!" Hamish said at once. "There are any amount of pleasant hotels to choose from and you'd have me there to keep an eye on you."

She smiled at his enthusiasm, but made a mental note to avoid Inverness like the plague. Fran Campbell, dangerous siren, was a figment of McAlister's unbridled imagination; all the same, there was enough truth in what he'd said to be taken seriously. Hamish *was* susceptible at the moment, and she must not encourage him in a friendship that he perhaps already saw as turning into a full-scale love affair. Himself, damn him, was right after all.

Chapter Six

It was Maggie who caught the force of all the frustration and mixed emotions troubling her brother's normally unruffled self-control. What sparked off the first quarrel they'd had since the fights of childhood was her unenthusiastic nod when he announced that he was off down to Kirktown, and would bring Fiona back for the evening. It reminded him of a grievance from the night before.

"It would be nice if you could seem to be welcoming her help," he pointed out somewhat acidly, "and while we're on this subject, it's high time you got your undisciplined staff in order again."

The unfairness of it stung Maggie out of the cold, lonely region she seemed to wander in at the moment. "If you're suggesting that Allie was rude last night, Fiona brought it on herself, I gather, by treating Elspeth like a half-witted servant. Allie wouldn't put up with that, and nor should I have done if I'd been in the room."

"That's Allie's version of it, I suppose – not the account I got from Fiona. I expect there was fault on both sides; they were hard-pressed and tired. But for heaven's sake keep your girl in check this evening, otherwise Fiona would be perfectly justified in refusing to come and help again. She's the last person to make a heroine of herself, but *we* needn't forget that she works hard all day long."

"I know, Neil, and of course I'm grateful," Maggie said more gently. "But don't put all the blame on Allie. She had no difficulty in getting on with Fran when *she* was working in the kitchen."

"And there's the root of the problem," McAlister pointed out. "Francesca Campbell made a friend of Allie, who's got above herself because of it."

Maggie's dark eyes fixed on him in astonishment made him look uncomfortable for a moment. "Who could have put such a spiteful idea in your head? The girls are friends to all of us, but they wouldn't dream of being impertinent, and nor would Fran encourage them to be. All she does is *not* treat them as if they were inferior – but you can't complain about that, because nor do you."

"And you're suggesting that Fiona does?" he asked coldly.

"Not exactly . . . but she can't help giving the impression that only *she* knows what to do in any situation."

There was truth enough in it to silence him for a moment, but finally he harked back to something he was sure about. "I shall be very glad, all the same, when Miss Campbell leaves Cullin."

"I shall be sorry," Maggie replied, uncooperative for once, "I wish she were going to stay."

"With her American friend? So that they can concoct some highly-coloured nonsense about life on a Hebridean island? My dear girl, it's the last thing we want."

Thinking the argument won at last, he stalked out of the kitchen, leaving her staring at a future she could scarcely bear to contemplate . . . Alan lost to her for ever, and Fiona Mackintosh becoming her sister-in-law, for ever telling her what to do. To be at odds with Neil seemed the last straw. She picked up her small son, suddenly overwhelmed by the need to have something warm and living to cling to. The tears that lay in wait all the time now, to betray her into a weakness she despised, blinded her to the fact that Fran, having parted company with Hamish in the courtyard, had seen her desolate figure through the kitchen window.

There were times when people needed to be left alone, but instinct told Fran that this was not one of them where Maggie Harding was concerned. She walked into the kitchen and headed in the direction of the kettle.

"Campbell's unfailing cure," she said calmly, ". . . a cup of tea works wonders when life looks a little grim."

Maggie tucked Keith back into his cot and scrubbed away her tears. "Sorry . . . I'm not usually quite so feeble. I was just thinking about life here after next weekend, as a matter of fact, with everyone gone except Colonel Forrester and Alice Milward. They're the nicest people, but I doubt if anyone could call them infectiously jolly!" Maggie's sad eyes stared out of a white, strained face. "Winter's coming, Fran. When it's dark by four o'clock and there are a lot of lonely night hours to get through, that's when you need a husband or a friend."

"You've got your brother," Fran felt obliged to point out.

"I know, and I couldn't ask for a better. But he's normally at Cullin House and when he marries Fiona I expect I shall see even less of him." She sipped the tea Fran had put in front of her, and tried to smile. "Tell me to count my blessings, and stop whining!"

"All right, I will . . . but that doesn't mean you're not entitled to grieve for what you've lost. You *must* grieve, Maggie, dear – anguish bottled up inside you because you think you have to be brave won't help you to get strong again. In the end you'll be able to manage . . . Cullin itself will help *you.*" Fran paused for a moment before adding, "But I'm afraid that in similar circumstances it wouldn't be the slightest help to me." Seeing Maggie distracted from her own problems by the contemplation of someone else's, she went on with her confession. "You have to be born to this island life to have any hope of coping with it! It's altogether too much for me . . . too beautiful, too isolated, too intensified in ways I never even thought about before Tod and I arrived here. I shall be thankful to get back to the mainland again."

There was a note in her voice that made Maggie stare at her more closely. It was strangely reminiscent of the near-desperation with which Neil had insisted that he wanted unwelcome guests to leave. Something more than mere incompatibility between two very distinct personalities seemed to have set up the tension she sensed in both of them. She had no way of knowing whether this was how Fran Campbell normally reacted to whatever seemed to threaten her habitual approach to life; but it certainly wasn't her brother's usual way of behaving. People that he didn't like he simply ignored.

Unsure whether to comment on what Fran had said or not, she offered a regretful confession of her own. "I was going to ask you to stand godmother to Keith . . . but perhaps it isn't a very practical idea if you don't like Cullin enough ever to want to come back!"

Fran hesitated for a moment or two, then decided that nothing but the truth would do. "I'd be his godmother like a shot, Maggie love, but it wouldn't be a popular choice. McAlister began by thinking I was Tod's chère amie. I put him straight over that, but he's now convinced that just for the hell of it I'm about to wreck Hamish's peace of mind instead. Your brother would prefer to see me quietly drown in the loch; failing that, I am to be run off the island!"

She tried to smile as she spoke, but there was no amusement in her face; resentment was visible, but it was mixed with hurt.

"There's a reason for what must seem a very *un*reasonable attitude, and you're entitled to know what it is," Maggie said quietly. "Neil was engaged to a girl three years ago – a southerner like you and almost as beautiful. He began by doubting that she'd ever transplant up here successfully, but he was lost in love, and she certainly seemed entranced by the idea of becoming mistress of Cullin. She was Colonel Forrester's niece as it happened. The wedding was to be in Gloucestershire and we were all to go – even Elspeth and Dougal, who insisted that Himself couldn't be properly married without them. Then a week before the wedding Neil got a letter from Vanessa calling it all off. He thought she'd suddenly got afraid of the idea of living here permanently and went rushing down to England to reassure her. She wasn't even there – she'd already left for America to join a very rich man who'd stayed at the Castle that summer."

There was a little silence before Fran spoke again. "Thank you for telling me . . . I see now why McAlister didn't exactly rush to welcome us when we arrived. Nice of him, at least, not to turn the Colonel away from his door afterwards."

"They were old friends, and Neil's friendships are for ever."

Like his enmities, Fran thought of saying, but Maggie must already know *that* about him better than anyone else. Instead, she put the subject aside and made an effort to sound briskly cheerful.

"I'm not sure yet where Tod and I will spend the winter, but I'll keep in touch by telephone. If I *am* allowed to be godmother I insist on knowing how my godson is progressing. Thank you for giving me a little share in him, Maggie."

She smiled and left the kitchen, went upstairs to enquire after the invalid, and then took refuge with Colonel Forrester in the dining room, as a way of avoiding a tête-a-tête with Hamish. It was tempting to ask whether the niece who'd jilted Himself so brutally had come to the sticky end she deserved, but the Colonel was eager to launch instead into a graphic account of his running battle with a wily trout that had been adjourned by both parties until the following day. Only when they were drinking coffee at the end of another slow and disorganised meal did Lionel Forrester manage to get his mind off fish and on to a subject that troubled him.

"Mrs Harding, now . . . how does she strike *you*, Francesca? I should hate to uproot myself from here, and so would Alice Milward, but I wonder whether we ought both to insist on leaving."

Fran pondered the question, then slowly shook her head. "I don't think so. I know Maggie seems frail at the moment, but she's getting stronger day by day. The rest of us will be gone by the end of the week, and then I suppose McAlister will go back to his own house as well. My own opinion is that she *needs* company . . . it would be a kindness if you stayed throughout the winter as usual."

The Colonel smiled his rare, shy smile, and retired to the billiard room a happier man; but Allie's mutinous face when she came to collect the coffee cups didn't suggest that all was well behind the green baize door.

"Come back, Fran Campbell . . . all is forgiven," she hissed in a stage whisper. "Yon . . . b . . . besom is in there telling us what to do until I could heave the plates at her. Elspeth's walked out of the kitchen, and she won't come back until Fiona's left for the night."

Fran's heart ached for Maggie, caught in the middle of the storm, but there was nothing she could do about it. She'd been told politely but firmly that she wasn't needed in the kitchen, and she wasn't going to give McAlister the chance to say it all over again. In fact, she hoped to leave Cullin Castle without even having to say goodbye to him.

She played her ritual game of Scrabble with Miss Milward in the library, lost as usual to a demon opponent who masqueraded as a genial and kindly soul, and then announced thankfully that she was going to bed. But with no more than one foot on the bottom tread of the staircase, she was halted by Neil McAlister, standing just behind her and holding the anorak she'd left hanging in the cloakroom.

"A little stroll, Miss Campbell?" The rain's stopped, and a new moon is rising over Beinn Mhor. Would a breath of fresh air not be good for you?"

"Kind of you to suggest it," she said with difficulty, "but it seems to have been a long and tiring day. I think I'll make do without more fresh air than I had this morning."

It was a mistake to remind herself of that disconcerting visit to Cullin House . . . it would be hard enough to erase from memory even if her mind could stop dwelling on it like a tongue continually touching an aching tooth. She saw his own expression change, but too briefly for any deductions to be made; he was so maddeningly difficult to fathom that she even felt an unexpected twinge of sympathy for Colonel Forrester's niece. Perhaps the poor girl had scarcely been told, had never really understood, how much he'd wanted her to share Cullin with him.

"If you're not too tired for a very short walk, I should be glad of the chance to talk to you," he said now, in his most formal manner. But the courtesy of it didn't amount to much, because he was holding out her jacket and her only option seemed to be to agree to put it on and go outside with him.

Reared among lamp-lit streets, she still wasn't prepared for the total blackness that awaited them beyond the range of lighted windows. Almost at once she tripped over a hidden tree root, and the next moment felt his hand clamped to her arm. But her pulse didn't quicken. Not the most extravagant imagination could have seen anything remotely amorous in that stern grip; she was simply a fool of a townee who couldn't be trusted to walk by herself in the dark.

In this unexciting way she was led to where the trunk of a fallen tree made a convenient seat by the edge of the loch. The wind as well as the rain had died away, leaving such stillness behind that even the smallest sounds could be heard – the rustling of each leaf and blade of grass disturbed by tiny creatures going about their nocturnal affairs. With her eyes finally accustomed to the night, Fran could distinguish shades of blackness, and make out the soft glimmer of the loch. Then the moon swung clear of the mountain's great shoulder of rock and laid a path of silver across the water. She held her breath, too entranced to speak, and not even aware of McAlister's inspection of her moonlit face. But at last she remembered why they had come out.

"You said you wanted to talk to me," she reminded him.

"Yes . . . did you mean it when you said that you couldn't wait to get away from Cullin?"

"It's Tod who wants to stay." She'd insisted on that once before; but it seemed necessary to make the man beside her understand that she could keep a level head despite even the blandishment of the scene in front of them.

"Would you stay with him?"

The grave question made her reply sharply. "Does it matter whether I would or not? From the moment we arrived you couldn't have made it more clear that we weren't welcome. You don't strike me as a man much given to changing his mind."

"Put with unusual moderation, Miss Campbell. What you really mean, I think, is that I'm as stubborn as a mule and constitutionally unable to admit that I might have made a mistake!"

"Something like that," she agreed, disturbed by the gleam of amusement that the moon now showed her in his face. Himself angry, she could cope with; Himself contemptuous it was a pleasure to confront. But Neil McAlister smiling might, like Cullin itself, be altogether too much for her. It was a relief when he went back to frowning over whatever occupied his mind.

"I *have* made a mistake," he said after a moment's silence. "I thought that Fiona's help would solve a temporary crisis for us – just until the season finishes. That hasn't worked out, and Maggie is being battered to death in the pitched battles between Fiona and the rest of the staff. I've had to suggest that Elspeth and the girls are better left to struggle on by themselves for the rest of this week; after that the problem will solve itself for the time being. My real anxiety is what happens from then on. I hadn't realised quite how hard this first winter without Alan is going to be for Maggie. Fiona will do her best to keep my sister company, but her job takes her all round the island, and frequently over to the mainland."

Fran bit back the words that trembled on her lips. If he wanted – as of course he did – to believe that the girl he thought of marrying would comfort his sister, instead of driving her mad, who was Fran Campbell to try to make him admit that he was making another mistake? She'd found nothing else to say instead when the man beside her spoke again, quietly, but with an effort that he couldn't quite conceal.

"I gather that to have *your* company for a while would make all the difference in the world to my lonely sister."

Fran sat perfectly still, but the effort not to run away from him made every muscle in her body protest. Run *now*, her heart seemed to be shouting . . . run to the sea and a boat, any boat, so long as it puts out away from Cullin; if she made her own mistake and stayed she might be bewitched into wanting to stay for ever. Even now, although she could still tear herself away, she might never quite recover from the separation.

"You haven't answered me," McAlister said after a long silence.

"If I . . . if I agreed to stay," she muttered between dry lips, "you'd have to let Tod stay as well. I promised to go on working with him – on the book you disapprove of so much."

"I realise that." The sadness in his deep voice told her what it cost him to reverse his decision. Cullin was his dear and precious inheritance, to be safeguarded for as long as he drew breath. But Maggie's need was desperate, and for the moment he must put her first.

"You still don't quite understand about Tod," she explained with difficulty. "He wears loud clothes, looks and sometimes sounds like any other brash American. But he's an honourable and truly gentle man. If those sound old-fashioned words to use, then so much the worse for the standards of behaviour that we've now come to take as normal. Cullin means a great deal to *him* as well; you have only to ask him not to mention it in his book and he won't do so. In fact, he'll probably not refer to it anyway. He perfectly understands that it mustn't be spoiled."

McAlister nodded, disconcerting her with a capitulation she hadn't been expecting. She was provoked into wanting to disconcert *him*. "Have you forgotten that Hamish will still be here as well? I am afraid he *is* making up his mind to fall in love with me, and even though you've decided that I'm some sort of female Dracula, red in tooth and claw, I don't have any desire to see him hurt."

"I doubt if I expressed myself quite so graphically," McAlister observed solemnly. "Hamish *is* a problem . . . another problem, I grant you; but for the moment Maggie has to be my main concern. I shall rely on you to deal with him as tactfully as you can – if there isn't one already, perhaps you could hint at some fictitious admirer in London, counting the days until you go home."

"Well that won't strain my imagination too much," Fran was pleased to agree, hoping that it left her with the last word.

She stood up, suddenly aware that this moonlit conversation had lasted long enough. The night, the serenely beautiful scene, and the sweetly-scented air required some different interlude, not this armed truce that seemed to be the best that they could manage. She felt weighed down suddenly with tiredness, or was it simply with regret for an opportunity that Hamish would certainly not have allowed to go to waste.

"I think I'll go back," she said almost desperately, "there's enough moonlight to see by now – you needn't fear that I'll take a header into the loch."

He merely held out his hand and she had to put her own into a clasp that felt so warm and strong and wonderfully secure that the instinct to run returned again, almost overwhelming her. With an effort that made her legs tremble she managed to walk beside him, but she could find nothing to say as they retraced their steps, and nor, it seemed, could he.

Back in the Castle courtyard again, he didn't immediately release her hand and she had to stare up at him.

"Thank you for agreeing to stay for Maggie's sake when I realise that you don't want to," he said quietly. "If it's any consolation I don't look forward to the next three months any more than you do."

She pulled herself away from him and walked indoors. Someone spoke to her as she passed blindly through the kitchen, but she was too occupied in not bursting into tears to answer them. London was another country; exiled from where she properly belonged, it looked like Shangri-la, desirable but unattainable.

Chapter Seven

Next morning Fran hesitated about offering her services in the kitchen, anxious not to give the impression that she reckoned they couldn't manage without her. But the thought of Elspeth having to cope alone while Maggie was occupied with the baby finally drove her into putting her head round the kitchen door. Elspeth *was* there alone, and there was no doubt about the welcome in her smile.

"I was afraid Maggie would be busy upstairs," Fran explained, "but it's also true that I wanted to be part of the team again! I haven't enjoyed the last two days nearly as much."

Elspeth looked faintly sceptical. "Do you say so, lassie? Speaking purely for myself, I'll be glad when this week is over. I'm not a natural-born fancy cook, ye ken . . . wholesome but plain is my motto, and it suits Himself well enough when we're back at the House." She put a mug of tea on the table in front of Fran. "You're going to bide, I hear."

"For a month or two," Fran was careful to point out, thinking that Elspeth made it sound as if she was to be there until Judgement Day. "I've never been away from London as long as this before."

"London? I've never seen it, lassie – don't know that I even want to; and I feel sorry for the puir souls that have to live their lives there."

Fran sipped her tea, briefly wishing that Elspeth and Aunt Ernestine could meet one day. A rare confrontation that would be, each of them respecting but totally misunderstanding the other. Then she wiped the grin off her mouth and got on with the pressing job of counting out slices of bread for toast.

Half an hour later the door burst open and Maggie rushed in, apologies already tumbling off her lips. The sight of the ordered kitchen, unrecognisable for the battlefield of the past two days, halted her in her tracks.

"Elspeth, you must have been up since dawn. I meant to be down much earlier, but Keith wouldn't . . ." then she stopped registering the fact that Elspeth was smiling and that Fran, enveloped in a flowered overall several sizes too large, was presiding over various pans on the Aga. She went over to disturb the cook by hugging her.

"Neil says you're not leaving," she said simply. "Dear Fran, I'm so glad."

"So am I." The words uttered themselves and were even true, Fran realised. Fear might still lie at the bottom of her heart, coiled like a snake and just as deadly, but for the moment a kind of joy was suddenly uppermost, and a light-headed feeling of reprieve. She would worry when the time came if Cullin made some demand that she couldn't meet, or left an image in her mind that she couldn't wipe away.

Maggie was looking worried again. "You and Mr Harriman are here to work . . . you mustn't spend all your time in here, helping me."

"We're on holiday until the hotel closes; till then I can please myself. It will be time enough to start pounding a typewriter after that."

"You'll be here for Chistmas *and* for Keith's

christening," Maggie remembered happily. "Neil and Hamish are his godfathers, of course."

"There's something to be thought about before that," Elspeth reminded her. "How do you feel about Hallow-e'en, my hinnie?"

A shadow dimmed Maggie's new-found brightness for a moment, then she did her best to shrug off sadness and smile at them. "I'd forgotten about it, I'm afraid. But of course we must celebrate it. We always do; and in any case it's something Mr Harriman shouldn't miss."

"You mean bobbing for apples, witches' masks . . . *that* sort of thing?"

Maggie smiled at the dubious expression on Fran's face. "Not quite. It's always the night the hotel closes for the winter and we have a special evening to say goodbye to our guests. Those who are still here know about it and come prepared. We dress for dinner and have a ceilidh afterwards – music, and Highland reels for anyone who feels energetic enough."

"Well, you can be sure Tod will, even if he has to dance by himself," Fran pointed out. "He's in the process of swallowing the local way of life hook, line and sinker. Offer him an eightsome reel and it will be like a call to arms." Then she smiled at the look of astonishment on Maggie's face. "What have I said to cause you so much surprise?"

"I was trying to picture a white-haired old gentleman doing an eightsome! Does he have the slightest idea how arduous they are?"

Fran's chuckle made Elspeth join in. "Dear girl, Tod may have white hair, but it's been like that since he was twenty-five. He's a remarkably spry fifty-two, energised by every vitamin known to the American pharmaceutical industry! I dare say he'll keep going in a reel longer than anyone else can."

She left the kitchen, still grinning at the idea, to go in search of the man himself, and found him in the hall, deep in conversation with McAlister. From the glow of happiness around him Fran knew that he'd already been told they were to stay on Cullin.

"I don't need to ask if you're better," she said, smiling at him and ignoring his companion. "You look as if you'd just come into a fortune."

"Better than that, Fran. Mr . . . McAlister here . . . no, dammit, I'll use a friendlier name – *Neil* has just been offering us the next three months at the Castle. Right now I could run clean over the top of Beinn Mhor without stopping to draw breath."

She saw even McAlister's stern mouth tug itself into a smile. He might still not want them there, but Tod's uncomplicated delight was hard to resist. No one but a bigoted fool could continue to believe that so wholehearted an admirer of all things precious to Cullin could intend to do them the slightest harm.

Over Elspeth's porridge in the dining room, they plotted out a plan of campaign for getting down to work. Tod listed headings of activity with a businesslike precision that reminded her of just how successful an author he was. On his own ground Mr Harriman was impressive enough to explain why he was now a wealthy man as well as a very nice one.

"I must make myself known to Mrs Harding after breakfast, Fran. There's yesterday's kindness to thank her for, but I must also see whether there's a small room somewhere that I can hire as an office."

"Bound to be. If there's one thing the Castle isn't short of it's rooms."

"Transport's got to be thought about, too," said

Tod, now getting down to things in earnest. "We shan't need to keep that car garaged on the mainland now, but we'll need something here for getting down to Kirktown."

Fran considered the problem for a moment. "What about making Colonel Forrester an offer? I doubt if he goes out much in the winter, except to take his usual walks. He might welcome the idea of having his car used occasionally."

"Brilliant – I'll tackle *him* after dinner when he's feeling mellow! Next thing is warmer clothes." Face shadowed for a moment by the fear that they might have to cross that dreadful stretch of water again, Tod tried to smile at her. "I suppose that means a trip to the mainland."

"Not for me," said Fran. "I can get my cousin to pack up extra things for me and ship them here. I'll only need the sort of waterproof that will keep out Highland rain, and a pair of boots built for tramping hills rather than city pavements, but I'm sure to be able to find those in Kirktown."

She broke off suddenly to signal to Maggie who had just come into the dining room. "My boss wants to meet you. Tod Harriman – Mrs Harding."

Tod leapt to his feet, pulled out a chair, and seated Maggie in it with what Fran could only think of as tenderness. She reckoned that they might make friends more easily alone, and wandered away to fetch more coffee from the kitchen. By the time she got back, Tod's health and Maggie's baby had been satisfactorily discussed, and they were getting down to less important matters. The question of rent for the 'office' turned out to be the biggest stumbling block, but Maggie finally gave in to the extent of accepting half of what Tod was anxious to pay. When she finally got up and left them he stared after her for so long that Fran had to repeat her question before he heard it.

"Is everything settled . . . can we start work on Monday?"

"Yes . . . yes, it's settled," he agreed with unaccustomed vagueness. "You know, Fran, if I was an artist I'd want to paint Mrs Harding. She's got the sort of face that would have haunted those old Italians. Maybe I should learn."

He *would* learn, if he set his mind to it; Fran had no doubt about that, but it seemed safe to air one reasonable doubt. "There may not be time – we're going to be rather busy on our own account. In any case, you've something else to learn first unless you're already familiar with Highland reels. We've got until Maggie's ceilidh on Friday to find out how they're done."

His eyes gleamed with joyous anticipation, as she'd known they would, and the afternoon was spent in the hall, being instructed by Allie and Dougal. Tod's only regret lay in the fact that he'd be performing in 'breeks' when it was obvious that the kilt was the only proper dress of a Highland gentleman.

Without too much argument from Maggie, and none at all from Elspeth, Fran resumed her place in the kitchen and everything there was peaceful and smooth until McAlister returned from a trip to the mainland the day before the party. That evening he caught her while she was eyeing the line of pheasants hanging up in the game larder. They'd been denuded of feathers by Dougal and looked slightly more cookable as a result, but she was wishing strongly that she'd dealt with just one pheasant before in her culinary life.

"Selecting your dinner, Miss Campbell?" McAlister's voice enquired smoothly behind her.

"I'm wondering how to cook it if you must know," she replied with absent-minded honesty.

His dark brows suddenly meeting in a straight line warned her of trouble ahead. "I imagine that the cooking of tomorrow's dinner has nothing to do with you."

"Then you imagine wrongly. We've agreed that Maggie must be left free to be the calm, unflustered hostess among her guests. Elspeth and I are going to do the cooking, and Dougal's wife will help us dish up and serve. Allie and Morag will be able to join in the fun all the sooner with another pair of hands to help."

"*We*'ve agreed," he repeated fiercely. "I suppose I know what *that* means. Miss Campbell has decreed, and everyone else agrees. You take too much on yourself, I think."

He spoke with a sharp explosion of fury that seemed out of all proportion to her crime this time. It would have been something to puzzle over if she hadn't been too occupied in holding on to her own temper.

"Just what do you recommend instead? That Maggie rushes backwards and forwards between basting of the pheasants in the kitchen and talking to her guests in the drawing room? . . . Or that Elspeth goes quietly mad trying to cope by herself? Or would you prefer to call in Miss Mackintosh again?"

She sensed him visualise for a horrified second, the domestic riot that would almost certainly ensue; even so he wasn't a man to yield ground easily. "At least it would be more seemly for Fiona to help," he insisted stiffly. "She belongs on Cullin."

Never before, in all their other acrimonious exchanges, had Francesca Campbell, who *didn't* belong, been quite so definitely rejected. She could feel her eyes pricking with tears that must on no account be allowed to fall, but amid the turmoil of mind and heart she clung to one thing – the hurt she felt was not connected with the looming figure in front of her. She was simply becoming infected with Tod's madness – wanting to belong, and being made to feel like a child standing for ever on the outside of a desirable shop window. Fiona Mackintosh was inside the shop, by right and by acceptance. It was hard not to hate her, and impossible not to feel envious. Fran took a deep breath and forbade herself the relief of shouting at McAlister; provoke her as he might, she would remain calm . . . the sophisticated incomer who found him absurdly out of touch with reality.

"Don't think I haven't got the message already that I'm an interfering southerner hellbent on meddling in your affairs," she said sweetly. "It's for the last time I promise you; after the weekend Tod and I will start work, and Maggie will resume the running of the Castle with no help from me. Take comfort from that, McAlister, and now leave me to commune with these poor dead pheasants."

She needed him to stoke her defiance with some fresh piece of Highland prejudice and male stupidity. It was treachery of the basest kind that he chose instead to smile at her, showing her for the first time the warm, shy heart of Neil McAlister.

"I doubt that you'll cease meddling for as long as you remain on Cullin, but less ungrateful people than me would call it true kindness. I didn't mean to sound so churlish just now, but when I invited you to stay on it wasn't so that you could go on being an upaid chef. You're a guest and should be treated like one. It's for us to do the extra work of the ceilidh, not you."

His voice was gentle, and as disarming as his smile, but

she shook her head. "Maggie took a lot of persuading . . . for heaven's sake don't tell her that she shouldn't have agreed." Fran hesitated and decided that, in this moment of unusual softness, she might as well take another bull by the horns. "I expect she's told you that I'm allowed to be Keith's godmother. Does that offend your principles more than you can bear?"

His smile disappeared as suddenly as it had come. "It offends my common sense," he said almost harshly. "The bairn needs someone *here*, not hundreds of miles away. I don't know what Maggie was thinking of."

She *hadn't* been thinking of Fiona – that was the rub, Fran realised. The girl that he'd chosen for himself ought to have been given a privilege that had gone to someone else. It was a slight to Fiona that she would find it hard to forgive, and he found it hard to forgive himself; but he refused to blame Maggie – it was all the fault of *this* insidiously appealing creature in front of him, with her golden hair and laughing eyes and easy, pleasant ways.

"I wish you'd never come to Cullin," he said deliberately. "I wish that more than anything else I could dream of except restoring Alan Harding to life again for my sister."

Then he turned and walked away, taking with him the memory of Fran's suddenly stricken face. He'd *meant* to hurt her, although he didn't know why. Yes, he did – for as long as she was there she'd be a thorn in his flesh, goading *him*, distracting Hamish, and undermining Fiona's rightful place among them.

Away from her and able to think more calmly, it didn't seem a sufficient enough tally of faults to justify the words he'd flung at her – he knew himself for a man who hated hurting other living creatures.

But *that* was Francesca Campbell's true fault . . . she was like those nymphs and sirens of old, putting spells on rational men and leading them off the paths of righteousness.

Chapter Eight

For the rest of that day and the next McAlister chose to spend all his waking hours at Cullin House. Just as anxious herself to avoid another encounter, Fran found that there was no need for her to keep out of his way. An end of term mixture of gaiety and sadness seemed to have descended on the rest of the hotel guests; they were getting ready to leave the morning after the party, and there were fishing rods to be cleaned and stored away for another summer; favourite walks to be taken for the last time; and expeditions to Kirktown in search of the tweed and hand-knitted sweaters, caps and gloves that must be taken home. Given them to admire, Fran agreed that the quality of the materials was beautiful and that every garment was knitted with meticulous skill. It was harder to enthuse about their colours and designs. Did they have to be so drab and ordinary? She wondered whether Fiona Mackintosh ever went to see what tempted the tourists who flocked into Edinburgh by the thousand every summer, much less to London to see what would sell there . . . certainly not these old-fashioned cardigans and unimaginative round-necked sweaters that had had their day twenty years before.

It was a temptation to meddle again, an outright invitation to interfere, which must be resisted because it would certainly raise a hornets' nest about her head.

But Fran's heart ached for the Cullin women who were surely capable of turning out irrestistibly attractive clothes, instead of such sombre-looking ones.

For the moment, though, there were more immediate problems to wrestle with – Maggie's 'special' dinner, and the supper that would be needed afterwards for all the extra guests arriving after dinner from every corner of the island. A ceilidh, apparently, was an occasion to which everyone reckoned to come, and there was nothing like Highland dancing for stimulating the appetite. The dinner menu was decided upon: smoked salmon, then pheasant with game chips, sprouts, roasted chestnuts and bread sauce, and a concoction to finish up with which mostly consisted of Drambuie and cream! The working party in the kitchen included several volunteers, among them Tod and Lionel Forrester, the latter surprised but delighted to find himself capable of helping, and Tod, as usual, infecting everyone with his own brand of gaiety. In the warmth and happiness of the kitchen Fran saw Maggie slowly but surely beginning to smile without effort; memories remained, but they were finding their rightful place in the background of her life.

By the end of the afternoon, pies, quiches, bannocks, and glistening bowls of fruit salad were lavishly lined up, Fran's Caledonian creams were safely in the refrigerator, and all the dinner vegetables were prepared. Now she had only the pheasants to brood over, while Allie and Morag put the finishing touches to the dining room, and everyone else went upstairs to dress. Amethyst-coloured napkins on every table exactly echoed the colour of bowls of heather, and snowy tablecloths and delicate crystal gleamed in the lamplight. The Castle was en fête, and doing its guests proud. It only remained for the pheasants in the ovens to turn, as required, from pallid white to delectable golden-brown, and she would have nothing to worry about.

Elspeth returned from a tour of inspection of the rooms to confirm that everything was ready. "Himself's back," she added contentedly.

"Back . . . from where?"

"He went down to Kirktown, to bring back the American lassies. One of them still has her ankle in plaster, but Neil thought they should be here."

It was a kindness that seemed to set the seal on a shining evening. Nothing would go wrong with the pheasants, Fran now realised; it was going to be that kind of evening. She was alone for a moment in the kitchen when the sound of bagpipes, hauntingly distant, grew slowly on the air . . . Dougal, back in his true role of piper to Himself, was leading his guests in to dinner. Mesmerised by the plaintive sound, Fran stood still to listen, aware that it wasn't only Tod whose heart and imagination were being caught by Cullin's way of life. She would go back to London, it was *her* place; but the suspicion was growing that even if she lived to be very old, she would forget nothing about these different island days.

The sound of Dougal's music suddenly came closer because someone had opened the kitchen door. Fran swung round expecting Elspeth, and found McAlister instead, heart-stoppingly beautiful in the splendour of full Highland evening dress. The adjective was right, although there was nothing effeminate about it for the man who stood there. She'd grown accustomed to the shabby kilt he always wore with the unselfconscious ease of a man dressed in his natural working clothes; but this was a McAlister she hadn't seen before, the gorgeous materials of velvet and lace oddly emphasising his masculinity.

"You look very . . . very grand," she murmured at last, thinking it high time one of them said something.

"Fine feathers on top . . . still the same awkward customer underneath."

"I don't doubt it," she agreed with a faint smile.

The glimmer of amusement she often found herself looking for lighted his eyes, but he'd promised himself tonight that he wouldn't be provoked by a girl he'd scarcely yet had a peaceful conversation with.

"Are you all right in here? Is there anything I can do to help?"

"I *hope* I'm right in saying everything's under control, but only time will tell! Go back to your guests, McAlister, and forget domestic worries . . . in any case you look much too splendid to be hobnobbing with the cook."

"You forget – being Himself, I can hobnob with whomever I choose."

"True, but you're a distraction. I think I shall do better on my own."

It was the truth. Tiredness was making her vulnerable, and Dougal's music played on emotions which were much too near the surface. If McAlister didn't take his disturbing presence away very soon, she'd probably end up bursting into tears.

"Promise me you'll eat some of your own dinner, and leave this blasted kitchen as soon as you can."

Damn him for the tenderness in his voice . . . it was almost the last straw. She made a great effort to smile, and look carefree while she did so.

"We're looking forward to the ceilidh, Elspeth and I . . . we'll be there, never fear."

Now, surely, he'd turn and go, with the little formal bow he often used. Instead, he took her hand and lifted it to his mouth. The gesture was as unselfconscious as the way he wore his Highland dress, and just as effective.

Tears were suddenly clogging her throat in earnest, but before they could give her away she was saved by Elspeth bursting through the door. McAlister dropped her hand immediately, and walked out of the room, leaving her to make a great business of opening the oven door to inspect the pheasants.

The next two hours disappeared in a feverish haze they could hardly remember afterwards. While Fran and Elspeth dished up and carved for dear life, Allie and Morag flew in and out, balancing piles of plates and vegetable dishes, and bringing back the empties which Annie McDougall dealt with in the utility room while singing at full throttle. It was a mad, exhilarating scramble they all enjoyed, safe in the knowledge that there were no disasters. Then suddenly the rush was over; everyone was at the last peaceful stage of drinking coffee, and all that remained was to clear the dining room and put the finishing touches to the buffet supper.

At last Fran hurried upstairs to change out of her working clothes, disconcerted to find that she strongly *didn't* want to join the party. Nothing so simple as tiredness tugged at her; the difficulty was Himself and the shattering effect he seemed to have on her. But if she gave in to a craven desire to crawl into bed, she didn't put it past him to notice she wasn't downstairs and come and drag her out again.

She coiled up her heavy plait of hair, retouched eye shadow, lipstick, and perfume, and then flung on a long midnight-blue velvet skirt and a shirt that seemed to be made out of snowflakes of lace. Outwardly, at least, Fran Campbell was herself again – cool, elegant, and so damned Londonish it wasn't true.

By the time she got downstairs the rooms were thronging with new arrivals, and the sound of fiddles tuning up announced that the next part of the evening was about to begin. Tod, resplendent in velvet jacket and bow tie, was thoughtfully on the watch for her, and immediately led her into the cleared hall where sets were forming for the first eightsome. The music was too toe-tapping to be resisted, and in a moment or two they were off, spinning and dipping, bowing and curtseying with the rest.

Maggie, with her tartan sash a splash of colour against the whiteness of her dress, was in another set partnered by someone Fran didn't know; McAlister was going down the dance with a flame-haired girl she *did* recognise – Fiona Mackintosh, transformed by excitement and happiness into striking beauty. She danced with a joyous abandon that not only infected everyone else but was an eye-opener to Fran. This wild, fiery creature was the real Fiona, not the controlled woman who chivvied the islanders into producing all those dreary cardigans.

It wasn't all as energetic as that; every so often the dancing was interspersed with music to be listened to, as someone casually picked up a fiddle or guitar and began to play, and everyone else sat quietly on the floor. Hamish, unable to dance because of his injured leg, revealed an unexpected talent for playing the piano, and Fiona partnered him on the violin in duets which would have done justice to a recital in Wigmore Hall. It was becoming Fiona's evening, in fact; there was no doubt in Fran's mind, and none in anyone else's she thought, that Fiona saw it as the perfect moment to stake her claim to being the future mistress of Cullin. She was doing it very well, behaving with the smiling assurance of a woman who was finally sure of her ground.

Fran sat with Tod, eating supper she didn't in the least want, only anxious to keep out of the way of McAlister and the girl who seemed glued to his side. Fiona occasionally looked across the room as if to make sure this demonstration of belonging wasn't being lost on an intrusive southerner; the southerner in question went on cheerfully smiling at Tod's flow of conversation, though she couldn't remember afterwards a single one of the things they'd talked about.

Supper was almost over when she looked up to see McAlister looming over her.

"The dinner was delicious, Francesca, and everything else has been perfect. We've a great deal to thank you for."

She wished desperately that he wouldn't stare at her so intently; that he'd go away and take Fiona with him.

"Are you enjoying the ceilidh, Miss Campbell," asked Fiona, ". . . or does it all seem very primitive and amateurish to someone used to London entertainment?"

"I . . ." Fran hesitated, unable to bring out the lie that she was enjoying herself, and tried another tack. "There was nothing amateurish about your performance with Hamish. You play beautifully together."

Fiona shrugged. "We get by among friends. But we haven't heard you perform yet. Everyone's supposed to contribute, you know, and I can't believe that Miss Campbell doesn't play half a dozen things perfectly."

It was said with a surface sweetness that almost but not quite concealed the knife-flick of her smile.

"Francesca has already contributed greatly," McAlister pointed out gravely.

"Of course, but only behind the scenes," Fiona insisted. "I'm sure she could perform just as well in the spotlight."

You mean, Fran thought, that you hope I can't and that I shall be led into making a complete fool of myself.

"I'm too spoiled by London," she said, with as much of a drawl as she could manage. "We don't have to provide our own entertainment there, so the result is that I don't even play a penny whistle."

"Maybe not . . . but she sings like a bird," said Tod, suddenly leaping into the ring. "I've heard her when she thought I wasn't listening."

"We shall look forward to it," Fiona murmured, giving him a flashing smile, and finally moving on.

"Tod – what possessed you to say that," Fran hissed in his ear. "I haven't the slightest interest in trying to compete with Fiona Mackintosh. She can play the violin standing on her head for all I care."

Tod looked at her flushed face, aware that more than just the irritation of being needled by a spiteful woman was upsetting her. She would normally have laughed at that, but now she was much nearer to tears.

"Let's forget about her," he said gently, "but I'd like these good people to have the pleasure of hearing you. We'll start off with the Eriskay Love Lilt. Don't tell me you don't know the words, because I've heard you sing it clean through."

He wandered over to the piano before Fran could haul him back, and beckoned to her. Short of bolting out of the room she hadn't any choice but to go and join him.

"Tod dear . . . this is ridiculous . . ." Her voice

faltered and died in the face of his joyous smile as he propped himself against the piano and pulled a mouth organ out of his pocket – it seemed that Tod had come prepared for the ceilidh, and that they were *both* going to make fools of themselves. Then he put the small thing to his mouth and a wistful arpeggio of notes silenced the chatter in the room.

"You'll know this one, ladies and gentlemen," said Tod.

He played the instrument like a master, the haunting, plaintive accompaniment weaving itself magically around the sweet, rich sound of Fran's voice. She wasn't a trained singer, but the notes fell as effortlessly as a bird's – like a choirboy's fed on cream, Maggie thought, listening to her. There was a little silence at the end of the song, then a roar of applause. Fran conceded 'My love is like a red, red rose' as an encore, and then firmly sat down, leaving Tod to change the tempo back to reels again. Hands came round her shoulders from behind, gently but irresistibly pushing her in the direction of the dance floor.

"Our turn, I think, Francesca," McAlister said quietly.

She went through the movements in a trance, preserved by heaven from forgetting what she was supposed to do next, waiting for the moments when the dance brought them together and their hands gripped and held. She didn't know whether it was paradise or purgatory, except that when it was over she wanted his hands to be still holding her. He led her off the floor, and back to Tod, and crossed the room himself to find Maggie. Fran found herself three feet away from Fiona Mackintosh, being stared at with a concentrated venom that made her blood run cold.

Chapter Nine

It was a relief to get away from the Castle next morning. McAlister was much in evidence among the throng of people in the hall, calmly bidding them goodbye and making sure that out of the mountain of luggage strewn around the floor they finally left with what belonged to them. With Tod beside her in the Colonel's stately car Fran drove down to Kirktown at a suitably decorous pace, while Dougal roared along in front of them with a bus-load of guests being delivered to the Mallaig ferry. She was grateful to have to force her mind to concentrate on the winding downhill road, otherwise it would have kept going over the night before, like a donkey tied to a treadmill. In some strange way she didn't yet want to face, the evening had made a subtle shift in relationships; all she was certain of for the moment was that things had changed, and that they had changed permanently.

She and Tod spent the morning in Kirktown, prowling round in search of the various items needed to equip the new 'office', tracking down a mac and boots for herself, and practically a whole new wardrobe of winter clothes for Tod. She could see he was sorely tempted in the matter of a kilt, but he finally put it down with a little sigh and walked resolutely away. A man had to have the figure for a kilt, even if his granny had given him the right to it.

Over a lunch of herrings cooked in oatmeal in a harbourside restaurant she found him untalkative for once.

"Why so thoughtful, Tod . . . did I spoil your appetite bringing you too near the water?" she asked with a grin.

"Hardly noticed it, to be truthful. I was still thinking about last night," he confessed. "It was a very special evening. I shall never forget the way Neil looked, and Mrs Harding was just . . . beautiful . . . brave and beautiful. Didn't you think so, Fran?"

She heard the wonder in his voice, and felt alarmed by it. He was no impressionable youth to be knocked off balance by a passing fancy; but their situation was complicated enough without Tod losing his heart to their widowed hostess.

"You've been keeping pretty quiet about the mouth organ," she commented, instead of answering his question. "I should have known better than to doubt that you could play it, but I didn't expect a virtuoso performance."

"Been playing it since I was kid," Tod explained casually. He hesitated, then came out with something else that occupied his mind. "You want to be careful of Neil's girlfriend, Fran. Intense sort of a woman, I reckon. My impression is that she's not overly fond of *you.*"

The well-meant warning brought back a memory she'd been trying to forget – the image of a pair of pale cat's eyes spitting hate. "Highlanders don't do things by halves," she remembered McAlister saying. She believed him, especially when it came to Highland women. A primitive clanswoman lay not far beneath Fiona Mackintosh's surface sophistication, and Fran didn't put it past her to stick pins into wax images of anyone classified as an enemy. It was odd to have been put into that category when it ought to have been obvious that she and McAlister could scarcely have a civil conversation together; but Fiona had mistaken the sort of electric charge that sparked between them. Fran shivered and went back to the grilled herring for which she had very little appetite.

"I think you're right about her wanting to see the back of us," she agreed quietly, "but it won't matter now that McAlister will be returning to Cullin House. We shall hardly see either of them in future."

"Pity if she marries him," Tod remarked thoughtfully, "but I guess that's what will happen."

His eyes wandered over Fran's face, but she was busy staring at a seagull drifting on the wind outside and her expression told him nothing.

By the time she'd coaxed the laden old car up the hill road, peace had descended on the Castle. There was no sign of Himself, and only Miss Milward and the Colonel were happily sitting by the fire, sipping tea. They had the contented air of hosts with the place to themselves again after the guests, pleasant but no longer wanted, had gone. Maggie had explained that they would now close off the public rooms and huddle together for warmth in the old tower part of the original Castle, and Fran had a moment's sharp doubt about the wisdom of staying there for the next three months. It suddenly seemed a long time to be locked in such quiet isolation; she was accustomed to the rush and bustle of London, and Tod was a good deal more gregarious than she was herself. They couldn't work all the time and if he became bored and lonely, he'd finally leave Cullin a disappointed man.

But by the next morning it was clear that she was worrying unnecessarily; like Colonel Forrester and

Alice Milward, Tod was even happier, if anything, with the new regime.

They began work in the office, sifting through the vast accumulation of their own notes, and the piles of leaflets, catalogues, and reference books that Tod had collected on their journey through Scotland. But first he made it clear what their working arrangement was to be.

"We can't slog at it all day long, Fran. Nine till one, flat out; then we leave it alone for the rest of the day. In a small community we have a duty to be sociable."

Fran smiled at this earnest statement, and forbore to mention that even on a desert island he'd find someone to be sociable with. Without in the least putting Jaime's nose out of joint, he managed to give the impression that he was there to be relied on when help was needed; and even more wondrous, in her opinion, was the way in which he treated Maggie. She was quite simply his liege lady, and her small son gradually began to give him more pleasure than he'd ever known. He'd looked ready to faint the first time Fran dumped a lustily-yelling baby in his arms, but by the time Maggie appeared, Keith was staring in fascination at Tod, who held him like a piece of Dresden china and played his mouth organ one-handed at the same time. From then on there was no doubt that child and man enjoyed each other's company.

It was Hamish who showed signs of resenting Tod Harriman.

"You'd think Keith was *his* nephew," he said crossly when he and Fran were out walking one afternoon. "Every time I turn round he's in the kitchen playing with Keith or wasting Maggie's time talking about his wretched granny. I wonder he gets any work done at all."

Fran swallowed the sharp retort that came to mind, aware that the man beside her was smarting under her ruling that the office was out of bounds to casual droppers-in.

"Wonder no more, Hamish," she murmured instead. "Tod works like a demon, and I should know because I have the greatest difficulty in keeping up with him. It's true he adores the baby . . . Keith is something absolutely new in his experience. But it also gives him pleasure to be helpful to Maggie. He only talks because she encourages him to, and he spends just as much time helping the Colonel with his stamp collection or listening to Miss Milward's flow of reminiscences."

"Oh, he's a paragon all right," Hamish said moodily. A moment later he looked ashamed of himself. "Sorry, Fran; quite uncalled for, I'm afraid. Mr Harriman's a very nice man . . . for an American!"

She smiled but shook her head at the afterthought. "He's nice by *any* standards," she insisted gently.

Hamish nodded, then came to stand behind her, his miserable expression suddenly changed to delight. "Look over there . . . oh heavens, what a sight!"

His hands on her shoulders pointed her in the direction of a glen running up the flank of Beinn Mhor. Above it, soaring with effortless power through the clear air, was the first eagle she had ever seen. Spellbound, she was even half convinced that she could hear the rush of air past its great wings. It turned out of sight behind the hill and she came down to earth again, dismayed to realise that Hamish's hands, still gripping her shoulders, had begun to tremble badly.

"Fran . . . you know why I was so snide about Tod, don't you?" His unsteady voice warned her that the trouble McAlister had predicted so correctly was upon her. Hamish was hellbent on throwing himself at her feet, and although she would have liked to say that his main ailment was not love but boredom, it would have seemed cruelly belittling to a man who tended to take himself and life very seriously.

Instead, she did the best she could with a perilous situation. "Tod is going to be able to stay here while *you* must soon return to Inverness, where eagles probably don't take to the sky above your head. Poor Hamish, of course I know why you were snide; I think you'd live here always if you could."

He tried to smile, but shook his head. "Try again, Fran. I don't like teaching, and I hate Inverness, but that isn't what I meant, and I think you know it."

"All right then – it's what's called propinquity," she said, trying to sound calmly matter-of-fact about it. "With time on your hands and half a dozen girls around to keep you entertained, you'd probably enjoy them all. As it is, dear Miss Milward isn't exactly competition, and you've got a bit stuck on me."

"Don't laugh at me, Fran. I'm not just stuck on you; I've fallen wholly and lastingly in love. You know it's so because you've been doing your level best all along to joke me out of it."

"Then I don't seem to have made a very good job of it," she said ruefully. "I'm not meaning to laugh, Hamish dear, but you've known me less than two weeks. It isn't long for falling 'lastingly' in love."

"Take me seriously, Fran," he shouted suddenly. "Don't you understand that I'm asking you to marry me?"

His hands slipped down her arms and locked behind her back, pulling her hard against him. She fought for a moment to avoid his seeking mouth, realised that she was simply inflaming him all the more by resisting, and forced herself to stand unresponsive under a shower of kisses that made her feel both ridiculous and sad. His hands finally slackened and fell away from her.

"Oh God," he burst out, "now I suppose I've made things a thousand times worse."

"No, but you haven't made them any better, either," she said with a passable attempt at lightness. His white, strained face was a reproach, though how she could have given him less encouragement than she had it was hard to know. McAlister had been cruelly unfair about that, but the fact remained that he was right about this sensitive man's capacity to get himself hurt.

"Hamish dear . . . please listen to me. You're at a loose end at the moment, still a bit off balance, and we've been rather thrown together in isolated and wildly beautiful surroundings. I can't think of a better recipe for letting emotions get out of hand. In a week or two you'll be back in Inverness, and in a month or two I'll be back in London; Cullin will seem like a highly romantic dream."

"You're wrong, Fran, and I'll prove it to you," he said stubbornly. "For the moment, though, I suppose I'd better take you home. No hard feelings for the caveman tactics just now?"

"No hard feelings," she agreed, and put her hand into the one he held out to her.

They retraced their steps in silence, Hamish wondering how Inverness was ever to seem bearable, and Fran wrestling with a problem of her own. Hamish's hand guided her carefully over stones and marshy grass . . . but it was the wrong hand. She was pierced to the point of pain by the memory of another walk back to the Castle, holding someone else's hand. What to do about *that* when she was back in London, and Cullin had become an inaccessible dream?

Her thoughts must have been powerful enough to

conjure him out of thin air. They hadn't seen him at the Castle since the morning after the ceilidh, but when she went down to the kitchen that evening to put the finishing touches to dinner, she glimpsed him and Fiona sharing the Colonel's pre-dinner drink in the small sitting room they now used instead of the hotel bar.

She was cutting out leaves and flowers of pastry to decorate the top of an enormous steak and kidney pie when the door opened behind her.

"What are you doing in here, Francesca? Is Maggie unwell?"

She put down the knife she was holding and thrust both hands in the pockets of her overall.

"Maggie's fine – taking a cup of tea with Dougal's mother who's poorly at the moment. I, as you see, am cooking supper. It's my turn."

"What do you mean, it's your turn?"

His voice was inhumanly devoid of anything but clinical interest in the question he was asking. A moment or two during a Highland dance, when she could have sworn that joy flowed equally through them both, were obviously figments of a disordered imagination. There was no joy in McAlister now, only passionless dislike.

"Maggie and I – by agreement, I hasten to add – take it in turns to cook the dinner. That way, Tod and I don't feel too badly about imposing ourselves on her here."

"By agreement perhaps, but by your suggestion, I don't doubt."

"I rather think it *was* my idea," Fran said airly.

A quick glance at his face suggested that she might have been wrong about 'passionless' – it would have given him a great deal of relief to be able to shake her till her teeth rattled; but he couldn't quite think of a sufficent reason. He had one more shot in his locker, though, and it was hurled at her like a cannonball after he had taken a deliberate look round the kitchen.

"I'm surprised Hamish isn't in here, 'helping', or at least keeping you from feeling lonely."

"What is that supposed to mean?" Fran asked with ominous quiet. "I get the feeling that it's intended to mean *something* which I shall greatly resent."

"I warned you early in our acquaintance not to supplement Mr Harriman's attentions by playing with Hamish. He's not used to London ways, and at the moment he's even less fair game than usual."

It felt as if she were being pelted with small, hard pellets of ice while her body flamed with indignation. If it hadn't been for the recollection of Hamish's outburst of the afternoon binding her hands, she thought she might have made a brave attempt at hitting McAlister.

"You know perfectly well the nature of Tod Harriman's 'attentions', so spare me any more gibes about that. As for Hamish, you said yourself that he must learn to cope with life. It isn't my fault that he's here; and I am here – if you remember – at your suggestion."

"Because I was given the impression that you wouldn't make matters worse by encouraging him. You're a dishonest cheat, it seems."

"And you are back at your favourite game of slapping labels on people," she shouted at him. "Instant judgements are your speciality – don't bother with facts, prejudice will do! As it happens, I refused Hamish's offer of marriage this afternoon as tactfully as I could . . . is that what you call encouraging him?"

"He came in looking so upset that I knew something

must have happened. Naturally he didn't mention the proposal, or the steamy love scene that Fiona almost interrupted accidentally. *That* is what I call encouragement. If you must have a man making love to you, for God's sake choose someone who won't be shattered when you shove an offer of marriage back in his face."

Fran held on to self-control with an effort that set every muscle trembling.

"Now I understand. It's Fiona who stood and watched our 'steamy' love scene and then came rushing back to give you a blow by blow account of it. I hope she wasn't too disappointed. I don't propose to discuss it with you or her, now or ever, and I don't give a damn what you think of me. All I ask is that you get out of my kitchen and eat dinner this evening somewhere where I don't have to look at either of you."

"*Your* kitchen, Miss Campbell?"

"I realise that you own this godforsaken, impossible island, and all that stands on it; for the moment, however, I'm the cook and this is *my* kitchen."

McAlister stared at her for a long moment, rage, disappointment, and something he vaguely recognised as jealousy, dying into an overwhelming sadness. The threat to peace of mind that she'd been from the moment she walked through the door of the Castle had never been more acute than now, when she faced him with flushed cheeks, bosom heaving, and huge dark blue eyes brilliant with unshed tears. She represented everything he distrusted in a woman, and who should know better than he what a sophisticated, beautiful southerner could do in the way of creating havoc? It didn't stop him almost nailing his feet to the floor in the struggle not to close the gap between them and pick her up in his arms.

"If I were a nervous man I might think it prudent not to eat anything you'd cooked this evening," he muttered at last.

"The name is Campbell – hated enough, but *not* Borgia!"

McAlister held up his hand, in a fencer's gesture of defeat.

"Before you run me through with a pastry knife, I was attempting to tease you."

His voice had changed, leaving only her of the two of them wrapped in unnecessary layers of hostility; she felt foolish and depleted at the same time. There was only one more thing she could say to whip up her own anger again, and probably his as well.

"If you feel it necessary to discuss me with Fiona Mackintosh in future, I should prefer *not* to have the conversation reported at second hand. I'm not much interested in *your* opinion of me, still less in hers."

"Take my word for it – I shall not discuss you with her or anyone else at any time," he said gravely. His mouth didn't flicker, but she was almost certain that his anger had melted inexplicably into amusement. With any other man she might have caved in and shared it, but the thought of him listening to Fiona's report was too painful to be laughed away. She picked up her steak and kidney pie, heroically resisted the temptation to throw it at him, and walked over to the oven instead. When she turned round the kitchen was empty and she could weep to her heart's content.

Chapter Ten

Either Tod seemed to sense her need to be feverishly busy or he was suddenly aware that three months were little enough time to get a book figured out and put together. Whatever the reason, Fran was grateful that their pace of working moved into top gear. She began to appear in the office well before nine o'clock, but he was always there, checking what had been achieved the previous day. Early on in their acquaintance he'd given her some of his other books to leaf through, and she'd found them informative, honest, and highly readable. But more and more it seemed to her that what he was now writing was *not* his normal formula of concise information, sensible advice, and vivid pen portraits of places and people.

Thinking about it one morning while they broke off for the coffee Maggie always insisted on bringing in, Fran suddenly fired a question at him.

"I don't believe this is going to be another 'Touring with Tod' – you've got a different sort of book in mind."

"If you've got more to say, I'm listening," he answered gravely.

Wishing she'd never started the subject, she was aware that she'd now have to go on with it. Tod took his work with a seriousness that had begun by surprising her, but she should have learned to expect it by now.

"My impression is that you're in the middle of a love affair." She was amazed to see him blush, and assumed that he thought her choice of words excessive. "You're writing the story of a sentimental journey that has become more important to you than you ever imagined."

He looked so relieved by the explanation that an even more extravagant notion took root in her mind. Tod's love affair was certainly with Cullin and all things Scottish but it began to seem very likely that it was with Maggie Harding as well. He'd been bowled over by his first sight of her, and subsequent acquaintance with her charm and kindness was completing his undoing. It would explain why Norfolk, Nebraska, seemed to have disappeared into the limbo of forgotten things as far as he was concerned.

"You're right, Fran," he said at last, while she was still busy fitting the pieces of the jigsaw into place. "What I'm doing now *is* a labour of love. I hope it will still inform, but not just on the level of what to do with a fortnight's tour. I want the people reading it to end up with an understanding of a country that's like nowhere else. Ambitious, maybe, on the strength of our own journey and what I soaked up from Granny's recollections, but I feel so strongly about it that I think I can do it."

"I'm sure you can, but the only thing that worries me is that it won't be what your readership is expecting to get."

"It doesn't bother *me*," said Tod. "This is my swan song, and I reckon that I can now please myself."

"You mean you're going to give up travelling . . . or, at least, give up writing about travelling?"

He hesitated a moment, then smiled at her sheepishly.

"Give up altogether, I think. You'll reckon I've gone mad, but I want to stay here. Every day I'm more certain of it."

Fran looked at him in astonishment. "Cullin . . . for the rest of your life, Tod? Are you sure?"

"I feel that I belong here," he said simply. "No ties to speak of in America, and more money than I shall ever want to spend. Why shouldn't I make an investment in the future of Cullin?"

It wasn't for her to ask him how closely Maggie was concerned in the future he was looking at, but a word of warning about McAlister had to be said.

"Have you talked to anyone else yet, Tod?"

"Nope . . . it's only just coming clear in my mind."

Her heart ached for a man who saw things in black and white. He loved Cullin, could afford to give up his work and live there; ergo, he would do just that. But what if Cullin didn't want him?

"Don't bank on it too much," she suggested anxiously. "There's Himself to consider – a man addicted to getting his own way if I ever saw one, and with very strong ideas of his own about the future of Cullin."

Tod smiled, aware of what she hadn't said. "Don't worry, Fran. I'm not about to try and turn the island upside down. All the same, Neil's got a battle on his hands to keep Cullin viable. He can't afford to turn down any help that comes his way – he knows that even better than I do."

Tod judged other people by himself, she feared. He almost certainly hadn't yet got the measure of a man who wouldn't compromise even if his life depended on it. She might have said that turning down help came naturally to Neil McAlister, but instead she merely murmured that she hoped Tod was right, and abandoned for the moment the delicate subject of his future.

The days settled into a peaceful routine: a morning's hard work; lunch in the kitchen with the 'family', which now surprisingly included Lionel Forrester and Miss Milward who refused to be left eating on their own; afternoons shopping in Kirktown, or out walking with Hamish; and quietly sociable evenings sharing books, music and conversation with the other inmates of the Castle. It was a world away from Fran's life in London, and the frantic rush to keep up with friends, and the newest film and the latest fashion. Every so often she tried to tell herself that she was missing it all, but a sneaking suspicion was growing in her mind that she would take one look at rush-hour London when the time came and burst into tears. Beinn Mhor's great head, draped in cloud, or clear against a constantly changing sky, was what she now looked for each morning, not Big Ben. Her ears had become attuned to quietness, and the song of curlew and plover. Most extraordinary of all, she'd grown used to a landscape barely sprinkled with other people. After the space and emptiness and limitless air of Cullin, she feared she might easily die of suffocation in a crowded underground train.

She went through the days swinging uncomfortably between happiness and dread, and mutely envious of Tod who at least had no doubts about what *he* wanted of the future. He became more serenely sure of it as time went by, and his contentment seemed to be infectious, making them all happily at ease with one another. Fran marvelled especially at the change in Maggie Harding, no longer recognisable for the haunted woman who'd come back from the mainland. In the middle of a bread-making lesson one afternoon, she stopped kneading dough, aware that she'd lost her pupil's attention.

"Fran dear . . . you're not watching."

"I know . . . I was looking at you! I was very alarmed about you when you first came back to Cullin, but I don't think I need be any longer."

"Largely thanks to you, and Tod," Maggie confessed immediately. "Life would have gone on somehow because I have Keith to look after, but there's actual happiness here again now; even the Colonel and Alice are enjoying themselves as they never have before. I try not to think of you going away."

"Maggie . . . Tod hopes not to," Fran suddenly blurted out. "He wants to stay for good. It means a great deal to him, so will you put in a good word for him with McAlister if you ever get a chance?"

"Has he said anything to Neil?"

"Not yet, but I think he's getting ready to, and I should hate him to get the frozen mitt from Himself in one of his Lord of the Isles moods!"

She grinned to take the sting out of her words, but Maggie stared thoughtfully at the dough between her hands.

"I wish I could make up my mind about you and Neil . . . sometimes you seem to hate each other; other times . . ."

"Other times . . . what?"

"I get a very different impression!" She was kind enough not to comment on the colour suddenly scalding Fran's face, and reverted to the subject of Tod. "I wonder what makes Mr Harriman so keen on Cullin, apart from the fond memory of Granny McDougall?"

It was a terrible temptation to tell her, but Fran nobly resisted the urge. Tod must be allowed to do his own wooing. "He feels at home here, and of course he's besotted with your son!" she said merely.

"Alan never was . . . at home here, I mean," Maggie

admitted sadly. "I have the feeling sometimes that it was thought wrong of him to go on that last expedition, but he could never have been tied down by things that other people regard as responsibilities. Keith was only born because I insisted on having a child to love when he wasn't here. I don't mean that Alan wasn't happy to have me and this place as a sheet-anchor to come back to, but the mountains were where his heart truly was. I knew that before I married him, so I have nothing to complain about. Hamish only climbed because he didn't want to seem less of a man than his brother. I mention that because it's obvious what he feels about *you*; you wouldn't have to fear that *he* would always be roaming."

Fran smiled at the hopeful expression on Maggie's face, but had to shake her head.

"I like him. He's a very nice man; but I wouldn't be able to marry him, even if I could see him happily transported to a life down south – which I can't, no how, as Allie would say!"

"Pity . . . I was hoping to get you as a sister-in-law."

Fran thought of asking about the one she was much more likely to get, then thought better of it. "McAlister is invisible these days . . . back at Cullin House, I suppose."

"He's away on the mainland, arranging for the sales of his Highland cattle. His strains are becoming famous now, and much sought after in places where strength and stamina are needed in cattle."

They finished making the bread and left it covered with damp cloths to rise while they took tea in to the four people in the sitting room locked in battle over the Scrabble board. On the way out of the kitchen Maggie thought of something else. "Sunday tomorrow, so you won't be working with Tod. Come to Cullin House with me, Fran. Elspeth says she hasn't seen Keith for days." In the face of Fran's obvious hesitation, she added, "Hen party . . . just us; Neil won't be back."

"In that case I'll come with pleasure," said Fran.

When they set off it wasn't quite a hen party, because Tod refused to be left behind, with Hamish also gone over to the mainland for a weekend visit. It was a late November day that had unaccountably strayed out of early October – still and serene, with sky and sea shading from aquamarine to sapphire. Fran drove, with Maggie beside her, and Tod in the back playing the baby to sleep with his mouth organ. A quick glance at the silent woman sitting next to her showed Maggie's face wet with tears.

"Something wrong?"

The quiet question made Maggie shake her head. "Just overcome with gratitude," she answered unsteadily.

"Oh well, if that's all . . ." Fran smiled at her, then concentrated on turning the car into the drive of Cullin House. The fact that McAlister's Land Rover was parked outside the door had scarcely registered before a tall figure came striding down the steps towards them. She looked reproachfully at Maggie but there was no time to accuse her of having been misled. Himself was already at the car door, lifting out his nephew.

He greeted Tod civilly, kissed his sister's upraised face, and stared at Fran, apparently without any pleasure.

"Maggie said you wouldn't be here," she found it necessary to explain.

"Which is the only reason you came," he agreed, to show that he had understood the message she wished to convey. “Don’t blame Maggie. I wasn’t intending to come back until tomorrow but my buyers were so anxious to conclude our deals that no persuasion was needed.”

“Nice for you,” said Fran. She fixed Tod with a firm blue eye, then turned to Maggie. “We’ll take a walk and be back by the time you’re ready to drive home again.”

“You’ll do no such thing,” said Maggie, looking horrified. “Mr Harriman wants to see Elspeth, even if you don’t. Anyway, she’s bound to have got lunch for us all.”

Aware that she’d been both rude and silly, Fran was about to apologise, but McAlister stepped into the conversation.

“We had a better idea. Elspeth wants the baby to herself, so a picnic barbecue awaits your pleasure on the beach. It seemed a nice enough day for one.”

That was that, Fran thought resentfully. Himself had spoken, and a picnic lunch in November was what they were going to get. She straggled into the house behind the rest of them, ashamed of her peevishness but unsettled, as always, by McAlister’s nearness. They drank sherry with Elspeth in the kitchen, collected the thermos of hot soup she had waiting for them, and then went down through the walled garden to the cove. Carefully sheltered from the breeze blowing off the water, a fire was glowing red under a grid on which cleaned, split mackerel lay grilling to perfection. There was a mouth-watering smell on the fresh, salt air, no sound except the smack of small waves against the sand at the water’s edge and the squawk of a reconnoitring seagull or two. It was impossible to go on feeling cross.

Fran perched herself on a convenient rock to sip

the mug of soup McAlister handed her, and decided that there were moments when life had nothing more to offer in the way of perfection. Even in the rain and wind of her previous visit to the house she had known instinctively what it would be like to live there. It was surely as close to heaven as anyone could hope to get. God have mercy on Fiona Mackintosh if she didn't feel properly grateful for what she was about to receive.

McAlister turned the fish with a deftness that indicated he was practised in the business of cooking in the open air, and Tod handed round plates with the only accompaniment needed of bread, salt, and wedges of lemon. The food was too good not to be concentrated on, and they ate almost without talking; but there was no sense of strain in the silences. They were four people under the spell of their surroundings, charmed into being at perfect ease with one another. When all the fish had been consumed and McAlister had carefully stamped out all trace of the fire, he found that only Fran was left still sitting on her rock, staring out to sea.

"You look like a wistful mermaid . . . land-bound when your heart aches to be out in the sea."

"Wistful, certainly," she agreed, still not looking at him. "I can't decide whether I'd rather be able to re-imagine this lovely place in after days or not have known it at all."

She heard the words fall into a silence he seemed disinclined to break; they'd given away far more than she intended, but even that scarcely seemed to matter now. "Maggie's taken Tod off to look for mussels," she added by way of changing the subject.

McAlister appeared not to have heard, though he glanced briefly in the direction of the two figures hunting among the small rocks left high and dry by the falling tide. He settled himself perversely on the not very large bit of granite she'd chosen herself, although the beach was strewn with other sitting places. She could feel the hardness and warmth of his body from shoulder to thigh, and despised herself for the fact that she was incapable of unconcernedly getting up and strolling away.

"I gather that you like Cullin House in these conditions," McAlister said eventually. "It doesn't look like this in January, with a great sea roaring across the North Minch and Beinn Mhor behind us sheathed in snow. We almost get blown off our feet struggling to the byres to feed the animals, and times enough when we think our troubles are over we have to dig the sheep out of unexpected falls of snow. It hardly gets dark at midsummer, but sometimes in midwinter it's a toss-up whether it will get light at all."

She turned to look at him and found that his eyes were fixed on her, not on the seascape in front of them.

"You mean I'm sitting here dreaming a lot of romantic nonsense about 'green days in forests and blue days at sea'; an effete Londoner wouldn't be able to cope with year-round life on Cullin – I think *that*'s what you're saying."

He shook his head with a rueful smile. "I don't think you're effete, but I doubt if you're seeing things with your usual clearness. Survival is balanced on a knife-edge here; we stay because it's where we belong, not because we feel sentimental about its unspoiled beauty."

"I hear you," she said lightly, "sentiment is out!" But it was one thing to agree, and quite another to rid her mind of the picture of Cullin House battened down to ride out a storm, curtains pulled in the drawing room, and Bess asleep on the rug in front of a huge log fire. For the moment it was hard to get excited about a centrally-heated box in Pimlico, but she insisted desperately to herself that it was only a matter of readjusting herself to London again. The man beside her now seemed to have abandoned conversation; instead he was whittling away at a piece of driftwood with his pocket knife, long brown hands sure of what they were fashioning so swiftly.

"A little memento of one 'blue day', at least, Francesca," he finally said, holding out to her the result – a gull, roughly carved but somehow alive with the grace and vitality belonging to a wild bird.

She glanced away from it, afraid of weeping; hadn't she just agreed that sentiment was taboo? God help her, please, to remember it and keep smiling.

But McAlister's attention was now fixed on the couple at the other end of the bay – not mussel hunting any longer because they too had found a rock to share.

"Mr Harriman seems to be much in evidence these days," he said abruptly. "I gather that my sister enjoys his company."

"You make it sound as if she shouldn't," Fran countered at once, suspecting snide criticism from Hamish or Fiona. "Tod adores the baby, and he's determined to help Maggie. Is there anything in that that requires officious interference?"

McAlister held up his hand. "Stop shouting at me, or I'll carry you down to the water and let you cool off in the sea. I'm damned if I ever met such a firebrand before."

She risked a glance at him and the glint in his dark eyes warned her that he hadn't just made an empty threat. He was more than capable of dunking her in the water.

"Sorry," she muttered, "but you aren't often at the Castle nowadays to see how much less unhappy Maggie looks than she did a month ago. Tod's kindness has a lot to do with that."

McAlister prudently chose to abandon a position that looked untenable. "It may be just as you say, but the fact remains that Mr Harriman, like yourself, won't be here in another month or two. I'd rather Maggie didn't become dependent on companionship that isn't going to last. Is that reasonable, or what you would prefer to call officious interference?"

The question left her wrong-footed as usual, since she didn't feel at liberty to tell him what Tod's intentions actually were.

"I'll withdraw the word officious if you'll agree not to interfere," she offered at last.

"It's a bargain, Francesca."

She was forced to take the hand he held out to her, then stopped breathing as his mouth left a kiss in her palm and he carefully folded her fingers over the spot where his lips had been.

"I think it's time you went home," he told her gravely.

For almost the first time in her acquaintance with him she felt able to agree completely.

Chapter Eleven

It was tempting, but not possible, to ask either Maggie or Tod outright about their blossoming relationship, but Fran was convinced that the picnic at the cove had at least moved them on from being landlady and guest to becoming friends. From then on it was noticeable that Tod made no bones about seeking Maggie's company, and that Hamish's occasional edged remarks bothered him not at all. The fact that they didn't seem to bother Maggie either was more significant, in Fran's considered view. She was keenly interested in the progress of the affair, and beginning to suspect that something more than friendship might finally come of it. Then Tod might get his heart's desire – a permanent tie with Cullin, an investment in its future, and best of all a woman and her son to love. Maggie would gain the care and companionship that perhaps had never been fully forthcoming from her marriage to Alan Harding.

It seemed so perfect an arrangement that Fran scarcely dared to think about it. She hadn't been inclined to superstition before, but in the very air she now breathed there seemed to linger traces of Celtic myths and folklore that conceivably still had the power to influence events.

The traces weren't always benevolent – a fact she was reminded of one afternoon while shopping in

Kirktown. Maggie had taken Tod to call on yet another McDougall relation and there was time to spare before she collected them. Lured as always by the harbour, she walked down to the restaurant there to look out of the window and drink tea. It was sheer bad luck, she reckoned, that Fiona Mackintosh should be there as well. The small room was almost empty and it would have been a studied insult to ignore her – or, worse an admission of weakness.

"I wondered where *you* were," Fiona said with a flashing smile as Fran sat down opposite her. "Maggie and that funny little American were too busy talking to notice me, but I passed them at least half an hour ago."

Fran ordered her tea, then looked across the table at a woman she was, uncharacteristically, beginning to hate. "If you're talking about Mr Harriman, Maggie is introducing him to another of his long-lost relatives," she explained with calm, remembering in the nick of time that she might herself have described Tod as a 'funny little American' at the beginning of their friendship. He had to be known to be valued properly, and Fiona had had no opportunity yet for that. "We haven't seen you at the Castle lately," she pointed out next, by way of changing a subject that could lead them into open dispute.

"Oh, I've been on the mainland . . . Neil has, as well. We both have to go regularly for different reasons, but being there together when the working day is over turns a chore into a pleasure we both enjoy!"

"I'm sure," Fran agreed politely. She wasn't clear whether she was meant to infer that shared evenings or shared nights were what Fiona and McAlister enjoyed together; from Fiona's reminiscent smile, probably both. Well, why not? Neil McAlister might behave at times like the natural successor to John Knox, thundering against a monstrous regiment of women, but she could all too easily imagine him in softer moments letting monkish self-discipline rip. An unwelcome image lodged itself in her mind of Fiona and Himself sharing some firelit, shadowy bedroom, and she was shaken by the fierceness with which her heart rejected it. But Fiona was inspecting her face with interest, and it was essential to find something less disturbing to talk about.

"I gather you look after the island's knitting industry," she said with an effort. "I suppose that's what takes you to the mainland. Is it really such a bore? I'd have thought it was a fascinating job – keeping in touch with what buyers want, and then guiding the women here accordingly."

Was it too subtle a hint, she wondered, that current fashions shouldn't be ignored completely? Not too subtle, but of no account, apparently, because the idea was waved aside.

"We don't bother about passing whims," Fiona said with magnificent assurance. "The whole point about Cullin's industry is that it's traditional. The women use patterns that are peculiar to the island, handed down from generation to generation. The last thing I should do is consult a fashion buyer."

The complacency of it was maddening, and the intention to put an ignorant incomer in her place crystal-clear. Fran went back to her tea, determined to leave the next choice of subject to Fiona. Unfortunately she harked back to Tod.

"It's kind of Maggie to shepherd Mr Harriman around, but I should have thought she had better things to do . . . especially when she knows how much Neil hates the sort of travel trash he's writing."

Fran had no licence to engage in battle over the island's knitting industry, but in the matter of Tod's literary output she *could* stand and fight. "You've read some of the 'trash', I take it?" she enquired crisply. "Let me know the names of the travel writers you're comparing Tod with before we go on with this argument."

"I'm not going on with it at all," said Fiona, sliding out of the corner she'd boxed herself into. "I don't mean to belittle what Mr Harriman does, but you know as well as I do that he's doing it under protest from Neil as far as Scotland is concerned. You can't possibly understand how hard we have to struggle to keep Cullin from being invaded by what Neil calls the barbarians."

"I think you're both a bit hard on the average run of tourists if you lump them *all* together as barbarians. The Castle guests are anything but that," Fran pointed out. "But as it happens, Tod is as keen to keep Cullin unsullied as you are; its name won't even be mentioned in a book which I can promise you is *not* going to be trashy."

The gauntlet had been flung down, and opposing sides taken. The duel was ostensibly about Tod, but both of them knew that he wasn't responsible for the dislike that flamed between them, annihilating any pretence of goodwill.

"Well, I've enjoyed our little chat," Fiona said, getting up from the table, "but I must be on my way. I hope Maggie eventually remembers that you're waiting for her, but I'm afraid she seemed very engrossed in her companion!"

"And I mustn't keep you from the design of some new woolly masterpiece," Fran countered sweetly. They now 'bled on both sides', but she felt unrepentant.

Hamish had obviously been carping about Tod, and she would have to try to make him understand that even if Maggie ended up by remarrying, it wouldn't diminish her memories of his brother. She was so unworldly a woman that no one, not even Fiona at her bitchiest, would be likely to suggest that Tod's wealth could be the attraction. But anyone who didn't know his mixture of kindness, intelligence, and sheer relish for life might wonder at a marriage between him and a woman fifteen years his junior. Fran paid her bill and went out into the dim afternoon wondering yet again how this interlude on Cullin would end.

Whatever happened, all their lives would have been changed by it . . . perhaps only with the exception of McAlister. *He* wasn't a pipe for Fortune's finger to sound what stop she pleased. One engagement fiasco might have made him cautious, but after the night of the Hallowe'en ceilidh no one could imagine that he hadn't committed himself to Fiona Mackintosh. She would be the next mistress of Cullin, and Fran prayed that Maggie could be happily settled with Tod before it happened.

When they'd started work on the book the winter had seemed to stretch almost into infinity – there were days, weeks, even whole months in front of them. But, towards Christmas, time suddenly began to gallop, despite the quiet routine of life at the Castle. The weather grew steadily colder, and with the wind veering to a different quarter Fran saw Beinn Mhor's head covered with snow for the first time. Everyone began to murmur darkly that they were in for a hard winter, and Tod smiled with anticipation, waiting for the exciting moment when some blizzard or great frost cut them off from the rest of humanity. He positively throve on the idea that it would be a splendid test of their resources to have to be self-sufficient. There was no doubt in *his* mind that they would all have a lovely time, and such was the joyous power of his conviction, that there was no doubt in anyone else's either – even Jaime, whose Highland temperament didn't naturally incline him to optimism, was heard to laugh out loud occasionally.

Fran was of the opinion that they were all more happily relaxed for seeing so little of Fiona and McAlister, but it wasn't a theory she aired in front of Maggie or Hamish, who might be expected to like their kith and kin. It was a thought that was bound to put her in mind of Aunt Ernestine. In the normal course of events in London they would have shared Christmas Day, or Fran would have driven her to visit some other member of the Campbell clan. She felt oddly reluctant to tear herself away from the close-knit little group at the Castle, but Christmas was Christmas, and she must at least offer to go south for a few days.

When she put this proposition over the telephone it met with an unusual silence at the other end. "I thought of coming up to see *you*," said Aunt Ernestine eventually.

"*Here* . . . on Cullin?"

"Where else? I take it that's where you still are?" Miss Campbell enquired trenchantly. She was aware of events taking place there of which she hadn't been properly informed, and was resentful of the fact.

Fran had a vision of her aunt, even if she survived the rest of the journey, being driven up the 'hill' from Kirktown by Dougal, his damp plaid and kilt steaming gently in the heat of his battered car while he pointed out the tracks of some small wild animal to a bemused passenger. Even more interesting was what Dougal would make of Aunt Ernestine, always supposing that he could understand a single word she said.

"You aren't exactly falling over yourself with enthusiasm," Ernestine observed after a while. "If you don't want me to come I can always stay here and grizzle all by myself."

Doubtful as she was, Fran couldn't help grinning at the familiar caustic note – she'd missed that kind of humour at the Castle. "I'd love you to come, but it's a gruelling journey to make in the middle of winter, and it's not exactly a swinging country house party you'd be coming to – we lead a quiet, peaceful life up here."

"Just my scene," Ernestine said untruthfully. "I'll fly to Glasgow, weather permitting, or take a night sleeper; you can meet me at whatever godforsaken place the steamer leaves from."

She'd done her homework, Fran realised, and was determined to come. To venture so far away from what she considered civilised life, she must be consumed with curiosity about her niece's stay on Cullin. With some important details settled and the conversation at an end, Fran went in search of Maggie.

"How do you feel about another guest for Christmas – my dear but eccentric aunt? She's got it into her head that she wants to come here instead of having me go home."

"I'd say bring a dozen guests rather than have you disappear. How is she eccentric, anyway?"

"She's what's called a character! But rather than try to explain her I shall let her burst upon Cullin in all her glory."

The days flew past to Christmas, with Elspeth borrowed to help Maggie make pies and puddings enough to feed a regiment, while Fran and Tod worked longer hours than usual in order to try to get ahead with the book. He could now see clearly the form he wanted it to take, and he was working with such speed and confidence that she found it hard to keep up with him. Perhaps always with this special landfall in mind, he'd read widely on the subject of Scottish history – knew its wounds as if they were his own, and rejoiced in its achievements. Wherever great deeds had been required in any far-flung corner of the globe there had always been Scots enough to accomplish them, apparently, and he wrote about them with passionate pride, insisting that his readers should see the beautiful but impoverished places from which these giants had originally sprung.

Confirmation that what he was writing was far from Fiona's 'tourist trash' came one day from a very unlikely source. They had wrangled amicably over the meaning of a Scots word, then consulted Elspeth in the kitchen. She offered an explanation neither of them had thought of and they were all still arguing and drinking coffee when McAlister walked in.

"Himself will know," Elspeth said confidently.

He asked to see the context in which the word was to appear and followed Fran to the office to look at the typescript. He read the paragraph in question, gave a verdict which clearly settled the argument, and then went on leafing through the pages.

"This is Mr Harriman's idea of a *tourist* guide?" he asked incredulously.

Fran shook her head. "Not really . . . it's Tod's swan song and labour of love – a prose poem, really, in praise of the land of some of his ancestors."

"It's remarkable," McAlister admitted slowly. "No wonder you bawled me out for being critical about it."

"That was on principle," Fran acknowledged, ". . . we hadn't started work then."

"You're a braw fighter for your friends, I'm thinking. It's a pity that the person you're always fighting is me!"

She shuffled papers on the desk, not wanting to look at him in case she saw him smiling at her.

"Maggie tells me that you have to go across to the mainland. I'll take you," he announced abruptly. "The road down to the harbour can be tricky in hard weather, and I've some business to attend to in Mallaig."

She blinked at this masterful attitude, not sure whether to take umbrage or just be grateful for the kindness that prompted it.

"I think I can probably get Aunt Ernestine here in one piece," she suggested at last, mildly.

The mildness didn't achieve a thing. "For once don't argue with me – just do as you are told. I shall take you to Mallaig and conduct you and your aged relative back to Cullin Castle."

Fran accepted with a gracious bow, and there the matter rested. She half expected that he might have forgotten by the time the day of Ernestine's arrival came, but he walked into the hall just as she was getting ready to leave. No doubt out of consideration for her aunt's advancing years, his car stood at the door, not the battered vehicle he usually drove. He was wearing what she recognised as his second-best kilt and tweed jacket, and the glint in his eye suggested that cares had been put aside for the day. He was not his workaday self, but a man who had for once given himself a holiday. She was grateful for the forethought that had led her to take care with her own appearance – new navy-blue trousers, a scarlet anorak and matching cap, made up, she reckoned, an outfit that was both eye-catching and appropriate.

"What a splendid couple we look," he observed as

they settled themselves in the car, "fine as fivepence, the pair of us."

"Wait till you see Aunt Ernestine," she felt obliged to point out. "She'll take the shine out of both of us."

He turned to smile at her, then concentrated on the road. After a night's hard frost, it was treacherous in the extreme, and in the darkness of early morning she realised that he'd had some reason to doubt her ability to cope with it. She allowed him to drive in peace, happy to know that for the moment, at least, they were at rest with one another, content to enjoy what had suddenly become a delightful excursion. It was almost Christmas, when excitement and joy went hand in hand; the sunlit, frosty world was beautiful; and happiness was tangible – a gift they offered each other.

The ferry was hooting impatiently as they parked the car, and they ran, laughing, for the gangplank. McAlister greeted everyone with his usual courtesy, but gradually shepherded Fran to the stern of the boat, where there was no one else to share the view with them. The rising sun turned the boat's wake to a froth of gold on the dark blue of the water, and Skye was a mauve shadow to the south of them. The air was icily cold against her face, but McAlister's body sheltered her from the wind. Etched against the sky, his profile had the grave beauty of a head on some old coin until he suddenly turned to intercept her glance and smile at her. Strange though it seemed, she felt almost sure that he was filled with the same delight that flooded her; it was like dancing with him at the ceilidh, hand-locked, although he wasn't touching her.

"I get the impression that you like being at sea," she remarked, by way of explaining to herself why he looked happy.

"Yes, though I like it even more when I'm crewing

my own small boat. I suppose islanders can't help being fascinated by the element that surrounds them."

"More so than by the island itself?"

"No . . . I love the hills, too, although I don't feel obliged to keep climbing them, Your true mountaineer must always be on the top, looking down."

"Like Alan Harding, I suppose?"

"I think so – high, lonely places became an addiction he couldn't do without in the end. Maggie understood that and never tried to suggest that he'd undertaken to take care of her as well. She just wanted him to be happy . . . he was a shy, charming man."

"But not an ideal husband," Fran pointed out. She was tempted to say that someone like Tod, who only wanted to consider *her*, must come as a pleasant surprise, but she was reluctant to spoil present harmony; Himself would probably never agree that he could do much worse than Tod Harriman for a brother-in-law. But the brightness of the day was suddenly dimmed for Fran by the memory of Tod's eager face whenever he looked at Maggie, and she was about to sacrifice harmony for the sake of her friend when a voice spoke behind them, forestalling what she would have said next.

"A word with ye, McAlister, when ye have a moment," the man standing there requested.

There was nothing to tell the rest of the world that they were on holiday, inside a magic circle separating them from other people. Her companion was still Himself, the man everyone looked to when they needed help. Fran smiled and wandered away, leaving them to talk. By the time a weighty discussion about a boundary dispute was finished the steamer was docking and Fran herself was deep in conversation with a fellow passenger.

"I'm sorry that I was forced to desert you," McAlister

said with the grave courtesy she had come to expect. "One conversation led to another, and another, I'm afraid."

"Don't worry . . . that poor man looked relieved to see you, and I've been very well entertained."

"Then I'm sorry on my own account," he said with a faint smile. "I've an errand or two while you seek out your aunt. If you'll both meet me at the hotel over there, we can have lunch before the ferry goes back again at three."

They parted company on the quay, and ten minutes later Fran was at the station watching the train from Glasgow arrive. A small crowd of passengers straggled along the platform, all of them shooting interested glances at the commanding figure of Ernestine Campbell. Her fringe below a white fur hat was redder than ever, a purple cape swirled about her in extravagant folds, and just hid the tops of shiny, black boots. Mallaig had probably never seen such a vision before and didn't intend to miss any of it now. Fran thought of McAlister waiting to meet a frail and elderly maiden aunt and laughed out loud.

"You were supposed to gasp with admiration, not fall about laughing," Miss Campbell pointed out acidly, grinning in spite of herself. "It's nice to see you looking so happy, though."

"Aunt dear – welcome to the Highlands! I was laughing at a thought of my own, not at you; but you're getting more admiration from your fellow passengers than is good for you anyway!"

She took her aunt's suitcase and led the way towards the station exit.

"What's next in this interminable journey – a hideous sea crossing, I suppose?" Ernestine suggested.

"No, lunch comes next, *then* the trip to Cullin. We're

being entertained by Himself, so I shall have to wait until this evening to hear all your news."

"You say it very blithely. Do I take it that the 'arrogant, tyrannical Highlander' – I quote from several of your letters – is less unbearable than you thought?"

Fran looked confused for a moment. "We still disagree a good deal, but in between times there are things about him that I'm forced to admire."

Ernestine digested this in silence, and then was too busy acknowledging the stationmaster's bow to pursue the matter further. McAlister was already at the hotel when they arrived. Fran looked at him so as not to miss the expression on his face, but was disappointed – he looked like a man who'd just won a bet with himself.

"Neil McAlister, Laird of Cullin," she said briefly ". . . my aunt, Miss Ernestine Campbell."

Ernestine didn't often find herself looking up at a man. She had to do so now, and Fran's impression was that she seemed not at all displeased by what she saw.

"I've heard a lot about you," she announced as he bowed over her hand.

"None of it good, I feel sure!"

He settled them at a comfortable distance from the fire and watched with enjoyment as Ernestine's cape was cast aside to reveal a shirt of black silk beneath a waistcoat and skirt of black and white Donegal tweed. If he wondered whether her luggage included any clothes more suitable for a midwinter stay on Cullin, his face didn't give the fact away. He nodded to the waiter, then registered Fran's astonishment as champagne nestling in an ice-bucket was put down beside him.

Aunt Ernestine registered it too. "You must have the

second sight, McAlister, unless my niece told you that I consider this the only apéritif worth drinking."

"You were expecting some poor little old lady," Fran muttered indignantly. "You as good as said so."

"Only until I saw the expression on your face." He poured the wine, trying to keep his mouth straight, and handed them both a glass.

"I shall drink to a happy Christmas for the Campbells," he said, raising his own glass. "May they long keep us wide awake on Cullin!"

Chapter Twelve

From that first surprising introduction, Ernestine and McAlister never looked back. His deadpan humour proved the perfect foil for her own sharp tongue, but there was more to the conversation than merry lunge and parry; she was interested in making him talk about Cullin, and intelligent in the questions she asked. Fran was content to listen, aware now that nothing about this perfect day could go wrong.

Ernestine bore the cold afternoon crossing cheerfully, but she was beginning to show signs of travel weariness by the time they were back on Cullin, driving up the road to the Castle. Fran occupied herself in the car with wondering how to suggest a rest before dinner tactfully enough for the idea not to be refused out of hand; but Maggie's kindness solved the problem with no difficulty at all. Ernestine was conducted to a bedroom, firelit and welcoming, and then brought the tray of tea that her soul secretly craved. Dinner would wait, said her hostess, until she felt refreshed enough to come downstairs.

"Nice people," Miss Campbell told her niece when Maggie had left the room, "nice place, too. I'm glad I came, and I can see why you don't seem to mind staying here."

Fran hesitated over how to answer, aware that Ernestine had been brought by a curiosity she would do her best to satisfy before she went home. In the end it seemed safer not to give away anything at all, and she merely smiled at her aunt.

"See you downstairs when you're ready," she said. "Tod will be waiting for you with a glass of sherry."

"I thought you led a quiet, peaceful life up here. It seems to be a continual round of dissipation."

"Oh, we break out occasionally!"

She left her aunt to drink tea and rest, and didn't see her again until Miss Campbell emerged, elegantly swathed in violet silk jersey, restored and in a mood to be entertained. Emboldened by his first slug of Tio Pepe, Tod advanced and stood on tiptoe to kiss her on both cheeks, while the Colonel's eye lit up at the sight of a lady of the right age group so obviously worthy of his mettle. She looked certain, moreover, to play a keen game of bridge, whereas Fran, who was his usual partner, could never be brought to take the matter seriously.

McAlister didn't put in an appearance, rather to Ernestine's regret, but Maggie explained that they were all invited to Cullin House for Christmas dinner the following day. Hamish limped in and settled himself by Fran's side as usual. Ernestine inspected him carefully and came to the conclusion that he was pleasant but too colourless to have provoked the change she found in her niece; it had, as far as she could see, to be McAlister who was the cause of that. Last to appear for dinner was Alice Milward, made even larger than life by the strange assortment of chiffon scarves and clanking jewellery that she added to her daytime layers of wool by way of dressing for dinner. When she was introduced, Miss Campbell took a second look at her, then put down her glass.

"Good God, it's 'little' Alice!"

Miss Milward blinked at a form of address that she hadn't heard, and certainly hadn't deserved, for fifty years. "Ernestine," she trumpeted with delight, not at all put out by the sight of a school friend who had weathered the years so much more elegantly than she had herself. They had much to catch up on, and Fran realised that it now wouldn't matter if all other entertainment failed; the business of reminiscing would keep them happily occupied for the rest of the evening. They all stayed up long enough after dinner to see midnight merge into Christmas morning, then retired to bed unaware that the world outside was quietly turning white.

Fran went down to the kitchen early next morning and found that, even so, she wasn't the first up. Keith, fed and happy, lay in his cot gurgling at the snow-light reflected on the ceiling; his mother stood staring out of the window. Fran went to stand beside her, linking her arm in Maggie's.

"It's Christmas . . . don't be sad," she said gently.

Maggie turned to smile at her. "I'm not. It looks so beautiful that I suppose I was wishing Alan could be here enjoying it too, but the truth is that he was a very solitary man – not what you'd call a sharer. That's what makes Tod such a new experience for me! He isn't just willing to share, he insists on it."

Fran agreed, then went to have a long and complicated conversation with her godson.

With Hamish in charge of the minibus they all made a hazardous journey down to Kirktown for morning service after breakfast. By the time they got back, the lower slopes of Beinn Mhor, looking like the snow-covered paws of some old, white lion, were dotted with children and toboggans. She spotted

McAlister there easily enough, making sure that none of them got into difficulties, while Fiona hurtled down the slope on a toboggan of her own which he courteously dragged up the hill again for her each time. There was no pleasure for one onlooker, at least, in watching them, and Fran was thankful when Hamish regretfully decided that his injured leg still wouldn't stand up to taking part in the fun and games. It was too bitingly cold to linger, and they soon went home to lunch and a quiet afternoon that filled in the time peacefully until they split up to get ready for the evening's festivity at Cullin House.

Alice was the first to reappear, looking mountainous but impressive in black velvet; Ernestine had chosen dark blue and green shot taffeta, irridescent as a starling's wing, and Maggie wore the white which became her black hair so strikingly. Fran's long skirt was in her favourite hyacinth blue, worn with a cashmere sweater of the same colour, so fine and soft that it might have been fashioned out of silk. If she hadn't known that she looked beautiful Hamish's expression when he caught sight of her would have told her so. She smiled at him with an affection that concealed her need for him to displace in her mind the memory of Fiona sitting in the snow laughing up at Neil McAlister.

Dougall had been sent over with chains for the minibus and instructions to drive them carefully over the snowy roads. It was Fran's first experience of setting off for a winter evening's pleasure in the Highland style – muffled up in greatcoat, scarf and boots, with satin sandals stuffed in her pocket. There were half a dozen other guests already at Cullin House when they arrived, people Fran recognised from the night of Maggie's ceilidh. Fiona, in another scarlet dress, had the air of hectic gaiety about her that a party seemed to inspire, and she ranged herself very pointedly by McAlister's side to welcome the party from the Castle. Ernestine's eye glinted at the sight of his Highland splendour and Fran could have told Fiona that her aunt had every intention of monopolising a man so worthy of her steel.

Cullin House was all that a house should be at any time, but grandly decked out for Christmas it looked its hospitable best; the glow of log fires and candles lit the beautiful, shabby rooms, and everywhere was the scent of beeswax and pine cones. Fran wandered about unnoticed, looking for Elspeth, and ran her to earth in the kitchen. It looked different now from her first view of it on a rainy autumn day, but everything about that visit was still vivid in her memory.

"Happy Christmas Elspeth! I'd offer to help but I'm under oath never to do any more interfering, and in any case, you look beautifully serene and unharassed."

"Everything's fine, lassie. Annie McDougall is helping me in here, and Allie's going to serve in the dining room." She looked Fran up and down and finally gave a satisfied nod. "You look out of place in here – you should be with the others, not letting you-know-who preen herself and take pride of place."

Fran gave her an affectionate grin, but shook her head and went away. She was of the opinion that Elspeth would quite simply die for McAlister if he should ever require it of her, but getting her to approve of Fiona Mackintosh as the mistress of Cullin was going to be much more difficult. She would be accepted in the end, of course; married to Himself she would bear him a child, and then Elspeth's loyal heart would be won.

At dinner it was becoming hard to meet him with off-hand friendliness; she seemed to feel ridiculously like a self-conscious adolescent again, and she was also aware of a pair of hazel cat's eyes observing every move she made. She took refuge with Hamish on one side of her and the minister on the other, knowing that Fiona would have no interest in either of them. Ernestine was having a rollicking time with her host at the other end of the table, but not even Fiona could see an elderly though compelling lady as a competitor, so there was no need to worry about that. Hamish began to look irritated because she wouldn't entirely neglect the minister, and when he did get her attention, said something that anchored her gaze on him as thoroughly as even he could wish.

"Maggie's looking very lit up tonight, I see."

"You sound displeased about it; don't you want her to be happy again?"

Her voice should have warned him, but he went on in a tone of stubborn disapproval.

"It's eight months only since Alan died; too soon for him to be forgotten. I'm not the only one who thinks so . . . Neil does, too."

"You're both entitled to your opinion, Hamish, but don't air it in front of me again," Fran muttered in a low voice. "Maggie won't ever forget Alan, but Cullin Castle is no place to live in on her own with a small child for company. You and McAlister might remember *that* when you're deciding how long she's required to stay grieving for the past."

"I'm not suggesting she must be alone for ever . . . but she must find a . . . a seemly companion when the time comes."

"Ah, now we come to the nub of the matter," she said furiously. "You don't consider Tod seemly, I take it?"

She was still careful to keep her voice low, but

McAlister at the other end of the table wondered what Hamish had said to make her look so beautifully angry; not, obviously, something that gave her any pleasure.

Hamish stared at his plate and wished that he hadn't been fool enough to start the conversation. When Fiona sharpened her tongue on Tod Harriman it was easy to agree with her, but he might have known that Fran wouldn't listen to criticism of someone she regarded as a friend.

"He's a pleasant enough man," he conceded stiffly. "But he's years older than Maggie, and ignorant of the ways of Cullin."

"Then let Cullin teach him," Fran interjected. "No one could be more willing to learn, and no one would take more loving care of Maggie and Keith. You ought to be grateful, instead of downright unkind, and that's my last word on the subject, Hamish."

She turned to the minister on her other side with a smile that made him forget he'd been neglected, while Hamish was left to struggle with the very deaf lady on his right.

After dinner there was music-making in the drawing room, with guests sharing in it with the same unself-conscious ease that had struck Fran on the night of the ceilidh. She was still not used to people taking it for granted in a small, isolated community that they must provide their own entertainment. Fiona and Hamish played, of course, and Tod made no fuss about pulling out his harmonica, but Fran shook her head when Hamish looked pleadingly at her from the piano. She felt reluctant to step into the limelight, and only gave in when Maggie made it impossible to refuse by publicly asking her to sing. She was rifling through a stack of music when McAlister strolled over to stand at her elbow.

"Host's perk . . . he's allowed to choose," he said solemnly. "Something soothing, I think. You were looking rather ruffled at dinner!"

He pulled out two of her own favourites, and put the music on the stand in front of Hamish. 'Jeannie with the Light Brown Hair' was known to everyone present, but the beautiful 'Green Hills of Somerset' was not, and they listened spellbound as the last soft notes faded into silence. Fran shook her head at the clamour for more, relented to the extent of singing 'Silent Night, Holy Night' for them in German, and then insisted that Hamish play more carols for everyone to join in. They were still singing when Elspeth came in to announce that coffee and hot mince pies were waiting for them in the dining room. There was a general drift out of the room, but Fran lingered by the piano, tidying the stack of music.

"What made you so angry at dinner?" asked a voice suddenly, just behind her.

She went on putting sheets of music together as if her life depended on it, until the pile was lifted out of her hands and dumped on the window seat, where it normally belonged. "Answer my question, please, Francesca."

"I don't think you have a right to ask it," she objected, still not looking at him.

"You're a guest in my house. I'm obliged to find out what upset you," he said quietly.

She forced herself to meet his eyes and immediately wished she hadn't. There seemed no way of breaking that locked glance without some physical effort that was almost beyond her.

"I was having a . . . a slight difference of opinion with Hamish," she muttered at last.

"I wish you would tell me what it was about, though of course you don't have to."

Fran hesitated a moment, then made up her mind. "Yes, I'll tell you, since Hamish said the point of view he was putting forward was yours as well. We were arguing about Tod as a possible husband for Maggie," she finished deliberately. "I gather from Hamish that you'd share his disapproval."

"I certainly should, if I thought there was the slightest chance of it happening."

"I think there's a very good chance of it happening, unless you all make Maggie feel that it would be a betrayal of Alan Harding."

"You, on the other hand, are promoting the match, I take it?" McAlister enquired with dangerous smoothness.

"Yes . . . interfering again, I suppose you'd say."

"That hardly describes it, I think. It may amuse you to meddle and matchmake up here, convinced that you can put a bunch of stupid islanders to rights; but kindly think what you're meddling *with* – people's lives in this case."

He still spoke quietly, but with a controlled fierceness that left her in no doubt of his anger; if he'd begun the evening with Christmas goodwill it was totally forgotten now.

"I know what you think I'm meddling with – Hamish explained it to me," she said with an indifference that she was far from feeling. "There's this grim Highland necessity to be seen to mourn for the months and years that are required until, with your approval of course, Maggie is allowed to choose some 'seemly' companion – Hamish's word, not mine."

She saw McAlister's hands whiten on the piano lid, but he couldn't allow himself the relief of shouting at her.

"Our ways are easily mocked by the smart, cheap world you live in . . . but, knowing the value of what we have here, I don't take any heed of that. Nor do I intend to discuss Mr Harriman. But since you pretend to have some affection for my sister, I will only say that you will be cruelly misguided if you encourage her to marry and go to live in America. This is where Maggie belongs, and where my nephew should be reared, in the knowledge that *he* belongs here too."

Torn now between rage and distress, Fran tried to hold her voice steady, and not to weep in front of him. "Far from mocking you, I'm more inclined to despair. Prejudice and arrogance aren't what will help Cullin to survive in today's admittedly tacky world; nor will they be much comfort to Maggie. You won't even consider the possibility that Tod understands what she needs to make her happy. All he asks of life is to be allowed to stay *here* and take care of Maggie and her son. But I'm sure you'll see to it if you can, that that doesn't happen."

"She was trembling now, too incensed to pick her words or remember that she'd given away more about Tod than she was entitled to. But McAlister's disbelief reminded her.

"Are you certain about that . . . about Harriman wanting to stay on Cullin?"

"Of course I'm certain. He'll want it even if Maggie chooses not to marry him. The dear foolish man thinks he can help . . . and imagines that his help will be welcome! What will you do – throw *that* in his face as well?"

The scorn in her voice flicked him like a lash laid

on bare flesh. With his self-control finally in tatters, his hands were on her shoulders, biting through the soft wool of her sweater, when Fiona's voice from the doorway made him release her and spin round.

"Your guests are looking for you, Neil. If you aren't ready to be dragged away from Miss Campbell I'll explain that you're otherwise engaged."

"No explanation is needed, Fiona. What you interrupted was a slight difference of opinion," he explained with heroic disregard for the truth. "Miss Campbell thinks I should welcome Mr Harriman's help in the running of Cullin."

Fiona sauntered into the room and tucked her arm through his. "It's what one imagines they *would* both think," she agreed with a pitying smile.

It left her, Fran realised sadly, with the last word. She followed them out of the room, longing for Christmas to be over. Her shoulders still hurt from the grip of his hands, but in some strange way she felt bereft without them. The truth was inescapable now – that the sooner she left Cullin the better. She couldn't regret having come – friendship for life with Maggie and with Tod, and an entrancing godson weren't gifts to be disregarded; but she could see that the future cost in pain and loneliness might be very high.

Chapter Thirteen

Snow would lie on the hills for the rest of the winter but elsewhere it had melted and the roads were clear by the time Fran and Tod took Ernestine over to the mainland for the journey home. Fran was quiet, her aunt thoughtful, and even Tod less talkative than usual, given so little encouragement by his companions.

"Another month or two and I'll be back in the firm," Fran said, when they were waiting for the train to leave.

Ernestine looked at her with unusual kindness. "You don't have to rush on my account – only on your own, I think."

She saw a great deal, Fran realised, this sagacious maiden lady, who as far as anyone knew had sailed through life untroubled by the emotional storms that threatened other people. Her usual mode of behaviour was simply to ask to be informed about what she didn't know, but for once she had been merciful. Fran had been aware of being observed, but Ernestine had held her fire, disinclined to probe a wound she feared was painful.

Sorry to see her go, Fran's farewell kiss was full of affection. "You don't have to worry about me, if that *is* what you're doing. As soon as the first draft of the book is complete Tod will be able to manage without me – then I shall be on my way back to London like a homing pigeon!"

It was cheerfully said, and the smile that went with it could easily be sustained until the train trundled Ernestine out of sight, but the return journey to Cullin was no more talkative than the outward one had been. Tod might, of course, have been enduring the sea crossing in stoic silence, but Fran's impression was that weighty matters on his mind even blotted out the discomfort of being afloat.

They settled down to work again but she realised that it had become a struggle for both of them. Tod was preoccupied, and she was aware that her Christmas-night quarrel with Neil had built a barrier that was uncrossable. She was on one side of a line that said 'Strangers keep out'. On the other side of it stood Himself, with Fiona by his side, linked by shared distrust of Francesca Campbell. It was strange to feel hated, as she knew she was by Fiona. It was much, much worse to face the truth about McAlister, who should have *known* that he could safely love her.

She went doggedly on, dragging Tod with her, and life settled down to its pre-Christmas routine, except that Hamish was declared fit for work again and unenthusiastically took himself back to his school in Inverness. Preparing dinner in the kitchen that evening, Fran found Maggie at her elbow, even though it wasn't her turn to be there.

"Thought I'd come and help," she said casually. "Nobody else, not even my son who's sound asleep, seems to need me at the moment."

"You mean you thought I *did* need you," Fran said with a rueful smile. "Was I looking very tragic?"

"Sad . . . a bit. Perhaps after Christmas is like having

post-influenza depression! Or did Hamish upset you, by any chance?"

"Well, I failed to steer him away from asking me again to marry him, and it's lowering to refuse a nice man and send him away unhappy. McAlister warned me it would happen, but I'm not quite sure what I could have done about it."

"Nothing at all," Maggie answered with unusual briskness. "Anyway, you've provided a counter-irritant. Hamish is inclined to melancholy, like a lot of Highlanders. Moping about you has taken his mind off losing Alan and worrying about me."

For a moment Fran was tempted to mention her argument with him about Tod, but that would mean inviting Maggie to confess whether she thought of marrying him or not. In the end she decided against it. McAlister had been right to the extent of saying that she had no right to meddle in other people's lives. A kind, intelligent woman had no need of interference from any of them; when the right moment came she would make up her own mind about Tod.

Maggie examined her friend's thoughtful face and wondered whether they had yet touched on what was really troubling her.

"I hope you don't take what *Neil* says too much to heart," she said finally. "He was a very young man when our father died. He had to be responsible for what he'd inherited, and it's become a habit with him to look after other people. I know that what you call his 'Lord of the Isles' manner irritates you at times, but I can't imagine what we should all have done without him."

Fran smiled in spite of herself – only gentle Maggie could reduce her fights with McAlister to the harmless level of irritation. "I seem to have discovered my

Highland blood up here and become quarrelsome; it's not how I usually behave!"

Maggie forbore to point out that it wasn't how her brother usually behaved either. She would have felt quite optimistic about such a stormy relationship if it hadn't been for Fiona, too firmly established as McAlister's future partner to ever be displaced now.

"Where is the great man, by the way?" Fran asked lightly. "He's been invisible since Christmas."

"Pinned down at Cullin House, poor laddie. Now that the winter's turned so hard again, it's a daily struggle to keep the livestock fed and the sheep dug out of snowdrifts. The thaw didn't last long, and the high winds we've got at the moment, combined with snow, make things difficult for them."

Fran had a vivid mental picture of Himself, snowflakes in his hair and melting on his brown face, wrestling bodily with an animal that hadn't had the wit to get itself out of difficulties; she could imagine him simply refusing to let it be lost, no matter what. The vision was clear and beautiful, and as much a part of him as the overbearing, arrogant self-assurance that had led her to cross swords with him so often.

On the whole she was grateful that he was too busy to check up on them personally at the Castle; that way she was more able to stay out of trouble. It also meant that they were likely to be spared Fiona's company, which she suspected didn't give Maggie a great deal more pleasure than it gave herself.

Work on the book took hold of them again, and she and Tod buried themselves in it each day. Then, in mid-January, the routine had to be interrupted by a trip to Kirktown for stationery supplies that they were running out of. She steered the Colonel's car gingerly down the snow-covered road, and eventually parted company with Tod in the town. While he was visiting his McDougall cousins she could make good a long-standing promise to call on Allie McConnell and her mother in their small cottage on the waterfront. They welcomed her with such warmth that it was impossible not to share the lunch they offered. Afterwards Mrs McConnell took up a piece of knitting she was working on, but Fran was conscious of her eyes more often on her own sweater – a Christmas gift from Aunt Ernestine. It was a lovely mohair garment, fashioned from a hazy mixture of blue and green – the colours of the sea outside the cottage window. Finally, Mrs McConnell asked if she might finger it.

"Beautiful," she said wistfully. "Now *that* would be a pleasure to knit."

"Fat chance," Allie snorted. "All you get handed out is fawn, and grey, and sludge green, and patterns that haven't changed in living memory. They're depressing enough to knit; what must they be like to wear!"

Fran remembered the dismal garments dutifully bought by the Castle's summer guests. The time would come, surely, when even loyalty wasn't enough to make them go on buying such things, even if the island women were prepared to go on making them.

"I gather the patterns are traditional," she suggested tentatively.

It produced another snort from Allie. "Traditional my foot! Fiona harps on that because she knows Himself thinks the old ways ought to be preserved. He's a grand man for almost everything to do with Cullin, but I doubt that he's very clued up about the clothes women want to wear."

Fran doubted it too, and it seemed craven not to give Allie moral support; but she'd already been warned out of this particular arena, and the last thing she wanted now was to be involved in a head-on clash with Fiona.

"Could you not discuss it with Miss Mackintosh?" she suggested. "There's no reason why she shouldn't listen to *you*. I'm afraid I should only do more harm than good. I'm looked upon as a stranger here, whose opinions are of no account."

"Fiona will listen, and then sweetly suggest that what I know about is waitressing. I can prove her wrong this time, though." Allie grinned at the thought of it. "I sent to London for a book of patterns – there's one in it just like the one you're wearing. By the time everyone's had a good look they're all going to know what they ought to be knitting."

Fran thought Mrs McConnell looked anxious, and rightly so. Her daughter was like a sturdy little mountain goat, impossible to persuade to go in any direction but the one she'd decided upon.

"Talk to Fiona first," Fran urged again. "She *is* still in charge, Allie dear, whatever you may think of the way she runs things. It's not just a matter of deciding whether to keep the old patterns; the dyers and spinners of the yarns all have to be involved. There's a lot to organise, and Fiona's the one to do it."

Allie agreed cheerfully enough, and there the subject of knitting was abandoned for the rest of Fran's visit.

A week later Maggie came back from Kirktown looking so worried that Fran had to ask what was wrong.

"I met Fiona in town – there's trouble among the knitters."

"What sort of trouble?" Fran asked the question, fearing that she already knew the answer.

"The younger ones especially are staging a revolt – brighter colours, more fashionable designs, before they'll produce any more work."

"Well, what they're given to do is pretty diabolical," Fran said reluctantly. "I can't say I blame them for digging their toes in."

"Fiona's of the opinion that you do more than not blame them. In fact, she's convinced that it's *you* stirring them up. She says you deliberately flaunt your 'trendy' clothes in front of them to make them feel dowdy and dissatisfied; worse than that, there's talk of designs from London being handed round."

Fran thought of Allie triumphantly brandishing her book of patterns, and remembered having gone soon afterwards to a film show with Tod in Kirktown. Her knitted dress had been simple enough by London standards, but she'd had the strong feeling that all the other women present were examining it stitch by stitch.

She was silent for so long that eventually Maggie spoke again.

"It sounds extravagant to say this, Fran – unbelievable, perhaps, to someone not born among our people here – but Fiona has persuaded herself into hating you. She has right on her side, she thinks, and you are simply meddling. It's a great pity that you had to get into a public fight with her."

"I didn't know I had. There was one occasion when I made a vague suggestion, but she took instant offence and I never mentioned it again. Then, when I visited Allie McConnell and her mother last week, the subject of the knitting cropped up again. But I promise you that all I did was urge her to talk to Fiona. That's the extent of my stirring up!"

"Well, let's hope it's a storm in a teacup," Maggie

said cheerfully, reluctant to admit that she didn't feel very optimistic. Fiona had been almost weeping with rage, and she wasn't a woman to sit down under what she took to be a deliberate attempt to wreck her running of the knitting industry. It had worked happily enough until a subversive, flashy Londoner had arrived, incapable of understanding the value of ancient traditions. Maggie was sadly aware that Fiona's opposition to the newcomer was more complicated than that, but even her own affection for Fran couldn't blind her to the fact that Fiona would have cause to feel betrayed if Neil didn't support her.

Fran returned to work with the unpleasant sensation that a sword of Damocles was hanging over her head. It fell a couple of days later, in the mid-afternoon, when she was restless and tired of sitting hunched over a typewriter, and insisted on walking the mile or so to the mail box with letters for posting. It was a bitterly cold, but fine afternoon, and she felt better for being out of doors by herself. On the way back she was overtaken by McAlister's Land Rover, which ominously pulled up in front of her. The door was held open in a way that allowed for no choice – she was expected to get in.

"No lift thanks – I'm taking a much-needed walk," she said briefly all the same.

"Get in, please . . . we're going to have a much-needed talk instead."

She was tempted to refuse, but a quick glance at his face told her that the only result would be an undignified chase which she would undoubtedly lose. The labrador, on the front seat as usual, foolishly made her welcome when she climbed in, and then sat with a head lodged in comfort on her knee.

"I think I'm in trouble again," she confided

to Bess, who flicked an ear to show that she agreed.

McAlister said nothing at all until he brought them to a stop in a passing-place along the road.

"I think we'll have our discussion here," he suggested grimly, "since you'll be shouting at me as usual in no time at all."

It sounded bitterly unfair, as if she was always the aggressor in a series of one-sided fights; but she wouldn't say so. Whatever the provocation she would stay calm and reasonable – only thus could she be sure of not saying something she would afterwards regret.

"I spoke to Mr Harriman this afternoon," McAlister said. "He told me his book is nearly finished. Since that is the case I feel able to ask you to leave Cullin more or less immediately."

His voice was so quietly reasonable that it took Fran a moment to register the enormity of what had just been said. After a long pause she managed to answer him, with her hands buried in Bess's coat so that he shouldn't see them trembling.

"Since I'm being made to feel like an erring housemaid about to be dismissed, may I know why?"

"You've been a trouble to *me* ever since you arrived on Cullin," McAlister said deliberately. "I was prepared to accept that because Maggie seemed to value your company, but I can't allow you to stay at the cost of disrupting everybody else's life as well."

"By 'everybody' I suppose you mean Fiona Mckintosh; I can't think of anyone else here that I might have upset."

"Immediately, yes," he agreed, aware of having no one to suggest if she challenged him.

"Then I can guess the reason. I'm thought to be

undermining the island's knitting industry, spreading sedition and unrest among its workforce!"

She had to sound flippant or burst into tears. But it was a mistake.

"It amuses you, doesn't it?" His voice was still quiet, but it held scorn that hurt like a touch of acid. "These poor benighted women stuck in their traditional ways need prodding out of them. It means nothing to you that the work they do is important simply *because* it keeps old ways and values alive. You would rather make them feel old-fashioned and inadequate."

"You seem as ready as Fiona is to imagine that I'm entirely responsible for whatever trouble has arisen."

"There was none until you arrived," he pointed out unanswerably, "and the women are insisting that they must make the sort of clothes *you* wear. It's grossly unfair, Francesca. The knitting was being allowed to die until Fiona stepped in and got it going again. The women were given work to do that didn't mean leaving their homes and children – can't even *you* see how valuable that was?"

Fran thought of Allie's treasured book of patterns obviously being hawked round among the knitters to show them the error of the ways that Fiona insisted upon. It didn't occur to her to explain how the revolt had arisen – Allie would need her job back at the Castle in the spring. In any case there *was* a sense in which she'd been to blame; she'd offered comparisons they couldn't fail to make, just by being there among them.

"I haven't really been trying to stir up trouble, but I doubt if you're going to believe that," she said quietly at last. "I don't even want Cullin's old ways to be changed. But I'll tell you something, McAlister, that you *must* believe. In this case we're talking about, the value of your tradition lies in just one thing – the inherited skill of these women. It does *not* lie in making them endlessly repeat designs that soon no one will want to buy. Then Fiona will have a much worse problem on her hands, and so will they."

She spoke so seriously that he couldn't even pretend to believe that she was trying to provoke him. All he was certain of was his own complete inability to know which of them was right.

"Fiona is confident that she can manage," he said finally, "provided she isn't undermined by interference . . . however well meant."

The last words were forced out of him by a sense of fairness that not all Fiona's complaints could quite demolish. They were enough to slay all resentments, leaving Fran only immeasurably sad.

"Then there is no more to be said," she commented when she could trust her voice. "If I'm allowed to stay until the weekend I can help Tod complete the first draft. After that he'll be able to manage on his own, and I can leave without letting him down. In fact I shall be *glad* to go – I've been away too long from where I belong."

She smiled as she spoke, in case he should guess that she felt riven by pain. He didn't answer and there was only silence to listen to, unbroken for once even by the bleat of a sheep on the hill or a curlew's long, liquid call – no, it was the guilbneach she listened for; Dougall had taught her the Gaelic name now. The sounds she missed *did* belong to Cullin, and she fixed her mind on them because anything was preferable to thinking about being sent away by a man who failed to understand that she would have done not the least thing to harm whatever he loved and believed in.

Then suddenly he began to speak again in a deep, melancholic voice. "Fiona believes that you deliberately caused unrest among the women. If you tell me it isn't so I must believe you . . . do believe you, because it isn't in you to be untruthful. But the damage you cause comes from not knowing what is at stake. Our only chance of keeping Cullin safe in a world that would sweep away its good, simple life is *not* to compromise, not to say that we'll accept some changes and reject others that we don't like. Perhaps we shan't survive in the end – fishing in our stormy waters, crofting on poor soil, cutting peat. . . . These aren't easy ways of earning a living, and too many of our young people may decide that they want a softer life elsewhere. Then Cullin will die, as other Hebridean islands have done. But for as long as there are men and women here who feel as I do we shall go on in the ways we know."

She felt imprisoned in the grief of knowing that, however arrogant his aims might seem, or however hopeless his fight against an encroaching world might turn out to be, there would be no place for *her* beside him, helping, fighting, and giving comfort if he failed.

Again, it was he who broke the heavy silence. "I'm sorry, Francesca. I should have liked to walk the glens with you in springtime . . . showed you where the seal cubs play in the bay . . ."

The broken murmur of his voice was more than she could bear.

"Damn you, McAlister – be quiet," she shouted desperately. Her hand found the door handle beside her, and she was out in a flash, running for dear life.

He let her go, but watched her until she was out of sight. It was better so, because he was sending her out of his life for a reason that had nothing whatsoever to do with Fiona's knitting patterns. Even more than his one-time fiancée had done, Fran spoke of a sophisticated, city life that was a world removed from Cullin. He wasn't fool enough to make the same mistake twice and think that, if he loved her enough, she would settle down here. Sooner or later she would get tired of it and go away, leaving him bereft. It was marginally less agonising to do it this way, by making the choice himself.

Chapter Fourteen

Fran reached the Castle consumed with a pain in her side from running too far, but the ache in her heart was far worse. She managed the last flight of stairs to her room, then collapsed on the bed, overtaken by a storm of weeping. At last, exhausted but calm again, she bathed her red eyes, put on too much make-up and then wiped it off again because it only made matters worse. It was time to go in search of Tod. She found him in the kitchen, neatly peeling potatoes for Maggie, but their conversation stopped so abruptly that she guessed they'd been discussing her.

"Perhaps you already know what I've come to tell you," she said quietly. "I'm going back to London at the weekend, having rather outstayed my welcome on Cullin . . . according to Himself!"

Tod didn't look surprised, but Maggie's shocked expression seemed to insist that they hadn't known what she'd come to say after all.

"Tod's just been telling me that Neil was asking how the book was going, but you must have misunderstood the rest, Fran love; Neil would never have asked you to leave – I can't believe it."

Tod's transparent face gave away the fact that *he* could, perhaps had even suspected the reason for the question McAlister had put to him. He was painfully torn, Fran thought, between loyalty to a friend and the inclination of his own heart. She must make it easy for him, because his choice mustn't be in any doubt.

"It's nothing to do with the book, Tod dear – McAlister is even rather impressed with that now; so there's no need for *you* to rush away. The difficulty lies with me – I'm thought to be upsetting Fiona!" Her pale mouth sketched a sort of smile. "It's time I went home in any case, and I was happy to agree that I could leave at the weekend without deserting my post!"

She found that it was all she could bear to say without bursting into tears again, and headed blindly for the door, leaving Maggie to stare white-faced at Tod.

"It's wicked to hate Fiona," she said slowly. "The poor girl has done her best; it's not her fault that she's tried to do it on what she thought were Neil's terms. But it would have been better for Cullin if she'd been less anxious to agree with everything he said."

Tod was strongly of the opinion that Fiona's efforts had been on behalf of Fiona Mackintosh, not of Cullin, but he was reluctant to say so to a woman who must sooner or later accept her as a sister-in-law. He had his own reasons for believing that Fran had spoken the truth when she said she was ready to leave; that being so, his only concern now was to comfort Maggie.

"Sweetheart, don't worry," he said earnestly, unaware of the endearment that came so naturally. "Fran's had enough of life on a Hebridean island, I reckon, but that isn't to say she won't come back for visits. Fiona and McAlister between them must tackle the trouble with the local ladies – that isn't *your* problem." He feared that Maggie's anxiety might have more to do with Fiona herself than with the future of Cullin knitwear, but on that subject no comfort was available – her brother had settled his own hash, as they said in Nebraska.

After a moment or two she managed a reply that sounded properly impersonal.

"Your own affection for the Hebrides is probably wearing a bit thin by now, but we all hope that *you*'ll come back for visits as well. If not, *I* shall have to learn to play the mouth organ to lull Keith to sleep at night!"

There was a long pause before Tod answered her, not in his usual eager way, but slowly, as if she must listen with care to what he said.

"I'll be leaving myself quite soon as a matter of fact – there are things piling up back home that need attending to. I didn't set out intending to stay away so long."

"Of course," Maggie agreed with determined cheerfulness, refusing for the moment to consider a future that included neither Fran nor this kind man she had foolishly come to depend on. "You'll be glad to get home."

An expression she couldn't read touched his face for a moment, then faded again leaving it with an air of desperate resolution she hadn't seen before.

"I used the word but Nebraska isn't where home is any longer." He came to stand in front of her, so that she had to look at him and be convinced of the truth of what he said. "Maggie, Cullin is home now . . . has been ever since I set foot on it. I shall come back the first moment I can . . . for good next time . . . and the only other thing I want in the world is to take care of you and Keith if you'll let me."

"I'm . . . I'm not sure what you're saying," she finally managed to murmur.

"Nor am I," Tod confessed with a shy grin. "I've

left it late in the day to ask a lady to marry me!" He took hold of her hands, but lightly, so that she could free herself if she wanted to. "Maggie, I'm years older than you are and I never was much to look at in any case. Even if you weren't still grieving for Keith's father there's no reason I can think of why you'd want to take a chance on marrying me. But I have to ask because people reckon on things being done properly up here, and I'd like the *right* to look after you. Will you promise to think about it while I'm away? If you turn me down – which I'm sure Himself and Hamish hope you will – it doesn't matter; I'll be somewhere nearby where I can still keep an eye on you."

She leaned forward to kiss his cheek, then blinked away sudden tears to smile at him. "You're the *kindest* man I've ever known, dear Tod. I promise I'll do my thinking, and whatever I finally decide, it will be *my* choice, not Neil's or anyone else's."

He kissed her hands, and then her mouth very gently, and walked away. It hadn't, he reckoned, been much of a proposal, but anything more would have been out of place, and there'd be years ahead enough to make it clear in a hundred ways how very much he loved her.

McAlister carefully avoided the vicinity of the Castle, but the evasion only provoked Maggie into bearding him in his den at Cullin House. He gave a little sigh as she walked in – the rare signs of his usually gentle sister on the warpath being too obvious to be missed.

"Fran's leaving at the weekend – but of course you know that," she began without preamble.

"Yes, I know," he agreed. "Both she and Tod Harriman seem to think her work here is finished."

"Perhaps . . . but that isn't why she's going in such a ridiculous rush."

Two pairs of dark eyes, similar in setting and intensity, met like fencers' swords engaging. He could only remember quarrelling with Maggie once before, and that had been for the same reason. It was something else to blame Fran Campbell for.

"If you know why Francesca is going I'm surprised that you don't realise how necessary it is," he said at last. "I surely don't have to make *you* understand that if we can't work together without disputes and ill feeling we are as good as lost."

"I understand that perfectly well," Maggie answered crisply. "What I *fail* to understand is why the trouble-maker is seen to be a girl whom everybody but you and Fiona manage to love without any difficulty at all."

There was a little silence before he found something to say. "She has easy ways, Maggie . . . beguiling ways that . . ."

". . . mislead us into thinking that she's full of grace and loving kindness – quite so! Ask Elspeth, Neil; ask Lionel Forrester or anyone else who's felt the better for knowing her, as I have."

"Fiona has not," he insisted desperately, ". . . and I owe *her* the duty of listening to what she says. No one could have worked harder for Cullin – for the future we're trying to preserve. *She* belongs here – Francesca will go back to London and amuse her friends with stories of our quaint, backward ways."

Maggie stared at his face before she answered him. "I doubt if you believe that, any more than I do. But there's one thing you must be sure of – it wasn't Fran who handed round the knitting patterns that caused so much trouble. Allie is the culprit – she told me so, in case I wouldn't want her back as a waitress. She didn't know that the blame had already been fastened on Fran."

He turned away from her and walked over to the window. From it he could see the cove where he'd sat with a girl one day and carved the figure of a seagull for her.

Anger spent now, Maggie went to stand beside him and was shocked by the unhappiness in his face.

"It's not too late to change things, Neil."

He looked down to offer her a strange, sad smile. "I'm afraid it is, my dear. I shall tell Fiona the truth about the patterns, and that will be my last word on the subject." Then in a voice that he strove to make normal again, he said, "Tod Harriman is a poor sailor, I believe. Tell Francesca, please, that I shall take her to Mallaig on Saturday."

Maggie left a farewell kiss on his cheek, unable to offer any other comfort, and went home to deliver his message.

"He wants to make sure I really go, I suppose . . . kind of him," Fran observed without gratitude.

Maggie looked distressed, torn between regret for Fran and loyalty to a brother who normally could do no wrong in her eyes.

"I think he was wanting to be helpful," she suggested gently.

"Let's give him the benefit of the doubt; in any case I'm sorry, Maggie dear, if I snapped at *you*."

She didn't refer to the subject again, only appeared at breakfast on Friday morning dressed for travelling and with her luggage, carried down by Jaime, already waiting in the hall.

"We finished work last night, so there's no point in hanging about," she explained quickly, not able to meet Maggie's eyes. "If I go now, I can be home in the morning before the shops close for the weekend."

"But Fran dear – Neil's coming for you tomorrow; I told you."

"I prefer it this way. Promise me you won't let him know until I've left Cullin." This time she did look at Maggie, and the stricken expression in her eyes made any more argument impossible.

With the taxi from Kirktown already at the door, goodbyes were necessarily brief – a hug for Tod, and a kiss for Maggie and Keith.

"At least you'll come back for the christening," Maggie said desperately.

"I'll . . . I'll do my best." She left farewell messages for Alice, the Colonel, and the girls, and then was gone almost before they'd brought themselves to believe that she was really leaving.

The night sleeper deposited her at Euston Station on a cold, wet February morning. Fran sat huddled in the back of a taxi, feeling cold and tired, and with the eerie feeling that she no longer belonged anywhere. Cullin didn't want her, London refused to accept her. The roar of traffic was a hostile assault on her eardrums, and the endless miles of steaming brick and stucco weighed on her to the point of desperation. This was her home, but it felt like a waking nightmare. She fled into her tiny flat in something near to panic, but there was no relief there; the walls seemed to be pressing in on her after the vast, high-ceilinged rooms of the Castle. She was only saved by the discovery that someone – her Campbell cousins, presumably sent round by Aunt Ernestine – had been there ahead of her to dust and air the flat. There were even flowers by way of welcome and food in the refrigerator. It was a piece of kindness that she thought saved her from raving melancholia. After a while she managed to pick up the telephone and ring her aunt, fairly confident at last that she could manage a conversation without weeping.

"I'm back, Aunt dear. Thank you for organising the twins for me; the flat's as clean as a new pin."

"All part of the Campbell service! Are you all right, Fran? You sounded odd the other day when you rang."

"A bit overwhelmed by London, otherwise fine," she said briefly. "I'll be reporting for work as usual."

The following Monday Ernestine thought she looked strained and thin, anything but fine in fact. It confirmed the suspicion that something not admitted to lay behind her sudden return to London. A question about Cullin received so brief an answer that Ernestine took the hint and dragged her niece's mind towards the future instead.

"Feel like looking after a 'helpless' male and two small children for a fortnight while his wife produces a third specimen? Not a sinecure, he admits, so you're free to refuse."

Fran's little shrug gave away the fact that it really didn't matter what she did. "Of course I'll go . . . where is it, by the way?"

"Sussex – rural but civilised, I'm given to understand."

She left for Cuckfield two days later, dismayed to find how relieved she was to be leaving London again already. She arrived at the address Aunt Ernestine had given her and found a pleasant house on the outskirts of the town; at least, it would have been pleasant but for the impression that an invading army had been camped in it for the winter. She was greeted with such gratitude by a male who was not only helpless but out-generalled at every turn by his demon offspring that the soreness of her heart eased a little. It was something to be needed.

The next two weeks were the most strenuous of her life, but at least there was no time to mope, and she finally went back to London with a feeling of real achievement. A chaotically disorganised house had been left clean and welcoming, and after several pitched battles Charlotte, aged six, and Thomas, two years younger, had conceded defeat. She even felt sad to say goodbye to them.

From then on there were only assignments that kept her in London. She slowly grew accustomed to city life again, but she was aware that she might never rediscover a relish for it. She was busy, but not quite busy enough to be sent to her bed to sleep the sleep of exhaustion. The memories of Cullin lay always on the margin of her mind, and Maggie's letters made homesickness flare up in her for a place that wasn't her home. She smiled at the world and doggedly went on working, but Ernestine Campbell had a shrewd idea of the effort it was costing. Something had to be done, and who better to take a hand than herself? Was she not a professional at sorting out the muddles that less clear-sighted human beings than herself made of their lives?

After considerable thought she began with a long telephone call to Cullin. Ruinously expensive though it might be, she didn't begrudge the cost – it yielded exactly the information she needed. A good general insisted on knowing all the facts before he planned his campaign – the strengths and weaknesses of the enemy, the lie of the land, the local support he could depend on. Armed with knowledge, Ernestine sat and thought, and finally smiled her crocodile smile – yes, unless her own troops proved unmanageably stubborn and stupid, she felt sure the battle could be won.

Chapter Fifteen

Easter was approaching when Fran reached the mews house one evening after a tiring day spent shepherding American Mid-Westerners round the sights of London. Suddenly McAlister's scathing question was in her mind . . . "Does it satisfy you indulging the whims of rich travellers?" At the moment the answer seemed to be no, and she went inside wondering whether it was time she parted company with 'Campbell's Comfort'. She walked into her aunt's sitting room and stopped dead in the doorway . . . she was hallucinating, going mad perhaps, because how could that long, lean man getting to his feet be *there* and not hundreds of miles away?

The world went dark, and swung away from her, while she ducked her head in an agonised determination not to faint. Finally she managed to look at them, with a smile of sorts pinned to her sheet-white face.

"Good evening, Francesca." His deep voice was just as she remembered, but it was not part of her memory of him that he should be wearing tweeds, and a school tie.

"What brings you to London . . . nothing wrong with Maggie, I hope?" she asked hoarsely, and saw him shake his head.

"Everyone is well, and I am heaped with loving messages for you. I usually make a business trip a couple of times a year, and Maggie asked me to try to persuade you in the course of this one to come back with me for Easter. She says you've been ignoring her pleas on the subject."

Fran thought guiltily of several unanswered letters and wished she'd had resolution enough to scotch the idea when Maggie first suggested it. Now it was going to be all the harder to refuse.

"It's kind of her . . . but Easter's out of the question, I'm afraid."

She spoke with a finality that bordered on being rude, and Aunt Ernestine's raised eyebrow indicated that she thought so too. But with no convincing excuse to offer, there was nothing to be done except say no with a firmness that couldn't be contradicted.

"My dear Fran – you're overdue for a holiday," said Miss Campbell, trying all the same. "There's no reason that I know of why you shouldn't go."

Fran's fragile self-control suddenly snapped. "There's every reason. I was told to leave Cullin forthwith. Now, apparently, I'm allowed to set foot on its precious soil again . . . until I do something else to upset McAlister and get booted out for a second time. Thank you very much, but the answer's still no. Go, stay, go – it's like being at the mercy of a demented traffic light."

Aunt Ernestine, who obviously thought this comment fair, turned to McAlister like an impartial umpire to see what he made of it. He might have been amused at any other time, but there was too much anger in Fran's voice now, and too much turmoil in himself. He wanted to shout at this girl for causing him so much pain, and so much doubt that she could ever be satisfied with himself and Cullin. He wanted more than anything in life to be allowed to love her; but he was almost certain that Ernestine Campbell was wrong, and that he would never be given the chance.

"I'm sorry . . . you make it sound as though we treated you very badly," he said awkwardly. "I expect we did . . . but there were reasons for that."

"They still exist," Fran pointed out sharply. "You distrust London women like me because one let you down once before . . . Maggie told me about that, otherwise I should have thought you were unbalanced on the subject. And no doubt Fiona Mackintosh is still there too, hating any newcomer who isn't safely wedded to a husband or the pursuit of a golf ball, or some unsuspecting fish. Tell me what's changed."

"Well, this much, at least – Fiona is giving up the island knitting industry; giving up the island, in fact. Since her efforts were not appreciated she felt free to take her undoubted talents elsewhere."

There was a long silence before Fran managed to answer him.

"I don't believe it. I thought *she* was wedded to Cullin, until such time as . . . well, what I mean is, that she had no intention of giving up." Fran had to change course rapidly, suddenly ashamed of exposing what she believed had been the extent of Fiona's ambitions. She glanced at her aunt, hoping she hadn't noticed the slip, and discovered that Miss Campbell was looking uncommonly pleased with herself. Preening was the word, Fran realised, with a growing sense of dismay.

"There's something that I think *you* know about," she suggested quietly. "Would you like to tell me what it is?"

Ernestine patted her red fringe, in no hurry to lose the limelight now that she'd got it at last, but also suddenly a little nervous. It wasn't an emotion she normally suffered from, and the effort to overcome it made her sound very off-hand.

"Do you think Glasgow for a branch of Campbell's Comfort?" she asked. "Or should it be Edinburgh?"

"You're talking in riddles. It's been a tiring day and I'd like to go home if you don't feel like being more explicit."

Suddenly aware that Fran was dangerously over-strained, Miss Campbell put questions aside and came to the point.

"You heard what McAlister said – Fiona was looking for a change from knitwear; I was needing someone capable and clever to run an agency in Scotland, so we've agreed on a year's trial." She saw the expression on Fran's face and conceded a little more in the way of explanation. "You *know* Americans and Canadians always insist on going there – look at Tod! With a Scottish branch office to call on, I shouldn't have had to struggle on alone without *you* for months."

She hadn't been left alone, and the subject of a branch office had never been mentioned before. Fran was suddenly in the grip of unaccustomed rage. Her aunt had always been masterful, but never devious before, never secretive and underhand. The discovery that she'd been all these things seemed for the moment even more upsetting than anything else; but unable to attack her in front of McAlister, anger could only be turned on him.

"I suppose you think I'm to blame for Fiona deciding to leave Cullin. Well, I *won't* be responsible for that. If you couldn't see how much she wanted to stay you must be even blinder than most men."

"What women want is more often than not a mystery to me," he admitted stiffly. "But this conversation isn't about Fiona. She accepted Miss

Campbell's offer, and that is that; we needn't discuss her further."

He knew that she was leaving Cullin with a bitterness that was directed almost entirely at himself – leaving her job there was in fact something of a relief. He'd become aware more slowly than he should have done of the real reason for her hostility to Fran. So stupidly blind had he been, in fact, that she'd had to point out to him herself what everyone else on Cullin took for granted. It had been an almost overwhelming shock; he believed he'd been as circumspect with her as he'd been with every other woman. But no one knew better than himself the closeness of island society, the care with which neighbours observed each other, and the speed with which rumours spread among even the most isolated communities. They all, it seemed, anticipated the day when Himself took Fiona Mackintosh to wife. He had, at last, made the offer that seemed inescapable, as warmly as he could. After staring at him for some time Fiona had finally thrown it back in his face, and then flung at him the news that she was leaving Cullin.

He put aside the memory of that interview to stare at another white-faced, angry girl.

"We needn't discuss *anything* further," Fran said finally. "I am going home; my aunt will be delighted to entertain you, I'm sure."

She began to walk towards the door only to find that he'd moved faster and was blocking the way. His dark face looked strained and sad, but she wouldn't be softened by it . . . couldn't allow herself to feel sorry for whatever ailed him.

"You haven't heard yet why I'm here," he said quietly. "I came to deliver two messages from Maggie since you seem to have given up answering her letters. Keith remains a heathen because you won't come to a christening, and she is threatening to postpone her wedding on Easter Saturday unless you're there."

Fran stared at him, anger and suspicion and grief all for the moment forgotten. "Tod was going home . . . do you mean that he's back on Cullin?" Happiness for Maggie bloomed suddenly in her face as she saw Neil nod.

"He stayed away for only as long as he was obliged to – the compulsion to return to the Hebrides was very strong, apparently."

The reply was made calmly, without pleasure, but without bitterness either; McAlister was accepting his new brother-in-law because he must. Fran decided that it would be stupid to start another quarrel by asking for something more generous – Tod would win him round in the end, simply by making Maggie happy.

"What is going to happen to the job Fiona is giving up?" she asked instead.

"Nothing for the moment. But finding a replacement for herself might be the first task her new agency has to handle."

Fran's expression said all too clearly what she thought of this suggestion, but before she could put the thought into words Ernestine intervened.

"We shall work on it together," she announced, neatly spiking her niece's guns.

The conversation hung fire for a moment until McAlister plunged again with an awkward lack of finesse that earned Miss Campbell's displeasure; he was a splendid laird, and a shyly charming companion, but she was obliged to concede to herself that a ladies' man he was *not*. "I delivered Maggie's messages but you haven't answered them, Francesca. Am I to have the pleasure of escorting you back to Cullin or not?"

Predictably, her aunt thought, the answer came.

"I shall arrive by Easter Saturday – you can promise Maggie that. But I need no armed guard to get me there. *You* are free to leave at once . . . I shall make my own arrangements."

She walked round him to the door, opened it, and left, leaving silence behind. At last McAlister found something to say.

"I'm afraid I didn't manage that very well – so Maggie would tell me."

"She'd be right," Ernestine agreed wryly, "but for once she could say the same of me. I got carried away with my own cleverness – I should have known that Fran would climb on her high horse. She'll come round in the end because she can never hold a grudge for long, but at the moment she's angry, with cause to be. It's as well your island is so inconveniently situated – that interminable journey will give her temper time to cool." She stared at his set face and softened her voice a little.

"You needn't be afraid to let her go alone – Fran doesn't give a promise and then break it. Now, shall we stop beating our breasts and drink to the happiness of Maggie and Tod Harriman?"

He agreed after only the slightest of hesitations, but refused Ernestine's next offer, of dinner at a restaurant nearby – this time with as much finesse as he could manage. The night train could easily be caught, and he would feel marginally less out of his depth with his face turned towards Cullin.

Ernestine bid him a cheerful goodbye, but looked grave when he'd gone away. She had to admit to a rare mishandling of her own campaign, which was bad enough; but she was also inclined to think that her troops had taken up positions from which they would refuse to be rescued. It was a failure all the more heartbreaking to contemplate when her intentions had for once been entirely unselfish.

With very little time in hand, Fran set out on her own journey the following morning, after a night's reflection that sent her to call at the mews house on her way to the station. She kissed her aunt by way of apology for the previous evening's display of ill temper.

"I can't stay more than a minute or two – my taxi is waiting; but I didn't want to go with you thinking I was still cross! The truth is that a Scottish branch is a brilliant idea, and I can imagine Fiona running it very well – without McAlister to please, she's very competent and sensible."

Ernestine stared at her for a moment – over-large eyes in a pale face testified to distress that had had to be wrestled with, and a composure that could easily be destroyed. Afraid for the first time in her life of saying the wrong thing, Miss Campbell nevertheless did her best for Himself.

"The poor man thought he was doing the right thing – he wasn't to know the arrangement wasn't working."

"He seems to have been far from right all round," Fran commented pleasantly. "I dare say Fiona will soon feel that she's much better off away from Cullin."

Abandoning a cause that seemed to be hopeless, Ernestine pecked her niece's cheek and walked out with her to the waiting taxi. "My congratulations to the happy couple, and I'll see *you* when I see you, no doubt."

"Early next week," Fran promised with a faint smile. "I shan't be needed to stay this time."

The day that followed seemed very long, but she

refused to let her tired mind linger on the thought it kept returning to – that a tedious, lonely journey might have seemed less so with Neil McAlister for company. She struggled not to remember a morning when they'd stared at a boat's frothing wake painted gold by the sun, and smiled because they were happy together. It was safer to think of Fiona, uprooted from what had been her home, because not even to *her*, apparently, would Neil McAlister entrust the privacy of his self-contained mind and heart.

After a night stop in Mallaig she caught the morning steamer, and settled down for a sea trip that was becoming familiar – a call at Portree on Skye, a briefer stop at Raasay, then on up the Sound towards Cullin. Even alone, and lonely, she was content to be there. The lovely prospect of sea and islands all about her was solace in itself; she'd missed it down south, with the deep, sad ache of someone who'd found but lost her heart's desire.

When the steamer tied up at Kirktown she looked for Dougal among the little crowd waiting on the quay, certain that Maggie would have sent him down. His great, kilted figure would have been easy to spot, but there was no sign of it, and she was beginning to feel disappointed when she saw the fair head of Hamish Harding instead.

He rushed to enfold her in a suffocating hug the moment she stepped off the gangway onto dry land.

"Fran, my lovely . . . Tod wanted to come, and so did Dougal and Colonel Forrester. I had to fight for the privilege of meeting you alone and unaided!"

"I'm honoured," she said smiling at him with warm affection. "Dear Hamish, you're looking very well, I think – the first term back at school can't have been an ordeal after all."

"It was unexpectedly embarrassing, as a matter of fact. Normally villainous boys had decided that they must behave like angels while I found my feet. The saintliness was wearing thin by the end of term, so I dare say they'll be themselves again after Easter." He stared at Fran, as if there might be something about her he'd forgotten, and found a change in her – gaiety was missing. "Are *you* all right . . . tired after the long journey?"

"I *was* tired," she admitted. "Now I feel fine, and very happy to be back."

He smiled, hoisted up her suitcase, and led the way to his car, while Fran breathed in the remembered tang of salt, tar, and cold, fresh air. The cry of seagulls was all about them, but the sound she waited for came later, as they wound their way up the hillside – the delightful bubbling sound of the curlews above the moorland slopes.

Maggie was out on the steps of the Castle entrance, waiting for them despite the misty afternoon rain that pearled her lashes and dark hair. Just behind her stood Tod, content to wait his turn at offering a welcome.

"Oh, dear girl, it's so lovely to see you again," said Maggie tremulously. "I was almost giving up when Neil said he'd go to London and *fetch* you if need be."

Fran registered the fact that there had been no 'business trip' after all, but refused to spoil this homecoming with the peevish thought that she'd been misled deliberately by McAlister. He had, as always, his own lordly way of doing things; if she couldn't accept that it would be better to stay away from Cullin altogether.

"I know I got very bad at answering letters," she admitted, "but *you*, Maggie love, were very sly – never a mention was there that Tod was back, with his hand in marriage accepted!" She kissed *him* warmly as well, and told him that he was supposed to look nervous, as well as effulgent with happiness.

Tod merely smiled more broadly still, and promised to do his best when the time came to stand before the minister.

There was no sign of Himself, and for that Fran was grateful.

Left in peace to settle into the room that had been hers in the tower, she followed her old habit and went to the window. The little loch was rippled silver by the wind, and above it the pinewoods led her eyes towards the shoulders and great head of Beinn Mhor, still powdered with winter snow. He was grand, but somehow benignly so, and the whole landscape stretched out as far as the sky contained nothing but peace and beauty. She was lucky to be here at all, luckier still to know that she'd be made welcome whenever she returned; it was more happiness than most people knew, and it would have to be enough. Fiona Mackintosh had expected more – a place in the heart and life of a man who'd given both to Cullin. Well, *she* wouldn't make that mistake herself; she'd dance at Maggie and Tod's wedding, see her godson christened, and then go away again without more grief than she could bear.

All her past habits reasserted themselves and she went downstairs very early the next morning, confident that Maggie would already be there, brewing the day's first pot of tea.

"I wasn't meaning to be sly about Tod," Maggie said when they were settled at the kitchen table. "I thought the christening would be enough to bring you back, and I would keep the wedding as a lovely surprise! While he was away I thought I'd come to the decision that it would be wrong to marry again

. . . greedy somehow, I suppose! Then when he came back, sooner than I expected, I saw straightaway what a fool I was being. He loves Keith and he loves me, and I knew it couldn't be wrong after all."

Fran smiled at her with huge affection. "I was terribly afraid that other people might put you off, but even Hamish seems happy with Tod now. It's harder to know what your brother thinks. Originally his objection seemed to be that an American would want to take you away from Cullin, but at least he must be aware now that nothing would prise Tod out of what he regards as paradise."

"Neil didn't try to put me off – but I think he hoped I'd remember how hard it is for incomers to settle down here permanently. Everything seems fine for a while; then the drawbacks begin to emerge – the long, dark winters, the sense of isolation from the rest of the world, and the unending struggle for most people to make a living here."

"All true for most incomers, but not for Tod," Fran insisted quietly. "If McAlister doesn't understand that he doesn't yet understand the man you're marrying."

"He *will* understand in the end," Maggie said with certainty. She looked at Fran's face – thinner than before, with a smile that came less readily – then looked away again. "The pity of it is that he's a stubborn man to convince now. Happiness might easily fly away while he is making up his mind to trust in it."

Not directly answering what Maggie had just said, Fran chose instead to follow where that train of thought led.

"You know, of course, what Fiona's going to do next. I'm ashamed to say that I was irked with Aunt Ernestine when she finally let the cat out of the bag. The agency is hers – she can make what changes she likes without consulting me; but it took me a little while to get over feeling like a jealous adolescent with her nose put out of joint!"

"We had some conversations with her about it," Maggie admitted, "and I might as well also tell you that Tod's taking a keen interest in the venture – to the extent of helping to finance it! He believes it's in everyone's interest to help Fiona make a fresh start away from the island. Neil is grateful, I think, but ashamed of being grateful. It's no wonder he stays at Cullin House, working himself into the ground."

There was silence in the room, broken only by the sound of Fran pushing back her chair. "This is no way to start the day before your wedding day – you're supposed to be upstairs, being waited on hand and foot by a bevy of handmaidens."

Maggie stood up too, but walked round the table to kiss her friend. "As handmaidens go you'll do very well."

After a breakfast shared with the Colonel and Miss Milward, her offer of help was refused. Maggie was adamant that she wasn't to set foot inside the kitchen to work.

"For once you're going to enjoy a rest and Cullin's beautiful fresh air. In any case, we're letting the new chef run himself in by preparing tomorrow's buffet lunch after the wedding. Half the island will turn up, but he insists he can work better on his own."

Fran left her and Tod to the task of acknowledging wedding presents and let herself out of the back entrance of the Castle, leading down through the park to the loch.

It was a shock to find the Land Rover parked there, and McAlister unloading cases of wine from the back of it. She was never prepared for the effect that the sudden sight of him had on her, and now matters were made ten times worse by the fact that, for all his long journey south, she'd hardly addressed a civil word to him in Aunt Ernestine's sitting room.

"Good morning," she muttered. "I've been sent out for the good of my health . . . a brisk walk in the fresh air, Maggie recommends."

"If you'll wait an hour I'll show you where the first primroses are to be found," McAlister suggested, chancing his arm.

Fran managed a cheerful smile. "Everybody's busy but me. I think the best thing I can do is keep out of the way." There were limits to what she could bear, and a primrose-carpeted glen with McAlister for company was one of them.

He looked up at the sky and frowned. "An hour might be too late, at that. The mist is closing in, so don't walk far."

About to nod and walk away, Fran thought of something she wanted to hear him say. "You didn't like the idea of Maggie marrying Tod once upon a time. Am I right in thinking you've at least got used to it?"

"Shall I apologise, Francesca . . . admit that you were right all along?"

"I don't want you to apologise," she said gravely, "just be glad that they're so happy together."

"I *am* glad, and pleased to have been proved wrong." The smile she hadn't seen for so long illumined his tanned face, making it hard for her to turn away from him and set off towards the loch. He was tempted to forget that a dozen tasks clamoured to be done and stride after her; but self-discipline was a habit ingrained in him now, and in any case although he sensed no hostility in her this morning, the slightest pressure would probably send her flying behind her barriers again. He must let her go in peace and bide his time.

Chapter Sixteen

An hour later Fran was on a flank of Beinn Mhor, looking back down the length of a glen that seemed to be enamelled in gold. But she'd walked far enough for her first morning back on the island and McAlister had been right about the weather. The soft, overcast sky was lower than when she'd started out, and trailing wisps of cloud were drifting down from the top of the mountain. She could see the path clearly enough, but it would be foolish not to start back immediately. Ten seconds later she was halted in her tracks by the sound behind her of an animal in distress – so sharp and piteous that she turned and began to retrace her steps without even thinking about it. The path she was on curved round a buttress of rock underpinning a shoulder of the mountain. On her right sparse trees dotted the hillside, climbing up to the corries and slopes of scree and tumbled rock that led up to a summit she could no longer see. The distinctive craggy head was now invisible, and Fran's heart missed a beat at the realisation that she was walking into, not away from, an advancing wall of cloud. She'd have given a great deal to be able to turn and run the other way, as fast as she dared along the narrow path, but the agonised sound somewhere ahead of her couldn't be ignored.

The path twisted again, so sharply that she almost fell over a large, shaggy ewe, hind legs on the path, the rest of her perilously canted over the edge as she scrabbled furiously at the stony slope that fell away down the hillside. The noise she was making had been enough to mask the other sound Fran now heard . . . the terrified bleat of a lamb caught in the brambles of a thicket of bushes springing out of the scree.

She was still wondering how to get herself down a sheer drop of ten feet or so without sliding the rest of the way into the valley when one more sound, soft and sinister this time, swished through the air, explaining the terror in the ewe's cries.

Fran looked up to see the heart-stopping sight she'd caught once before when Hamish had pointed out to her the flight of a golden eagle. The hungry bird was quartering the hillside in search of food, and if it hadn't already done so it would at any moment mark out the lamb trapped in the brambles. She thought the eagle in flight the most majestically beautiful thing she'd ever seen, but she couldn't watch it carry away the tiny creature bleating at her from the bushes. She saw the bird disappear into the cloud, heard the rush of wings as it turned and beat along the hillside again, and without conscious thought slid over the edge of the path.

She went feet first, praying that the little thicket that had caught the lamb would be strong enough to hold her as well. She was briefly aware of pain as the rough scree of the slope bit into her hands, then with her heels desperately jabbing into the crumbling surface of the ground, she clung to the bushes, anchoring herself to the thickest branch she could see. At least she and the lamb were there together, but it was laborious work freeing a creature too petrified to help itself, while she didn't dare release her hold on her thorny but precious stem. She didn't dare look up either, but the agonised cries of the ewe up above told her that the eagle was still around. It wasn't the moment to wonder whether hunger or hunting instinct would cause it to attack the human being who deprived it of prey; but the mist that had frightened her ten minutes ago had suddenly become a friend.

The struggle up the slope towards the path again, with the lamb zipped inside the front of her anorak, was something that haunted her long afterwards. It was accomplished on hands and knees, and for every three feet she won from the hillside, two were lost as the loose scree beneath her hands and knees gave way and let her slip down again. She was trembling with the combined effort of crawling, swearing and praying by the time she'd inched her way near enough to the edge of the path to unzip the lamb and heave it up to join its mother. The piteous baa-ing ceased immediately; she heard the patter of their feet scrabbling off along the path, and then silence, complete and terrifying.

The world was not only silent, but now invisible. While she'd been struggling with the lamb things had changed: the mist had multiplied as if some giant hand had been beating up limitless white of egg all around her, and she was in the middle of a vast, damp meringue; even the bushes she'd clung to so lovingly ten minutes ago had disappeared, and her only point of reference was the ground beneath her knees and the edge of the path whose overhang above her head entirely defeated her.

The white, noiseless world deprived her of the use of all normal senses, and she was left merely with the instinctive conviction that it would be madness to do anything but stay where she was. But she felt her way slowly along the face of the slope, searching for some hollow in the ground that would give her a less precarious lodging, and finally found what she was looking for: a small ledge of rock whose back rose sheer again to the level of the path. She wriggled into it with a sob of relief; she was now in no immediate danger of falling off the mountain, and screened from even the most maddened eagle. Her wristwatch was missing, presumably caught somewhere in the middle of the bramble bush, and she could only guess at the time that had passed since she'd left McAlister in the Castle courtyard.

It grew increasingly cold, and her lacerated hands were beginning to sting abominably. To take her mind off them she railed out loud at a man who was supposed to have a duty to go in search of lost citizens. Had he taken the slightest note of the direction she'd set off in? Did he know, or care, that she was alone and hurt on his damned mountain, and beginning to feel extremely frightened? Anger helped . . . it was better than the fear of ruining Maggie's wedding, of being found too late, if she was found at all. It was much, much better than the knowledge in her mind that she might die without the chance to tell Himself of the dreadful mistake he'd made – that all they'd needed for complete happiness was for him to have a little faith in her. But even anger was eventually dulled by the hypnotic whorls of mist that, shifting before her eyes, brought the fresh anxiety of falling asleep. She was almost mesmerised enough to miss the sound of a voice calling her name when at long last it came.

"Fran . . . ces . . . ca . . ." The syllables, long drawn out and haunting, were muffled by the blanketing mist, but only one person in the world called her Francesca.

"I'm here." It came out as a hoarse croak, and she tried again and again, desperate that he would move away without hearing her.

"Keep calling so that I can find you," McAlister's voice was nearer this time.

"Down below the path," she shouted, indignant that need didn't bring him to her like a homing pigeon.

Then she heard the scrape of his boots on the path above her head, and suddenly his hands were on her shoulders, hard and warm and infinitely reassuring.

"Put your hands in mine," Neil instructed briefly, "then roll over onto your knees so that I can pull you up. You can't fall because I shall be holding you."

"I might drag you over," Fran objected, made argumentative by her sudden reluctance to leave the little hollow that had come to feel so safe.

"Hardly . . . Bess is here too, hanging on to *me*!"

She somehow did as she was told, anaesthetised by sheer relief to the pain of having him grip her damaged hands. A moment later he'd hauled her up over the edge and stood holding her, but not with anything that felt like tenderness. The idea of finding happiness together seemed a feverish fantasy born of fear; he looked merely tired and angry.

"Did you not hear me say the mist was coming down? Couldn't you just once have done as you were bid?"

The roughness of it saved her from bursting into tears, but when his fingers gripped her torn hands again, euphoria fled and she gave a wince of pain that made him turn her palms upwards to look at them.

"I'm sorry," he murmured unsteadily. "It's not the moment to be shouting at you, is it? Your hands look as if you'd been crawling for miles."

"Instead of shouting at all, you'd do better to take care of your lambs, McAlister."

"My *what*?"

"Lambs . . . one of them fell over the edge and got stuck in some brambles; by the time I got it out the mist had come down and I was stuck myself. Now I'm sick of this wretched mountain, and I should like to go home."

He misunderstood her, as she'd known he would. "For the moment I can only return you to Cullin Castle, and even that won't be comfortable. For that distance I must carry you across my shoulder, I'm afraid."

"I'd rather walk," Fran said distinctly, ". . . in fact I *insist* on walking."

It would be better for her, he realised, if she could manage it . . . she *would* manage it. She didn't belong on Cullin; did extravagant things, took risks that proved how unfitted she was for island life. But if only courage had been required, he knew how fittingly she might have stayed for ever.

Fran had no clear recollection afterwards of the journey back – only of the need to force her legs to function, of the exhaustion that dragged at every step, and of the warm, hard arm across her shoulders which kept her from giving up the struggle. With Bess walking at their heels like the well-trained shadow she was, they moved through a silent, eerie world that would have ruled out conversation even if either of them had felt capable of making any.

But the mist was beginning to thin by the time they were down on level ground, skirting the lochan. With a feeling of passionate relief she could see the grey, slate roof of the Castle tower emerging above the streamers of whiteness that now drifted in the gentle breeze. Up above, the frightening blanket of mist would remain all day, but with the suddenness typical of Hebridean weather, away from the hills the atmosphere might soon be crystal-clear again.

She was scarcely aware of people in the courtyard,

of Maggie murmuring over her, and of being lifted into the Land Rover. Only the painful session in Dr Calum McConnell's surgery brought her fully awake, to endure having grit and dirt washed out of her cut hands, and be given the tetanus injection he insisted on.

"Now, bed for you," he said when the ordeal was over, ". . . and I'd recommend it tomorrow as well – you'll not be feeling quite the thing for a day or two."

Fran managed to smile at him. "Thank you, but I have a wedding to attend in the morning – it's what I came all the way from London for."

"Save your breath, Calum," McAlister suggested, seeing him about to remonstrate. "You aren't yet well enough acquainted with Miss Campbell to know that however nicely she thanks you for your advice she will almost certainly ignore it."

Fran heard the edge to his voice and knew herself still unforgiven for having caused so much trouble and anxiety. It seemed not only very unfair in the circumstances, but strangely unlike him – she still had a vivid recollection of almost her first evening on Cullin when he and his friends had gone without complaint or the least resentment to search for two lost Americans. But she had no energy left to argue with him, and no inclination either. It was safer to sit quietly beside him on the journey back up the hill, in a haze of sadness and exhaustion that had become almost pleasant because, wrapped in it, nothing now seemed real.

Maggie was at the door again, waiting to take charge. "Bed for you," she said echoing the doctor, after one glance at Fran's white face.

"A shower first, please, if you'll give me a hand," Fran pleaded. "It was kind of Dr McConnell not to complain of the fact, but I smell rather strongly of sheep!"

She walked into the hall with Maggie, turned round, unable to leave McAlister so abruptly, and found him already gone without waiting to be thanked. It was the last straw, sending her up the stairs closer to tears than she'd been all day. Clean again with Maggie's help, she obediently drank the broth brought up to her, and agreed that all she needed now was sleep.

It was actually far from being what she needed, and she lay awake for a long time, watching the firelight flickering on the ceiling, and thinking her way through the muddles and misunderstandings of the past months. Like the mist outside, the haze in her mind had disappeared, leaving only certainties behind. There were two that should have matched, but didn't; they made a third that was all too simple to understand. Accepting it at last, she closed her eyes against the cruel enticement of a firelit room that should surely have been shared, and wept herself to sleep.

It was early evening when she woke. The dusk that filled the glen outside had seeped into the corners of the room, but the glow from the hearth kept the shadows at bay. Someone had been careful to keep the fire going and, glancing round, her eyes discovered who it was – McAlister's long shape had somehow folded itself into one of the window seats, but his head was turned away from her to face the darkening view outside.

She knew that she must confess to being awake, must thank him calmly for rescuing her, and make it clear that she would soon leave Cullin and not trouble him again. But the words that formed themselves said none of those things.

"Neil . . . that eagle – would it have taken the lamb?"

The hoarse question brought him to his feet, to cover the distance between them in a few quick strides. Her eyes staring up at him were full of remembered horror, and he understood fully now what had happened up on Beinn Mhor. It was tempting to be economical with the truth, but he couldn't for more than a moment or two contemplate offering her the comfort of a lie.

"I've known it happen," he admitted gently, "especially after a harder winter than usual when food has been short. Natural laws have to be about survival, you see, not sentiment. Don't be put off island life because of them."

She shook her head, trying to smile. "I can certainly bear the visits needed to keep an eye on my godson – in fact, I shall insist on them. But I'll try *not* to be a nuisance in future."

It seemed likely that he would relinquish his post now and go away, but instead he perched himself on the side of the bed. As he did so Fran saw what he would also be unable to miss – the little wooden gull that he'd carved for her the day they'd had their picnic in the cove. It stood, as it had done ever since he gave it to her, on the table by her bed, looking ready to lift its spread wings in flight. Feeling by turns feverishly hot and icily cold, she tried to find something to say that would ignore it, explain it, or laugh it away; but Himself spoke first.

"I wasn't the only one looking for you – the other men were out on the hill as well. Hamish, especially, was very distressed. He'd like nothing better than to take care of you, but I expect you're aware of that."

Fran could hear no accusation in his voice this time; it was completely neutral, taking care to point out what he thought she ought to know.

"Inverness isn't Edinburgh or London," he went on doggedly, "but you'd find many of the amenities you're accustomed to there."

He still stared at the little gull, not at her, wishing with all his heart and soul that he could be sure of understanding what it meant . . . or even if its presence there meant anything at all. His failure – as he saw it – with Vanessa Forrester had left a scar that wasn't yet healed. Fiona had accused him of being a fool where women were concerned, and he seemed to have proved her right by giving his heart to a girl who belonged in Bond Street and the Rue de la Paix. They'd done nothing but misunderstand each other, and the undoubted fact that everyone else on Cullin reckoned he should keep her there by brute force, if necessary, was no help at all to a man who in this one, crucial aspect of his affairs had lost whatever confidence he'd ever had.

"Inverness could be stuffed with every amenity known to woman and I still wouldn't want to live there," Fran said finally. "Hamish is a very nice man who will make some other girl the best of husbands . . . but not me. He's known that for some time, McAlister – you don't have to do his wooing for him."

He *was* looking at her now, and she marvelled that she'd ever thought his face shuttered and unrevealing. Astonishing tenderness blazed there, and a shy, rueful humour that she hadn't known he possessed.

"You called me Neil a moment ago . . . could you not make a habit of it? Maggie had a lot to say after you went home . . . and so did my Elspeth. I was given to understand from *her* that only lifelong loyalty to the laird of Cullin prevented her from following you to London. Coming from a woman who regards it as a sink of depravity, you'll realise the depth of trouble I was in for sending you away, and she's scarcely spoken to me since."

Fran listened but she was unable to smile, because

the moment was too fraught with hope and uncertainty. Perhaps she was still light-headed from the morning's adventure, or misled by the passionate longing of her heart?

"I know why you sent me away," she said gravely, ". . . you didn't think I was what Cullin needed. But you couldn't have thought that about Fiona – why did you send *her* away?"

"I didn't – she chose to go. I even offered to marry her because she claimed it was what was generally expected, and I couldn't let her be humiliated in front of everyone she knew. She guessed the truth and knew how meaningless my offer was; but she was tempted to punish me by accepting, she said, so that *she* could later jilt me as publicly as Vanessa had done."

"But she changed her mind about that?" Fran could scarcely bear to ask, imagining the painfulness of the confrontation.

"Yes . . . I think she understood that I'd have loved her if I could. But that was always going to be difficult, and it became impossible from the moment *you* set foot in my life."

There was silence in the shadowy room, broken only by the sound of logs settling on the hearth. Hope was growing stronger in her heart but she had to make sure.

"I'm still the London woman . . . the sort of southerner you don't trust after Vanessa," she reminded him desperately.

He smiled then, and suddenly she had no doubt at all. "You're the light of my life, mo gràdlach. If I could say it to you in Gaelic, my tongue would run free as a bird, but I must ask in English if you will marry me and stay to infuriate, and bewilder, and enchant me for the rest of my life?"

Fran reflected for a moment and remembered the expression that Elspeth reserved for occasions requiring the utmost heights of enthusiasm.

"I think I'd like it fine," she agreed primly at last.

He couldn't touch her bandaged hands, scarcely dared to touch her at all for the bruises Calum's inspection had revealed, but her lovely mouth wasn't hurt, and *that* he could safely lean forward to cover with his own. It seemed, after a long moment of question and response, as if nothing more was needed, but he framed her face gently in his brown hands so that she had to look at him.

"I can't promise you an easy life, my heart, or even that Cullin will survive; but for as long as it can be made to, this is where my work is. Even loving you as I do, I can't abandon my responsibility for the people who belong here."

"I don't want you to," she said with quiet certainty. "*I* can't claim to belong here yet, but I shall in time." Then she smiled radiantly at him. "I'm not sure that Aunt Ernestine will be altogether pleased – I rather think *she* had a fancy to be 'Herself of Cullin'!"

"I know," he admitted, "I . . . that's why I'm anxious to settle for the niece instead, as the lesser of two evils!"

Misled by his grave expression, she nearly made the mistake of protesting, until a gleam of amusement in his eyes gave him away.

"What else is amusing you?" she enquired suspiciously.

"I'm thinking I should have had the courage of Ernestine's convictions and sounded out the minister about two weddings for the price of one tomorrow!"

"A truly Scottish thought!" But her smile faded quickly. "I know you weren't serious, but I should like Fiona to have the chance to settle into her new life before we seem to be flaunting our own happiness. In any case, I must clear up things in London and bring my aunt back to see us married." She saw a sudden shadow on his face and reached out to him with her bandaged hand. "There's nothing to fear, Neil. I *shall* be back, because my label is securely tied this time. I'm 'McAlister's woman' for as long as I live."

He leaned over to kiss her again. "'McAlister's wife' has an even better ring. But now I must let you sleep, my dear one, which is what I was supposed to do all along according to Maggie's clear instruction. Her cup of happiness will overflow when I tell her you'll soon be here for good, but Elspeth, being the thrawn, unforgiving lassie she is, will take longer to come round."

"You can leave *her* to me," said Fran with immense contentment, "and the knitting rebels, too. You'll see, McAlister – all shall be well. All manner of things shall be well, on Cullin!"

Looking at her, he had no doubt of it now.